D0397763

VOL. FOUR

WINGS OF
THE WIND

TURN OF
GLORY

AL LACY

Multnomah Publishers

BATTLES OF DESTINY, Volume 4
published by Multnomah Publishers
A division of Random House Inc.

© 2007 byALJO PRODUCTIONS, INC.
International Standard Book Number: 1-59052-948-0

Compilation of:
Wings of the Wind © 1997 by ALJO PRODUCTIONS, INC.
ISBN 1-57673-032-8
Turn of Glory © 1998 by ALJO PRODUCTIONS, INC.
ISBN 1-57673-217-7

Cover Photography by Steve Gardner, www.shootpw.com

Multnomah is a trademark of Multnomah Publishers,
and is registered in the U.S. Patent and Trademark Office.
The colophon is a trademark of Multnomah Publishers.

Printed in the United States of America

For information:
MULTNOMAH PUBLISHERS
12265 Oracle Boulevard, Suite 200
Colorado Springs, Colorado 80921

07 08 09 10 11 12 13 14 — 10 9 8 7 6 5 4 3 2 1

Novels by Al Lacy

JOURNEYS OF THE STRANGER SERIES:

Legacy
Silent Abduction
Blizzard
Tears of the Sun
Circle of Fire
Quiet Thunder
Snow Ghost

ANGEL OF MERCY SERIES:

A Promise for Breanna
Faithful Heart
Captive Set Free
A Dream Fulfilled
Suffer the Little Children
Whither Thou Goest
Final Justice
Not by Might
Things Not Seen
Far Above Rubies

Novels by Al and JoAnna Lacy

HANNAH OF FORT BRIDGER SERIES:

Under the Distant Sky
Consider the Lilies
No Place for Fear
Pillow of Stone
The Perfect Gift
Touch of Compassion
Beyond the Valley
Damascus Journey

MAIL ORDER BRIDE SERIES:

Secrets of the Heart
A Time to Love
The Tender Flame
Blessed Are the Merciful
Ransom of Love
Until the Daybreak
Sincerely Yours
A Measure of Grace
So Little Time
Let There Be Light

SHADOW OF LIBERTY SERIES:

Let Freedom Ring
The Secret Place
A Prince Among Them
Undying Love

ORPHAN TRAINS SERIES:

The Little Sparrows
All My Tomorrows
Whispers in the Wind

FRONTIER DOCTOR SERIES:

One More Sunrise
Beloved Physician
The Heart Remembers

DREAMS OF GOLD SERIES:

Wings of Riches
The Forbidden Hills
The Golden Stairs

A PLACE TO CALL HOME SERIES:

Cherokee Rose
Bright Are the Stars
The Land of Promise

BOOK SEVEN

WINGS OF THE WIND

BATTLE OF ANTIETAM

To my sweet little niece,

Pami P-Nut,

who hangs on the breathless edge of anticipation

for another one of Uncle Al's novels to come off the press

(I think).

I love you, P-Nut!

✳ ✳ ✳

PROLOGUE

On September 3, 1862, four days after the Confederate Army's stunning victory at the Second Battle of Bull Run, General Robert E. Lee sat down and pondered the situation. In the aftermath of routing the Federals for the second time within thirteen months, on the same battlefield, two courses lay before him: Go forward or go back.

The decision was not easy. His men were weary and tattered.

Lee considered what it would mean to go back. He would withdraw south below the Rappahannock River. There he could rest his exhausted army, which as one of Lee's generals phrased it, "had been marching, fighting, and starving" since the Seven Days' Battles around Richmond, Virginia, in late June.

To stay in northern Virginia and rest his troops was out of the question. Thousands of foraging soldiers had already stripped the fields there, and the Confederate supply lines were overextended. Lee lacked the wagons to carry sufficient food for his army and fodder for his horses over the one-hundred-mile route from Richmond. If he withdrew, he would have to drop below the Rappahannock to find crops to feed his men.

To make this move, however, would allow the Union Army of

the Potomac to reorganize and perhaps launch another drive against the Confederate capital at Richmond.

Lee reasoned that if instead of withdrawing he forged ahead and invaded Maryland, he could achieve his immediate military objectives. Such an invasion would not be with the purpose of occupying Union territory, but rather to harass the enemy on his own soil. Lee could feed his army and horses on Maryland's rich autumn harvest while luring the bulk of the Federal forces away from Washington, preventing another enemy march on Richmond before winter set in.

Lee knew the Union cause was at its nadir. A strike and a victory on Union soil could very well turn the tide for the South and win independence for the Confederacy. Ever since the Baltimore riots early in the War, there had been signs of pro-Confederate sympathy in Maryland. Many Marylanders were serving in the Rebel army. Their presence on Maryland soil could rally the citizens of that state on the side of the South.

Lee reasoned that another advantage might be gained by his invasion of Maryland. There was growing opposition to the Civil War throughout the North. An invasion of Confederate troops across the Potomac no doubt would strengthen anti-war Democrats in the upcoming November elections and so galvanize discontent that President Abraham Lincoln would be forced to settle for peace.

Furthermore, reports from abroad indicated that European powers were watching Lee's progress intently. Great Britain and France had greeted the recent Confederate victories with favor. A successful foray into Union territory might induce the British, as well as the French, to accord the Confederacy diplomatic recognition and even intervene in the War on its behalf.

In spite of all these potential advantages, Lee had to weigh one great drawback: the frightful condition of his army. In addition to the men's physical and mental weariness, they were short on supplies and feeble in the means of transportation, because so many horses had been killed in the last three months of battles. And the men needed clothes and shoes.

Still, Lee reasoned that the morale of his men had never been higher. The recent rout at Bull Run had their spirits high, and the spirits of the enemy troops were at an all-time low.

Lee made his decision.

He wrote a long letter to President Jefferson Davis. It began: "The present seems to be the most propitious time since the commencement of the War for the Confederate Army to enter Maryland."

With those words, Lee announced his intention to carry the conflict onto enemy soil for the first time in the Eastern theater. Little did he know that his campaign on Union soil would culminate in the fiercest single day of combat in American history.

The letter was sent to Jefferson Davis by midday, September 3. Lee was so certain Davis would sanction the invasion that he prepared his army that afternoon and moved them north on Thursday morning, September 4. It took them the better part of three days to move fifty thousand men onto Union soil, along with what wagons and animals they had. As the ragtag army's last troops were wading across the Potomac on September 6, President Davis's sanction of the invasion was in writing and in Lee's hands.

To meet the Confederate threat, President Lincoln commanded General George B. McClellan to move his Army of the Potomac westward.

Eleven days later, on September 17, 1862, the two armies clashed head-on along the banks of Antietam Creek near Sharpsburg in western Maryland. Of all the days on all the battlefields where American soldiers have fought, the most terrible in loss of life and limb was on that bloody Wednesday in the pastoral Maryland countryside.

When the fighting ended at dusk on September 17, 5,818 men lay dead and 17,292 lay wounded in the meadows and fields and along the banks of Antietam Creek. The creek flowed crimson with blood while the wounded moaned and cried out for water.

Night came, bringing a mournful chorus of suffering from the lantern-lit tents, barns, sheds, and houses where weary surgeons, aided by equally exhausted nurses, removed bullets, stitched up bayonet wounds, and sawed off mangled limbs. The same mournful chorus came from the deeply shadowed hollows, woods, fields, meadows, and roads where the wounded and dying men of both armies lay beyond the reach of help.

Near midnight, Confederate Major General Thomas J. "Stonewall" Jackson sent his young aide, Henry Kyd Douglas, on an errand across the fields in the pale, misty moonlight. Later, Douglas wrote:

> The dead and dying lay as thick over the land as harvest sheaves. The pitiable cries for water and appeals for help were much more horrible to listen to than the deadliest sounds of battle. Silent were the dead, but here and there were raised stiffened arms; heads made a last effort to lift themselves from the ground; prayers were mingled with oaths, the oaths of delirium; men were wriggling over the earth; and the midnight hid all the distinction between the blue and the gray.
>
> My horse trembled under me in terror, looking down at the ground, sniffing at the scent of blood, stepping falteringly as a horse will, avoiding human flesh; afraid to stand still, hesitating to go on, his animal instinct shuddering at this cruel human mystery.

The Civil War's bloodiest battle left the residents of the Maryland countryside in and around Sharpsburg stunned and sleepless for days. It was a full week before all the dead had been buried and the wounded had been carried away. The stench of decaying flesh hung in the air for a long time, even after the bodies had been interred. It took the powerful sense of death's awful presence even longer to fade.

Within the next few weeks and months, several thousand more

men died of their wounds, or of disease brought on by the wounds.

As I write, several history books lay at my fingertips. In these written records is abundant evidence that the battle along Antietam Creek was the most bitter and savage of the American Civil War.

However, the mercy and compassion of men and women of the medical profession on both sides shone through. The story of one of those gallant physicians began in the small town of McCann's Run, Virginia, in May 1840.

BATTLE OF ANTIETAM
SEPTEMBER 17, 1862

ONE

Five-year-old Hunter Newman Jr. stood at the door of his mother's bedroom, fear clouding his eyes. His arms and legs felt heavy and his pulse raced as he watched Thora Kemp and Bessie Caterson labor over his mother.

Florence Newman had come down with a severe case of typhoid fever. It had been two days since Dr. Riley had examined her.

Hunter bit down hard on his lower lip when his mother rolled her head and shook as if she were penetrated to the core by incredible cold. Was he going to have another living nightmare, as when his father had died almost a year ago in a hunting accident?

Although Hunter had been only four years old at the time, he had taken his father's death hard. For the first three months after his father was killed, Hunter had awakened his mother and baby sister two and three times a night, screaming. Though the nightmares had almost stopped by the time his father had been gone six months, Hunter still remembered, and he trembled at the thought of them.

Now Hunter stood at his mother's bedroom door and looked on in horror as her rapid breathing grew raspy and shallow. She was so pale. Emblazoned in Hunter's mind was the picture of his father's body in the coffin. Hunter feared his mother would die and leave him, too.

Thora and Bessie tirelessly bathed Florence in cool water, trying to reduce her fever. Dr. Riley, the only physician in a thirty-mile radius, had left medicine when he'd been there last and told Bessie and Thora what to do to help keep the fever down and relieve her suffering as much as possible. If she got worse they were to send for him.

While the women continued to wring out cloths in the cool water, Bessie whispered, "Hunter's at the door. The little guy looks scared out of his wits."

Without glancing at him, Thora said, "Why don't you take him outside and talk to him? I'll look after Florence."

Bessie wiped perspiration from the sick woman's brow for the hundredth time that day and handed the cloth to Thora.

Florence laid glassy eyes on Bessie and asked with thick tongue, "Is Hunter all right?"

"He's just worried about you, honey. I'm going to talk to him."

Florence swallowed hard, trying to focus on Bessie's round face. "Tell him...tell him I'm going to be fine."

Bessie nodded and turned away. She walked quietly to the small sandy-haired boy and said, "Hunter, let's go out and see how Jane Louise and little Lizzie are doing."

Hunter shook his head. "No, ma'am, please. Mama's gonna die. I don't want to leave her."

Bessie bent down to Hunter's height, looked him in the eye, and said, "Your mama's awfully sick right now, but Miss Thora and I are working on her. Jesus will help us to make her well. Come on, let's go see about little sister."

Hunter stiffened, gazing toward his mother. Thora spoke to him gently, "Hunter, it will make your mama feel better if you go outside and see about Lizzie."

Florence rolled her head on the hot, damp pillow and choked out the words, "Son...Miss Thora's right. And let Miss Bessie talk to you."

Hunter nodded and let Bessie take his hand. "Come on, honey," she said. "You can come back and see Mama later."

Hunter glanced once more over his shoulder as Bessie led him away from the door and through the house to the porch. It was early May in western Virginia, and in spite of the heavy gray sky, the air was warm.

Jane Louise, Thora Kemp's fifteen-year-old daughter, was sitting on the porch swing, holding little Lizzie Newman. Lizzie was two years old and, in contrast to Hunter, had dark eyes and hair. She was chewing on the hand of her rag doll when she saw her brother. "Hunna!" she said, and smiled.

Hunter dearly loved his little sister. He managed a crooked grin. "Hi, Lizzie."

Jane Louise gave Bessie a look and said, "How's she doing?"

"Not very good right now. Your mom's staying with her so I could bring Hunter out here for a while."

Hunter let go of Bessie's hand to stand close to his little sister. "Mama's real sick, Lizzie, but Miss Bessie says she'll be okay."

Lizzie nodded as if she understood, then held up her rag doll. "Hunna wan' play wif Daisie?"

"No, Lizzie. You play with her."

"Hunter," Bessie said, dragging two straight-backed chairs close to the swing, "come and sit down so we can talk."

The boy climbed up in the chair, looking at Bessie with eyes longing for assurance, and waited for her to speak.

Bessie leaned close and took both of his hands in hers. "Hunter, in the Bible Jesus said, 'I will never leave thee nor forsake thee.' Do you know what that means?"

Hunter adjusted his position slightly. "Mm-hmm. Mama read that to me out of the Bible not very long ago. It means that Jesus is always with us, even though we can't see Him, and He will never ever go away."

"That's right, honey." Bessie smiled, squeezing his hands. "Jesus won't ever leave your mother, either. He's right here to take care of her."

Some of the fear went out of Hunter's eyes. He knew that Bessie Caterson and her husband, Bill, had a close relationship with his parents—as members of the same church and as good friends. Bill Caterson and Hunter Sr. had spent a lot of time together. Bill had been on the hunting jaunt along with two other men, Zack Peterson and Dave Mullins, when Hunter Sr. was accidentally shot and killed by Zack Peterson. Shortly thereafter, the Petersons had left McCann's Run and moved to Richmond.

The Catersons, along with widow Thora Kemp, had stayed especially close to Florence and the children after the accident. Bessie knew that Hunter Jr. had been asking Florence a lot of questions about Jesus and the cross and sin but didn't yet understand it all. Bessie prayed quickly for guidance as she chose her words carefully. "Hunter, Jesus loves your mother, and He loves you and little Lizzie. And because He does, He will always watch over all three of you."

Hunter looked at the porch floor, his mind working out what she had said. At the same time, Lizzie wanted off Jane Louise's lap to play. Lizzie carried her rag doll to the edge of the steps and looked back at her brother. "Hunna pway wif me."

"He will pretty soon, sweetie," Bessie said. "We're talking right now."

Lizzie nodded and looked down the dusty road to the east. Her attention was drawn to a horse and buggy in the distance.

At last Hunter said, "Miss Bessie…"

"Yes, honey?"

"If Jesus is going to take care of Mama, why couldn't He take care of Papa when Mr. Peterson's gun went off and killed him?"

Bessie's heart ached for the boy. "Well, honey, it wasn't that Jesus couldn't take care of your papa. He could have kept that gun from firing."

Hunter searched her eyes as he asked, "Why didn't He want to keep Papa from being killed?"

Bessie silently asked God for wisdom, but before she could put the words together, Jane Louise spoke up. "Hunter, Jesus wanted your papa up in heaven with Him. He had a special place of service for him there. So your papa is with Jesus now, serving Him in heaven."

Hunter pondered Jane Louise's words for a long moment, then said with quivering lips, "Maybe Jesus wants to take my mama to heaven, too…and she's gonna die like Papa did."

Bessie and Jane Louise exchanged a glance as if to decide who would answer. It was Lizzie who got them off the hook. "Tom!" she squealed, pointing at the rider turning off the road toward the house.

The two-year-old laid down her doll and clapped her hands as Tom dismounted from his horse and picked her up, lifting her above his head. "You're just getting cuter every day, Lizzie!" he said.

Hunter, who considered sixteen-year-old Tom Jackson his best friend, slid off the chair and bounded down the steps. Tom held Lizzie in one arm and hoisted Hunter up in the other. For the first time that day, Hunter smiled and relaxed. "Can I help you chop wood, Tom?" he asked.

"You sure can!" Tom drawled. "It always goes faster when you're there to pick up the wood and stack it."

Tall, black-headed Tom Jackson lived with his Uncle Cummins and Aunt Ophelia Jackson at Jackson's Mill, some four miles west on the road toward Clarksburg.

Tom's father, Jonathan, had been a lieutenant at the head of a cavalry company in the War of 1812, and several men on his father's side of the family had fought in the American Revolution. As far back as Tom could remember, he had wanted to be a soldier. He was planning on a military career once he finished high school. He had already contacted his congressman, desiring entrance into West Point Military Academy.

When Tom's father died of typhoid fever at the age of thirty-five, Tom was only three. His mother, Julia, died three years later, and Tom was obliged to live with his Uncle Cummins and Aunt Ophelia. His siblings went to other relatives.

Cummins Jackson was a hard-drinking man, but Ophelia was a

member of the Presbyterian Church in McCann's Run and had taken Tom to church with her ever since he had come to live with them. At nine years of age, Tom had asked Jesus Christ to be his Saviour.

For the past year—since Hunter Newman Sr. had been killed—young Tom had come to the Newman house twice a week to do the necessary chores, such as chopping wood, cleaning the chicken house, weeding the garden, repairing worn and broken things. He knew the Newman family well from church, and did the work for Florence without pay.

While holding the Newman children in his arms, Tom looked at Bessie and Jane Louise. "How's Mrs. Newman doing?"

Bessie frowned. "Not very good, Tom, I—"

"Oh, Tom! I'm so glad you're here!" Thora had come out onto the porch. "I heard your voice from the back room. We need your help."

"Yes, ma'am?"

Thora looked at Bessie. "Her fever is getting worse…much worse." Then to Tom, "Will you ride to Smithburg and bring Dr. Riley? He told us to send for him if Florence's condition worsened."

Hunter's face turned white as Tom set him down and placed Lizzie in Jane Louise's arms. Tears welled up in Hunter's eyes and he dashed up the steps of the porch and bolted through the door, heading toward his mother's bedroom.

Tom vaulted into the saddle and galloped away as Thora turned to Jane Louise and said, "Run to the parsonage and bring Pastor Poole! Hurry!"

As Thora and Bessie, who carried Lizzie, approached the bedroom, they could hear Hunter sobbing, "Please don't die, Mama! Please don't die!"

"Hunter, listen to me," Thora said. "Tom is going after Dr. Riley. He will come as quickly as he can."

Florence was shaking with chills, even as perspiration flowed down her brow. She clumsily patted her son's tear-streaked face and said in a slurred voice, "Hunter, don't cry now."

Soon Lizzie leaned forward in Bessie's arms, extending a small hand toward her mother, and broke into tears. "Mama-a! Mama-a!"

"Hunter," Florence choked out, "you're scaring Lizzie. She needs to see you be strong. Remember, you're the man of the house."

Hunter had taken pride in that title since his father's death and had done his best to live up to it. His mother's reminder took hold, and he looked around at Lizzie. She was sniffling, her eyes fixed on him.

He slid to the floor and walked over to her, waiting for Bessie to lower his little sister to the floor. Then he put his arms around her and said, "It's okay, Lizzie. Jesus is here with us, and Dr. Riley's coming."

TWO

Inside the Riley Clinic in Smithburg, nurse Linna Bittner finished bandaging a small boy's hand and gave him a piece of horehound candy.

Dr. Riley's wife, Alfreda, sat in a chair against the wall looking on, commending Timmy for being such a brave boy and not crying. Alfreda often stopped by the clinic during her daily walk.

When Timmy and his mother had reached the door, Linna offered a final word of admonishment. "No more playing with your mother's butcher knife, Timmy."

"Yes, ma'am," he said, looking at his bandage as he followed his mother outside.

Alfreda sighed and said, "Boys will be boys."

"Oh, won't they," Linna said with a chuckle, her Scandinavian accent coming through. "I'm sure we treat ten times as many boys for cuts, bruises, and broken bones as we do girls."

"Well, Chet and I raised three boys and two girls. I think between those three boys, one of them always had a splint or a bandage or iodine showing somewhere." A faraway look came into Alfreda's eyes as she sighed again and said, "Sometimes I wish they were still little and running around the house."

"They do grow up fast," Linna said, as she cleaned the examining table. "Seems like just yesterday that my two girls were little. And now, here they are married and both expecting their first babies."

"Well, honey, I'll say this—the first time you hold one of those precious grandchildren, you'll be glad your daughters grew up and got married. When I start pining for the days when they were little, I remember that if they hadn't grown up, I wouldn't have those wonderful grandchildren. Why, I remember when our first grandchild was born—"

Alfreda's sentence was cut short by the sight of a surrey pulling up in front of the clinic. Linna followed Alfreda's gaze, focusing on the man who jumped down and, instead of helping the woman, hoisted a wheelchair from the back of the surrey.

Linna squinted and frowned slightly. "I don't recognize either one of them. I wish Dr. Riley was here. Who knows what kind of problem I might face with a wheelchair patient."

Alfreda suddenly stood up, smiling. "Oh, I know them," she said, and hurried toward the door.

Linna followed and stood just inside the doorway as Alfreda moved onto the porch. Linna judged the man and woman to be in their late thirties. As the man eased the woman into the wheelchair, Alfreda hurried to them. "Jason! Ellie! How wonderful to see you!" She embraced the man and leaned over to put her arms around the woman.

Linna heard the man say, "Some people on the street told us where you live and where the clinic is...we went to the house first. When we found no one home, we figured you might be here."

"Linna," Alfreda said, "I want you to meet Dr. Jason McGuire and his wife, Ellie. Linna Bittner has been the doctor's nurse ever since he came here to go back into private practice."

Linna stepped forward as Jason began to pick up the wheelchair. "Here," she said, "let me help you."

"It's all right, ma'am. Ellie's not heavy. I'm used to it, but thank you anyway." As he spoke, he lifted the wheelchair and set it on the porch.

Once inside, Jason looked around the clinic expectantly. "Is Dr. Riley here?" he asked.

"No," Alfreda said, "he's at a farm some twenty-five miles south of here, delivering a baby, and there's no way to know when he might be back. Can you stay for the day?"

"No reason we can't," Jason said. "I noticed a hotel as we drove into town. We'll even stay the night if that's what it takes to see Dr. Riley."

"If you stay the night, it won't be in the hotel. You'll stay with us—we have plenty of room."

Ellie spoke up. "We…we wouldn't want to be a bother, Mrs. Riley. We—"

"Hush, now!" the older woman said in mild rebuke. "You could never be a bother." Then, turning to the nurse, Alfreda said, "Linna, I'm sure you know that Doctor taught at Harvard Medical School before he came here five years ago…"

"Yes."

"Well, Jason—I mean Dr. McGuire—was one of his students. One of his most brilliant students, I might add."

McGuire shook his head modestly as Alfreda continued to speak. "Dr. McGuire is a prominent physician and surgeon in Boston." Then, looking at Jason, she asked, "You are still practicing in Boston?"

"Yes, ma'am."

Alfreda nodded. "And to what do we owe this wonderful visit?"

"Well, we're on a little vacation," he said. "Ellie's parents live in Parkersburg, and we came here to see them. They moved from Hudson, New Hampshire, about a year ago. We sure couldn't get this close to the Rileys without stopping by."

"Oh, I'm so glad you did," Alfreda said. "Chet is going to be so happy to see you! Well…why don't we just mosey on over to the house so Ellie can be comfortable?"

A half-hour later, Alfreda Riley and her guests were sitting in the parlor, sipping tea and talking of old times at Harvard. When the talk began to dwindle, Alfreda looked across the tea table and said, "The last time we saw you—what was it, nine years ago?—you were talking about adopting a child. I assume it has never come to pass."

"Ah…no, it hasn't," Jason said.

"Are there still plans to do so?"

"We decided against it," Ellie said. "It was my decision actually. I'm afraid I wouldn't be able to care for a child properly from a wheelchair."

"I offered to hire a nanny," Jason said, "but Ellie wouldn't hear of it."

"I don't want to bring up a child with a nanny as its mother. If I can't be a mother to our child, I'd rather not try it at all."

"I can understand that," Alfreda said.

"So tell her what you *are* doing, honey," Jason said.

A broad smile spread over Ellie's slender face. "Well, to satisfy the motherly instinct the Lord put inside me, I work with sick and injured children at Boston Hospital, where Jason does his surgeries and sends his patients."

"Well, wonderful!" Alfreda said.

Ellie hunched her shoulders and tilted her head. "It's not the same as actually being a mother, but I can handle what I do from the wheelchair. The work is very satisfying."

"I'm so happy for you, Ellie," Alfreda said. "What a wonderful way to spend your time."

Tom Jackson bent low over his horse's neck and pushed her hard. His heart was heavy for Florence Newman and her children. "Lord, that dear lady and those sweet kids have had an awful hard time of it since Hunter was killed. I'm not questioning Your ways. You know that. But I'm asking You to take care of them…and if in Your wisdom You see fit to take Mrs. Newman home to heaven, please take care of those little children. Give them a good Christian home to be raised in."

Twenty minutes later, young Jackson galloped into Smithburg, ignoring the gawking people, and made a beeline for the clinic, skidding the puffing mare to a halt. He slipped from the saddle and bolted through the door.

Linna Bittner, busy with filing, greeted him with, "Tom! What's wrong?"

"It's Florence Newman. Her typhoid fever's getting worse. She needs Dr. Riley immediately!"

"I'm sorry," Linna said, pulling a folder from the drawer. "Doctor is not here. He's delivering a baby twenty-five miles south of here."

Tom's countenance fell. "Ma'am, it's really bad. Mrs. Kemp is worried that Mrs. Newman will die if she doesn't get help. What am I going to do?"

"Tom, I don't know what to tell you. The mother at the farm has had some serious complications carrying her baby. Her life and the baby's may be at stake, too. I'm not sure what to do. If only there was another doctor nearby. But the nearest one is—"

Tom saw Linna's eyes widen.

"Yes?"

"There's a doctor and his wife from Boston visiting Mrs. Riley at this very moment," Linna said.

"He's a regular-type doctor?"

"Yes. Physician and surgeon. If Florence can be helped, he can do it."

"Then I'll go ask him."

"Tell Dr. McGuire that I sent you. Explain about Florence, and I'm sure he will go with you. Tell him to stop here if he needs any medicine."

Pastor Nelson Poole sat beside Florence's bed while Thora and Bessie bathed her face and arms. He had prayed with Florence upon arriving at the house, then sat down and read Scripture to her. Now he was speaking in soft tones, trying to encourage her.

The fear Hunter felt at seeing his mother so deathly pale and hearing her ragged breathing was taking its toll. He pictured the last time he saw his father in the coffin. Now it was his mother he saw lying there, lifeless and chalky white.

Wild panic filled him. He felt his pulse pounding at the back of his eyes, on top of his head, in his throat. A cry was working its way up when the pastor turned and saw the panic on Hunter's face.

"Hunter," Pastor Poole said calmly, "why don't you go outside and see if Tom and Dr. Riley are coming?"

Hunter had been out to check the road six times already, but he obediently turned to go. As he passed through the parlor, he saw that Jane Louise was sitting on the couch with Lizzie asleep in her arms. He shifted to walking on tiptoe, and Jane Louise smiled at him.

Outside Hunter looked westward and saw Mr. Wykopf's Guernsey cow crossing the road. Bertha was always getting out. Hunter wondered why Mr. Wykopf didn't mend his fences. Then he saw a rider galloping his way with a surrey following.

Hunter charged through the front door and yelled, "Tom's coming with Dr. Riley, Jane Louise!" He bolted down the hall into his mother's room and repeated the good news.

Bessie and Thora sighed with relief. Pastor Poole patted Florence's clammy arm and said, "You hear that, Florence? Doc Riley's here."

The sick woman ran a dry tongue over chapped lips and nodded. Bessie gave her water and said, "You're going to be all right, now, honey. You'll see."

***

Tom Jackson skidded his lathered and panting mare to a stop and dismounted while the surrey was bouncing up behind him. Hunter stood waiting beside Bessie and Jane Louise.

Bessie fixed her eyes on the man at the reins and said, "Tom, that's not Dr. Riley…"

Tom walked with Dr. McGuire up the steps and said, "Mrs. Caterson, Jane Louise, this is Dr. Jason McGuire. He and his wife just arrived in Smithburg to visit the Rileys. Dr. Riley is delivering a baby way out in the country."

"Ladies," McGuire said, touching his hatbrim. His gaze settled on Lizzie and Hunter. "And these are Mrs. Newman's children?"

"Yes," Tom said, laying a hand on Hunter's head. "The little lady is Lizzie, and this little friend of mine is Hunter."

Dr. McGuire looked at Lizzie with kind eyes and stroked her cheek. "Hello, Lizzie. You're sure a cute little thing. I wish I had a daughter like you."

Lizzie smiled, warming up to the doctor immediately.

McGuire then looked down at Hunter and placed a hand on his shoulder. "Hunter, eh? That's a strong masculine name, and you look like you're all boy. I wish I had a son like you."

Hunter managed a smile. Jason McGuire eased down on one knee and looked Hunter straight in the eye. "I'm going to do everything I can to help your mother. I want you to know that."

"Thank you, sir. My papa died when I was four. I don't want my mama to die."

"I know about your papa, son. Tom told me. I'll do everything I can for your mama."

Hunter reached out with both arms, and McGuire gave him a hug. Then the doctor patted Hunter on the back and said, "Let's go see about your mama. Will you take me to her?"

Bessie and Jane Louise followed as Hunter took the doctor's hand and led him inside. Tom trailed along.

Dr. McGuire set his black bag on the bedstand and Florence looked up with languid eyes. "Mrs. Newman," he said, "I'm Dr. Jason McGuire. I'm from—"

"I heard, Doctor. If you studied under Dr. Riley, I trust you completely."

"Thank you, ma'am. Now let's check your temperature."

Dr. McGuire placed a thermometer in Florence's mouth and checked her pulse. He also quickly checked her eyes and throat and listened to her heart. He read the thermometer and placed it back in his medical bag, his expression remaining impassive.

He glanced from time to time at the children who looked on and then set soft, gentle eyes on Florence and said, "Mrs. Newman, I understand from Tom that you are a Christian."

Florence smiled slightly and nodded.

"I just want you to know that I am too, ma'am. Jesus Christ saved me when I was nineteen years old under the fiery message of a Baptist preacher."

Pastor Poole stepped closer, smiling, and laid a hand on McGuire's shoulder.

Tom excused himself, saying he would go do the chores around the Newman place. "Want to help me, Hunter?" he asked.

Dr. McGuire saw Hunter's hesitation and said, "You go ahead, son. It'll be good for you to spend some time with Tom."

The five-year-old nodded and walked to his mother's side. "Mama, I'm gonna help Tom with the chores. I'll be back pretty soon."

"That's fine, honey," Florence said hoarsely. "You go ahead."

Soon the sun was setting, and Florence's fever rose higher. The doctor made no comment when he read the thermometer.

"Worse?" Thora mouthed silently from the other side of the bed.

The doctor nodded.

The room had been silent for some time, except for the sound of the women dipping cloths in water and wringing them out. Florence swallowed with difficulty and fixed torpid eyes on McGuire. "I'm...I'm not going to make it, am I Doctor?"

McGuire hesitated, then said, "I cannot lie to you, ma'am. You won't make it through the night."

Thora and Bessie exchanged sorrowful glances, then looked at their pastor. Nelson Poole's face was pale.

No one had noticed that Hunter had returned to the open doorway and heard what the doctor said. He blinked rapidly, as if startled by a loud noise, and charging toward the bed, he cried, "No! No, Mama, no-o, please don't die! Mama-a!"

He managed to climb onto the bed before anyone could stop him and threw his arms around his mother, continuing to call her name.

Dr. McGuire feared that typhoid might be contagious, in spite of what the medical experts were saying. He wanted to pull the boy away from danger but refrained.

Jane Louise, still carrying Lizzie, had come back into the bedroom. Even though Lizzie didn't know exactly what was going on, Hunter's sobs upset her and she began to wail.

Florence kissed Hunter's forehead and said calmly, "Honey, you have to be brave. You're making Lizzie cry. C'mon, now. Be Mama's big boy."

The sandy-haired child nodded and released his hold on his mother. She was going to die, but for her sake, and for Lizzie's, he would be brave.

THREE

D r. McGuire looked at Nelson Poole and nodded toward Florence. The doctor had done all he could; she needed her pastor now.

McGuire laid a firm hand on Hunter's shoulder and looked down into widened, fear-filled eyes. He tried to smile at Hunter but couldn't quite manage it.

"Florence," the pastor said, "you're in the Lord's hands. He will not fail you now. He—"

"I know that, Pastor," she whispered. "I have no fear, even as David in Psalm 23. My Shepherd is with me. You...you will see that the children are taken care of?"

Poole was not sure what he was going to do about the Newman children, but he nodded silently.

Florence saw his nod, and said, "Would you let the children come and sit beside me?"

Jane Louise carried Lizzie to the bed and Dr. McGuire helped Hunter to climb up.

The dying mother raised a shaky hand and stroked Lizzie's cheek. "Mama loves you, sweetheart," she said. "Jesus will take care of you and brother."

Lizzie leaned over and hugged her mother's neck, then straightened back again into Jane Louise's arms. The two-year-old was touched by the emotions in the room, but didn't understand what was happening.

But Hunter knew. He embraced his mother, fighting the urge to cry. He swallowed hard and bit down on his lower lip.

Florence ran her dull gaze from one child to the other, then lifted her eyes toward heaven and said in a half-whisper, "Thank You, Lord, for being so good to me. You saved my soul when I was thirteen. You gave me such a good husband…and these two wonderful children. Please, Lord, take care of Hunter and Lizzie."

Florence looked at the pastor's Bible on the bedstand. "Pastor," she said, "would you read my favorite praise verse? Psalm 104:1. I love the way it exalts the Lord."

Tom Jackson was now in the room. Tears were streaming down his face as Nelson Poole read the words, pushing them past the lump in his throat:

Bless the LORD, O my soul.
O LORD my God, thou art very great;
thou art clothed with honor and majesty.

"Thank you, Pastor," she whispered. "The third verse is also one of my favorites. Would you read it to me?"

Hunter recalled so many times that his mother had referred to that verse in the past year, especially on a windy day. She would look heavenward and say, "Hunter, see those big white clouds up there? Psalm 104 verse 3 says Jesus makes the clouds His chariot. And sometimes He steps out of His chariot and walks on the wings of the wind, looking down at us. The day Papa left us, Jesus came walking on the wings of the wind, reached down, and lifted Papa up into His mighty arms and took him home to heaven."

Hunter felt Dr. McGuire's hand squeeze his shoulder. He liked this man who reminded him of his father—strong yet gentle.

Florence spoke again, her hoarse whisper even weaker. "Hunter…Jesus is coming on the wings of the wind to take me to be with Him and Papa. But someday, Son, He will walk the wings of the wind and bring us together again—all four of us." She swallowed with difficulty and tried to speak again, but her strength was gone.

Hunter looked up at Dr. McGuire, then at the pastor, who had a grip on his mother's hand. Florence's chest rose and fell a few more times, then her head fell to one side and she stopped breathing.

Pastor Poole placed her hand gently on the bed and stepped back to allow Dr. McGuire room. The doctor checked for a pulse but could find none. He pulled the sheet up and covered Florence Newman's chalky-white face.

A strangled moan escaped Hunter's lips and his whole body trembled. He could hardly breathe.

The kindly doctor turned and said, "She's with Jesus now, Hunter." He dropped to one knee to be able to look into Hunter's eyes. "Jesus will make everything all right for you and Lizzie, Hunter. You'll be happy in your new home."

"Who are we gonna live with, sir?"

McGuire looked to the pastor, ran his gaze to the women, then back to the pastor. "Have some arrangements been made for their care?"

"Not yet, Doctor," Poole said. "We were so confident God would spare Florence's life."

Hunter ran from the room, his heart pounding in his ears as he ran. When he was deep into the woods, he threw himself on the ground beneath a giant oak tree and sobbed out the pain in his young heart.

"Aren't there any relatives who could take them in and adopt them?" Dr. McGuire asked.

"None that I know of, Doctor," Poole said, softly. "I'll do everything I can to find someone to adopt them, but everybody around here is poor."

"I'll talk to Bill," Bessie Caterson said. "Maybe we could adopt Lizzie. I...I haven't told any of you this, but Bill and I just learned yesterday that we're moving to Greensboro. Pastor, you knew Bill had applied for a job there. With Florence so sick, I just haven't thought to tell any of you that the letter of acceptance came yesterday. We'll be leaving in a few days. He'll be getting a raise in pay, so he just might go along with adopting Lizzie. But we couldn't afford to take both of them. I love Hunter too, but I think for me, Lizzie would be easier to raise."

"I'd hate to see Hunter and Lizzie separated," Tom said. "They are brother and sister. They should be raised together."

"By far that would be best," Poole said. "The children shouldn't be separated."

"I'm a stranger, here," put in Dr. McGuire, "so I have no say in anything about this. However, I'd like to put in my two cents' worth. I agree with Tom and Pastor Poole. Hunter and Lizzie should be raised together. Of course there may be no choice. They must have a home, even if it means separation. But one thing's for sure, they must be adopted by Christian people."

Jane Louise was sitting on a straight-backed chair, holding a squirming Lizzie, who pointed toward the body that lay covered on the bed and said, "Mama."

"We ought to move to the parlor," Thora said. "And someone ought to check on Hunter."

Quickly the women moved through the house, calling the boy's name, but there was no reply.

Darkness had fallen, and the stars were twinkling in a velvety black sky. Tom ran to the backyard, calling for Hunter, and the pastor and the doctor checked in front and down the road. When everyone had returned to the parlor, they began to talk about scouring the town.

"Before you do that," Jane Louise said, "you'd best look in the forest. Florence has told Hunter over and over not to go there—even in the daytime—but he told me more than once that he feels close to his father out there."

"Have you any idea where, Jane Louise?" the pastor asked. "It's a pretty big forest."

"Well, I've never seen the spot where his father was killed, but that's where he goes." She put a hand to her temple. "I'm trying to remember what he said about it. I think there's a huge oak tree there…and a small stream that runs by it."

"I know the place," Tom said. "I'll light a lantern and go after him."

"We'll light a couple of lanterns," the pastor said. "I'll go with you."

"I…ah…would like to go along, too, if you don't mind," Dr. McGuire said. "I want to be sure the little guy is found before I head back for Smithburg."

Hunter had no more tears to cry and was sitting with his back against the oak tree. Owls hooted, and strange night sounds filtered through the forest, but the boy was too wrapped up in his grief to be afraid of the night around him.

Memories of his father and mother rushed through his mind. He was glad, at least, that his mother had been able to talk to him before she died. His father, on the day he had died, had walked out of the house with his musket in hand, saying he would bring some meat home that evening.

The boy's mind once again ran to Lizzie and what would happen to the two of them. Who would take them in? Pastor Poole loved them, and so did Mrs. Poole, but they already had three children. Maybe five would be too many. The parsonage was pretty small.

Hunter wouldn't mind living with Tom Jackson, since they were best friends. Tom's Aunt Ophelia was a nice lady. She always cried in church. Tom had told him she cried a lot because his Uncle Cummins wasn't a Christian, and she didn't want him to go to hell. Hunter had seen Uncle Cummins a few times. He was always using bad language and he was real crabby. For sure, Uncle Cummins wouldn't let Lizzie and Hunter live in his house.

He thought of the different families in the church. He liked everyone. Well, except for Mrs. Ballard. She always smelled strongly of something like flowers, and whenever she kissed his forehead she left it wet. She talked so loud it hurt his ears, and in church she sang louder than everybody else. Anyway, Mrs. Ballard was real old. His mother had told him she was forty-six. Anyone that old wouldn't want children living in her house.

And, of course, he wouldn't want to live with somebody who didn't really love him and Lizzie.

Love. He suddenly thought of Dr. Jason McGuire. Dr. McGuire hardly knew him, but he sure did show Hunter that he loved him. So much like Papa. A warm feeling came over Hunter when he remembered Dr. McGuire saying, "I wish I had a son like you."

But Dr. McGuire lived in some big city somewhere, and was awfully busy with his work. Besides, maybe Mrs. McGuire wouldn't—

Hunter lifted his head and listened. Someone was calling his name. It sounded like Tom. Hunter got up and looked toward town. He could see twin lights winking through the trees. Then he heard it again: "Hu-u-nter-r!"

It was Tom's voice, all right.

Hunter wondered who else was with Tom. Probably the pastor. Would he be angry? Hunter hadn't meant to upset anybody.

The lights were getting nearer. Hunter cupped his hands to his mouth and shouted, "I'm over here!"

It took only seconds for them to hurry toward him. Hunter saw Tom carrying a lantern, and Pastor Poole carrying another. It was the third man whose presence pleased Hunter the most. Dr. McGuire hadn't left yet for Smithburg. He had come with Tom and Pastor Poole to find him.

"Hunter, we were worried about you," Tom said.

"You shouldn't have run off like that, Hunter," Poole said. "Especially into these woods at night. There *are* wild animals out here, you know."

"Yes, sir. I…I just wanted to be near Papa. He was killed back there by the big tree. I—"

"It's all right, son," Poole said. "You gave us a pretty good scare though."

The boy dipped his chin. "I'm sorry."

Dr. McGuire moved forward and said, "Come on, son. We'll take you back home now." The doctor picked Hunter up and cradled him in his arms.

There was something about being in Dr. McGuire's arms and hearing his voice that went all the way to Hunter's heart. It was the closest to a father's touch he'd felt since his father died.

As they walked back toward town beneath the towering trees, Poole said, "Hunter, when we get back, we'll arrange a place for you and Lizzie to stay tonight. I'm calling a special meeting of the church tomorrow night to find a family who will adopt you and Lizzie. How does that sound?"

Hunter hesitated and then nodded his head.

When they arrived back at the Newman house, Bill Caterson was sitting at the kitchen table with Bessie and Thora, holding a sleepy-eyed Lizzie. Jane Louise had gone home. Everybody smiled and felt a moment's reprieve from the sad events of the day when they saw Hunter in Dr. McGuire's arms.

Bill said, "Hey, Hunter, you really had us worried."

Hunter did not reply, but when Dr. McGuire started to put him down, his little arms tightened on the doctor's neck. McGuire sat down near the table with Hunter on his lap.

Tom and the pastor doused their lanterns and remained standing as Bessie introduced Dr. McGuire to her husband.

Bill then turned to the pastor and said, "I was just telling Thora that Bessie and I'll take the children for the night."

"Did the ladies tell you I'm calling a special meeting of the church tomorrow night to find a family who'll take Hunter and Lizzie?"

"Yes," Bill said, looking down at the sleepy little girl in his arms.

"Pastor, Bessie and I would love to adopt both of these children, but even with my new job in Greensboro, we couldn't afford it. I agree that the ideal thing would be for them to both be adopted into the same home, but if that doesn't work out, we'll take Lizzie. Bessie feels she's best suited for raising a little girl."

Poole nodded. "I understand. I'm trusting that the Lord will work it out according to His will." He rubbed his tired eyes and said, "We'll have Florence's funeral day after tomorrow."

Dr. McGuire gave Hunter a squeeze and lowered him to the floor. "Well, folks, I've got to head for Smithburg. I haven't seen Dr. Riley yet. Sure hope he's home when I get there."

Everybody followed the doctor onto the porch where he turned and bent down to hug Hunter once more, saying, "I'll be praying that you'll be adopted into a real good home, Hunter. Good-bye."

Hunter nodded, wishing Dr. McGuire didn't have to go. McGuire told the others good-bye and turned toward his surrey. Nelson Poole called after him, "Oh, Doctor! Florence didn't have much in the way of money. If you'll give me a figure, I'll take a special offering at the church to see that you're paid."

McGuire paused and raised his hand in a wave. "No charge. The smiles I got from Lizzie and the hugs I got from Hunter are pay enough."

FOUR

T he night was dark except for the shimmering stars as Dr. Jason McGuire drove west toward Smithburg. The clip-clop of the horses' hooves echoed across the fields and was swallowed up in the dense stands of trees that lined the road.

McGuire could not shake the heaviness he felt for the Newman children. He would have adopted them in the blink of an eye if he could have. But with Ellie in a wheelchair, it was out of the question.

He considered talking to Ellie again. A nanny would make it possible. But he remembered Ellie's words the last time he had suggested adoption and hiring a nanny. McGuire shook his head. His desire was an island, gradually succumbing to the tides of reality.

When the surrey pulled into Smithburg it was after midnight, and most of the town was asleep. But he saw light glowing in the Rileys' parlor windows.

As McGuire guided the team toward the barn, a side door of the house opened, sending a slanted shaft of light into the darkness. He recognized the silhouette of the elderly physician and heard a familiar voice call out, "Jason! That you?"

"Yes, sir."

Riley walked toward him as he drew the surrey to a halt beside the elder doctor's buggy. McGuire slid from the seat and the two men embraced, pounding each other on the back.

"I just got back about half an hour ago," Riley said.

"Get the baby delivered all right?"

"Mm-hmm. What about Florence?"

"She…ah…she died."

"Oh, I'm so sorry."

"She was critical when I got there. I knew when I took one look at her that she would never pull through. Went peaceful, though, with her faith anchored in her Shepherd. Pastor Poole was with her."

"Praise the Lord. I assume the preacher will see to it that the children are placed in a good home."

"Let's talk about it after I get these horses in the corral. Can I buy some feed from you?"

"It'll cost you somewhere around fifty thousand dollars," Riley said.

"Charge it to the dust and let the rain settle it," McGuire bantered back.

Moments later, the two friends entered the house and broke the news of Florence Newman's death to Alfreda and Ellie.

"Pastor Poole is calling a special meeting of the church tomorrow night," McGuire said. "He's going to see if there's a family who will adopt them."

"Do you know if the prospects are good?" Riley asked. "The folks in that area are pretty poor."

"He knows it might be difficult. You know Bill and Bessie Caterson?"

"Sure do."

"They're moving to Greensboro, North Carolina, and they've offered to adopt Lizzie if no family will take both children."

"Separate them?" Ellie said. "That would be terrible. Mrs. Riley told me about their father being killed a year ago. And now they've just lost their mother. Certainly they shouldn't be separated."

"I agree," Jason said, "but they may have to be separated if one family can't take both of them."

"Be a shame," Riley said.

Ellie's eyes misted and her lips quivered. "Poor little dears. Mrs. Riley said the boy is five and the girl two."

"Yes," Jason said. "And they're both beautiful children. I especially got attached to Hunter. Wonderful little boy. Little Lizzie is pretty as a picture. Captured my heart with her smile."

Ellie was quiet for a moment, then looked at her husband. "I would say let's adopt them, but there's no way I could take care of them…at least the little girl. A two-year-old would be out of the question. I guess the boy might not be a problem for a mother in a wheelchair."

Jason's heart leaped in his breast. He turned to his wife and said, "Really? You think you could handle a five-year-old boy from your wheelchair, Ellie?"

Ellie smiled at him warmly but didn't comment.

He shrugged his shoulders and said, "Surely some family in the church will adopt them both. Of course, if they don't, the Catersons will adopt Lizzie and take her to North Carolina. Then…ah…someone in the church certainly will adopt Hunter."

"Of course," Ellie said.

Silence prevailed.

Jason cleared his throat. "On the other hand, maybe the poor little fellow will be left out in the cold."

Ellie sighed. "Well, if that happens, I guess we'd just have to take Hunter back to Boston with us."

Ellie's words started a riot inside Jason. Was she serious? No, she couldn't be. Dare he ask her? After all, even a five-year-old would demand a lot of attention. It would be too much to put such a load on Ellie. Of course, with a nanny…

"Jason," Alfreda said, "have you had anything to eat? Chet ate supper at the farm where he delivered the baby."

Food was the furthest thing from Jason's mind. "Oh…ah…no,

BATTLES OF DESTINY

4 0

ma'am, but really I'm not hungry."

"You're sure? I could fix some leftovers from the supper Ellie and I had."

"No. Really. I'm fine, thank you."

"Well, then," Alfreda said, sighing. "It's late. We'd best get to bed."

"Sounds good to me," Ellie said.

When Jason neither responded nor moved, Ellie said, "Sweetheart—"

Jason was lost in his own thoughts. He returned to reality with a start when he heard his wife say, "Sweetheart, where have you been? We've been talking about retiring for the night."

"Oh! Sure. I guess we'd better. We sure appreciate you two taking us in like this."

"Happy to do it," the older physician said. "After all, you and Ellie are just like family—like our own kids, you know."

Jason smiled. "Thank you."

Riley cocked his head. "Jason…"

"Yes, sir?"

"Your mind is still in McCann's Run, isn't it?"

Jason rubbed the back of his neck. "I…I just have to know if those little ones find a good Christian home. Tell you what. If you don't mind, Ellie and I will stay a little longer than we had planned. We'll drive over to McCann's Run day after tomorrow and see how the church meeting turned out."

"Of course we don't mind," Alfreda assured him. "Do we, Chet?"

"Not in the least. In fact, I'll just take Jason to the clinic with me tomorrow. Maybe since he's one of those hotshot big city doctors, he can teach this old country doctor something."

"Not in a million years," Jason said. "You've already forgotten more than I'll ever know." Then to Ellie: "Is that all right with you, sweetheart? Staying over and going to McCann's Run on Saturday?"

"Certainly. You're not alone in this, darling. I too want to know if those dear children will be adopted."

On Friday evening the members of McCann's Run Presbyterian Church gathered in their white frame building with the steeple on top. The pastor was in conversation with Thora and Jane Louise Kemp and Bill and Bessie Caterson, who sat on a front pew with the Newman children. Thora's other children were on the pew behind her. Tom Jackson and his Aunt Ophelia were on the front pew across the aisle.

At seven-thirty on the dot, Nelson Poole stepped behind the pulpit, called the meeting to order, and asked one of the men to open in prayer.

Four people slipped in just after the "Amen." Poole waited for them to take a seat, then said, "All of you know why I've called this special meeting." He looked over the congregation and did a quick survey, telling himself there were three families missing. He was about to proceed when a couple filed through the door. The sound of wagons rattling to a halt outside told him more were arriving.

Poole waited patiently for the others to enter. These people were farmers, and he understood the necessity of getting cows milked and stock fed after working in the fields all day. The three missing families were now in their pews.

"All of you know why I've called this special meeting. You've had time to think about the situation and make it a matter of prayer, so I'll get right to the point. Do we have a family willing to adopt Hunter and Lizzie Newman?"

People looked around at each other, waiting for someone to speak up. When no one did, the pastor said, "Mrs. Poole and I would love to do it, but you all know the size of the parsonage, and you all know my salary. We just can't do it."

A man stood up. "Brother Jenkins," Poole said in acknowledgment.

"Pastor, Audrey and I would love to adopt those precious kids, but we already have five. I just don't know how we could afford two more."

Others stood up one at a time, expressing the same reality. They couldn't afford to adopt even one of the Newman children, let alone both of them.

"Well, folks," Poole said, "since there's no one who can adopt Hunter and Lizzie, I have an alternate plan. I would like to see them stay together, so how about if we pass them from family to family a week at a time? That wouldn't impose a financial burden on anyone. With our small house, it will mean a couple of children sleep on the floor, but we can manage that when our turn comes. In fact, Mrs. Poole and I will take them the very first week."

A low rumble of discussion among the people went on for the better part of a minute, then Bill Caterson stood to his feet. "Pastor," he said, "the offer Bessie and I made to you last night still stands. We will adopt Lizzie. I wish we could afford to adopt both of them. We'd sure do it if we could. I don't like the idea of them being shifted from home to home every week. I know this would keep them together, but they need a home and family to call their own. That's what Bessie and I wish to do for Lizzie. We'd like to know that we have your blessing and the blessing of the church on our adopting her."

There was much discussion, but the final consensus of pastor and congregation was that the Catersons should adopt Lizzie and give her the home and security she needed.

Several families volunteered to take Hunter for a week at a time, and Mrs. Poole wrote down their names. The pastor then told the volunteers that his wife would set up the schedule and post it on the church bulletin board so each family would know when it was their turn.

When the meeting was dismissed, Hunter began to cry, saying he didn't want to be separated from his sister.

Bill Caterson knelt down beside Hunter and said, "North Carolina isn't real far away. We'll try to work it out so we can have you down once in a while to spend a few days with Lizzie. Would that make you happy?"

The boy nodded, wiping his tears.

"Then we'll work on that," Bill said, patting the boy's arm.

Tom Jackson sat beside Hunter with his arm around the boy, and the families who had volunteered to take Hunter gathered around him, letting him know they would be glad to have him in their homes.

The next day, Jason and Ellie McGuire arrived in McCann's Run at 9:30 A.M., figuring they would talk to the pastor before the funeral. But as they rounded the corner on the dusty street where the church stood, they saw wagons, buggies, and surreys pulling into the church-yard.

"Looks like they have their funerals early around here," Jason said.

Inside the white frame building, a closed coffin decorated with flowers rested on a stand in front of the pulpit. People quietly filed in while the woman at the pump organ played a hymn. Six men who had volunteered as pall bearers sat on a front pew. Across the aisle on the second pew, Bill and Bessie Caterson, with Lizzie, were sitting with Mrs. Poole. Hunter sat next to Mrs. Poole with Tom Jackson on his other side.

In an attempt to avoid looking at the coffin, Hunter kept turn-ing around to glance toward the rear of the church. He happened to be looking that way when he saw Dr. McGuire enter, pushing a lady in a wheelchair. His heart beat faster. He looked up at Mrs. Poole and whispered, "Dr. McGuire just came in. Could I please go see him for a minute?"

"All right," she replied, "but don't stay very long. The service will be starting in a few minutes."

Hunter looked up at Tom as he slid off the pew and said, "Dr. McGuire's here!"

"Yes, I saw him," Tom said.

Mrs. Poole leaned toward Tom. "Maybe you'd better go with him so he's sure to come back in time."

"Yes, ma'am. Come on, Hunter."

Compassionate eyes from the people in the pews watched little Hunter Newman as he walked in front of Tom Jackson to the back of the church. There was a space behind the last row of pews, then a final pew was positioned against the back wall. Jason had parked Ellie's wheelchair next to the side wall and was just sitting down beside her when he saw the little boy hurrying toward him with Tom on his heels.

Ellie McGuire watched her husband lift the bright-eyed child into his arms and felt a lump rise in her throat when she saw how Hunter clung to Jason's neck. Then Jason set the boy down and said in a subdued voice, "Hunter, this is my wife, Ellie. Ellie, this is Hunter Newman."

Hunter was taken aback for just a second at the sight of the doctor's wife in a wheelchair, but he covered his surprise quickly. She was very pretty, and he could tell by the look in her eyes that she liked him.

Ellie opened her arms, smiling. "Could I have a hug?"

Hunter complied, squeezing her neck hard. Tom greeted Ellie, then took the boy back to the front pew.

As her husband sat next to her, Ellie leaned over and said in a soft whisper, "I can see why you had such an instant attraction to the boy. He's precious."

Later, at the cemetery, when the graveside service was over, the McGuires waited patiently while the mourners moved past Hunter and Lizzie. Pastor and Mrs. Poole stood close by and also greeted the people. The McGuires were listening as the pastor explained what had happened at the church meeting.

"I hate to see Hunter and Lizzie separated," Jason McGuire said, "but I'm glad Lizzie will have a good home. But this bouncing Hunter from family to family bothers me. He needs a permanent home, too."

"I agree," Poole said, "but we don't have any choice. At least he'll have good care. I can assure you of that."

McGuire rubbed his chin for a few seconds and then said, "Pastor, would you excuse us for a moment? I need to talk to Ellie alone."

Jason leaned close to Ellie and said, "Darlin', I…I really feel the Lord wants us to—"

"Adopt Hunter?" she said.

"Yes. It's been all I could think of for two days."

"I realize that. And I agree with you that the circumstances seem providential for Hunter to have parents and for us to have a son."

"Do you mean it?"

"As long as there's no talk about hiring a nanny. I told you Thursday night that I could handle a five-year-old from my wheelchair. If Hunter becomes our son, I don't want some nanny raising him. I want us to raise him. I'll be everything to him a mother can be, I promise you."

Jason's whole body tingled. "All right. Let's talk to the pastor."

McGuire saw Poole looking their way and motioned to him. As he approached McGuire said, "Pastor, would there be any objection to Ellie and me adopting Hunter?"

The preacher's eyes widened. "Why, of course not. I think it would be wonderful. My only concern is the…the wheelchair. Can you handle a five-year-old boy, ma'am?"

"I can," Ellie said firmly.

"Well, I certainly can be a character witness for you, if you'd like to take care of it on Monday at the same time the Catersons adopt Lizzie."

"The only thing left is to present this to Hunter," Jason said. "I want him to be in total agreement."

"Certainly," Poole said, turning to call to the boy. "Hunter, would you come over here?"

He had been watching the McGuires and Pastor Poole and he came on the run.

His eyes flitted from Ellie to Jason to Nelson Poole as the pastor said, "Hunter, Dr. and Mrs. McGuire would like to talk to you about something very important."

"Yes, sir."

McGuire dropped to one knee and said, "Hunter, as you can see, Mrs. McGuire—Ellie—is in a wheelchair."

"Yes, sir," Hunter said, setting his sky-blue gaze on Ellie.

"And...well, Hunter, she can't have babies and be a mother like other women. Like your mother did. So we don't have any children."

"Yes, sir."

"Thursday, when I came to your house to see if I could help your mother, I saw right away that you are a very special boy. You've been taught well by your parents. You're respectful to your elders, and you're a good brother to your little sister. Well, Hunter, we just told Pastor Poole that we will adopt you, if you want to be our son."

Hunter's smile spread from ear to ear. "Oh, yes, sir! Yes, sir!"

Jason took the boy in his arms and held him, trying to keep from breaking into tears. "Then on Monday, Hunter, Ellie and I will go with Pastor Poole to the county magistrate's office and adopt you."

"Oh, thank you, sir!" Hunter rushed to Ellie to give her a hug and thank her too. Then he said to both of them, "Couldn't you adopt my sister, too?"

Jason explained that the Catersons had already set their hearts on adopting Lizzie, and that Ellie's being confined to the wheelchair would make it impossible for her to take care of a two-year-old. He promised Hunter that they would make arrangements with the Catersons for Hunter and Lizzie to see each other often.

The next day, the McGuires attended the services at McCann's Run Presbyterian Church. The news was out, and people looked on with pleasure as they saw Hunter sitting on the pew next to Dr. McGuire and his wife.

Pastor Nelson Poole preached on adoption, showing from the

Bible that Christians are not only born into God's family by receiving Christ into their hearts, but they are also given the status of heirs of God and joint-heirs with Christ through adoption.

On Monday, Nelson Poole accompanied the McGuires and the Catersons to the county magistrate's office, and the children were legally adopted. Bill Caterson assured Dr. McGuire they would keep in touch by mail. McGuire told them he would finance any trips to Boston the Catersons could make, and that from time to time, he and Ellie would come to Greensboro with Hunter.

Early the next morning, Bill and Bessie loaded their wagon and were ready to pull out. The McGuires had driven to McCann's Run with Hunter so he could say good-bye to his little sister. Pastor Poole and Tom Jackson were also there.

While Ellie looked on from the surrey seat, Jason led Hunter by the hand to the Caterson wagon.

Tears were streaming down Hunter's cheeks as he hugged his little sister and said with shaky voice, "Good-bye, Lizzie. I love you."

Hunter's tears caused Lizzie to start crying. "Wuv you," she said, sniffling.

Bill handed Lizzie back to Bessie. "God bless you all!" he said, as he climbed aboard.

"We'll write you as soon as we get settled in Greensboro!" Bessie called.

As the wagon pulled away, Jason picked Hunter up and held him.

"It'll be all right, Son," Jason told him. "We'll make sure you get to see Lizzie real often."

When the Caterson wagon was out of sight, Jason said, a quaver in his voice, "Well, I guess we'd better get going."

Tom moved close to Hunter and laid a hand on his shoulder. "Well, little friend," he said, blinking back tears, "I don't know when we'll see each other again, but I'm going to pray that the Lord will make it happen."

The best friends hugged and told each other good-bye, then the surrey moved west and Tom was lost from Hunter's view.

FIVE

It was Sunday afternoon, May 20, 1855. The sky was threatening rain over Cambridge, Massachusetts, and had forced the graduation exercises of Harvard Medical School indoors.

The great auditorium was slowly filling up as family and friends of the graduates made their way inside hoping to find choice seats. A section directly in front of the platform was roped off for seating the graduates.

Dr. Jason McGuire, his hair now streaked with silver, wheeled Ellie through the front door and down the center aisle. Ellie was as pretty as ever, even with a few lines added to her face and some threads of silver in her hair.

When they came near the section just behind the roped area, a young man with a white armband greeted them.

"Good afternoon, folks. This section is reserved for the immediate family of the graduates. Do you have a ticket?"

"Yes," Jason said with a smile, reaching inside his European-made black suit. He produced two tickets and handed them to the young Harvard student. "Our son is graduating today, young man. Would there be a place where I could stash this wheelchair? I'd like his mother to sit in one of the seats."

"Of course, sir. I'll take it over there by the west wall for you."

Other people were filling in the special section as Jason lifted Ellie from her chair and placed her in one of the opera-type seats.

Soon the auditorium was packed, and at three o'clock the band struck up a lively march and the school officials filed onto the platform, clad in gowns and mortarboards with tassels swinging. When the faculty and staff of the Harvard Medical School and top officials of the university were seated, the band struck up an inspiring processional.

Everyone on the platform rose to their feet, and then the audience stood. The standing audience blocked Ellie's view of the graduates as they moved down the aisle from the back of the auditorium, but she would be able to see her son when he passed her row.

Ellie saw Jason's mouth quiver and watched him brush moisture from his cheeks. Then Hunter came into view, looking like a prince to Ellie. Just the sight of him was enough to start her crying softly from joy and pride.

Hunter had grown into a tall, athletic young man. He stood two inches over six feet and was ruggedly handsome.

When the graduates were all in their places, the president of Harvard University introduced Dr. Gabriel Rains, pastor of Boston's Broadway Baptist Church, asking him to say the opening prayer.

Rains's prayer exalted Jesus Christ and asked His blessings on the graduates who would go out to serve mankind. At his "Amen," the great audience sat down, and the ceremonies began.

After the commencement address, the graduates walked to the side of the platform to receive their diplomas in alphabetical order.

When the name "Hunter Newman McGuire" was called, tears spilled down Ellie's cheeks. Jason put an arm around her as Hunter walked to the center of the platform to receive his degree. Jason leaned close to whisper, "That boy has made me so proud."

When the graduation exercises were over, and the graduates were being swarmed by their families and friends, Hunter McGuire hurried back to where he knew his parents were seated. As he approached them through the crowd, Jason smiled and said, "Hello, Dr. McGuire."

Hunter embraced his father. "Thank you, Dad, for being my inspiration all the way through medical school. I hope I can be half the physician and surgeon that you are."

"You'll be ten times what I am, Son."

Hunter then leaned over and wrapped his arms around the woman who had so wonderfully cared for him. As he held her close, he said into her ear, "I love you. Thank you for being my mom."

"Thank you for being such a wonderful son," Ellie said warmly.

"Hey, Hunter! If you don't quit hugging that beautiful lady, her husband will probably break your neck!"

Jason laughed as Hunter turned around to face John Brinton with his fiancée, Betty Miller. "Well," Hunter said with a chuckle, "if it isn't *Doctor* John Brinton."

"Yes! And don't you forget it, *Doctor* Hunter McGuire!"

The McGuires offered congratulations to John for his graduation and imminent marriage. Betty then turned to Hunter and said sincerely, "I've said this several times before, but I must say it again. Thank you for caring enough about John's eternal destiny to lead him to Jesus. If you hadn't won him to the Lord and brought him to church, we would never have met."

"My pleasure, Betty," Hunter said, then blushed as she raised up on tiptoe and planted a kiss on his cheek.

Ellie smiled at Betty and said, "Well, dear, by this time two weeks from today, you'll be Mrs. Dr. John Brinton."

"That's right," Betty said. "John and I will have been husband and wife for nearly two hours by this time in two weeks." She turned and said, "And Hunter is going to be best man!"

"I disagree with that," John said. "If Hunter was the best man at the wedding, *he* would be the one with the bride!"

Everyone laughed.

John clapped a hand on Hunter's shoulder and said, "Well,

Hunter, maybe you'll catch the bride's bouquet and finally find a woman who'll have you!"

Hunter playfully clipped his dark-haired friend on the chin and said, "Oh, yeah? I've had women swarming all over me since I was ten years old. I have to beat them off with clubs."

John waggled his head. "Well, lah-dee-dah! How come you aren't the one getting married, then, Romeo?"

"Simple. The right little gal hasn't yet walked into my life. When she does, I'll know it, and grab her."

"Well, I hope she shows up before you're sporting a cane and living in a rocking chair!"

No rain had fallen yet, but the dark clouds were still hanging low as the McGuire surrey rolled off the campus with Hunter at the reins. Ellie sat between her two men.

"Son," Jason said, "I want you to know how proud Mom and I are of you. What a joy to watch our boy walk across that platform and receive his degree. And on top of that, to hear you listed as an honor student."

Ellie turned to smile at her son and saw the shadow of sadness that suddenly clouded Hunter's face.

"Hunter…what's wrong?"

"I…I sure wish Lizzie could have been here to see me graduate."

Jason reached around Ellie's back and squeezed Hunter's shoulder. "I wish she could have too, Son."

The Brinton-Miller wedding took place as scheduled on Sunday afternoon, June 3. After the reception in the fellowship hall at Broadway Baptist Church, John and Betty stepped out the door where a decorated buggy waited with a "Just Married" sign on the back.

The crowd looked on gleefully as the young unmarried women

collected, each one hoping to catch the bride's bouquet. There was much laughter as Betty tossed the bouquet into the air and it bounded off hands and fingers for a few seconds before a young woman caught it. Then the crowd made two lines for the bride and groom to run between so they could pelt the couple with rice on their way to the buggy. Hunter McGuire had rice in both hands.

Just before John and Betty started their run, one of Betty's friends dashed up to her with a second bouquet and whispered in her ear. When the couple headed for the buggy, ducking their heads against the flying rice, they paused long enough for Betty to toss the bouquet straight at Hunter. He caught it in a reflexive movement and stood with a bemused look on his face as everyone laughed.

He continued to hold the bouquet, turning it in his hands as the buggy bounded down the dusty street, noisily dragging old pots, pans, and buckets.

SIX

Afternoon sunshine cast long shadows across the Virginia countryside as the train chugged toward Lexington on Wednesday, June 6, 1855. Dr. Hunter McGuire was about to begin his internship at the Kurtz-Aaron Medical Clinic.

As the coach rocked soothingly, Hunter let his gaze roam over the rolling landscape. Wildflowers picked up the gold of the lowering sun and the evening breeze tufted the grass. His eyes and ears were attentive to every tangent and curve, to the rhythm of the wheels on the rail joints, to the flow of the train along the smooth tracks.

Suddenly the rear door of the coach opened and closed with a brief rise in volume of the clacking wheels. The conductor's high-pitched voice filled the coach, "Lexington, ten minutes! Lexington, ten minutes!" and then was gone as the man passed through to the next coach.

The train ran on without breaking stride for another five minutes, then the engine's long whistle blast fled by the window in gusty waves, and the town came into view.

Soon the engine was chugging into the depot with the bell ringing. When the brakes squealed and the engine released steam with a loud hiss as it came to a halt, the young doctor stretched his arms and yawned. The other passengers were gathering their belongings as Hunter hoisted his long, muscular frame and stood up in the aisle. He reached for his bag and hat in the overhead bin and moved slowly toward the front of the coach.

When he stepped onto the platform and ran his eyes over the crowd, he spotted a short, thick-bodied man with carrot-red hair. When their eyes met, the man broke into a smile and hurried toward him.

"Dr. McGuire," he said, extending his hand. "Weldon Kurtz."

It felt good to hear the 'doctor' adjoined to his name. Hunter knew it would take awhile to get used to it.

As they shook hands, Kurtz said, "You look exactly like the daguerreotype you sent with your application. Couldn't have missed you. Dr. Aaron and I have certainly been looking forward to your working with us at the clinic."

"Not as much as I've been looking forward to it," Hunter said with a grin.

"I assume you have more luggage."

"Yes. There's a trunk in the baggage coach."

"Well, let's go get it."

The doctors had acquired a nice room for Hunter at one of Lexington's best boarding houses. Dr. Kurtz got him settled there, then took him in his buggy to a restaurant where they were to meet Dr. Bryce Aaron for supper.

Aaron was waiting for them, leaning against his buggy. Hunter knew it was him when he smiled and raised a hand in a friendly gesture. He was about Kurtz's height, but was quite slender and balding. Hunter climbed down, and the two men shook hands and introduced themselves.

After they had begun their meal, Dr. Aaron said, "Well, Dr. McGuire, you've come to a very busy clinic. We have the only facility of its kind between Roanoke—fifty-five miles to the south—and

Staunton—thirty-five miles to the north. I hope you've come expecting a lot of hard work. We're getting busier all the time."

"I welcome hard work, Doctor. I want to do my part while I'm interning here, and I want to learn as much as I can."

Kurtz winked at Aaron and said, "We were hoping you'd be the one to teach *us*, Doctor…being a graduate of Harvard and all."

"Especially a Harvard graduate who graduated in the top five of his class," Aaron said, and winked back.

Hunter's sand-colored eyebrows arched. "And just how did you learn that?"

Aaron took a sip of coffee. "Oh, we received a letter from a certain person who thought we ought to be aware that we've hired a genius."

Hunter tilted back his head and laughed heartily. "Okay, so my mom thinks I'm a genius. You know how mothers are."

"Yes," Aaron said with a chuckle, "we both have them."

"But seriously, Dr. McGuire," Kurtz said, "we're quite pleased to have you interning at our clinic."

"Thank you," Hunter said humbly. "The pleasure is mine."

Dr. Aaron looked at Hunter with a steady, pleasant expression. "In your application you said you were Virginia-born."

Hunter swallowed his bite of food. "Yes, sir. McCann's Run. It's in the western part of the commonwealth. Rural area. About halfway between Parkersburg and Clarksburg."

"You left there when you were pretty young, I recall."

"Yes, sir. I was five."

"Was your father practicing in that area up until that time?"

"No. It's a long story, but I'm a McGuire by adoption. My real father died when I was four, and my mother died a year later. Dr. Jason McGuire just happened to be in the area when my mother was dying, and he filled in for the family doctor. The McGuires adopted me and took me to Boston."

"You were the only child?" Kurtz asked, lifting his coffee cup to take a sip.

"I had a sister. Lizzie. Younger than me. Someone else adopted her. So how many employees do you have in the clinic?"

Both doctors took the hint and left the subject alone.

"Well, let's see," Aaron said. "We have three certified medical nurses on staff, and three nurses' aides. One of those aides is working toward her C.M.N. We have a janitor who comes in and cleans once a day, and a receptionist who works the day shift. She also does the filing work, takes care of the books, and does the banking. So we have eight employees."

"As you might guess," Kurtz said, "we work one C.M.N. and one aide on each of the three shifts. We have ten beds in one ward at the clinic, so the teams of two can pretty well handle it. Dr. Aaron and I normally work the day shift, but we both live close by, so if we're needed at any time during the other two shifts, we can easily be contacted."

Hunter nodded. "In our correspondence, you mentioned your plans to one day become a full-fledged hospital."

"Most assuredly," Kurtz said. "We figure we're maybe four years away from realizing that dream. But we'll make it by then, won't we, Doctor?"

"I have no doubt," Aaron said. "And it will be sorely needed by then, the way the population is growing around here."

The meal was soon finished and Dr. Aaron reminded his partner that they had a patient to check on before bedtime. Kurtz told him to go ahead, he would drive Dr. McGuire to the boarding house. Aaron bid McGuire good night; he would see him just before seven o'clock when the day shift started.

As Hunter rode with Dr. Kurtz through the dimly lit streets of Lexington, he said, "I've known for years that the Virginia Military Institute is here. I didn't notice it when the train pulled in."

"It's up on a hill that way," Kurtz said, pointing. "You can see it in daylight if you know where to look. See that cluster of lights up there?"

"Mm-hmm."

"That's it. You'll see the cadets around town a lot. Always in their uniforms. We treat one every now and then. Fine young men. Courteous and well disciplined."

Kurtz drove past the clinic so Hunter could see it, then headed toward the boarding house.

The next morning the sun was just above the tree-lined hills when Dr. Hunter McGuire left the boarding house and headed toward the clinic. The air was cool, and birds were singing in the trees.

A few of Lexington's citizens were on the streets as Hunter walked, and they responded warmly as he greeted them. When he reached the clinic, he entered the front door and found the reception area deserted. He moved past the reception desk, through a set of double doors, and into the hallway. A pretty lady in white was coming his way, carrying a bundle of sheets and pillowcases. She wore no cap, which identified her as the nurse's aide. When her glance fell on the tall young man, she stopped and smiled. "Good morning, Dr. McGuire. Welcome to the clinic, and to Lexington."

"Well, thank you, ma'am. But how do you know me?"

She giggled and said, "Us single girls have been studying your picture. The one you sent with your application."

Hunter blushed. "Oh. I didn't know the doctors had made it public."

The young woman set the bundle on a nearby table and extended her hand. "I'm Rita Watkins, nurse's aide."

Hunter gripped her hand lightly. "I'm happy to meet you, ma'am."

At that moment, a nurse appeared, coming from what appeared to be the ward at the end of the hall. Rita Watkins introduced Hunter to Molly Mulvane, who was in her early fifties. She explained they were about to go off duty when nurse Carolynn Atherton and nurse's aide May Godfrey came in. Both called the new intern by name before they were introduced. Again Hunter blushed, but found them to be charming ladies.

Then the doctors came in together, followed by young Doralee Chambers, the receptionist.

The day started off with Dr. Aaron giving Hunter a tour, acquainting him with the layout of the building and the normal routine of the day shift. Aaron explained that he and Dr. Kurtz wanted him to work the day shift for a month, the evening shift for the next month, and the night shift for a month after that. This schedule would give him a working knowledge of the differences in each shift.

The rest of the day was anything but dull. First Hunter was called upon to treat an elderly man who had fallen off a horse and broken his shoulder. Dr. Kurtz watched to see if Hunter could handle it and he passed with flying colors. Next was a teenage girl who had seriously cut her hand while learning to cut up chickens for canning. According to Dr. Aaron, Hunter did a perfect job of treating the cut, taking stitches, and bandaging.

Then a middle-aged man was brought in with heart failure, and Hunter worked side by side with Dr. Aaron for nearly four hours. In spite of their efforts, the man died, and Hunter had a first lesson in how to harness his compassion and grief and work with professional objectivity.

When three o'clock came, Hunter was worn out more from emotional strain than the hours he had put in. He was working with Dr. Kurtz on one of the elderly patients in the ward when Carolynn Atherton walked up and said that nurse Maude Edwards and aide Jodie Lockwood were in the building and she and May would be leaving for the day.

A few minutes later, a matronly woman in her early fifties came into the ward.

Dr. Kurtz looked up and said, "Maude, I want you to meet—"

"Dr. Hunter Newman McGuire," Maude finished for him, smiling at Hunter. "Glad to meet you, Doctor. Only I think you're better looking than Doralee was able to describe. She's not much with words."

Kurtz chuckled and said, "Maude, I think you're too old for him."

"I know that, Doctor, but I'm trying to help the single girls around this place find husbands."

"You count me out, Mrs. Edwards," Hunter said with a grin.

"Oh?"

"Yes, ma'am."

"And why's that? You a confirmed bachelor?"

"No, ma'am. But I—"

Maude turned around to see what had cut off the young doctor's words.

A petite young woman smiled at the small group and then fixed her attention on Hunter. "Hello, Dr. McGuire. I'm Jodie Lockwood, the nurse's aide for this shift."

Hunter McGuire was so struck with the young woman that he could hardly breathe. He guessed she was about eighteen. She had jet-black hair, deep-brown eyes, exquisitely noble features, and a blinding smile.

Jodie extended her hand and Hunter took it, returning her smile. "It's a pleasure to meet you Miss Lockwood. It is *Miss* Lockwood?"

"Yes."

"Jodie's the aide Dr. Aaron told you is working on her C.M.N. certificate," Kurtz said.

"Oh, yes. That's great, Miss Lockwood."

"How has your first day been?" she asked.

Hunter paused, thought on it, then said, "Well-l-l…it's been…ah…educational, to say the least. But all in all, it's been enjoyable. And I'm sure excited about working here."

That night, Hunter had a hard time getting to sleep. The fascinating face of Jodie Lockwood wouldn't leave his mind. He told himself that if she wasn't a Christian, the first thing he would do was give her the gospel and do everything he could to lead her to the Lord.

He told God that he knew something completely different than anything he had ever experienced before had happened deep inside him the instant he laid eyes on Jodie. He had dated many young women in his church in Boston. Some were pleasant company, and he enjoyed being with them, but he had never felt anything like this.

Hunter finally fell asleep sometime after midnight. When he woke up the next morning, seeing Jodie was foremost on his mind.

Hunter chatted with Jodie at shift-change time on Friday and learned that she was seventeen. Even though she was a year younger than he had presumed, it made no difference. She was quite mature for her age. He was also thrilled to learn that she wasn't seeing anyone.

On Saturday, after an exhausting shift, Hunter and Carolynn Atherton were in the ward room attending an elderly woman when Jodie and Maude Edwards came in to start their shift.

Jodie came over to stand beside Hunter and looked at the patient, then glanced at Hunter. "Good afternoon, Dr. McGuire. What happened here?"

"Mrs. Caldwell fell out of bed a few moments ago," Hunter said. "I can't find anything broken, but she banged herself up some. And how are you this beautiful day?"

"Just fine. Hello, Carolynn."

"Hi, Jodie."

Jodie glanced at Hunter again and said, "Dr. McGuire, before you leave, I need to see you for a moment."

"All right. We're about through here. I'll come find you."

Ten minutes later, Hunter found Jodie by the reception area talking to Doctors Aaron and Kurtz. As he walked toward them, she broke off the conversation politely and said, "There you are."

Both doctors waited as Jodie said, "I'll only detain you a moment, Dr. McGuire."

I wish you'd detain me for the rest of my life, Hunter thought. Aloud, he said, "My time is yours, Miss Lockwood. Did you want to talk in private?"

"Oh, no. That won't be necessary."

Hunter felt a jab of disappointment.

The doctors were still standing there as Jodie said, "I just wanted to ask if you were planning to attend church services tomorrow."

"As a matter of fact, I am," he said. "I'm going to First Baptist."

Jodie's eyes lit up. "Well, that's exactly where I was going to ask you to come…as my guest. Will you? Come as my guest that is?"

"Well of course!"

The doctors moved closer. "Forgive me, Dr. McGuire," Dr. Kurtz said. "I was going to invite you to First Methodist Church, but just hadn't gotten around to it."

"And I was going to invite you to Oaklawn Presbyterian with me and my family tomorrow," Dr. Aaron said.

"No forgiveness necessary, gentlemen," Hunter said. "But since Jodie asked me first, I'll go as her guest."

"So you're a Baptist, eh?" Aaron said in mock dismay.

"Smart man," Jodie said with a giggle.

"Hah!" Kurtz said. "If he really had good sense, he'd be a Methodist!"

Everybody laughed, then Hunter said, "There isn't any church going to take a person to heaven. Only Jesus can do that."

There was a twinkle in Jodie's eye as she said, "Even if being a Baptist isn't what takes a person to heaven, I figure as long as I'm going to make the trip, I might as well go first class!"

The three men laughed heartily.

"Dr. McGuire," Jodie said, "we have a lot of fun kidding each other around here, but let me say seriously, these two wonderful men are a joy to work for. You will come to love them dearly when you've been here awhile."

"I'm already getting quite attached to them," Hunter said.

"Will you need a ride to church in the morning?" she asked.

"No, thank you. My landlord said I could use one of his buggies anytime."

"And you know where the church is?"

"Yes. I saw it when Dr. Kurtz first took me to the boarding house."

"Well, Sunday school is at ten, and the preaching service is at eleven. The Sunday evening service starts at seven."

"Thank you, m'lady," Hunter said, bowing slightly.

Jodie curtsied.

Hunter bowed again, excused himself, and headed for home.

The Sunday morning church services were a joy and an inspiration to Hunter. He liked the pastor's preaching, and he liked the warm, friendly people. He was pleased to see a good number of cadets from the Virginia Military Institute in attendance.

Jodie introduced Hunter to Mr. and Mrs. Walter Blevins, who rented a room to Jodie in their home. The Blevinses invited Hunter to have Sunday dinner with them.

During the meal, Jodie offered to take Hunter on a tour of the town. Hunter accepted, saying they could use his landlord's horse and buggy.

The day couldn't have been more beautiful as Hunter and Jodie drove through the streets of Lexington and around its perimeter. How much better the birds sang since he had met Jodie Lockwood! The sun shone brighter and the air smelled sweeter.

As Jodie directed Hunter through the wealthy neighborhood, he ran his gaze over the fancy mansions with their high fences and superbly manicured yards, then looked at her and said, "It sure was a joy to find out you're a Christian, Miss Jodie."

"And for me to learn the same about you. And I'm glad you like the church."

"It's great."

As they left the wealthy section, Jodie pointed up the hill to the west and said, "There's V.M.I."

"Impressive."

"Mm-hmm. They call it the West Point of the South."

"Oh? I wasn't aware of that."

"Quite a setup, they have. On some days, you'll hear the cannons."

"Cannons?"

"They teach them cannoneering, along with the use of muskets and handguns. The cannon field is set up near the foothills of the Appalachian Mountains a few miles west of the Institute."

"That's interesting." Hunter paused, then said, "Have you dated any of the cadets?"

"A few. They're nice young men. Very polite and gentle-manly …like yourself. I suppose you dated lots of young women in Boston."

"Some."

Hunter wanted to blurt out that he had never met a girl who so thrilled and captivated him as she did, but he kept it inside. They were now back in the center of the business district, where the tour had officially started.

"Well," Jodie said with a sigh, "that's about it. You've seen Lexington now. How do you like it?"

Hunter aimed the buggy toward the section of town where the Blevins lived.

"Fine. It's a real nice town." He wanted to add that the best thing about Lexington was that Jodie Lockwood lived there.

Jodie sighed again, and said, "I'm sure going to miss it."

Hunter wasn't sure he'd heard her correctly. "What did you say?"

"I said I'm sure going to miss Lexington."

"Y-you're leaving?"

"Yes. Next Friday. I'm moving to Baltimore."

SEVEN

J odie's words were like a battering ram to Hunter's midsection. "Baltimore? How...how come?"

"Well, I've been with Dr. Kurtz and Dr. Aaron for the past fourteen months working toward my C.M.N. certificate. You probably know that means I'm halfway there. But my real desire is to also earn my C.S.A. certificate."

"Surgeon's assistant," Hunter said. "But that certificate can be earned only under a surgeon who is on the staff of a hospital approved by the American Medical Association."

"That's right. Have you heard of Dr. Benjamin Karr?"

"He's Baltimore's most prominent surgeon. One of the best in the whole country. Has his own clinic."

"He's also on staff of the hospital in Baltimore and the one in Washington, D. C. Both are approved by the AMA. So Dr. Kurtz, bless his heart, contacted Dr. Karr and asked if he would hire me and allow me to finish my C.M.N. training there while also gaining time and experience toward my C.S.A. certificate."

Jodie seemed so excited that Hunter put a smile on his face and managed to hide his disappointment.

Jodie's words came faster now. "The Lord had it all planned, Dr.

McGuire. On the same day Dr. Karr received the letter, one of his potential C.S.A.s told him she was quitting in two weeks to get married. So…as of a week from tomorrow, I'll start to work for Dr. Karr! Isn't it wonderful?"

"Sure, that's great," he said. "I'm real happy for you." Lord, forgive me for lying. I'm not happy about it at all.

In the days that followed Jodie's announcement, Hunter hardly noticed the singing birds or sunshine or the smell of Virginia's fresh air. His heart was like a dead thing in his chest.

Each day when Jodie arrived for the evening shift, Hunter spent as much time with her as possible and had to act as if he were happy for this turn of events in her life. He desperately wanted to tell her he loved her, but it had to remain his secret for now.

At nine-thirty Friday morning, Jodie came into the clinic accompanied by Mr. and Mrs. Blevins, who were taking her to the depot to catch the train to Richmond. There she would board another train for Baltimore.

Hunter wished he could be with Jodie right up to the minute she boarded, but it was out of the question. He was on duty. And as far as Jodie and the others knew, they were just friends…barely acquainted.

Carolynn Atherton and May Godfrey came from the ward and joined the three doctors to tell Jodie good-bye. Carolynn and May embraced her and wished her the best, then excused themselves to get back to their patients.

Hunter looked on as tears misted Jodie's eyes when she moved close to Kurtz and Aaron and said, "I owe you two so much. Thank you for all you've done for me. She hugged them both as they expressed their wishes for her great success.

Then Jodie turned to Hunter and said, "It was a genuine pleasure to meet you, Dr. McGuire. I can see a wonderful future for you. God bless you."

"God bless you too, Miss Jodie," he managed to choke out. "I know you will do well as a surgeon's assistant."

Jodie smiled up at him and said, "If you're ever in Baltimore, look me up. It would be nice to see you again."

Hunter's smile felt painted on. "I'll do that."

Suddenly, she opened her arms. "I've hugged everyone else good-bye around here, do you mind if I do the same with you?"

The painful thudding of his heart seemed audible to Hunter as he felt Jodie's arms around him and he pressed his hands to her back.

Suddenly she was out of his arms and saying in a brisk tone, "Well, folks, we'd better get going."

The Blevinses moved out the door first, and Jodie followed while the doctors watched them walk to the surrey. Mr. Blevins took his wife's hand to help her aboard while Jodie waited.

Hunter saw his chance and hurried up to Jodie. "Here, Miss Jodie, allow me."

"Why, thank you, Dr. McGuire."

Hunter held on as she eased onto the seat.

Jodie smiled at him and said, "Good-bye, Doctor."

"Good-bye." Hunter wanted to cry out that he loved her, but all he did was stand and watch as the surrey pulled away and turned the corner. Jodie waved one more time before the surrey carried her from view. He felt as if she were taking his heart with her, and the pain wrung a groan from him.

When he returned to the clinic door, the doctors were still where he had left them. There was a sudden rumbling like thunder, and Hunter glanced up at the clear sky, then looked at the doctors as they chuckled.

"Cannons," Kurtz said.

"Oh, yes. Miss Jodie told me the Institute trains the cadets in cannoneering."

"It's been a couple of weeks since we've heard them," Aaron said. "You ever handle a gun, Dr. McGuire?"

"As a matter of fact, I do," Hunter said. "Or I should say I did.

In my growing up years, my dad took me hunting in northern Massachusetts and southern New Hampshire. I got pretty good with a musket. Dad also taught me how to use a handgun."

"Well, remind me to stay on your good side," Kurtz said.

The three doctors laughed, then Aaron said, "Well, gentlemen, we've got work to do."

One night, about a week later, Hunter read his Bible, then doused the lantern and crawled into bed. Lying there with moonlight streaming through the window, he prayed, "Lord, I've got to be honest with You. I don't understand. Surely You didn't let me meet Jodie and fall in love with her just to tear my heart out? I've never felt about any girl like I feel about her. And I believe she would've fallen in love with me if we'd had enough time together.

"It just seems to me that it was Your hand that brought us together and that You mean for me to have Jodie for my wife, Lord Jesus. So I'm asking You to keep her from falling for someone else till I can tell her how I feel...and You can help her to love me, too."

On a rainy afternoon, when Jodie had been gone for over a month, Hunter arrived at the clinic for the evening shift just as a wagon marked "Virginia Military Institute" hauled up and came to a stop. A uniformed man was sitting in the bed of the wagon.

"Sir, are you one of the doctors here?" the man asked.

"Yes. I'm Dr. McGuire. May I help you?"

"Yes, Doctor. We have a very sick cadet here."

Hunter looked into the wagon bed and saw a ghostly pale young man, gritting his teeth and clutching his midsection.

"Let's get him inside," Hunter said.

"Doralee," Hunter said as he and the uniformed men entered the reception area, "this young man may have an acute attack of appendicitis. Would you find one of the doctors for me, please?"

Hunter hurried the cadet into the surgical room and onto the operating table.

"Have you been vomiting?" Hunter asked him.

"Three times...before we left the Institute," he said, and groaned.

"I'm going to probe in the lower abdominal area. It may hurt a little, but it's the only way I can find out what I need to know." To help keep the patient's mind off the pain, he asked, "What's your name?"

"Willie...Crane."

"How old are you?"

"Nn-n-n-ngh! Nineteen!"

"Where you from?"

"Rich...mond."

"So you're planning a military career?"

Suddenly Willie stiffened and let out a scream.

Nurse Maude Edwards came running just ahead of Dr. Aaron.

"What's going on?" Aaron said, plunging through the surgery door.

"Cadet Willie Crane here has appendicitis, Doctor," Hunter replied.

"Normal symptoms?"

"Yes, sir. The pain is right where it's supposed to be...and he vomited before they brought him here."

Aaron moved closer. "Let me check."

"Please do. If I'm wrong, I sure want to know it."

Aaron probed the painful area and made Willie scream again, then turned to McGuire. "It's appendicitis, all right. Nurse, prepare the patient for surgery. We'll go with chloroform."

Maude nodded and began to gather the needed materials.

"I'll have to ask you gentlemen to go to the waiting room," Aaron said to the two men who had brought Crane in. "It's just down the hall."

Both men headed for the door and disappeared.

Willie groaned and said, "Doctor, will I be all right?"

"I believe so, son," Hunter said. "But if we wait much longer, you might not be. The nurse is going to get you ready for surgery."

Dr. Aaron motioned for Hunter to move into the hallway. Once they were out of earshot from Willie Crane, Aaron said, "I want you to do the surgery."

Hunter's eyes bulged. "But, Doctor, I…the only appendectomies I've done were on cadavers. I observed several on live patients in medical school, but I think I should observe some more before I actually do it."

Aaron smiled. "Wasn't one of your reasons for choosing to intern here was that you would do surgery much sooner than in a hospital?"

"Well, yes, sir. But I didn't expect to do it *this* soon!"

"Can't learn to swim by watching someone else," Aaron said. "Got to hit the water yourself. Of course, I'll be right at your side to give any advice or instruction you may need."

"Whew! I thought you meant I'd be on my own."

Aaron laughed. "Only when you're completely ready for that."

During the surgery, Dr. Aaron stood by ready to offer assistance if needed. It wasn't. Hunter had performed the operation flawlessly.

Late in the afternoon on the day after the operation, Hunter was on the opposite side of the ward from Willie Crane's bed, tending to another patient. His back was to the door and he didn't see the nurse's aide enter with a tall, dark-haired man in uniform.

Hunter heard Willie say weakly, "Hello, Major. It's nice to see you."

"I had to come and see how my number one cannoneer is doing," a voice replied.

Hunter finished his task and started toward the door. As he drew near Willie's bed, it struck him that there was something familiar about the dark-haired man. The major stood almost as tall as Hunter and was slender but muscular. He had an angular, craggy face and dark brown, close-cropped hair with short side whiskers. But it was the deep-set, blue-gray eyes and the way he stood that seemed most familiar to Hunter.

"Dr. McGuire," Willie Crane said. "I'd like you to meet my favorite professor at the Institute, Major Thomas Jackson."

"McGuire?" Jackson said, cocking his head and squinting as he took in Hunter's sandy-colored hair and sky-blue eyes. *"Doctor* McGuire? Not the adopted son of Dr. Jason McGuire of Boston?"

Hunter's skin tingled and his pulse quickened. "Tom? Tom Jackson of Jackson's Mill?"

The two men embraced and clapped each other on the shoulders. Willie watched and smiled, surprised to learn they were friends. The six other patients in the ward looked on with interest.

When the two men finally turned back to Willie, the major explained to him that he had not seen the doctor in fifteen years. In fact, Dr. McGuire had been only five years old.

Tom rested a hand on Hunter's shoulder and said, "I want to hear about your family, and all about you. Could we get together for an evening meal?"

"I'm on the evening shift for another three weeks, but how about Sunday? You don't have school up there on the hill on Sunday, do you?"

"Sure don't. How about right after Sunday morning church services day after tomorrow?"

On Sunday the two old friends ate together and began to get acquainted all over again. They talked of times Hunter could recall, then he filled Tom in on his adoptive parents, his graduation from Harvard Medical School, and his internship at the Kurtz-Aaron Medical Clinic.

Tom had graduated from West Point in 1846 as a second

lieutenant and was assigned to an artillery unit in the U.S. Army. The United States had just entered into war with Mexico, and he was sent immediately into that country to fight. He fought under the famous war hero, General Winfield Scott, and became fast friends with Captain Robert E. Lee, who was now making a name for himself in the U.S. Army as a full colonel. Hunter had heard of Lee and was impressed that Jackson knew him.

By the time the Mexican War had come to an end in July 1848, Tom had risen to the rank of major. Now he was professor of artillery tactics and philosophy of war at Virginia Military Institute.

Hunter smiled. "I've heard your cannons over there in the foothills."

"Some folks in these parts complain about the noise, but the only way to train men to fire the big guns is to have them fire the big guns."

Hunter smiled again and sipped his coffee. "How about marriage, Tom? Don't tell me you haven't been caught by some pretty lassie."

Sadness filled the major's eyes.

Hunter saw it and said, "Oh, Tom, I'm sorry. I—"

"No, no, no. Don't be. You would have no way of knowing. She had the same name as your adoptive mother."

"Ellie?"

"Ellie Junkin, oldest daughter of Dr. George Junkin. He's been a Presbyterian minister for several years, then became president of Washington College right here in Lexington."

"I've been by the campus many times."

"I met Ellie at church soon after coming here. We were married by her father at Oaklawn in 1853. Ellie died the next year, Hunter, giving birth to our first child, who was stillborn."

"Tom, I'm so sorry."

Tears misted Jackson's eyes. "I miss her something fierce. The Lord's given me peace, though. I know my Ellie is in a lot better world than you and I. Maybe someday the Lord will bring another mate along for me, Hunter. I don't know. That's in His hands."

Tom took a deep breath, let it out slowly, and said, "What about your little sister, Lizzie? How's she doing?"

It was Hunter's turn to look sad. His voice was heavy as he said, "I haven't seen her since the day the Catersons drove away from McCann's Run to go to North Carolina."

"*What?*"

"It's true. Within a month after my adoptive parents took me to Boston, Dad sent a letter to Bill and Bessie Caterson at Greensboro. The letter came back with a note on its face, saying there were no Catersons in or near Greensboro."

"How could that be?"

"Several months later, Dad made a trip to Greensboro and came upon the man who had hired Bill. The Catersons never showed up, and their prospective employer never heard anything afterward."

Jackson shook his head, frowning.

"Dad went to McCann's Run and asked if anyone there had heard from the Catersons. It was as if the three of them had disappeared off the face of the earth. Dad talked to the Ritchie County sheriff, and he said there was no way he could investigate the disappearance, and no other sheriff's department would, either. There's a lot of territory between McCann's Run and Greensboro. So, with no further avenues to pursue, Dad returned to Boston."

"And that's it? Nothing since then?"

"Nothing."

"What do you think happened?"

"I have no idea. It sounds like foul play, but I've never given up that Lizzie is still alive somewhere. God knows where she is. I've prayed daily that the Lord will bring us together again—as my birth mother would put it—'on the wings of the wind.'"

Jackson scrubbed a hand over his face. "Well, Hunter, with God all things are possible. You just keep praying, and don't give up."

*** *** ***

As time passed, Tom and Hunter spent much time together and became close friends again. The major was known for loving to debate theological issues, and he and Hunter had a good time together doing so.

Hunter became acquainted with several young ladies at church, and even dated some, but there was a guard on his heart. He believed that somehow, in God's sovereign way, He would bring Jodie Lockwood back into his life. Several times a day, and especially at night, Hunter thought about her and prayed for her.

Many times Hunter came close to writing to her at the Karr Clinic in Baltimore, but he was afraid it would make him look as if he was trying to push himself on her.

He also contemplated asking for time off to make a trip to Baltimore. But when he recalled her parting words, he told himself it was an "if you're in the neighborhood" invitation. It would seem too bold on his part to go there just to see her.

EIGHT

By January 1856, Dr. Hunter Newman McGuire could stand it no longer. He would write a friendly but casual letter to Jodie. When she replied, it would give him an open door to write again and slowly build toward the lasting relationship he wanted with her.

He sent the letter to the clinic in Baltimore on January 10. Then he prayed and waited. When there was no reply by April 1, and the letter had not been returned by the postal service, his heart sank. He decided to try again.

Again there was no reply.

More than a year passed, and finally Hunter decided he would take some well-deserved time off and go to Baltimore. Whether it seemed bold or not, he had to tell Jodie he loved her.

Hunter arrived at Baltimore's Union Station on September 9, 1857. The row of horse-and-buggy rigs in front of the station made him think of Boston. He raised a hand and caught the first cabbie's attention. The cabbie snapped the reins, clucked to his horse, and pulled up beside Hunter.

"Welcome to Baltimore, sir. Where can I take you?"

"Do you know where the Benjamin Karr Clinic is?"

"Of course, sir. I can have you there in about twenty minutes."

Baltimore was sizzling in the heat, and Hunter fanned himself with his hat as the buggy carried him through the streets. They pulled up in front of the clinic and Hunter noted by his pocket watch that the trip had taken twenty-two minutes.

"Will you want me to wait, sir?"

"Won't be necessary," Hunter replied, alighting with bag in hand. He paid the cabbie, crossed the board sidewalk, and entered the clinic. It was an impressive building, with a large reception area painted in bright colors and decorated with fresh flowers. Several people were waiting. Hunter approached the receptionist, and she smiled pleasantly.

"May I help you, sir?"

"I hope so. I'm Dr. Hunter McGuire from Lexington, Virginia. "Would you know if Miss Jodie Lockwood is in? I'm a friend of hers."

The receptionist looked puzzled. "Are you asking if a Miss Jodie Lockwood works here, Doctor?"

"She came here over a year-and-a-half ago to finish her C.M.N. work and gain her C.S.A. certification."

"I see. Well, Doctor, the present staff—including myself—has been here only three months. Miss Lockwood was not here when we took over the clinic, I can tell you that."

"Took over the clinic?"

"Yes, sir. Dr. Jeremy Clayton bought the clinic from Dr. Karr."

"But it still says Benjamin Karr Clinic on the sign outside."

"Yes, sir, but— Oh! There's Dr. Clayton. He can answer your questions."

The receptionist intercepted the stout middle-aged man coming through the door and introduced him to Hunter, explaining that Hunter was looking for Jodie Lockwood.

Dr. Clayton invited Hunter to his office. When they were

seated, Clayton explained that he bought the clinic from Dr. Benjamin Karr three months previously and brought in his own staff. Since Dr. Karr's name was so well known, he decided to leave the name of the clinic as it was, with Dr. Karr's permission. Dr. Karr had gone to Switzerland in semi-retirement and to do some teaching in a medical school in Zurich.

Dr. Karr's staff had scattered. He knew that all of them had left Baltimore but hadn't the slightest idea where any of them had gone.

"Dr. Clayton," Hunter said, "would there be a file around here that might have a record of Miss Lockwood? Something that might give me a clue as to her whereabouts?"

"Well, I don't know. Let's take a look."

McGuire followed Clayton into another office and waited while the man searched through folders in a file cabinet.

"Ah! Here's Miss Lockwood's file," Clayton said, lifting the folder and laying it on a nearby desk. He shuffled through the papers, pausing and read a little, then flipped pages and read some more. "Well, your Miss Lockwood finished the required time and Dr. Karr recommended her for the C.M.N. and C.S.A. certificates. According to this, she came here having completed fourteen months' work for the Kurtz-Aaron Medical Clinic in Lexington, Virginia."

"Yes, sir, I am aware of that. I'm doing my internship with Doctors Kurtz and Aaron."

"Oh, I see."

"That's where I met Miss Lockwood. Do you see anything there that would indicate where she went after receiving her certificates?"

Clayton looked through the folder again. "No, sir. All it says is that she received her certificates last April 27. There's no indication where she might have gone."

"Hmmm. Almost five months ago." Hunter felt keen disappointment. He thought for a moment, then said, "Dr. Clayton, do you have an address in Switzerland where I might contact Dr. Karr?"

"I have the address of the school where he's going to teach, but he won't start until a year from this fall. He and his wife were going to tour Europe for a year."

Hunter thanked Dr. Clayton and left the clinic. He rode back to the depot and raked his mind for a solution. If he only knew where her family lived, they could probably tell him where she had gone. Maybe Doctors Kurtz and Aaron could help. They probably had that information in their records.

Hunter arrived back in Lexington and explained to the doctors what had happened in Baltimore. When the doctors checked the file, they saw that Jodie had listed Athens, Tennessee, as the nearest town to her country home. They recalled that she had received a letter telling her that both her parents had drowned in a boating accident. By the time the letter arrived, her parents had already been buried. The doctors offered Jodie time off to go home, but she declined, saying there was no need since the funeral was already over.

That night, Hunter knelt beside his bed and prayed, "Lord Jesus, Your Bible says that the steps of a good man are ordered by You. How can I believe anything but that You ordered Jodie's steps *and* mine when You let us meet? You haven't taken my love for her out of my heart, and You know I can't get her out of my mind. Please bring whatever is needful into my life to lead me to her."

Hunter was now working the day shift at the clinic. Kurtz and Aaron had built an addition to the building, adding ten more beds. They hoped it wouldn't be long before they could convert the clinic into a full-fledged hospital.

Late in the afternoon on the day after he arrived back from Baltimore, Hunter left the clinic and started walking toward the boarding house. He looked up to see Tom Jackson in a buggy with Mary Anna Morrison beside him. Hunter smiled to himself. For the past four months, Tom had been courting Mary Anna, who, like his first wife, was the daughter of a Presbyterian minister.

Hunter liked Mary Anna. She had a pleasant way about her, and in the four months that Tom had been seeing her, she had brought a brightness to his eyes that Hunter had not seen since their boyhood days.

Tom brought the buggy to a halt. "Hello, Doc. Welcome back."

"Afternoon, Major. Miss Mary Anna."

"Doc, we meant to get to the clinic before your shift ended and offer you a ride home. I want to know about your Baltimore trip, and Mary Anna and I would like to talk to you."

"I'll take you up on it," Hunter said, climbing in beside Mary Anna.

Jackson clucked at the horse and headed for the boarding house. "Actually, Doc," Tom said, "we'd like to take you out for supper and do our talking."

Hunter laughed. "Well, far be it from me to turn down a free meal!"

"I figured you'd like to freshen up first. Right?"

"Yes. It's been a harrowing day."

"Well, I'll ask right off, then. Did you find Jodie?"

"No. She's no longer at the clinic, and no one there could tell me where she is."

Hunter explained the situation at the Karr Clinic in Baltimore and then what he had learned from Aaron and Kurtz.

Tom sighed as he looked past Mary Anna to his friend, and said, "Hunter, I can only offer you Tom Jackson's opinion…"

"I value your opinion."

"It seems to me that the Lord has other plans for you. Certainly if He wanted you to have Jodie for your wife, He would let you two get together. Just seems to me that the Lord must have someone else in mind for you to marry, and that's why you've hit this rock wall. Wouldn't you say?"

Hunter nodded slowly. "What you say is sensible, Tom, but I love that girl so much. Being without her is tearing me up."

"It wouldn't if you'd give your heart a chance to reach out to someone else."

"Easier said than done, ol' pal. You know I've dated several girls. Nice Christian girls. But when I'm with them, my mind is on Jodie."

"Hunter," Mary Anna said, "there are a lot of women who would give their eyeteeth to have a man who loved them like you love Jodie."

"Yes'm," Hunter said, sliding from the buggy. "Would you two like to come in and sit in the parlor while I freshen up?"

The Appalachian Café on Main Street was just beginning to fill up when Hunter, Tom, and Mary Anna arrived. Tom waited until the food was delivered to the table and he had thanked the Lord for it before saying what was on his mind.

"Well, Doc, you probably know what we want to talk to you about."

Hunter grinned. "I think I'm about to hear a wedding announcement."

Mary Anna laughed. "This doctor is awfully smart, Tom."

"Don't have to be very smart to see what's been going on between you two the last few months. And may I say I'm very happy for both of you. So when is the day?"

"Depends on you," Tom said.

"Me?"

"Yep. Will you be in town on Sunday afternoon, December 20?"

"I will if that's the day of your wedding."

"Good. It's hard for a fella to be best man at his friend's wedding if he's somewhere else," Tom said.

Hunter smiled and looked at Tom. "I'm deeply honored that you'd want me to be best man."

"We both want it, Hunter," Mary Anna said.

Tom Jackson and Mary Anna Morrison were wed at Oaklawn Presbyterian Church on Sunday afternoon, December 20, 1857.

Dr. Hunter McGuire—still dreaming of Jodie Lockwood—buried himself in his work.

When the new year came, serious trouble was brewing within the United States. The slavery question was becoming a heated issue. Twelve years previously—in 1846—the Northern states had outlawed the institution of slavery. The Southern states refused to follow suit because of the enormous impact it would have on the Southern economy.

One day in late January, things were unusually quiet at the clinic. Doctors Aaron and Kurtz were sitting in Kurtz's office after lunch, discussing the slavery issue when Hunter came in from a house call. He hung up his hat and coat in the hall and entered Kurtz's office carrying a rolled-up newspaper in one hand and his medical bag in the other.

"How's Mr. Benkleman?" Kurtz asked.

"Just a bad cold. He'll be all right. Have you gentlemen seen today's *Sentinel?*" Hunter unrolled the paper so they could see the front page.

"More about the slavery controversy?" Aaron asked.

"Yes. They're about to get into fistfights in Congress. A couple of Northern congressmen made speeches yesterday and just about had those politicians swinging at each other. The Northerners say we're immoral for embracing slavery, and they're going to force us to give it up. I really haven't paid a lot of attention to this issue, have you?"

"Well, Doctor," Aaron said, "we've never had much industry here in the agrarian South, and a high percentage of Southern money is tied up in plantation and cotton futures. To pay workers' wages for labor would break the plantation owners' backs financially."

Weldon Kurtz picked up where Aaron left off. "I don't know if you're aware of it or not, Dr. McGuire, but there's a growing demand for cotton in the U.S. and in Europe. The plantation owners see an opportunity to greatly strengthen the Southern economy because of this increasing demand."

"I've picked up on it now and then in the newspapers," Hunter said. "So now things are heating up because the Northerners are opposed to plantation owners using slave labor to accomplish their financial goals."

"That's it," Kurtz said with a nod. "So they accuse Southerners of being immoral to try to force them to abolish slavery. If this doesn't work, they'll turn to stronger measures."

"I'll guarantee you the people of the South will not bend to Northern pressure," Aaron said. "The Northerners will never be able to force abolition below the Mason-Dixon Line. We'll fight them first."

"From what I see in the paper, I think you're right," Hunter said.

"We're bowing our necks," Kurtz said, "not because we're all in favor of slavery, but because the Northerners are infringing on our states' rights. It's nobody's business up north to tell us how to run our economy."

"I agree," Hunter said, "but I can't say I agree with one human being making chattel of another."

Aaron nodded. "We both feel the same way, but we also understand that the South's economy would suffer a devastating blow if slavery was abolished. The main thing is, those folks up north need to keep their noses out of our business. We're not going to let them dictate abolition to us."

When another year had passed, the name of abolitionist John Brown showed up in the newspapers. By the spring of 1859, Brown had shed blood in Kansas and Missouri over slavery, then turned his attention to Virginia.

As the months passed, the violence grew worse. On October 17, 1859, Brown and a group of his followers seized the U.S. Armory at Harper's Ferry in defiance of the pro-slavery Southerners, killed five civilians, and took hostages. The U.S. Marines were called in, with

Colonel Robert E. Lee in command. Brown refused to surrender, and the Marines attacked.

Eleven of Brown's men were killed, including two of his sons. The rest were captured. Brown was tried at Charleston for treason against the Commonwealth of Virginia and sentenced to hang. His execution was set for December 2, 1859.

Virginia governor Henry A. Wise called for the Virginia Military Institute's Corps of Cadets to stand guard in Charleston while the hanging was carried out. Major Thomas Jackson took his artillery attachment from the Institute to comply. Brown was hanged without intrusion by fellow abolitionists, and Jackson led his men back to Lexington.

War fever, however, was on the rise. Abolitionists in the North were angry over John Brown's execution. As the new decade dawned, the battle over states' rights grew hotter among political leaders. In the next several months there was verbal skirmishing between the Northerners and Southerners in Congress, and as the verbal battle spread to the people, the threat of violence became a reality.

When Abraham Lincoln was elected president of the United States on November 6, 1860, it was all the Southerners could take. In the four-month interval between Lincoln's election and his inauguration on March 1, 1861, South Carolina seceded from the Union, followed immediately by six other deep-south states, and together formed the Southern Confederacy.

On February 4, delegates from the seceding states convened at Montgomery, Alabama, to frame a constitution, establish a provincial government, provide for armed forces, and elect Jefferson Davis president of the Confederate States. Davis was a West Pointer and a Mexican War hero. He was also a former U.S. Senator, as well as former U.S. Secretary of War.

It was apparent that other Southern states would secede.

Two days after Lincoln's inauguration, Jefferson Davis, on authorization from the Confederate Congress, issued a call for 100,000 volunteers for military service. Thus the Confederate States Army was born.

The Confederate Army immediately went to work by seizing Federal property within Southern borders, including forts, arsenals, and customs houses.

At Charleston Harbor, South Carolina, Major Robert Anderson—the Federal commander of Fort Sumter—resisted the demands of Confederate authorities that he surrender the fort.

By dawn's early light at 4:30 A.M. on April 12, 1861, a ten-inch mortar shell whistled in a high arc from the Charleston shore and exploded inside Fort Sumter. The American Civil War had begun.

Confederate shore batteries commanded by General P. G. T. Beauregard bombarded Fort Sumter for forty hours before Anderson finally surrendered. More Southern states seceded, and the armies of the North and South drew up their war plans.

On April 20, Major Jackson received orders from Confederate authorities to bring the entire student body from Virginia Military Institute to Richmond, where they would be inducted into the Confederate Army. They were to begin their march at 12:30 P.M. on Sunday, April 21.

Because this would not allow time to attend services at the local churches, Major Jackson set aside the hour between 6:30 and 7:30 that morning for cadets who wished to have their own time of prayer and Bible reading. He had also asked Hunter to come to his house before he and the cadets left for Richmond.

When Hunter arrived, he joined Tom and Mary Anna in the kitchen, and they prayed together.

Afterwards, Tom opened his Bible and said, "Both of you know that my faith is in the Lord Jesus Christ for my salvation. I have told Mary Anna, Hunter, that I had peace when I fought in the Mexican War, and I know I'll have the same peace in this one. If the Lord sees fit to take me to heaven from a bloody battlefield, I'm ready to go.

My sins have been washed away in the precious blood of God's Lamb, and I do not fear dying."

Tom found the page he wanted. "Here. Second Corinthians five, verses one through four. 'For we know that if our earthly house of this tabernacle were dissolved, we have a building of God, an house not made with hands, eternal in the heavens. For in this we groan, earnestly desiring to be clothed upon with our house which is from heaven: If so be that being clothed we shall not be found naked. For we that are in this tabernacle do groan, being burdened: not for that we would be unclothed, but clothed upon, that mortality might be swallowed up of life.'"

By this time Mary Anna was wiping away tears.

"Mary Anna," Tom said, "you're my beloved wife. Hunter, you are my best friend in this world. I just wanted to leave you both with this Bible passage and for you to hear it read by my own mouth. Should the Lord see fit to take me Home, please remember that I went in perfect peace, my mortality being swallowed up of life."

While Mary Anna and Hunter walked with Tom to the spot where he and his men would begin their march to Richmond, Tom said, "Doc, if this war goes full-scale, which it could, the Confederate Army is going to need doctors. I'm asking you to consider being a volunteer if the need arises."

"We haven't talked about it, Tom," Hunter said, "but it bothers me to have my parents on one side of this conflict, and me on the other."

Jackson nodded. "There's going to be a whole lot of this kind of thing as the war progresses."

"Mom and Dad have been very understanding about my situation. They know I'm against human beings owning other human beings, but they also know that my allegiance belongs to the South. From what they've said, I know it's not going to divide us if I carry my medical skills to the Confederate battlefields. So if I'm needed, let me know."

NINE

O n April 18, 1861, Lincoln was in the East Room of the White House, listening to eyewitness accounts of the bombardment of Fort Sumter, when there was a tap on the door.

Lincoln's young private secretary, John Hay, entered. Hay was a slight man, with dark curly hair and mustache. "You asked me to let you know if Senator Blair had been able to talk to Colonel Lee, sir."

"Yes?"

"He did, sir, and the Colonel has arrived."

Lincoln thanked the men for their reports and waited for them to exit the room before telling Hay to show Colonel Lee in.

Seconds later, Lincoln's craggy face crinkled in a smile as he moved toward the silver-haired man, his hand extended. At six feet four inches in height, Lincoln towered over most men, and Lee was no exception.

Colonel Robert Edward Lee had seen Lincoln only from a distance and was stunned to see how gaunt the president looked up close. As he shook Lincoln's hand, he drawled, "I am glad to make your acquaintance, Mr. President."

"Same here," Lincoln said, his deep-set eyes appraising the fifty-five-year-old army officer. "Come...sit down."

As Lee sat on a plush, overstuffed chair, Lincoln said, "Colonel, I'll get right to the point of my asking for this meeting."

"Yes, sir?"

"I've been going over your military record, and I like what I see. Since we are now at war with the Confederates, I'm searching for the right man to put in command of the Union Army. I believe you are that man. What would you say to that?"

Lee's countenance sagged, and he cleared his throat. "Mr. President," he said, in his soft Southern accent, "I am honored that you would see me capable of commanding the Union forces. However, I must tell you that just two days ago I drew up my letter of resignation from the United States Army. I was about to present it to the 'powers that be' when Senator Blair approached me, saying you would like to see me. In respect to you, I came immediately, planning to turn in my resignation later today."

Lincoln passed a lean hand over his mouth. "Then I must ask you to reconsider, Colonel. I am genuinely interested in making you the commander of the Union army."

"My decision to resign did not come easy, Mr. President. I am a man who has always loved his country, and if you have examined my military records, you know I served well in the Mexican War."

Lincoln nodded. "That's the reason you attracted my attention. I see military genius in you, Colonel. I would like to employ it for the Union cause."

Lee sighed. "Mr. President, I am a native-born Virginian, as you probably know. Virginia is a Southern commonwealth, and the Virginia Peace Convention passed an ordinance of secession yesterday. I cannot and I will not fight against my own people. I mean no disrespect, Mr. President, but I must decline your offer."

Lincoln's eyes clouded. There was a break in his voice as he said, "Colonel Lee, it disturbs me greatly to think of you as my enemy."

"I feel the same way about you, sir," Lee said, "but I guess that's the way it is."

There was a moment of awkward silence between them, then

Lincoln rose to his feet. "I'm sorry it turned out this way, Colonel. Perhaps this war will be short-lived and we can soon be friends again."

Lee extended his hand. "You have my deepest respect, Mr. President. May God grant both you and President Davis the wisdom to make it short-lived. If you don't, this land we love will be a cauldron of blood."

Colonel Robert E. Lee's prediction began to come true the very next day when Federal troops from Massachusetts arrived in Baltimore, Maryland. They had to march from one depot to another to board a train for Washington. Angry Southern sympathizers, carrying Confederate flags, threw bricks and rocks at the soldiers. When the soldiers answered back with guns, the citizens started shooting too. By the time it was over, at least four soldiers and nine civilians were dead, and hundreds more were injured and wounded.

That same day, the U.S. Armory at Harper's Ferry, Virginia, was evacuated by the Federals when they learned that a swarm of Virginia troops were coming to take it by force.

On April 20, Colonel Lee sent a wire to President Jefferson Davis, offering his services, and was immediately appointed commander of the Confederate Army of Virginia. Lee went to work to build a strong fighting force.

On April 27, Major Thomas J. Jackson was promoted to colonel and was given eleven thousand men. On May 1, he was ordered to the armory at Harper's Ferry to guard it in case the Federals tried to take it back.

At the same time, Major General Joseph E. Johnston was made commander of the Confederate Army of the Shenandoah. Brigadier General Pierre G. T. Beauregard had already been appointed commander of the Army of Northern Virginia.

During May and June, skirmishes took place in western Virginia, Missouri, and along the Potomac River in Maryland. On

July 11, the first major battle took place at Rich Mountain, Virginia, with Major General George B. McClellan leading the Federals. Lieutenant Colonel John Pegram led the Confederates. Pegram's unit was put on the run by McClellan's troops, but not without leaving dead and wounded Yankee soldiers on the mountain.

Jefferson Davis knew heavy battles were imminent and he needed to strengthen the Army of the Shenandoah, especially. He had great confidence in Colonel Jackson. On July 12, he promoted him to Brigadier General and gave him command of the First Brigade, Army of the Shenandoah under General Johnston.

In the middle of the afternoon on July 15, a rider in a Confederate Army uniform galloped through Lexington and halted in front of the Kurtz-Aaron Medical Clinic. He pulled a sealed brown envelope from a saddlebag and headed for the door.

"Hello, Lieutenant, may I help you?" Doralee Chambers asked from the reception desk.

"Yes, ma'am. I'm Lieutenant Paul Morgan, First Brigade, Army of the Shenandoah. I have a very important message for Dr. Hunter McGuire. Is he in?"

"Yes. He's with a patient at the moment. I'll tell him you're here and see how long he thinks it might be."

Doralee returned in less than two minutes. "Dr. McGuire said to have a seat, Lieutenant. He will be with you shortly."

When Hunter entered the reception area in his white frock, Morgan rose to his feet. "Dr. McGuire? I'm a courier from Brigadier General Thomas Jackson, sir."

Hunter's eyes widened. *"Brigadier General* Jackson, eh? I learned only recently that he had been promoted to colonel."

"Well, he's now commander of First Brigade, Army of the Shenandoah."

"Oh? So he's not at Harper's Ferry any longer."

"That's correct, sir. He's camped with the brigade over by

Manassas. General Johnston, commander of the Army of the Shenandoah, is on his way there with the rest of his troops. General Beauregard is leading his Army of Northern Virginia to the same place right now. This could be a real bloody battle, sir."

McGuire looked at the envelope in Morgan's hand. "And you have a message for me from General Jackson?"

"Yes, sir." Morgan placed the envelope in Hunter's hand. "He asked that you read it in my presence and respond. I'm to ride back immediately and give him your answer."

Hunter pulled out the letter, and read silently:

Dear Hunter,

You said to let you know when I needed you to come. We are about to engage in a furious fight with the enemy. There will be many men killed, and many wounded. I need you. The Confederate soldiers need you. Please give Lieutenant Paul Morgan your reply. I am anxiously waiting.

Yours expectantly,
Tom

At sunset on July 17, Brigadier General Thomas Jackson was sitting in Major General Johnston's tent on the bank of Bull Run Creek, near the town of Manassas.

"It's hard to say how many men McDowell will come with," Johnston said, "but we'll give them a fight they won't soon forget. They'll know they've got a tiger by the tail when we get through with them. We'll—"

"General Johnston, sir," came a voice from outside the tent.

"Yes?"

"General Jackson's courier is here and wishes to see him."

Jackson sprang off his chair and went outside. Johnston followed. Jackson stepped out into the light of the setting sun and saw his old friend standing with Lieutenant Morgan. He was speechless for a few seconds, then said, "Hunter! I didn't expect you to come this soon!"

"I told Doctors Kurtz and Aaron that I would be volunteering my services to the army whenever you sent for me, Tom—er, excuse me...*General*. By the way, congratulations on your two promotions since I saw you last."

"Thank you," Tom said, and grinned.

"Anyway, Kurtz and Aaron were prepared for me to go. You probably don't know that since I finished my internship they made me a junior partner in the clinic. Plans are that when it becomes a hospital, I'll become a full-fledged partner."

"I didn't know, but congratulations."

Tom Jackson then introduced Hunter to General Johnston. As they shook hands, Johnston said, "Dr. McGuire, I've been hearing a lot about you from General Jackson. Welcome to the Army of the Shenandoah."

"Thank you, sir."

"I can't tell you what it means to have you volunteer your services. You do understand, though, that the Confederate government will pay you for this."

"Tom—there I go again—General Jackson advised me of it, sir."

"We know we aren't going to match financially what you receive in Lexington, but—"

"That's no problem, sir. My heart is with these men. I want to do my part in this war."

"Well, your part is very essential—saving lives."

"Every one I can, sir, even if it's a Yankee soldier."

Johnston grinned. "Your friend here told me that's how you feel. And I have nothing against that. He said something like this: 'An enemy is no longer an enemy when he is wounded and incapable of fighting against us.' Do I have that right, General?"

"Exactly," Jackson said.

"Doctor," Johnston said, "we hope to have this war over with soon. I want to see you go back to that clinic and make good with your career." He nodded solemnly and continued to speak. "Because of General Jackson's recommendation of you as a physician and surgeon, I am officially appointing you as Corps Medical Director under his direct command. We have other doctors coming, but most of them are less experienced than you. They will take orders from you. I'll let you and General Jackson work out the details. He'll show you what we have in the way of medical supplies."

There were many skirmishes between the Federals and the Confederates during the next five days. Then, on July 21, the two armies clashed head-on along the banks of Bull Run Creek. Thirty-five thousand Union troops led by Major General Irvin McDowell stormed against twenty-four thousand Confederate troops led by Brigadier General P. G. T. Beauregard, and eighty-five hundred troops led by Major General Joseph E. Johnston.

It was a hot, humid day as the two sides battled it out. Bodies were strewn on the bloody fields—some dead, some wounded—as cannons boomed, muskets flared, and powder smoke filled the heavy air.

Among the Confederate losses was Brigadier General Bernard Bee, commander of Third Brigade, Army of the Shenandoah. Bee was killed ten minutes after he gave Tom Jackson the nickname—Stonewall—that would stay with him for the rest of his life.

During the heat of the battle, Bee and his brigade were spread out on a hillside, firing at Union soldiers attempting to ascend the hill. On top of the hill, some fifty yards above Bee and his troops, was General Jackson's artillery, firing at enemy artillery positioned in a heavily-wooded area. The Union infantry below were trying to take out the Confederate cannoneers and their leader.

Jackson courageously stood erect amidst a hail of bullets so he could see where to direct his cannoneers to fire. General Bee shouted above the din, "Form! Form! There stands Jackson like a stone wall! Rally behind the Virginians!"

Only seconds after Bee was shot and killed, a cannonball exploded near Jackson. Shrapnel whistled on both sides of him, a molten fragment hitting his left hand, ripping into the middle finger, and another red-hot chunk catching the tail of his coat.

Jackson stuck his bleeding hand into his pocket and remained where he stood, just like a stone wall.

When there was a respite in the fighting, the general left a colonel in charge and rushed onto the back side of the hill where a hospital tent had been set up. There were already several wounded Confederate soldiers lying around it and inside on the tent floor. When Jackson entered the tent, a young doctor looked up and said, "I'll be with you in just a second, General."

Jackson nodded. "I don't believe I know you."

"I'm Dr. Bruce Dean, General."

"Where's Dr. McGuire?"

"He's on the field somewhere, doing what he can for the wounded who can't make it to the tent. Now, General, let me take a look at this. Well, you're out of this battle. This finger will have to come off immediately. I'll get some chloroform and—"

"You're not cutting this finger off, Doctor," Jackson said. "It isn't that bad."

"Oh, but it is, sir. If I don't amputate right away, it can very well result in your death."

"How much experience do you have with this kind of wound?"

"Well, not much, General, but I *am* a medical doctor, and—"

"Just wrap it up. I've got to get back to my post. I'll have Dr. McGuire look at it later."

Dean's mouth turned down. "If you insist. But I'm telling you, the finger has to come off."

As Jackson headed back, the Yankees started to come at the hill again. When the general's men saw him, they shouted, "Three cheers for General 'Stonewall' Jackson! Hip-hip-hooray! Hip-hip-hooray! Hip-hip-hooray!"

Further down the slope, General Bee's men—now commanded by Colonel Efram Smith—joined in and began shouting at Jackson, calling him "General Stonewall."

It was midafternoon when the Union troops found themselves outgunned and outmanned in spite of their greater numbers. They turned back toward Washington in hasty retreat.

By dusk, all was still along Bull Run Creek, except for exultant Confederates who rejoiced over their victory…and the wounded who moaned and cried out in pain.

At the hospital tent, Dr. Hunter McGuire and Dr. Bruce Dean labored over the wounded men. Darkness fell and they continued to work until two other doctors showed up from another brigade to help. While they worked by lantern light, they discussed the new nickname for General Jackson.

Jackson stepped up to the tent and overheard his old friend say, "Well, gentlemen, I'll tell you what. I've known the man as long as I can remember. We grew up in the same rural area. If there ever was a man who deserved to be called 'Stonewall' it's him. He—"

"Hello in the tent," came the familiar voice. "You have a wounded general out here."

Hunter stepped outside and noted his friend's bandaged left hand. He examined the finger in the presence of Dean, who was embarrassed when Hunter pronounced that all it needed was some stitches. Hunter had Dean take the stitches, and Jackson alleviated some of Dean's embarrassment by commending him for doing a good job.

When Stonewall Jackson and the rest of the Confederates sent General McDowell and his battered troops retreating to Washington, the Northerners—who thought they would make short order of the ragtag Confederate armies—now recognized they had a genuine war on their hands.

Because of the rout at Bull Run Creek, President Lincoln relieved General McDowell of his command and replaced him with Major General George Brinton McClellan.

The following year there were hundreds of skirmishes between Union and Confederate troops, including some in Missouri and as far west as New Mexico.

In November 1861, Stonewall Jackson was made commander of the Army of the Shenandoah and promoted to major general.

While almost countless skirmishes were taking place east of the Mississippi River on Southern soil, General McClellan—after much prodding by President Lincoln—finally moved his army to the peninsula between the York and James Rivers in Virginia. His orders were to attack Richmond, which had become the Confederate capital in May 1861.

General McClellan had received improper information from Union intelligence, which reported that his army was vastly outnumbered by General Johnston's Army of Northern Virginia. McClellan moved at a snail's pace, taking two months to advance to the outskirts of the Confederate capital. He spent a third month sitting in front of the enemy's fortifications without launching an attack.

McClellan's reluctance to move on Richmond had President Lincoln furious.

During the same period, Stonewall Jackson was driving Union forces from the Shenandoah Valley. In late June 1862, Jackson brought his army back to the Richmond front to participate in the Seven Days' Battles, June 25 to July 1.

At the same time, General Johnston's new command attacked General McClellan's troops repeatedly and drove them all the way back to Harrison's Landing on the James River.

The Union forces were taking a sound beating. President Lincoln was frustrated that his top field commander seemed reluctant to carry the battle to the enemy. As Lincoln put it to General Henry W. Halleck, whom he made General-in-Chief over all Union land forces on July 11, "McClellan has the slows."

Lincoln was pleased with Major General John Pope's performance in the Peninsular Campaign, and ordered him to form the Union Army of Virginia, which would carry the battle to the Rebels in central and western Virginia. McClellan and his troops were ordered to stay close to Washington to stand guard. McClellan was furious that Pope would be sent to the field and he planted in one spot, but obeyed Lincoln's orders, remaining in charge of the Union Army of the Potomac.

Pope led his troops into battle at Manassas against Stonewall Jackson's Army of the Shenandoah August 29–September 1, which became known as the Second Battle of Bull Run.

When Lincoln learned of the fight going on at Manassas, he ordered McClellan's Union Army of the Potomac to rush to Pope's aid. McClellan was too late arriving, however, and the Confederates whipped Pope's army. The Second Bull Run victory resulted from the courage and masterful strategy of Stonewall Jackson, whose name was fast becoming a household word, not only in the South, but also in the North. Almost every day his name was on the front pages of newspapers reporting on the War.

In Washington, President Lincoln was sorely disappointed in Pope's performance at Manassas. He sat down with Halleck and vented his frustration. Halleck began bringing up names of other Union generals as possibilities to replace Pope.

Lincoln listened, but didn't respond.

When Halleck had exhausted his list, Lincoln said, "I have an idea, General. Since we're short on men who are capable and experienced enough to lead our military forces, I'm going to relieve General Pope of his command and merge his Army of Virginia with General McClellan's Army of the Potomac. General McClellan will be commander of the entire force."

"Mr. President," Halleck said, cautiously, "you have me in this position because you respect my military opinions."

"Of course. There's something you wish to say?"

"Yes, sir. My concern is not with the merging of the two armies into one. After the defeats we've been experiencing, I'm sure that would serve to unite our men in a big way. But McClellan, sir. Haven't we had enough of his reluctance? You said yourself, Mr. President, that he has the slows. Surely there's another general who could head up the newly formed Army of the Potomac."

Lincoln rubbed his tired eyes. To Halleck, the president's cheekbones seemed to protrude even more than they had the day before, and his eyes seemed to have sunken deeper.

"General, there's not a man you've listed who can lead men like McClellan can once he *does* take them into battle. You won't argue with that, will you?"

"No, sir. But what can we do to light a fire under him, so he'll move like we want him to?"

"Let's have a meeting with him," Lincoln replied. "I'll prod him hard."

TEN

On Monday, September 1, 1862, Major General George McClellan was called from the army camp just outside of Washington to meet with President Lincoln and General-in-Chief Henry Halleck in the east room of the White House.

Lincoln and Halleck were standing up when John Hay ushered McClellan into the room. McClellan was a small man, only five-feet-five. His men affectionately called him "Little Mac" outside of his presence. The president and Halleck shook hands with McClellan, then sat down at a table for their meeting.

"General," Lincoln said, "I called you here so the three of us could discuss the demoralized condition of our troops."

"It certainly concerns me, Mr. President," McClellan said. "The Confederates have fought like wildcats. It seems nothing we do discourages them, or even slows them down. They come into each battle with a vengeance, and even though they must be just as weary, worn, and hungry as our men, they seem to fight all day long as if they were more than human."

"It's all in the mental attitude, General McClellan," Halleck said. "My personal opinion is that neither you nor General Pope have instilled the proper mental attitude into your men. This is nothing less than a lack of leadership. Everything rises or falls on leadership. Certainly you will agree with that."

McClellan was nervous under Halleck's penetrating gaze. "It is the truth, General Halleck. I must agree with it."

Halleck looked at Lincoln, who seemed willing to let him continue. "With General Pope, in my opinion, it was a lack of military strategy. His men lost confidence in him in the Manassas battle. With you, General, I see something different. When you are in battle, you have a keen mind for strategy and a way of keeping your men fired up to fight. But the problem—and I know Mr. Lincoln agrees with me—is your lack of taking the fight to the enemy. To put it bluntly, General, you're too slow. Conse-quently, you allow the Confederates to outmaneuver you, and when you do, you lose the battle. This is what's demoralizing your men."

Abraham Lincoln fixed his deep-set eyes on McClellan and waited for a reply.

McClellan squirmed a bit and cleared his throat. "Mr. President, General Halleck, what appears to be slow moving to you is simply my style of military strategy. Rushing into a battle without proper preparation can prove devastating."

"So can waiting too long," Halleck said.

The discussion continued for some two hours. Finally McClellan agreed to take another look at his tactics and make the necessary adjustments.

Halleck was not satisfied and was about to say so, when Lincoln said, "All right, General McClellan, that's good enough for me. Now, let me explain what I have in mind."

The president laid out his plan to relieve General Pope of his command over the Union Army of Virginia and merge that army into the Union Army of the Potomac. McClellan would retain his position as commander.

Little Mac was pleased, and agreed that it was a smart move.

Henry Halleck was dismayed that McClellan would be the top man of the newly merged force, but kept it to himself.

"All right, General," Lincoln said. "You are the chief field commander of the combined forces. I'm depending on you to reorganize the demoralized army and to rally it into the fighting force that it no doubt can be. You must lead them to victory by crushing General Lee's armies and bring this war to a swift end."

"I'll give it my best, Mr. President...my very best."

On Tuesday, September 2, General Lee met with Generals Jackson and Longstreet. The Confederate Army of the Shenandoah was still camped outside of Manassas.

"Gentlemen," Lee drawled, "there will never be a better time than right now to take advantage of the low morale of the Union troops."

"Can't argue with that, sir," Longstreet said. "We've got them with their tails between their legs."

"So what do you have in mind, General?" Jackson asked.

Lee paused a moment, then said with a slight grin, "March our troops onto Northern soil and launch an attack."

Both men showed surprise.

"Too bold, you're thinking?"

"Well...no, sir," Jackson said. "I think it's a great idea. That would shake them even more. Just where do you have in mind to make the attack, sir?"

"Maryland," Lee replied. "At least start there. Maybe carry it into Pennsylvania. I think we need to strike while the iron's hot. In my mind, putting our footprints on Union land would further demoralize them. They've brought the war onto Southern soil, let's hand it back to them."

"I like it!" Longstreet said.

Jackson was a little less exuberant. "How soon, sir?"

"Right away. Next few days."

"But our men are tired, sir," Jackson said. "They need shoes. And they could use new uniforms. Some of them are in pretty bad shape. Shouldn't we let the men rest up for a while before we march into Maryland? We're a little low on ammunition and supplies, not to mention food."

"We can't wait," Lee said. "Yankee morale is at an all-time low. I'm aware that our men are tired, but they've got heart, General. They can do it. And like I said, we've got to strike while the iron's hot."

"I understand," Jackson said, "and I agree, sir. Our men have heart like no soldiers I've ever seen. Just what are your objectives?"

Lee smiled. "Well, let me make it clear that I'm not interested in occupying Union territory. I just want to harass them and take the spirit out of them. As for ammunition and supplies, we can lay our hands on some pretty quickly from Richmond. And we can feed the troops from the fields of the Maryland farmers. Lincoln's troops are doing that to our farmers every day.

"Not only that, but the invasion would lure most of the Federal forces away from Washington, thus preventing another enemy march on Richmond when they decide they're ready to fight again."

"Good thinking," Jackson said, grinning.

"So, gentlemen, the opportunity to level a powerful blow to Billy Yank's breadbasket is at our fingertips. We've got to move quickly."

"Have you discussed this with President Davis?" Longstreet asked.

"Not yet. I wanted to get your reaction before I moved ahead with the plan. Since you now see the importance of striking quickly, I will write President Davis a letter and send it with a courier tomorrow."

"How many troops are you planning to take into Maryland, sir?" Longstreet asked.

"Fifty thousand."

"Exactly *which* troops?"

"Let me answer that question by explaining a big change I have in mind."

Lee shared with the two generals his plan to merge Jackson's army with the Confederate Army of Northern Virginia. He would then divide the combined armies into two corps of five divisions each. Jackson would head up one corps, and Longstreet—whom Lee called the "Old Warhorse"—the other. The fifth division in Jackson's corps would be the army's cavalry, under the command of Major General James E. B. (Jeb) Stuart.

"It would be my pleasure to have General Stuart's cavalry a part of my corps, sir," Jackson said.

"Then you're in agreement with my entire plan, General Jackson?"

"Indeed, sir. Let's hit those Yankees where it hurts most—at home."

Lee turned to Longstreet. "And you, General?"

"One hundred percent, sir. Let's deal Billy Yank some real misery."

On September 3, General Lee wrote a long letter to President Davis, outlining his plan as he had spoken it to Jackson and Longstreet, and sent it by courier that very day. He admitted that his men were in tattered uniforms and needed shoes, but expressed his confidence that they would fight with everything in them. He closed the letter by affirming this would be the South's most powerful move since the Civil War began.

Next, Lee merged the two armies, then divided them into two corps of five divisions each. The weary soldiers were exuberantly in favor of their leader's plan.

On September 4, as the Confederates prepared to march toward the Potomac, General Jackson moved his troops to the camp just outside Leesburg, Virginia, where the rest of Lee's army was collecting. Wagons were coming in from Richmond, loaded with ammunition and supplies.

As his men set up tents for their brief stay, Jackson moved among them, speaking words of encouragement.

Presently, General Lee appeared and explained to Jackson that in the re-formation of the Confederate army, he was placing Major General Ambrose Powell Hill as commander of Jackson's Second Division. There would be five brigades under Hill. Four of the brigades were already in the camp. The one Lee had designated as First Brigade was on its way from North Carolina under the command of Brigadier General O'Brien Branch. Lee had actually sent for Branch's brigade three days before the second Bull Run battle. Now they would make a strong addition to I Corps' Second Division.

Lee then handed Jackson a description of the makeup of his entire I Corps, giving him the names of all the commanding officers and their units. The official count of all officers and fighting men under Jackson and Longstreet was 49,981.

A slow grin spread across Jackson's face. "Well, General, you still owe us nineteen men. Didn't you say we'd go across the Potomac with fifty thousand?"

Lee chuckled. "You're a real stickler," he said, and walked away.

Jackson called a meeting of his division commanders, Generals A. R. Lawson, Ambrose P. Hill, John R. Jones, Daniel H. Hill, and Jeb Stuart. When the meeting was over, the sun was low in the western sky. The generals scattered to pass on the information to their unit leaders.

When General Hill returned to his division encampment, he found that his First Brigade had arrived. Its commander, Brigadier General Branch, was waiting for him. After shaking hands, Hill told Branch the information from General Jackson that he was about to pass on to his brigade commanders.

"Quite a hero General Jackson's turned out to be, sir," Branch said. "I like that name Stonewall."

"It fits him, that's for sure."

"You're going to have this meeting with your brigade commanders right now, sir?"

"Yes."

"Could I have about half a minute? Then I'll go with you."

"Sure. I can wait."

"Thank you, sir." Branch glanced toward the spot where the First Brigade was pitching tents. "Corporal Stedham! Will you send Major Dayton over here right away?"

The corporal nodded and dashed in the other direction.

To Hill, Branch said, "Major Dayton studied under General Jackson at Virginia Military Institute, sir, and was wondering if the general was on the grounds. He'd really like to see him again."

The young man hurrying toward them was tall and ruggedly handsome. As he drew up, Branch said, "General Ambrose Hill, I want you to meet Major Rance Dayton."

Dayton extended his hand and expressed pleasure over making his division leader's acquaintance.

"Major Dayton," Branch said, "General Hill was just in a meeting with General Jackson, so he is indeed on the grounds."

"Oh! I've got to see him. Do you think it would be all right to look for him, General Hill?"

"I don't know why not," Hill said, pointing across the camp to the west. "That's his tent over there. The larger one."

Stonewall Jackson was talking with Hunter McGuire when his aide called through the tent flap, "There's someone here to see you, General. You said it was all right to interrupt."

"Certainly," Jackson said, rising from his chair. "You don't have to go yet, do you, Hunter? Come on out while I see who this is and what he wants."

"Might be Abraham Lincoln, Tom," Hunter said, and chuckled. "Maybe he wants some advice on how to whip hardheaded Southerners."

What the general saw was a familiar face grinning at him. "Well, I'll be! Rance Dayton! How are you, you scalawag?"

"I'm sorry for interrupting you and this gentleman, sir, but I just had to see you. I arrived about an hour ago with the First Brigade to serve in General Hill's division."

Jackson suddenly noticed Dayton's uniform. "And you're a major already!"

"Yes, sir. And commander of the Eighteenth North Carolina Infantry Regiment."

"Well, Major Dayton, I want you to meet the closest friend I have in this world, Dr. Hunter McGuire. Dr. McGuire is Corps Medical Director. He and I have known each other since we were boys."

As McGuire and Dayton shook hands, Jackson explained to Hunter that Dayton had studied at V.M.I.

"Let's see, Rance—I mean Major," Jackson said. "What year was it you graduated? About '57 or '58?"

"June 4, 1858, sir."

"So what did you do after graduation?"

"Returned to my home in Fayetteville, North Carolina. I decided to go into law enforcement and was hired as deputy sheriff of Cumberland County by Sheriff Tucker."

"So you left your deputy job to get into the War, is that it?"

"Not quite, sir. Sheriff Tucker retired early in 1860, and even though I was pretty young, I ran for sheriff and got elected. Of course, when the War broke out last year, I felt it was my duty to get into it, especially since I'd graduated from V.M.I."

"You plan to stay in the military when the War is over?"

"No, sir. I'm going back into law enforcement. Thought I might go out west and take up marshaling one of those tough cattle towns."

"You're not married, I take it."

"Ah…no, sir. Had one on the line, but she decided she didn't want to marry a man who wore a badge. So she married—pardon me, Dr. McGuire—she married a doctor."

Hunter grinned. "Some women just have good sense."

Rance noticed five young soldiers from his regiment crowding close, eyeing Stonewall Jackson with looks of admiration.

"Hello, guys," he said with a chuckle. "I know what you're here for." To Jackson, he said, "General, these men are part of my regiment, and you're their hero. I've told them all about my V.M.I. days, studying under you, and they've read about you in the papers down in Fayetteville, where we all grew up together. They've been almost as excited as I have since learning we'd be assigned to your corps, and they want to meet you."

Jackson greeted the five men warmly and then introduced them to Hunter.

"You men better treat Dr. McGuire real good," Jackson said, "because one of these days he could be treating *you!*"

Hunter watched the five young soldiers walk away and noted how new their uniforms looked compared to some of the other men's. He turned to Jackson and said, "I'm concerned that so many of our men need shoes. I've been treating sore feet ever since we got here."

"I know, Hunter, but I don't know what can be done. General Lee wants to cross the Potomac and take the fight to the Federals right away. There's no time to get shoes shipped in."

"General," Rance Dayton said, "I happen to know that our regiment brought along about a dozen extra pair of shoes. I can let you have those."

"We'll take them," Jackson said with a smile.

"And be very thankful for them," Hunter said. "A dozen fewer men with sore feet is significant."

"I'll get them to you right away, Doctor. Do you want them delivered to you?"

"Yes. I'll pick the men with the sorest feet and see if we can get them fitted."

Hunter shook Dayton's hand again and excused himself.

"Rance, come on into the tent and sit down," Jackson said. "Let's talk about old times at V.M.I."

"You sure you have time, sir?"

"A few minutes, anyway. Come on in."

They sat on straight-backed wooden chairs next to a frail table that served as Jackson's desk.

"Sir, I have to tell you, when I saw in one of the Southern newspapers that you had been dubbed 'Stonewall' at First Bull Run, I thought to myself, 'Fits my favorite professor perfectly.'"

Jackson let a smile tug at his lips. "You think so, eh?"

"I know so, sir. When I sat in your classes and watched you on the artillery practice field, I saw a rare strength in you. If I had to go into battle, I knew I'd want you to be my leader."

"Rance, I appreciate your kind remarks, but let me say that whatever is in me that makes me like a stone wall comes from the Lord."

Dayton grinned. "That sounds like you, sir."

"Then you do remember the times I talked to you about your need to open your heart to Jesus and let Him save you, Rance." Jackson's eyes were full of compassion. "Have you done so?"

"Well, sir...no, I...I haven't. General, I know what you're saying is right. And I will think about it."

"You don't need to think about it, Rance. You need to do it. Just tell Jesus you're a sinner in need of salvation. Tell Him you believe He died for you on Calvary and rose from the grave so He could save you. You once told me you believed it. Do you still?"

"Yes, sir."

"Then act upon your head belief and make it heart belief, Rance. You can settle it right this minute, if you will."

Rance cleared his throat. "I'll sure think on it, sir. And... thank you for caring about me." Rance stood up and shook the general's hand. "I really will think about it."

"Just don't die while you're thinking about it," Jackson said.

"Yes, sir. I must get back to my men now. God bless you, sir."

Jackson watched his former student walk away in the dull light of dusk. "Keep him pressured, Lord. I want to see him saved."

ELEVEN

The Army of Northern Virginia, led by General Robert E. Lee on his white horse Traveler, marched north through Leesburg. It was a sunny, clear morning for the long procession of men, horses, mules, wagons, caissons, and cannons on wheels. Stonewall Jackson and James Longstreet, sitting straight-backed and proud in their saddles, rode on either side of the general.

The bands of both Corps marched in one unit, playing D. D. Emmett's song, "Dixie," as the Confederate army marched along Leesburg's main thoroughfare. Hundreds of cheering spectators lined both sides of the street. People stepped up and handed food to the soldiers and spoke encouraging words about their move onto Maryland soil.

One stout woman shouted from a balcony, "The Lord bless your dirty ragged souls! Show Billy Yank that fancy pressed uniforms aren't everything!"

Many of the soldiers raised their muskets and shouted back that they would do that very thing.

Hunter McGuire rode in a medical supply wagon driven by Corporal Lanny Dixon not far behind the three generals. There were four other medical supply wagons belonging to I Corps further back in the line, each manned by a doctor who was under Hunter's authority as Corps Medical Director. General Longstreet's II Corps also had four medical supply wagons, a Corps Medical Director, and four doctors.

All eight wagons had received supplies from Richmond, and some supplies had been donated by doctors in Leesburg. Hunter was grateful his new medical kit had arrived—he was sure he would need it once they invaded Northern territory.

"They tell me you know General Stonewall quite well, Doctor," Corporal Dixon said to Hunter.

"Since I was a small child. He's eleven years older than I am. He was my hero then and he's my hero now."

"Mine, too. The thing I admire most about General Stonewall is his courage to stand up for the Lord."

"He's no coward, I'll guarantee you that. And he's sure not ashamed to let it be known that he loves Jesus."

"I passed by his tent late the other night on my way to sentry duty and heard him praying for his men. Really touched my heart."

"He cares about his men, Lanny, not only their lives and limbs, but their souls. Too bad there aren't more generals like him."

When General Lee was two miles outside of Leesburg, he twisted around and looked back along the line of nearly fifty thousand men, animals, and equipment on wheels. The tail end of the line was just leaving the outskirts of the town. There was a new light in his men's eyes. This march and what it meant—taking the War to the Federals on their own soil—had energized them.

Lee veered his army eastward toward the Potomac River, planning to cross at White's Ford about five miles from Leesburg. The Potomac was a half-mile wide at the ford, and as usual for early September, about five feet deep. The river was fringed by lofty trees in full foliage and the banks were flower-strewn and green with grass.

It would take considerable time to get his entire army across—at least a full day. The wagons, cannons, and caissons would take the most time and effort. They would have to cross single file because the ford was narrow and the river bottom grew deeper just a few feet on both sides of it.

Lee called a halt as he and Jackson and Longstreet reached the west bank of the Potomac just before noon. When the entire army had collected, Lee explained that he wanted to move as much of the army as possible onto the Maryland side before dark.

The first troops stepped in with their muskets held carefully out of the cool water, which felt good to their sore and blistered feet. The rest of the army cheered, excited to be taking the offensive against the enemy who had stepped onto Southern land well over a year ago.

At dusk, with the larger part of his army still on the Virginia side, General Lee settled his men down for the night.

The next day, as one of General Jackson's units was crossing the broad river, a team of balky mules hitched to one of the caissons stopped about forty yards out and refused to budge. Jackson shouted to the driver that he was holding up progress. The driver shouted back that he had tried everything he knew, but this was the most stubborn team of mules he had ever seen.

"Major Harmon," Jackson said to one of the men near him, "ride out there and help that driver get those mules moving."

"Yes, sir." Harmon snapped a salute and gouged his horse's sides, splashing into the Potomac and forcing his mount past the tangle of halted wagons. When he reached the mules, he leaned over and grasped the bridle of the nearest one and jerked it hard, letting loose a blast of profanity. It took less than half a minute for the mules to respond to the major's tirade and surge forward. Harmon touched his hat brim and smiled when the driver thanked him. As Harmon rode back, he glanced toward General Jackson and noticed the displeasure on his face.

"The ford is clear now, General. There's only one language that'll make stubborn old army mules understand on a hot day that they must get out of the water."

Jackson continued to scowl as he said, "Just because some foul-mouthed soldiers in this army use that kind of language to make mules obey doesn't mean it's necessary, Major. The tone of your voice is what they respond to. You could shout 'Rhubarb!' in the same tone of voice and they'd respond."

Harmon looked chagrined. "Sorry for the profanity, sir."

"Apology accepted, Major, but that doesn't clean out my ears."

"Excuse me, General," Harmon mumbled. "I...I need to go check on some of the wagons in my unit before they reach the water."

It took a day and a half to get the entire army and its equipment onto the Maryland side. The sun was going down on Saturday, September 6, as the band members crossed over, holding their instruments above their heads.

Lee was sure that by now his crossing onto Northern soil had reached even the ears of Abraham Lincoln.

On Friday afternoon, September 5, news of the Confederate crossing of the Potomac hit Washington like an artillery shell.

Ever since the previous Sunday, when reports of the debacle at Bull Run had come in, panic had prevailed among the federal officials, including President Lincoln and his General-in-Chief, Henry Halleck. The crossing of the Potomac suggested that the Confederates were about to move on Baltimore, which would be only a prelude to an attack on Washington.

Word of the Confederate invasion spread fast among the Union troops and stirred their ire. In the past few days, since their beloved "Little Mac" had been appointed commander of all Federal troops around Washington, morale had begun to lift. Lincoln had no man among his military leaders who could come near the degree of popularity McClellan enjoyed with the troops.

Lincoln told McClellan that he was expecting him to bring the men out of their depression over so many lost battles and to turn them into a crack fighting unit as they had once been.

Spurred by Lincoln's trust in him and by Lee's brazen crossing of the Potomac, McClellan began marching the bulk of his restructured army northwest toward Maryland on Saturday, September 6. He took six corps with him—eighty-four thousand troops—leaving two corps behind to defend Washington.

It was eleven o'clock on Sunday, September 7 when General Lee led his army of nearly fifty thousand men to a spot about two miles south of Frederick, Maryland. They would make camp there after they marched through the town. There were Marylanders among Lee's troops, and he wanted to see what kind of reception his army would receive. Not only did Lee want to test the degree of Southern sentiment as reported by the newspapers, he also wanted to impress the Marylanders with the size of his army.

By noon, the long column was marching into Frederick with Confederate flags snapping in a hot, stiff wind that had been building since early morning. The double-sized band played "Maryland, My Maryland," and people of all ages began to line Main Street. Church services were letting out, and the crowd began to swell by the hundreds. Soon there was a combination of jeers by pro-Union people and cheers by those who favored the South.

As the procession moved slowly through town, the boos and hisses seemed louder than the cheers, and Lee realized the newspapers were guilty of either false or mistaken reporting.

Just as he and his two main generals passed Frederick's First Baptist Church, angry pro-Union men began throwing rocks and bricks. The band stopped playing, trying to protect themselves and their instruments.

Lee didn't want a confrontation with civilians. He called for his adjutant, Colonel Robert Chilton, and told him to ride back along the column and tell the men to protect themselves as best they could, but not to retaliate.

A brick sailed through the air and bounced off the side of Hunter McGuire's wagon, striking a small boy who had just come out of the church ahead of his parents. Hunter saw the boy go down. He leaped from the wagon and knelt beside the unconscious child. The rock-throwing stopped, and the army procession kept moving.

"I'm a doctor," Hunter said to the well-dressed men and women who pressed close. "Do any of you people know this boy's parents?"

McGuire heard someone close by shout, "Nurse Lockwood! Nurse Lockwood, Timmy Jones is hurt!"

Hunter's head jerked up as he rose to his feet, lifting the small, limp form in his arms, and looked toward the church.

"Timmy's parents are over there on the porch," someone said.

Hunter peered over their heads and saw a woman bound off the porch of the church building, a young couple on her heels. She hoisted her skirt slightly and lost her hat to the stiff wind as she ran toward him.

When Jodie Lockwood saw the tall, sandy-haired man who was cradling Timmy, her face blanched.

"Dr. McGuire!" she said. "I…I'm so glad to see you!"

Hunter's throat felt tight.

The boy's parents closed in, frozen with fear. "Oh, Timmy! Howard, he's dead! He's not breathing!"

"He's breathing, ma'am," Hunter said, his own emotions stirring like a whirlwind within him. "But he's unconscious. I'm a doctor. Is there a doctor's office near?"

"Mr. and Mrs. Jones," Jodie said, "this is Dr. Hunter McGuire. I recommend him without reservation. Let's get Timmy to Dr. Roberts's office."

"May I carry him, Doctor?" the boy's father asked.

"It's best that I do, Mr. Jones. I need to keep pressure against the head wound until we can get him to the doctor's office."

The man nodded and took his wife by the hand. "Come on,

Lillian. Timmy's going to be all right."

General Jackson suddenly appeared on foot. "I saw the boy go down, Doc. How is he?"

"Hard to say. I'll know more when I can examine him. I suspect he has a concussion. Miss Lockwood, here, is a nurse, and she's about to take us to the doctor's office."

"We'll set up camp at that spot south of town," Jackson said. "Meet us there when you can."

"Will do. Let's go, Miss Jodie."

Jackson's eyes widened. *Jodie Lockwood?*

The crowd looked on as Hunter and the Joneses followed Jodie down the street.

Without breaking stride, Jodie turned to Hunter and said, "I'm Dr. Harvey Roberts's nurse at the Frederick Medical Clinic. It's just in the next block. Dr. Roberts was called out of bed in the middle of the night by a rider from Sharpsburg. There's no way to know when he'll be back."

"I'll do everything I can for Timmy, if the parents will give me permission," Hunter said.

"Miss Jodie's word is good enough for us, Doctor," Howard Jones said. "We trust you. Do whatever you have to for our son."

"Here we are," Jodie said, as they arrived at the clinic. "I dropped my purse when I jumped off the church porch, but there's a key hidden around back. I'll use it to go through the back and open the front door."

The Joneses remained in the waiting area while doctor and nurse took Timmy into the back room. Ten minutes later, Jodie opened the door and stuck her head out. "Timmy's going to be fine. Dr. McGuire is taking stitches in the gash, and we'll be through in just a few minutes."

"Thank you, Lord," Timmy's mother said on an exhaled breath.

When the door opened again, Hunter emerged with Timmy in

his arms. The boy's eyes were a bit glazed, but he recognized his parents and reached for them. Lillian Jones talked in low tones to her son as he lay in her arms, his bandaged head on her shoulder.

"He's going to be all right, then, Doctor?" Howard Jones asked.

"Yes," Hunter said, smiling. "He's got a concussion, but it will clear up. Took eight stitches to close the gash. Timmy should rest for a few days…not do the things active boys his age usually do. Have Dr. Roberts check him by Wednesday. He'll know when to take the stitches out."

Both parents nodded.

"Timmy will be drowsy for a while, but keep him awake till bedtime this evening. If he becomes nauseated, alert Nurse Lockwood. I'll be at the Confederate camp just south of town, at least for this evening. Call on me if you need me."

"We will, Doctor," Lillian said. "Thank you so much."

"What do we owe you, Doctor?" Howard asked, reaching for his wallet.

"Not a thing. It was my pleasure." Hunter winked. "Of course if you'd like to add a little extra to the offering plate in this evening's service…"

"I'll do it!" Howard said, as they left.

When the door clicked shut, Hunter and Jodie slowly turned to face each other.

TWELVE

I can't tell you how nice it is to see you again, Doctor." A sweet smile lighted Jodie's face.

Hunter caught himself just short of making a fool of himself. "It's wonderful to see you again, Miss Jodie. I…I've thought about you many times since we met—how long has it been?"

What do you mean, McGuire? It's been exactly seven years and three months. And you've thought about her millions of times.

"So you've been working for Dr. Roberts since you finished at the Karr Clinic?"

"Aren't you amazing? You even remember where I was going when I left Lexington!"

"Some things I guess we never forget," Hunter said. Even as he spoke, he could hardly believe he had found Jodie after all these years.

Jodie told Hunter about earning her C.M.N. and C.S.A. certificates at the Benjamin Karr Clinic, and then getting hired by Dr. Roberts. Hunter thanked God for bringing them together again.

"So what about your career?" Jodie asked. "How long have you been an army doctor?"

"Since July 17 of last year. When I finished my internship almost five years ago, Kurtz and Aaron made me a junior partner. And they plan to take me in as a full-fledged partner when the clinic converts to a hospital. Of course, everything is on hold until this war is over."

"So you've been there for some battles."

"Yes…the two at Bull Run Creek have been the bloodiest, but we don't know what's to come."

"Oh, I hope it doesn't last much longer! Today was my first glimpse of General Lee. He looks quite distinguished, doesn't he? And if I remember the newspaper pictures correctly, I think the man who came to ask about Timmy was Stonewall Jackson."

"That's him, all right. Tom—General Jackson and I are old friends. We knew each other as boys."

"Well, I'm impressed, Doctor. It isn't everybody who can say they're old friends with the now-famous Stonewall Jackson."

"No, I guess not. He's the one who asked me to volunteer my services, and he coerced General Johnston into appointing me Corps Medical Director."

Jodie laughed. "I'm sure there had to be coercion." She studied him closely for a moment, then said, "Dr. McGuire, have you married?"

"No. No I haven't. And I'm surprised that you're still *Miss* Jodie Lockwood. Surely you've had many proposals?"

Jodie turned toward a pair of straight-backed wooden chairs nearby. "Do you have time to sit down, Doctor, or do you need to get to the camp?"

"I have time," he said, adjusting the chairs so they faced each other. "Here, allow me." Hunter seated Jodie, then took the other.

Jodie smiled. "To respond about the 'many proposals,' Doctor, I have met several fine Christian men over these years, both in Baltimore and here in Frederick. And…well, there have been a few marriage proposals. But in each case, I just couldn't accept."

"I see. Go on."

"I couldn't accept for two reasons. Number one, in each case I had no peace from the Lord about it. That would be enough right there to keep me from accepting a proposal. The second reason was that I didn't feel the kind of love for any of the men that goes with deciding to get married."

"That's important," Hunter said. "Marriage is a lifetime proposition. Certainly both people should have a deep and abiding love for each other."

"Dr. McGuire, may I ask why you haven't married?"

Hunter chose his words carefully. "Well, Miss Jodie, several years ago I fell head-over-heels in love with a very special young lady. Beautiful inside and out, and a devoted Christian. But she went far away, not knowing how I felt about her. I tried to find her so I could tell her of my love, but it was as if she had vanished off the face of the earth."

"Oh, I'm so sorry," Jodie said. "You…you still don't know where she is?"

Hunter had prayed for this moment, longed for it seven years and three months. "I haven't known where she was until about an hour ago."

It took two or three seconds for Hunter's words to register in Jodie's mind. Suddenly her heart seemed to stop and she felt a blush start at the back of her neck and envelop her body. Tears filled her eyes.

"Miss Jodie, I'm sorry. I didn't mean to upset you. I—"

Jodie shook her head and finally spoke. "You haven't upset me, Hunter. I…I mean, Doctor. It's not that at all. I don't know how to say this except to just come out with it. Within a few days after I left Lexington, I found myself thinking of you constantly. Soon I realized I had fallen in love with you, but I had no way of knowing how you felt about me.

"I wanted to write to you in the worst way and say that I loved you, but it would not be proper to speak first, so I prayed and asked the Lord that if He had chosen you for me, He would bring us together in His own time and His own way. I couldn't believe He would let me meet you and fall in love if He hadn't given you the same kind of love for me. I—"

"Oh Jodie…" Hunter dropped to his knees in front of her. "God was keeping us for each other all along. I love you, Jodie! I love you!"

Jodie threw her arms around Hunter's neck. Their tears mingled as their lips met softly, sweetly. He held her for a long time, then rose to his feet. "Jodie, I feel like I'm dreaming," he said.

Jodie looked up at Hunter with shining eyes. "I almost gave up," she said. "As time passed, and the Lord hadn't brought you back into my life, I began to think it wasn't God's will for us to be together."

Hunter took her in his arms again and spoke softly. "I prayed so hard, and sometimes horrid thoughts pierced my mind—thoughts that you had already married. Somehow I just couldn't accept those thoughts. Somehow I knew in my heart that the Lord had let you come into my life long enough for me to fall in love with you, and someday He would bring us together and let you learn to love me, too."

"I don't have to learn, darling," Jodie said. "I've been loving you for seven years."

They stood in each others' embrace, savoring the sweetness of it, then Hunter said, "Jodie, I sent you two letters while you were still at the Karr clinic. I guess you never got them."

"No, Hunter. I'd have been the happiest woman in the world if I'd received them."

"But they never came back. I wonder what happened to them."

Jodie was silent a moment, then said, "I think I know what happened. We had a receptionist at the clinic who handled all the mail. She was an atheist. She became quite angry when I witnessed to her about Jesus and told her the Bible says those who say there is no God are fools. From that time on she made life as miserable for me as she could. Dr. Karr finally fired her not long before he sold the clinic. I'm sure she intercepted your letters."

"I know about Dr. Karr selling the clinic to Dr. Clayton."

"You do?"

"I couldn't stand not seeing you, so I took a few days off to go to

Baltimore. When I arrived at the clinic, no one knew you. Dr. Clayton found your records, but there was nothing to indicate where you might have gone. And now, on a windy Sunday, the Lord has brought you to me, as my mother would say, 'on the wings of the wind.' That's from—"

"Psalm 104:3. It's one of my favorite verses!"

"It was one of Mom's, too. She used it a lot. Before she died she said she was going to heaven to be with Dad, but that one day Jesus would come walking on the wings of the wind and bring us all back together—Lizzie, Mom, Dad, and me."

"Lizzie? Your sister?"

Hunter nodded, sadness capturing his eyes. "My father had been dead a year when Mom died. Lizzie and I were adopted by different families. I was adopted by a doctor and his wife from Boston. That's where I grew up. Lizzie was adopted by a family in McCann's Run, Virginia, where we were born. She was only two years old. They left for North Carolina right after the adoption but never got there. They just disappeared without a trace."

"Oh, Hunter, that's awful."

"I guess I never asked you where you're from, Jodie. Your family, and all that."

"Well, I was born and raised in the South. Southeast Tennessee, just outside of Athens."

"In the country, eh? A real Tennessee plow girl."

Jodie grinned. "I guess. Well, anyway, I wasn't raised in a Christian home. Neither of my parents were Christians. They both drowned while boating on Lake Chicamauga after I had moved to Lexington. My roommate in Lexington, who was like a sister to me, took me to First Baptist Church, and that's where I came to know the Lord."

"Bless her heart," Hunter said. "Do you have any siblings?"

"No. I wish I did. Would've been easier if I'd had brothers or sisters to help share the grief when my parents died. What about you, Hunter? You probably still think about Lizzie a lot."

"Every day."

The clock on the wall caught Hunter's attention. "Guess I'd better get back to the camp. It's nearly three-thirty. Tom—I mean, General Jackson is going to wonder what's happened to me."

Some of the light went out of Jodie's eyes. "How long will General Lee stay camped out there?" she asked.

"Probably not long. I don't really know what he's got in mind. All I know is that he's brought his army here to harass the Yankees."

"When will I see you again, Hunter?"

"I'd love to say I'll be here tonight for the church services, but since I don't know what's being planned, I'd better say look for me when you see me coming."

As he spoke, Hunter rose from his chair, lifting Jodie's hand. Without hesitation she moved close and put her arms around him. Hunter smiled and folded her close. "If I'm dreaming, Jodie, I don't want to wake up."

They kissed lingeringly and then Jodie lay her head against Hunter's chest. "So we don't know when we'll see each other again," she said.

"I'm afraid there's no way to tell. We may march a long way tomorrow. But I know where to find you now, and I'll be back just as soon as I can. And…"

"Yes?" she said, leaning back to look into his face.

"If you move elsewhere, tell *everybody* in town where I can find you."

She laughed. "I'm not planning to move, but you have my word on it. I won't be so hard to find again."

"Before I go, let's thank the Lord for bringing us together." Hunter took Jodie's small hands in his own and closed his eyes.

"Dear Lord," he began, "I must ask You to forgive me for all the times I doubted You, even when I prayed so hard that You would bring Jodie to me. We both thank You from the depths of our souls for guiding our lives and for bringing us together in Your own time and Your own way. We don't know when this awful war will be over, but You do. Please protect Jodie. Keep her, I pray, in the hollow of Your mighty hand, and let us be together again very soon. In the precious name of Jesus, we pray. Amen."

Hunter held Jodie close as she wept. When she had gained some composure, she blinked against her tears and said, "I'll show you the boarding house where I live. It's on the way south out of town."

As they walked along Main Street, Hunter kept an arm around Jodie's shoulders. Soon they were at the outskirts of Frederick. Grassy meadows and fenced farm fields spread out before them, and they could see the white tents of the Confederate camp some two miles in the distance, beneath tall trees.

"Jodie, if it's at all possible, I'll come into town and see you before we break camp and move out. If I don't come, you'll know I just couldn't do it. But know this much for sure…you'll see me the first opportunity I get."

"Then I will live for that moment, darling," she said, softly.

Hunter headed down the road and looked back after walking about thirty yards. Jodie remained where he had left her, and he could see tears glistening her cheeks.

When he was almost out of sight from her, he paused and looked back again. She stood in the golden light of the late afternoon sun, waving at him. As he waved back, his heart seemed to swell with love for her. "Lord," he said, "I love Jodie more now than ever."

General Lee's adjutant, Colonel Chilton, met Hunter as he approached the camp.

"Yes, Colonel?" Hunter said, as they drew abreast.

"General Lee asked that you stop by his tent, Doctor. He's located beneath those tall elms."

Hunter thanked the adjutant and started for the general's tent, greeting soldiers as he went. General Lee was outside, talking with Stonewall Jackson, when Hunter walked up.

"You wanted to see me, sir?"

"Yes, Doctor. Both General Jackson and I are concerned about the boy. Is he all right?"

"Yes, sir. He has a concussion and needed some stitches to close up the gash on his head. But he'll be fine."

"That's good news." Lee turned back to Jackson. "You and General Longstreet meet with me first thing in the morning. Right after breakfast."

"We'll be here, sir," Jackson said, and started to head back to his Corps. Hunter bid General Lee good evening and walked away beside his old friend.

When they were out of earshot from any of the soldiers, Jackson said, "Hunter, unless I misunderstood what I heard in town today, that was your Jodie Lockwood, wasn't it?"

Hunter's face was beaming. "It was, Tom. God brought Jodie to me right there in the middle of Main Street!"

"And?"

"Tom, you won't believe it."

"Try me."

"She's been in love with me all this time. Said she knew it only days after arriving in Baltimore, but didn't think it proper to write to me, not knowing my feelings. She just prayed like I've been doing all these years. She's had opportunities to marry, but God picked her for me, Tom…and He saved her for me!"

Jackson halted abruptly.

"What's wrong?" Hunter asked.

"You *did* ask her to marry you, didn't you?"

"Well, no. I…I didn't take it that far today. But when I see her again, I sure will. Fellow has to use a little discretion, Tom."

"But you have no doubt she'll say yes?"

"None whatsoever."

A wide grin spread over Jackson's face. "Well, my friend, let me say that I sure am glad I was wrong. It looks like the Lord did have Jodie picked out for you. I hope the two of you will have a marriage as good as Mary Anna's and mine."

When Hunter looked at all the men in I Corps whose sore feet needed his attention, he knew he wouldn't be able to see Jodie again that evening.

After finally climbing into his bedroll just before midnight, he could hardly sleep for thinking about her. He'd found her, and she was in love with him.

At the boarding house in Frederick, Jodie stared up at the dark ceiling, marveling at the miracle of meeting Hunter again. The Lord had brought him to her, just as she had prayed He would. Hunter hadn't brought up marriage, of course. But when he did, she had her answer ready.

At his tent in the Confederate camp, General Lee was wide awake. Just before darkness fell, he had received an intelligence report from Jeb Stuart's scouts that the Union Army of the Potomac had left Washington on Saturday, led by Major General George B. McClellan. "Little Mac" was headed on a straight line for Frederick with eighty-five thousand to ninety thousand troops.

THIRTEEN

D aylight came across the Maryland sky in changing sheets of color. Sunday's wind had died down to a moderate cool breeze, but would grow hot again as the day progressed.

Generals Jackson and Longstreet finished breakfast and started for their commander's tent. General Lee was seated with a map before him.

"Good morning, sir," Jackson said. "You look tired."

Lee sighed. "Please sit down, gentlemen. I didn't sleep at all. Too much to do. After you two were in your bedrolls last night, General Stuart's scouts rode into camp. They estimate that at least eighty-five thousand men left Washington Saturday and are headed this direction."

"Are you surprised, sir?" Longstreet asked.

"Not that they're coming…only the number. It doesn't deter me from harassing the stuffing out of the Federals, but it does change the way we're going to do it."

Jackson and Longstreet noted the map on the table, folded to focus on Washington, D. C., and the states of Virginia, Maryland, and Pennsylvania.

"As you gentlemen know," Lee said, "it's been in the back of my mind that if all went well in our invasion, we might drive our troops as far north as Pennsylvania."

He picked up a small twig and pointed at Frederick on the map. "My thinking is this: From Frederick we could move part of our army northwest across Catoctin Mountain—right here—and South Mountain—here—to Hagerstown, Maryland. From where we sit to Hagerstown is approximately twenty-seven miles."

Lee moved the twig's tip as he spoke. "Right here is the path of the Cumberland Valley Railroad. By moving our army northwest, as I just indicated, we would be shielded on our right flank by these mountains. We would follow the path of the Cumberland Valley Railroad, which curves seventy miles northeast from this point to Harrisburg—Pennsylvania's capital."

"And I think I see what you've got in mind," Jackson said. "Just west of Harrisburg lies the Susquehanna River and the key bridge of the Pennsylvania Railroad. You're after the bridge."

Lee smiled and rubbed his tired eyes. "You get a good grade in class today, Thomas J."

"Sure!" Longstreet said. "That bridge is vital to McClellan's supply line."

"That's correct," Lee said. "The destruction of the bridge would sever a vital Union supply route between east and west and weaken McClellan considerably.

"Now, to implement my plan, we'll have to safeguard our own lines of communication and supply against Union cavalry raids. Here's what I've come up with: We can shift our lines westward into the Shenandoah Valley behind the protection afforded here by the Blue Ridge Mountains. But first we'll have to deal with two Federal outposts that stand virtually astride my intended supply route in the Valley."

Jackson was ahead of his commander again. "You're speaking of Harper's Ferry and Martinsburg, sir?"

"Yes. I'm kicking myself for not keeping troops at Harper's Ferry when I brought you away from there, General. Now we've got to take the place from the Federals again. They've got twelve thousand troops camped there. Fifteen miles northwest of there—right up here—is Martinsburg, where the Federals have a twenty-five-hundred-man garrison. In order to eliminate these two threats, we'll have to temporarily split our army in two. General Longstreet, you will take three of your divisions—Hood's, Walker's, and Jones's—and begin the first leg of the movement into Pennsylvania. You will cross South Mountain to Boonsboro, halfway to Hagerstown. I will go with you.

"Meanwhile, General Jackson, you will take the other two divisions of II Corps—McLaw's and Anderson's—and all of your own I Corps and take over the Union garrisons at Harper's Ferry and Martinsburg. When you've accomplished that, our entire army will converge on the banks of the Susquehanna right at this point. We'll destroy the bridge at Harrisburg, then cut south, fortify ourselves, and clash head-on with McClellan's under-supplied army."

James Longstreet shifted his big frame on the chair and shook his head. His words had a slight biting edge to them. "General, I don't like dividing our forces."

Lee blinked, and Jackson's head came up. Longstreet was known for speaking his mind, but this bold statement surprised the other two men.

"I don't like it because it weakens us," Longstreet said. "I think whatever we do, we need to keep our forces together."

"In this situation, General," Lee said, "it's the only sensible thing to do—blow up the bridge at Harrisburg, cutting off Union supplies from McClellan's army, and neutralize Harper's Ferry and Martinsburg to keep our own supplies coming unhindered. My plan will work because there's no way the Yankees at those two outposts can stand against the numbers we'll throw at them."

"But what if McClellan gets past the point you indicated on the map where we'd cut south to meet him?" Longstreet asked. "Then we'd have to chase him down, which would give him time to fortify.

We've got to remember, General, that if General Stuart's scouts are accurate in their estimation, McClellan has us heavily outnumbered."

"But you're forgetting something—McClellan's temperament."

"Sir?"

"The man is slower than the seven-year itch. He's an able military leader, I'll give him that, but he's a very cautious one. Believe me, we'll easily have time to come south from Pennsylvania and wait for him when he reaches this point, right here. Big surprise for McClellan! By that time, we'll have all his supply sources cut off. Since we're outnumbered, it's the only way we can come out the victors."

Longstreet darted his eyes to Jackson. Stonewall grinned at him. "I believe our esteemed leader is on target here, General."

Longstreet stared at the map in silence, his face rigid.

After a few moments, Lee said, "Well, Old Warhorse, are you with me?"

Longstreet's face muscles relaxed. "Of course, sir, but reluctantly. I just don't hanker to split our forces. However, you are the boss of this outfit, so I'll comply."

Lee glanced at Jackson, grinned, looked back at Longstreet, and said, "You're a good man, and I appreciate the fact that you aren't bashful about expressing your opinions."

Longstreet smiled slightly. "Bashful, sir, I am not."

Lee rose from his chair. "Well, gentlemen, I'll put this plan into writing and make it an order. Then I'll have Colonel Chilton make a copy for the head officer of each division."

"You haven't said when we'll split the army and move out, General," Jackson said.

"Well, it's going to take Colonel Chilton several hours to make all the copies once I get the original into his hands. I'd say we should plan to move out at sunrise on Wednesday."

Longstreet masked his surprise. He had expected they would move out tomorrow. Waiting until Wednesday would give McClellan another day to march his troops westward.

The sun had set that evening when Jodie Lockwood finished drying the last supper dish and placed it in the cupboard. She removed her apron, hung it on a wall peg in the small kitchen, and picked up the lantern.

When the knock came at the door, her first thought was that Dr. Roberts needed her to help with a medical emergency.

It was Hunter, with a bouquet of wildflowers in his hand.

Jodie's face glowed as she greeted him. "Oh, I'm so glad you're here! And those flowers…they're beautiful!"

"Not as beautiful as you. When God made you, He did His most excellent piece of work."

"Aren't you the flatterer." She raised up on tiptoe and kissed Hunter softly. "Come in, darling. I'll put these flowers in water."

Jodie wore a simple cotton print dress, but to Hunter it was royal attire. He followed her to the kitchen and lifted the dipper from the water bucket while Jodie took a small vase off the cupboard shelf and extended it toward him.

"Only about a third, Dr. McGuire."

He poured the water carefully and grinned. "Yes, Nurse Lockwood."

Jodie slipped the stems into the vase and set it on the cupboard. Then turning to Hunter's embrace, she declared, "I'll never throw them away. When they begin to wither, I'll press them in a book and keep them always."

Hunter looked into her eyes, the amber glow of the lantern playing on their faces. "I love you, sweet Jodie."

"And I love you, my darling Hunter."

After his tender kiss she stayed within his arms.

"Hunter, I'm so glad you didn't have to leave. Do you know yet when General Lee will be moving his army out?"

"Word is it'll be Wednesday morning at daylight."

"Then can you come a little earlier tomorrow night and let me fix you a nice meal?"

"I can arrange that. What time?"

"How about six o'clock?"

"Six o'clock it is. I'll look forward to it."

"I've been told I'm a good cook. I hope you will agree."

"If it's you cooking it, it has to be good."

"Dr. McGuire, you are what is known as a diplomat."

"Well, since yesterday just about noon, I've been known as the happiest man on earth. If that makes me good at diplomacy, so be it. How about going for a walk? There's a half-moon up there in God's big starry sky."

"I'd love it."

Windows glowed with lantern light as Jodie and Hunter strolled hand-in-hand beneath a canopy of stars and listened to the seemingly millions of crickets playing their nightly music.

"Isn't God's creation wonderful?" Jodie said. "Everything around us is so beautiful."

Hunter squeezed Jodie's hand. "If it were only as peaceful as it looks tonight," he said.

Soon they were at the town's south edge and they could see the winking fires in the army camp.

"I hate to think of the coming battle," Jodie said, her voice low. "This war is so senseless."

"War is always senseless. I don't know why people can't just live and let live."

"Because Jesus said there would be wars and rumors of wars all the way up to the end time. But I'll sure be glad when this one is over."

"It would be a lot easier for a married physician and surgeon to have a normal life than following these armies around," he said.

Jodie looked up, trying to see Hunter's expression in the pale silver light. "Just any married physician and surgeon, or one that I know personally?"

"The one who is so in love with you that sometimes he thinks his heart is going to burst right through his chest. Will you marry me, Jodie?"

Jodie had practiced her answer, but now it came out totally different. "Oh, darling, I…I…What am I stammering for? Of course I'll marry you!"

Hunter took her in his arms and kissed her long and tenderly. He felt her warm tears on his face. He held her against him and pressed the side of her head to his chest. They stayed that way for a long time with only the sound of the night breeze in the nearby trees and the music of the crickets.

Hunter broke the silence. "Let's talk about our engagement. We want to be right and proper in it. Do you think four or five months is long enough? I mean, it's not like we're fresh out of high school."

"I'm sure four or five months would be proper," Jodie said. "And maybe by that time the War will be over."

"I hope so. But even if it's not, we'll get married anyway. That is, if you don't mind being married to an army doctor who follows the battles."

"I don't mind."

"I knew you'd say that. We can set the exact date later, but for now we'll say January or February."

They had turned back toward town when Jodie stopped abruptly and pulled at Hunter's hand. "Hunter—"

"Hmm?"

"You will be careful, won't you? I know you're not right out in the middle of the battlefields, but bullets and cannon shells can travel a long way."

"I'll do my best to keep this engaged man alive, sweetheart."

"You do that."

On Tuesday morning, September 9, Colonel Chilton stood over General Lee as the Confederate Army leader signed the copies of his plan. At the head of each page were the words *Special Orders Number 191.*

When he had signed the last order, Lee looked up at Chilton. "Colonel, I ask you to personally deliver these to each division commander."

"Yes, sir."

"Tell each man that the orders pinpoint our movements over the next several days, and they are to guard the papers with care."

"I understand, sir."

"Since I talked this plan over with Generals Jackson and Longstreet this morning, I've had a change of mind. I'm putting Major General Daniel Hill's division with General Longstreet's three divisions into Pennsylvania. If either General Jackson or General Longstreet questions this change, tell him to come and see me at once."

"Yes, sir."

Stonewall Jackson and Hunter McGuire stood talking outside Jackson's tent when the general suddenly chuckled. "So she's going to give you a sample of her cooking, is she? What are you going to do if it's bad?"

"It won't be. That sweet petunia couldn't do *anything* bad."

Jackson shook his head. "Son, the love bug has bitten you with real sharp teeth."

"General Jackson, sir," came a voice from behind them.

Jackson pivoted as Colonel Chilton approached. "Good morning, Colonel."

"Good morning, sir. And good morning to you, Dr. McGuire."

Chilton took some folded papers from the stack he was carrying and extended them toward Jackson. "This is General Lee's Special Order, sir. You know about it. He said to tell you that he made a change after he talked with you and General Longstreet. If you have any questions, you are to see him immediately."

"All right. Thank you."

When Chilton was gone, Jackson smiled at Hunter. "Well, my friend, I guess I'd better read this over. You and Jodie have a good time this evening. The fact that you're going to get a home-cooked supper makes me miss my Mary Anna even more."

"Well, I'd invite you along, Tom, but—"

Jackson laughed. "Sure you would! Now get out of here! I've got important work to do."

Hunter walked away, a broad smile on his face.

Jackson entered his tent to read the special orders. When he saw that General Lee was taking one of I Corps' divisions with him into Pennsylvania, he sat down to write a note to General Hill.

Jackson copied the orders word-for-word on a fresh piece of paper and added a note at the bottom to make sure Hill understood that he was in agreement with Lee's last-minute change.

He signed the note, folded the paper, and stepped outside to scan the men milling about camp. He spotted Lieutenant Garth Mallory walking in his direction.

"Lieutenant!" Jackson called.

Mallory's head lifted and he hurried to Jackson. "Yes, General?"

"I need this very important paper delivered to General Daniel Hill. Would you see that he gets it right away?"

"Certainly, sir." Mallory accepted the folded paper, and Jackson thanked him then returned to his tent.

As Mallory threaded his way among the tents, he spotted a corporal who was in Hill's division. He hailed the corporal and explained that General Jackson had given him a note to deliver to General Hill. Would the corporal do it for him…he had some other things to tend to.

The corporal took the note, pulled three cigars from his shirt pocket, and carefully wrapped the note around them. He placed the small bundle back in his pocket and told Mallory he would deliver the note to General Hill.

***

That evening Jodie answered Hunter's knock wearing a two-piece dress of cobalt blue sateen. It had a pointed basque waist and a lace Byron collar and cuffs, and small silver buttons. Her mass of jet-black hair was elegantly upswept, with trailing curls.

Hunter was enchanted.

"Come in, darling," Jodie said. "Supper will be ready in a few minutes."

Hunter moved through the door, his eyes sweeping over her. "Jodie, you look gorgeous! I love your hair like that…and that dress—"

"I wanted to dress in a special way for you tonight. I hope it pleases you."

Hunter took her in his arms and kissed her.

Later, after they had given thanks for the food and begun to eat, Hunter told Jodie the army would be pulling out in the morning at dawn.

"Oh, Hunter. I'm going to miss having you so close."

"I'm going to miss being so close," Hunter said. "And I'm going to miss this scrumptious cooking. Couldn't we get married right now and just run away from all this?"

Jodie grinned. "I wish we could. Do you really like my cooking?"

"Couldn't be matched this side of heaven."

As the meal progressed, the happy couple talked of their wedding and the future that lay before them.

Later, when the dishes were done and the kitchen cleaned up, Hunter and Jodie took a walk in the moonlight, this time through town to the north. Since Hunter had no idea what would become of the Confederate invasion of Maryland—and he was sworn to secrecy concerning Lee's push into Pennsylvania—he couldn't tell Jodie when he would see her again.

When they returned to the boarding house, Jodie wept and clung to Hunter. He kissed her soundly, told her once again that he loved her, and walked away into the night.

***

At dawn on Wednesday morning, September 10, 1862, General Lee's army had finished breakfast and the men were hastily pulling down tents and loading wagons. The tattered soldiers, refreshed after four days' rest, were in a cheerful mood.

By the time the sun was up, Lee and his troops had begun their move. To further impress the citizens of Frederick, he marched his fifty thousand-strong army through town.

The combined bands played "The Girl I Left Behind Me" as people gawked from windows, while others stepped out onto porches and still others lined the street. Both Union and Confederate flags waved. There was booing and hissing mingled with cheers, but as Lee had figured, there were no rocks or bricks thrown.

Hunter sat on the wagon seat next to Corporal Lanny Dixon. As they drew near the clinic, Hunter looked for Jodie. Suddenly he spotted her, standing next to a distinguished-looking man he presumed was Dr. Roberts.

Hunter smiled and waved. Jodie pointed him out to Dr. Roberts, then blew him a kiss.

To conceal his real objective of heading southwest to Harper's Ferry, Jackson marched his troops north as if they were going with Lee. When they were out of sight from Frederick, he turned them around, veered west, and dropped down into a shallow valley.

FOURTEEN

General Lee's strategy was sound, but his estimate of McClellan's movements was in error. He was not aware of the pressure Abraham Lincoln had put on McClellan to step up the pace. The eighty-four thousand troops of the Union Army of the Potomac drew near Frederick from the south at midafternoon on Friday, September 12.

Major Generals Ambrose E. Burnside and Joseph Hooker flanked McClellan as they rode.

General Hooker let his ice-blue gaze roam the area ahead and said, "General McClellan, sir, that open area fringed by tall elms looks like a good place to make camp. Should be enough room for all of us there."

"Looks good to me," McClellan replied.

As they drew nearer, Hooker rose up in his stirrups. "Sir, there have been tents and a large number of men here."

"Lee!" McClellan said. "He camped here, and not long ago!"

Joe Hooker was the first to dismount and scan the area. "I'd say by the way the grass looks and by the depth of the footprints in the soft dirt, they left here two days ago, three at the most."

"Well, if this place was good enough for Bobby Lee, it's good enough for George B. McClellan. General Burnside, ride back along the column and tell them we're camping here."

"Yes, sir." The balding general with the muttonchop whiskers wheeled his horse about.

That night McClellan met with his Corps leaders. The major generals stood in a half circle, facing their leader. A large fire burned close by.

"Gentlemen," McClellan said, "I have not yet decided how long we will camp here. I'll make that decision after I send some scouts out in the morning. When they find Lee, we'll make our move. However, in the morning, we're going to march our entire column through Frederick. If I know Bobby Lee like I think I know Bobby Lee, he's already done that to impress the people. Well, George McClellan will not come behind Bobby Lee in anything."

At the same time McClellan was picking his camp site south of Frederick, Robert E. Lee was doing the same for his four divisions at the base of South Mountain, some fifteen miles northwest.

When Lee's tent was set up, he stepped inside and sat down, rubbing his chest. Colonel Chilton, who was carrying in the general's bedroll, noticed the grimace on Lee's face.

"General, sir, you're in pain. Shall I get one of the doctors?"

Lee took a deep breath and winced. "That won't be necessary, Colonel, thank you. I'm just having a little pleurisy. I've had it before."

"Sir, I really think I should go get Dr. McGuire."

"No, really," Lee said. "I'll be all right in a minute or two."

"Sir, at the risk of being hanged for disobeying my superior officer, I *am* going to fetch Dr. McGuire." With that, Chilton was out of the tent and gone.

Lee smiled, then winced again from a spasm of pain.

Five minutes later, Hunter was listening to Lee's heart with a stethoscope while Colonel Chilton stood by.

When Hunter had finished, he said, "General, it's not pleurisy. You have an irregular heartbeat. Has any doctor ever told you this?"

"No."

"Well, sir, this is going to sound impossible, but my advice to you is to try to relieve yourself of too much pressure."

Lee smiled. "I've got a war to fight."

Hunter reached into his black bag and pulled out a small white envelope. "I'm going to give you a sedative, General. I want you to take half of these powders right now and the other half in the morning. Hopefully, you'll feel better by then. I'll check on you again tomorrow."

Hunter was about to leave when rapid, pounding hooves were heard outside. Colonel Chilton stepped out and called back, as the horse skidded to a halt, "It's one of General Stuart's scouts, sir."

"Show him in," Lee said.

The scout introduced himself as Sergeant Harland Bailey, and told Lee that another scout had asked him to bring the message that a large unidentified part of McClellan's Union Army of the Potomac was marching south from Pennsylvania toward Hagerstown.

Lee's hand went back to his chest. "How has McClellan managed to do this? It hasn't been that long since he pulled out of Washington. There's no way he could have sent part of his army into Pennsylvania last Saturday and had them there already heading south toward Hagerstown!"

"All I know is what the scout told me, sir."

"Well, I've got to believe him. Colonel Chilton, go bring my division leaders, quick!"

Lee was shouldering into his shirt when Hunter stopped him. "Sir, we need to get this sedative into you now."

Moments later, General Lee, back in shirt and coat, met with his division leaders. Since Hagerstown was to be the springboard for Lee's invasion into Pennsylvania, he told the generals they would pack up immediately and ride through the night to get there. He would take three divisions, totaling sixteen thousand men, leaving

Major General Hill's division of five thousand at South Mountain to guard the rear.

Hunter McGuire insisted on going with Lee to keep an eye on him. Lee did not argue.

At sundown in the Union camp, the tents had been pitched and the cooks were building fires to start supper. A delegation of Frederick businessmen, upon hearing that the Federals were making camp on the same spot where the Confederates had been, had come to the camp and now gathered in front of General McClellan's tent, talking to him.

McClellan's weary soldiers sat on the ground to rest, and some stretched out to catnap. Two soldiers—Sergeant Bloss and Corporal Mitchell of Burnside's IX Corps—sat under an elm, discussing where Lee might have taken his army.

"Maybe they got cold feet and circled back south," Mitchell said.

"That would be something," Bloss said. "Maybe this time they'll all drown in the Potomac."

"Yeah. Sure would make it easier on—"

Mitchell was staring at something in the tall grass a few feet away.

"See something?" Bloss asked.

Mitchell stood up and headed into the grass. "Some kind of package over here," he said.

Bloss watched Mitchell pick up something white and heard him say, "Well, whattaya know? Some dumb Rebel lost three cigars. They're wrapped in—" Mitchell slipped the paper off the cigars and suddenly tensed. "John, c'mere! Look at this!"

Bloss got to his feet and took the paper from Mitchell's fingers. As he scanned the message, his eyes widened. "Do you realize what this is?"

"Yeah! We need to get it to General McClellan!"

"Let's take it to General Burnside first. It'd be best if he took it to General McClellan."

Burnside's aide told them the general was in conference and could not be disturbed. Bloss and Mitchell headed for their own division leader, Brigadier General Samuel D. Sturgis.

General McClellan was still in conversation with the businessmen from Frederick when he noticed three soldiers hastening toward him. He recognized General Sturgis, who was carrying a white sheet of paper.

"General McClellan," Sturgis said, "Sergeant Bloss and Corporal Mitchell have found something you must see immediately."

McClellan excused himself to the businessmen and angled the paper toward the last rays of the sun. His grip on it tightened as he saw the heading: *Special Orders Number 191, Headquarters, Army of Northern Virginia, September 9, 1862.*

Soldiers began to gather as word went round the camp that something important was happening. McClellan lifted the paper over his head and shook it, laughing heartily. "Talk about a stroke of good fortune. This is more than I could ever have hoped for!"

"What is it, General?" asked one of the businessmen.

"A special order from Bobby Lee to his division leaders! He has split his army, sending Stonewall Jackson to Harper's Ferry and Martinsburg to capture our outposts there. Lee is with the rest of his army, headed toward Pennsylvania to blow up the Pennsylvania Railroad bridge at Harrisburg. We got 'em where we want 'em! Now we'll crush the Confederate army!"

McClellan then asked Bloss and Mitchell how and where they had found the paper. He commended Mitchell for his sharp eye, and told him he would be a sergeant when he woke up the next morning.

When McClellan turned back to the businessmen, he said, "I need to use the telegraph in town. Can you gentlemen—"

"I run the telegraph office, General," one of them said. "It's yours to use, free of charge."

"Thank you, sir. I need to wire President Lincoln and tell him the news."

McClellan hastened into town and sent a wire to Lincoln, saying he would send trophies of the victory when the Confederates were vanquished.

On his return to the camp, McClellan moved among the men, waving the lost order and stirring them up by shouting, "With this paper, I will whip Bobby Lee!"

Lee's three divisions—including Stuart's cavalry—arrived at Hagerstown at dawn on Saturday morning. Stuart sent two scouts north to see how close the Federal troops were.

The day passed while the men caught up on their sleep in shifts. Jeb Stuart insisted that General Lee get some sleep, saying he would awaken him when the scouts returned.

Lee slept for about three hours and was up again, waiting with Stuart at the edge of camp. It wasn't until sunset that the two scouts returned. When they saw Lee and Stuart, they drew rein.

"We couldn't find any Union troops anywhere," a scout said. "The reason we've been gone so long is because we wanted to make sure. We went several miles into Pennsylvania and covered broad swaths separately. The report you received, General Lee, was erroneous."

Lee was so relieved that he felt no anger toward the scout who had made the false report. He thanked the men, then turned to Jeb Stuart. "General, we'll camp here for the night and return to General Hill's division at South Mountain in the morning."

Four hours later, when all the men except the sentries were in their bedrolls asleep, General Lee was just slipping off his boots when he heard footsteps and a low voice. "General Lee, sir, I assume you're still awake."

"Yes."

"It's Corporal Tom Humphrey, sir—one of the pickets. There's a gentleman here from Frederick who would like to see you. He says it's important."

"Just a moment, Corporal."

Lee pulled on his boots, straightened his shirt and coat, and opened the tent flap. He could see two figures standing in the dark. "You rode all the way here, alone, from Frederick, sir?"

"Yes, General. My name is Stephen Cunningham. I own the Cunningham Hotel in Frederick."

Lee shook the man's hand and bid him sit on one of the wooden folding chairs inside the tent. Cunningham then said, "I'm afraid I'm a bearer of bad news, General, but somebody had to come and tell you."

Lee's brow furrowed. "Bad news?"

"Yes, sir. General McClellan and some eighty-four thousand troops arrived about noon today and are camped on the same spot where you were."

Lee's eyebrows arched. "Arrived today?"

"Yes, sir. Some of the pro-Union businessmen in town decided to go to the camp and talk with McClellan. I went along to see what I could learn. Although my wife and I have lived in Maryland for thirty years, we were born in Alabama, and our sympathies lie with the South."

"I'm glad to hear that, Mr. Cunningham. So the bad news is that McClellan is camped at Frederick?"

"Well, no, sir. The bad news is that one of McClellan's men found a copy of an order you issued to your division commanders on September 9. It was numbered 191. McClellan now knows your plans to destroy the railroad bridge at Harrisburg, and he knows that General Jackson has been sent to capture the Union garrisons at Harper's Ferry and Martinsburg."

Lee felt the strength go out of him. He put a shaky hand to his forehead. "Well, Mr. Cunningham, this *is* bad news. I thank you for riding all the way here to let me know."

"I felt it was my duty as a loyal Southerner, General. I'll be heading back home now."

As Cunningham rode away, Lee turned to Humphrey.

"Corporal, I need you to awaken General Longstreet. Tell him I must see him right away."

Suddenly Lee and Humphrey heard a stirring in the darkness to the south, then a horse blew and a voice came from the same direction.

"General Lee! Sergeant Rick Wells, sir. On picket duty. I have Lieutenant Charles Simeon from General Hill's division at South Mountain with a message for you."

Even as Wells spoke, Simeon handed him the reins and approached the general. "Sir, General Hill sent me to advise you that an enormous number of small campfires can be seen toward Frederick from the southern tip of South Mountain. He's sure it's the Yankees, sir. The fires are within about a mile and a half of our camp."

Lee spoke to Humphrey. "Corporal, I not only need General Longstreet, I need his division leaders."

Humphrey nodded and disappeared.

Lee then turned to Simeon. "Lieutenant, tell General Hill to move his division into Turner's Gap within South Mountain. He'll be best fortified there."

"Yes, sir."

"Tell him I scrutinized the gap as we passed through. It would be advantageous for him to get his artillery up on the west side. The flat rock formations will allow plenty of room and a clear shot where the Yankees have to expose themselves to enter the gap from National Road. Got it?"

"Yes, sir."

"Tell General Hill he must hold the gap at all costs. We will begin our march from here at dawn and get there as soon as we can."

Four sleepy-eyed generals were heading toward Lee's tent, buttoning shirts and pulling up suspenders as Lieutenant Simeon galloped south out of the camp.

"Come in, gentlemen," Lee said. "I've got news for you, and we've got planning to do."

While his division leaders were digesting the new information,

Lee told Jeb Stuart to send a courier immediately to Stonewall Jackson and inform him of the recent developments. Jackson was to hurry his capture of Harper's Ferry and Martins-burg, and then rush to South Mountain.

Lee discussed the situation with his division leaders, trying not to show discouragement. They would push hard for South Mountain at daybreak. Dan Hill was going to need all the help he could get.

It was about an hour before dawn when General Hill stood at the north edge of his encampment with his brigade leaders beside him. They were Brigadier Generals George B. Anderson, Alfred H. Colquitt, Samuel Garland, Roswell S. Ripley, and Robert Rodes.

National Road was barely visible at the point it plunged into the mountain. They talked in low tones about the coming battle, and periodically glanced toward the Yankee camp where only a few fires flickered now. Suddenly they heard the sound of thundering hoof-beats echoing out of the gap.

"He made good time," Colquitt said.

"That's why I sent him," Hill said evenly. "Simeon's a good horseman."

Lieutenant Simeon delivered his message, and Hill turned to his brigade leaders. "All right, gentlemen. You heard General Lee's orders. We've got to move out before dawn when Billy Yank will attack, sure as anything. We've got to be ready to meet them at Turner's Gap."

By the time the sun was coming up on Sunday morning, September 14, General Hill had his division positioned for battle at Turner's Gap in the heart of South Mountain.

Hill climbed to a high point where he could see the southern entrance of the gap. There were no Yankees on the road yet. He ran his gaze along National Road, noticing that there was good enough defensive ground around the defile where National Road crossed the mountain. Even a small force could make it hot for the attacking troops.

However, as he studied the entire area, he noticed that his division was vulnerable on both flanks. Two roads branched off National Road near the eastern base of the mountain. One was the Old Sharpsburg Road, which angled to the south and crossed the range at Fox's Gap, a little less than a mile from Turner's Gap. A rough farm road left the Sharpsburg road part way up the slope and made a loop farther to the south before turning back and continuing along the top of the ridge through Fox's Gap to Turner's.

The second branch, the Old Hagerstown Road, made a circuit to the north, rejoining National Road at the crest. From it, too, there ran a wide, looping farm road, presenting the Yankees with still another flanking route. Hill decided that to hold Turner's Gap at all costs meant spreading defenders across a good three miles to cover all five roads.

The terrain of South Mountain was irregular, pocked by ravines and hollows, and marked by rounded peaks. The slopes were heavily wooded and thick with undergrowth and tangles of mountain laurel. Where the ground leveled off near the crest, a number of farms had been carved from the forest, their fields and pastures bordered by split-rail fences and stone walls. It would be a difficult place to maneuver troops and direct a battle, but it had to be done.

General Hill hurried to where his troops were setting up their defenses and explained what to do to be able to hold the gap against a massive Union force.

He quickly dispatched Garland's and Colquitt's brigades toward the other four roads to cover them against enemy approach.

Every unit was in place by six o'clock. Thankful that the Federals had not attacked at dawn, General Hill climbed even higher than before and looked to the south. What he saw left him breathless. Spread across the valley were Federal troops in all their array.

Hill set his jaw as he headed down toward his men. Billy Yank was going to find out that Johnny Reb might be low in number, but he was high in fighting spirit.

FIFTEEN

J ust before eight o'clock that Sunday morning, General McClellan was sitting at a folding table outside his tent, sipping hot coffee and talking to General Burnside.

Late the day before, McClellan had learned from his signal stations on hills south of Frederick that the Federal garrison at Martinsburg had been captured by Stonewall Jackson's forces and that Harper's Ferry was presently under siege. McClellan had spent Saturday afternoon developing his plan of attack. He intended to relieve Harper's Ferry and pounce on the scattered units of the Confederates.

To accomplish these goals, he would first have to get his massive army across the Catoctin Mountain, just west of Frederick, and the more formidable South Mountain a dozen miles beyond. McClellan had guessed that Lee would learn of his arrival at Frederick when Lee passed through Turner's Gap. He would know the Federals were on his trail, and fortify himself near the small town of Boonsboro, just north of South Mountain.

On Saturday night, McClellan had sent the bulk of his army to camp near the southern tip of South Mountain. They were then to move on to Boonsboro and wipe out Lee's forces. Once that was done, they would go after Jackson's I Corps, wipe them out, and take back Harper's Ferry and Martinsburg.

At Frederick, McClellan held in reserve twelve thousand men. These he would bring with him to Harper's Ferry to help the other sixty thousand finish off Stonewall Jackson's I Corps. The War would soon come to an end, and George B. McClellan would go down in history as the General who polished off Bobby Lee.

"General McClellan," Burnside said, "shouldn't I go ahead and take my Corps through Turner's Gap? That would give us more momentum when we go after Jackson at Harper's Ferry."

McClellan and Burnside were not friends. It was known by every man in the Union Army of the Potomac that they simply tolerated each other. Burnside had felt all along that McClellan was too slow to attack, as did President Lincoln and Henry Halleck. Burnside had been pleased that McClellan had actually hurried his army from Leesburg to Fredericksburg, but he was already seeing signs of the old "slows" returning.

His suspicions were confirmed when McClellan replied, "No, General, I want your Corps here in reserve."

"But, sir, General Franklin's twelve thousand will be enough reserve. I really think I should take my men and head over South Mountain, now."

McClellan's expression turned sour. "I'll be the judge of that, General. In my thinking, it's best that you remain here in reserve. Please don't argue with me. You'll move out when I—"

McClellan's words were cut off by the rapid pounding of hooves. A rider galloped toward them from the north, and seconds later they recognized a lieutenant from General Pleasonton's cavalry.

"General McClellan!" the lieutenant shouted, thundering to a stop. "Lee wasn't at Boonsboro. He was waiting for us at Turner's Gap, and we've got a hot battle going on! The Rebels have the advantage of high ground, and they're going to be hard to dislodge. We can't tell if it's all of Longstreet's Corps in the gap or just part of it, but General Pleasonton wanted you to know about the battle. He figured you might want to send more men."

McClellan brushed a hand across his face, smoothed his mustache, and said, "You ride back and tell General Pleasonton I'm sending General Burnside's Corps immediately."

Burnside felt a warm glow flow through him but showed no emotion. "I'll round up my men and we'll be on our way in a jiffy, sir," he said.

The battle at Turner's Gap was indeed a hot one. Although the Confederates had the advantage of high ground, the Federals had the advantage in numbers.

General Hill was perched on a high spot above Turner's Gap, his adjutant, Colonel Barry Hucklesby, at his side. They were standing in a rock cleft, peering south at the swarm of blue uniforms pressing in a V shape into the mouth of the gap.

From further out, the Union artillery was arcing shells onto the Confederates' first line. Suddenly a screaming shell came close to where Hill and Hucklesby were positioned and burst a few yards below them. They felt its hot, brutal breath as they ducked, then heard the hiss of flying pieces of rock and the whine of shrapnel all around.

Hucklesby's ears were ringing as he straightened up. "You all right, sir?"

"Fine," Hill said, quickly looking back toward the battle. Through the smoke he saw ghostly figures moving toward the mouth of the gap. The Yankees had plenty of men. No matter what the Rebels threw at them, they just kept coming.

A hot wind was beginning to blow, and soon the smoke parted, revealing the green fields to the south speckled with bodies in blue uniforms. The outnumbered Rebels were fighting hard, and their guns were taking a toll on the Yankees.

But Union artillery was doing the same to the Confederate army. When the Union musket balls couldn't reach the enemy, they arced shells over the natural rock fortresses.

Hill could also see Brigadier General Samuel Garland moving amongst his men, shouting encouragement and directing them to fill in gaps in the lines when others went down.

Down the National Road at the mouth of the gap, the Confederates were facing assaults from the right, left, and front. Bullets buzzed all around, and cannon shells exploded, sending deadly hot canister whistling every direction.

Hill studied the whole scene and said to his aide, "Colonel, if Generals Lee and Longstreet don't get here soon, we're done for."

He put binoculars to his eyes and looked north, then used the binoculars to scan the scene below. "Colonel..."

"Yes, sir?"

"We need more men at Fox's Gap. Go down there and tell General Hood to take his brigade over there on the double. He's got to plug a hole the Yankees are opening in our lines."

Hucklesby had been gone no more than a minute when Hill saw General Garland take a bullet and go down. Hill watched two of Garland's men carry his body a few feet away and lay his hat over his face.

By one o'clock the Southerners were feeling the pressure of the overwhelming odds. To make matters worse, in the distance they saw long columns of Federals marching toward South Mountain from Frederick.

Twenty minutes later, as the columns drew near, the Union soldiers recognized their esteemed leader riding beside General Burnside. McClellan's presence excited his troops. When the front of the columns drew near the battle, McClellan veered his mount to the side of National Road and drew rein. The passing columns of men cheered him as they marched toward the mouth of the gap.

* * *

By three o'clock, General Hill could see that his exhausted men were on the brink of collapse. The Yankees had enough men that they could fight in shifts. There were no such breaks for the Rebels.

Then, seemingly at the last moment, General Longstreet's troops came into view from the north. They were dusty and tired after their long march over rough terrain, but ready to join in the fight. Hill dashed down amongst his men, shouting that help had arrived.

As Longstreet's troops approached the base of the mountain, closing in to reinforce Hill's gallant troops, the weary men cheered at the sight of General Lee. His presence and the reinforcements put new life in their fight.

Now that Lee and Confederate reinforcements had arrived, McClellan studied a map of the South Mountain area and made his decision. Thus far, his troops had made no serious attempt to force Turner's Gap or flank it. At 4:00 P.M., McClellan sent General Joseph Hooker's entire I Corps, except for one brigade, to make a wide flanking movement to the north. The unit he held back was Brigadier General John Gibbon's "Black Hat Brigade." Gibbon and his men were ordered to rush the Confederates headon at Turner's Gap.

Although the addition of Longstreet's troops was a boon to Hill's meager force, the arrival of twelve thousand more Federals did much to offset it. Still the weary Confederates gallantly fought on.

By sunset, Gibbon's Black Hat Brigade still had not penetrated Turner's Gap but were battling it out several hundred yards below the summit with General Colquitt's brigade.

WINGS OF THE WIND

Soon the Confederates on the north side of the gap were under heavy fire from the troops McClellan had sent to that side.

Brigadier General Robert Rodes of Hill's division, with 1,200 men in his 26th Alabama Brigade, plus 150 cavalrymen sent by General Jeb Stuart, had to cover a difficult spur of the mountain that extended north from National Road, dipping into a ravine, then rising to a commanding peak nearly a mile away.

Two divisions from Hooker's I Corps were coming at them with such a wide front that Rodes knew he was flanked by a half-mile on either side. He had to slow the Federals down.

He called to the leader of the 150 cavalrymen, a captain named Errol Taylor, and told him to lead the way on horseback with thundering guns as he sent four hundred skirmishers into the woods and fields at the base of the mountain.

Taylor led his men as directed by Rodes and indeed took a toll on the Union soldiers approaching the base of the mountain. The four hundred roaring guns of the skirmishers did their part as well, and dropped dozens of Yankees who would never rise again.

But the massive numbers of Yankees kept coming. On Rodes's right, the Federal division under Brigadier General John Hatch was advancing along the Old Hagerstown Road. A split-rail fence ran alongside a cornfield at the side of the road. Hatch and his men became engaged in a fierce contest at the fence with Rodes's men, including some thirty cavalrymen.

Hatch fell, severely wounded, and was immediately succeeded in command by Brigadier General Abner Doubleday. Rodes had lost several men in the first few minutes of fighting at the fence and pulled his men back to regroup and make a charge.

As a ruse, Doubleday ordered his men to lie down quietly behind the fence. Rodes and his men rushed forward, suddenly wondering where the Federals had gone.

The 26th Alabama Regiment met a sweeping volley from the hidden Federals that sent them rushing backward, leaving their dead and wounded along the fence.

* * *

When the sun's rim was disappearing below the horizon, Robert E. Lee was with James Longstreet, observing the battle on an elevated rock ledge. It was obvious the Confederates were losing ground.

"General," Lee said, "we are simply too well outnumbered, and there's no sign yet of Jackson. As soon as it's dark, we'll withdraw from here. We don't have a chance."

"I agree, sir. I'll spread the word."

At dusk, as the Federals began to set up camp, small groups of men went out to pick up their wounded.

Captain Errol Taylor was concerned over his five men who had gone down at the fence. If they were alive, he wanted to bring them in. He approached General Jeb Stuart with his request. "Sir, I know that since we're pulling out after dark we can't do anything about our dead. But some of my men may still be alive. Is it all right if I take a couple of men and go see?"

"Of course," Stuart said. "But be careful. Those Yankees might decide to get themselves some more trophies. Take a half-dozen men with you. If you run into any Yankees, get out of there quick. Even if it's only a handful. Understand?"

"Yes, sir."

Taylor chose his six men and they rode hard in the fading light. They found the five cavalrymen at the fence, their horses standing close by, looking on with ears pricked.

Taylor slid from his saddle, and Lieutenant Dirk Melby followed. The others stayed on their horses, watching for any sign of the enemy.

When Taylor and Melby had examined the last man, Taylor looked back and said, "All dead. Let's take their horses and head back."

Suddenly one of the mounted men shouted, "Yankees!"

A swarm of infantrymen came out of the woods in the dusky light, raising their rifles. Taylor and Melby dashed to their horses and vaulted into their saddles as Yankee guns spit fire.

"Go, men!" Taylor shouted.

Lieutenant Melby and the others gouged their horses' sides, putting them to an instant gallop. As they thundered away, Melby expected to see Taylor pull up beside him, but the captain was still sitting in the saddle, looking back at the Yankee soldiers running toward him.

"Lieutenant Melby, what's he doing?" one of the other cavalrymen said. "Why didn't he come with us?"

"I don't know! But if we go back, we'll only be taken prisoners. Let's go tell General Stuart!"

The Union soldiers who dashed toward Captain Taylor were part of an infantry regiment led by Lieutenant Adam Welch. Welch held his service revolver on the Confederate officer astride his horse. The rest of the men had their rifles leveled on him as they drew up. Those who were closest could see by the insignias on his collar and sleeves that he was a captain.

Taylor's horse nickered and bobbed its head as Welch barked, "All right, Captain, off the horse! You're our prisoner! Drop that rifle!"

When the captain continued to look off in the distance, Welch got irritated. "I said off the horse, soldier! *Now!*"

Sergeant Phil Rowan squinted at Taylor's face. "Wait a minute, Lieutenant." Rowan reached up and waved a hand in front of Taylor's eyes.

"Lieutenant! He's *dead!*"

"What?"

"Never saw one any deader. There's a bullet hole in his temple."

Welch finally saw the dark hole in Taylor's temple. "So there is. But how's he staying in the saddle?"

Sergeant Wallace Ulrich stepped up and tried to take the rifle from Taylor's death grip.

"I can't get it loose, sir," Ulrich said.

Welch took hold of the reins and pulled, but Taylor's dead fingers held them fast. "We've got to take him down, men. Sergeant Rowan, steady his body while I pry the reins from his fingers."

When the men had lowered the body earthward, it preserved the same position as in the saddle.

"Lieutenant, I've never seen or heard of anything like this," Ulrich said.

"Nor have I," Welch replied.

"I read something about it once, Lieutenant," one of the infantrymen said. "Can't recall the medical term for it, but it's something about death form, or figure, or shape. I guess it's happened a few times, especially on battlefields."

"Well, it's a new one on me," Welch said. "Let's take him to General McClellan. This is one for the books."

A slender crescent moon hovered overhead, giving off its meager light as Generals Lee, Longstreet, and Stuart stood together, listening to Lieutenant Melby.

"It doesn't make sense, Lieutenant," General Lee said. "Why would he just sit there?"

"Sir, we have no explanation for it. Captain Taylor leaped into his saddle at the same time I did and said, 'Go, men!' When I looked back, he was still sitting there, just waiting for the Yankees to come to him."

"Well, if any of you are thinking deserter, you can forget it," Jeb Stuart said. "Not Errol Taylor. Something snapped in his mind. That's all there is to it."

At that moment Hunter McGuire approached. "General Lee, sir…"

"Yes, Doctor?"

"We've got the wounded in the wagons. They're awfully crowded, but we have no choice."

"Do you have many near death?"

"Yes, General. We'll probably lose several before we get to Sharpsburg."

Lee sighed. There was a long pause, then he said, "Well, let's move out."

Under cover of darkness, the remaining Confederate troops slipped away down the western slope of South Mountain with the silver-haired commander in the lead. Lee had sent a courier to Stonewall Jackson, explaining what had happened at South Mountain, and that he was leading his troops to Sharpsburg, Maryland, along the banks of Antietam Creek. Jackson was to bring his I Corps there as soon as the military posts at Martinsburg and Harper's Ferry were secured.

As Lee rode beneath the night sky, he moved his lips in prayer, asking God not to allow Jackson to fall into a Union trap, too. A deep-settled peace came over him as he prayed.

The defense of South Mountain had proven costly. Lee could only estimate at that point, but he feared he had lost over two thousand men in the battle, and he had not yet asked Dr. McGuire how many were wounded.

Lee was considering letting his men rest at Sharpsburg until Jackson arrived. Then he would take his battered army back into Virginia and put an end to his invasion scheme.

When morning came, General McClellan was not surprised to learn that the Confederates had pulled out. He gathered his six Corps leaders at his tent and said, "Gentlemen, we've put Bobby Lee on the run like a dog with his tail between his legs. As you know, I have scouts already trailing him. It wouldn't surprise me if he's headed for the Potomac. I've a feeling he's licking his wounds, and he'd like to lick them on home ground. Well, good enough.

"So, our next move is to head for Harper's Ferry and Martinsburg and lick Tommy Jackson the same way. Only we'll just go ahead and annihilate him." He glanced toward the horizon and added, "Let's be ready to pull out in thirty minutes."

Ten minutes later, a courier galloped into the Union camp and slid from his saddle where McClellan stood with Generals Porter and Hooker.

McClellan recognized him as being from his signal corps near Harper's Ferry. "You have news for me, Corporal?"

"Yes, sir. I'm sorry it has to be bad news."

"Well, let's hear it."

"Our garrisons at Martinsburg and Harper's Ferry are both in Confederate hands, sir. They have surrendered and are prisoners."

McClellan's face turned crimson. He looked at his generals with fire in his eyes. "Well, this throws a different light on things. We'll go after Bobby Lee and wipe him out first. As soon as the scouts return, we'll find out just where he's heading to cross the Potomac. Maybe we'll catch up in time to drown them before they can step on Virginia soil."

McClellan's scouts returned at ten o'clock and told him that Lee was not heading for the Potomac, but rather seemed to be on a beeline for Sharpsburg. McClellan made a quick decision. He would follow Lee and wipe him out on Maryland soil.

Because of his superior number of troops, McClellan did not hurry the men as they began the march westward.

SIXTEEN

Dawn came gray and dismal on Monday morning, with a soft rain falling. Jodie Lockwood awakened, stretched her arms, and said, "Good morning, Lord. We needed this rain, but you surprised me with it."

She padded to the dresser and leaned close, smiling at her reflection. "You fortunate woman! Hunter McGuire loves you. Just think of it. In a few months, you'll walk down the aisle and become Mrs. Doctor Hunter McGuire."

She wheeled about and hurried to the small table beside her bed where her Bible lay. She picked it up and held it to her breast, closing her eyes

"Thank You, Lord," she said aloud. "You've been so good to me. Thank You for keeping Hunter from falling in love with some other woman. He's mine, all mine, and You gave him to me. Thank You, oh, thank You!"

The rain was a gentle drizzle as Jodie walked to the clinic, humming a nameless happy tune.

Inside, she folded her umbrella and deposited it in the closet just

BATTLES OF DESTINY

1 5 8

as Dr. Roberts came from the back room. His face was somber as he bid her good morning

"You look sad, Doctor. Is something wrong?"

"You haven't heard."

A knot started to form in Jodie's stomach. "Heard what?"

"There was a big battle at South Mountain yesterday."

"Not good for our side?"

"No. Just the Southern grapevine, but folks in that area said Lee's troops were vastly outnumbered. Lots of bodies in the fields and on National Highway leading in and out of the gaps when the sun went down yesterday. Most of them were in gray uniforms."

The kindly physician moved close to Jodie and touched her shoulder. "I know what you're thinking. I won't say army doctors aren't in danger on those battlefields, but you can be thankful your young man is in medicine and not in a uniform."

"I am, Doctor, but with bullets and shrapnel flying all around—"

"Jodie, didn't you tell me God had kept Hunter for you for seven years?"

"Yes, sir," she said, fighting tears.

"Well, then, I believe He isn't going to let anything happen to him now. Sounds to me like the Lord's got it all worked out. Just trust Him."

"I do, Doctor, but—"

"No buts, dear. Either you trust the Lord's mighty hand in your life and Hunter's, or you don't. Which is it?"

"You'd have made a good preacher, Dr. Roberts," she said with a slight smile. "Maybe you missed your calling."

Roberts chuckled. "No. I'm doing what I'm supposed to. And speaking of such, my nurse is supposed to be preparing the examining room for Mrs. Ballard, who is due here in about five minutes."

"Oh, yes! I'll get right to it."

All day long, as patients came into the clinic, they talked about the battle at South Mountain. Jodie wished she knew where Hunter was, but so far the Southern grapevine had not supplied that information. It was the last patient of the day, a pro-Union man, who told them. While Jodie and Dr. Roberts worked on him, he bragged that the Confederates got whipped at South Mountain, and expressed his curiosity as to why Robert E. Lee had moved his army to the banks of Antietam Creek near Sharpsburg.

Word was, the man said, that General McClellan was on their trail. Some people were saying that part of Lee's army was elsewhere with Stonewall Jackson. If Jackson was on his way to Sharpsburg, and McClellan was headed for the same place, and Lee was already there, a whopper of a battle was coming.

The rain had stopped late in the afternoon, but dark clouds still covered the sky as Jodie walked home. She thought of Sharpsburg, just sixteen miles west. Was Hunter there with Lee? Or was he with Jackson? Most likely he was with Jackson. She thought of asking for time off to take a ride to Sharpsburg, but dismissed it, telling herself Hunter was Jackson's Corps Medical Director. Certainly he would be with his old friend.

But where was Stonewall Jackson?

It was noon on Monday when Lee's wet and bedraggled troops plodded through mud to the banks of Antietam Creek. They were less than a quarter of a mile from Sharpsburg when they made camp and set up their tents in the rain.

Lee and his officers were heavy-hearted. They had left their dead lying in the fields, the woods, on the rocks in Turner's Gap, and on National Road. But it was imperative they pull out when they did, or there would have been more dead men to grieve over.

Eight wounded men had died on the journey from South Mountain, and graves were hastily dug along the creek's edge. Before the dead were in the ground, two more men had died.

Hunter and the other Corps physicians labored without rest all day long, amputating shattered limbs, removing bullets and shrapnel, stitching up wounds, and doing what they could to relieve the pain and suffering.

Generals Lee, Longstreet, and Hill were in Lee's tent with the rain pattering softly on the canvas roof. They were discussing Lee's planned retreat into Virginia once Stonewall Jackson and his Corps arrived.

Lee was very discouraged, and he blamed himself for the defeat at South Mountain.

"General, sir," Dan Hill said, "it certainly wasn't your fault that your order got lost. Some soldier was just downright careless."

"That's for sure," Longstreet said. "I think we need to find out who he was and put him under discipline."

Lee raised a palm, shaking his head. "No, gentlemen. What's done is done, and if I had not insisted on putting the order in writing, none of this would have happened. The blame is on me. I should have had a meeting with all the division commanders and given it to them orally, making them memorize it."

"General Lee!" a voice called from outside. "Messenger here from General Jackson, sir!"

Longstreet opened the flap and let the man in.

"Yes, Sergeant?" Lee said.

"General Jackson wants you to know that all is secured at Martinsburg and Harper's Ferry. He is leaving General A. P. Hill's division to hold the prisoners, sir. There are 14,500 of them. General Jackson is leading the rest of his Corps toward Sharpsburg at this moment. They were to leave about ten o'clock this morning."

Lee gripped the man's upper arm and said, "That is good news, Sergeant." He took a step back. "You're soaked to the skin, son. I'll fix it so you can use a tent to dry out."

"Thank you, sir, but there isn't time. General Jackson wants me to meet up with him and advise him of any plans you have."

Lee rubbed his bearded chin, looked at both Longstreet and Hill, who knew he was planning to retreat back into Virginia, and replied, "Sergeant, you tell General Jackson we're going to make a stand right here and have it out with McClellan. Tell him to come as quickly as he can."

Thirty minutes later, Lee stood in his crowded tent, looking into the faces of Major General Longstreet and his five division leaders, and Major General Hill, who was actually part of Stonewall Jackson's I Corps.

"Gentlemen," Lee said, "I had in mind to lead this army back into Virginia as soon as General Jackson arrived. But I've changed my mind. McClellan is on his way here, and we're going to show him how Southerners can fight."

They all nodded their agreement. The generals were not of a mind to retreat.

"Now, gentlemen, I know we saw General McClellan move with speed when he came to South Mountain, but I doubt he will do that again. And I have no doubt that General Jackson will be here quickly. All right, gentlemen. Let's make ready for Little Napoleon."

Stonewall Jackson and his troops arrived at the Confederate camp on Antietam Creek on Tuesday morning, September 16, just before ten o'clock. Longstreet's troops cheered their arrival, and General Lee was there to welcome them.

Jackson had brought 27,500 men with him, leaving General A. P. Hill and four of his six brigades at Martinsburg and Harper's Ferry—a total of 1,500 men.

There was no sign yet of McClellan.

Lee told General Longstreet to meet with all division leaders of I Corps and fill them in on the plans. He then took Jackson to his tent.

Lee motioned to a chair. "Sit down, General."

"If it's all the same to you, sir, I'll stand. I've been in that saddle a long time."

"Oh, certainly. Sorry…I didn't think about that."

"It's all right, sir. Since we're going to fight McClellan here, what do I need to know?"

"I'll fill you in after I hear the details of your capture of Martinsburg and Harper's Ferry," Lee said.

Jackson filled his commander in on the story, making sure his men received the credit due them. Lee smiled as he listened, nodding his approval.

At last Jackson said, "General, there were six men of the Eighteenth North Carolina Regiment who voluntarily went above and beyond the call of duty. In the dead of night, while trooper Everett Nichols was on sentry duty, he discovered that some two dozen prisoners were missing. Somehow they had managed to escape from a small shed.

"Nichols awakened his regiment commander, Major Rance Dayton, who roused the other four, and Nichols got a man from the regiment to fill in for him on sentry duty. They caught the escapees at dawn and brought them back."

Lee's brow furrowed. "How did they ever track them down in the dark?"

"That, sir, I cannot answer. Major Dayton was a student of mine at V.M.I., so I know him well. He's exceptionally intelligent and resourceful."

"Well, that was fine work, to say the least. Dayton and those men are to be commended."

"I'd like for you to say that in person, if you don't mind, General. That kind of soldiering needs to be encouraged."

"I'll be glad to."

Five minutes later, Jackson led the six men into Lee's tent and introduced them to their supreme commander.

"Major Rance Dayton," Lee said, "you and troopers Billy Dean Baxter, Chuck Carney, Hank Upchurch, Everett Nichols, and Buford

Hall have my highest admiration for what you did. I want to commend you for a job well done. Those Yankees who escaped could have caused all kinds of problems had they been able to get to some part of the Union army. I want you to know that I'm very grateful for men like you. God bless you."

Major Dayton took a half-step forward, back straight, shoulders squared. "General Lee, let me say for these men and for myself that it is a privilege to fight under your command. We are honored, sir. And if called upon to go beyond the call of duty again, we will gladly do so."

When Rance Dayton and his men were gone, Lee gave Jackson the details of his battle plan for meeting McClellan's army.

"I'm aware that it went bad for you at South Mountain, General," Jackson said. "What were our losses?"

"As of this morning, the best we can tell, the number of our men killed or missing is about twenty-seven hundred. The wounded we brought with us were about five hundred. Dr. McGuire and his staff have worked extremely hard to save as many lives as possible, but we've had twenty-seven more die since leaving South Mountain. A burial detail is digging more graves downstream right now. Dr. McGuire sent his staff to bed at four this morning. They slept maybe three hours, then went back to work. I believe Dr. McGuire is sleeping right now."

"Good. He'll need to get some rest. There'll be a lot more work for him when we engage McClellan."

Lee was doing some mental calculations. "With our losses and General A. P. Hill's division absent from us, we'll have about forty-five thousand men to face McClellan. I have no way of knowing his losses at South Mountain, but I'm sure they were nothing like ours."

"We'll be ready for them, sir," Jackson said. "Anything else we need to discuss right now?"

"No…just one thing to say, though."

"Yes, sir?"

"I'm sure glad you're here."

"Thank you, sir. I am, too."

"Let's give those blue-bellies a fight they won't forget."

Robert E. Lee had shaken his discouragement and still had hopes of gaining a victory on Northern soil. As his division commanders took their positions, the forty-five-thousand-man force in tattered uniforms were spread over an area of four miles.

The ground Lee chose for battle promised strong defensive positions, though hardly impregnable ones. Its most prominent feature was the tree-lined Antietam, which flowed in a north-south course a short distance east of Sharpsburg before joining the Potomac three miles south of the town.

The Confederates were situated all the way from the bend of the Potomac, which enclosed the little farming community, along high ground behind the swift-running Antietam Creek. Both of Lee's flank troops rested on the banks of the muddy Potomac, and the undulating of the Sharpsburg ridge afforded his men good concealment from any Union artillery which might be placed to the front.

The four-mile-long position was well strengthened by farms, stone walls, split-rail fences, waist-high outcroppings of limestone, and little hollows and swales. Northeast of town there was an old sunken road so deeply worn down by wagon wheels that it offered a good spot for riflemen to lay low and snipe at enemy troops. There were also several clusters of woods, each covering about an acre of ground. Amid all of these natural concealments were open fields.

Although the Confederate line would be stretched thin, Lee took advantage of another geographical feature. Just west of the long ridge was a major north-south road—the turnpike connecting Hagerstown, Sharpsburg, and Harper's Ferry. It would provide a perfect route for shifting troops back and forth rapidly.

Lee had chosen a heavily wooded area midway between his

flanks to set up the hospital tents and place medical supply wagons. Open fields lay on three sides of the wooded area, and the creek on the other.

Antietam Creek was a defense barrier of sorts. It ranged in width between sixty and one hundred feet, and was fordable in only a few places. There were three bridges, however, that crossed the creek within the battle area, each about a mile apart. Lee saw to it that the lower bridge, a mile southeast of Sharpsburg, was directly beneath strong Confederate positions on the bluffs overlooking the creek.

The middle bridge, on the road to Boonsboro, was subject to Confederate artillery fire from the heights near Sharpsburg. The upper bridge, some two miles east of the Confederate artillery, was more difficult to cover. Lee would have to leave that bridge vulnerable to Union use.

As Lee had predicted, McClellan came after them slowly. Two Federal divisions McClellan had sent ahead arrived in the area just after dark on Monday night. They pitched camp some five miles east of Antietam Creek. Their orders were to wait for the rest of the army and not engage in hostilities unless forced to do so.

Midafternoon on Tuesday, General McClellan rode at the head of his troops as they approached the Sharpsburg area. He was in high spirits. He had failed to save Harper's Ferry, but at South Mountain he had won what he described to his men as "a glorious victory." And if the letter he had received that day by courier from the White House was any indication, he was back in the good graces of his president.

McClellan reached into his coat pocket to read the message for the third time since the courier had ridden away. It said: "God bless you and all with you. Destroy the Rebel army, if possible. A. Lincoln."

McClellan's scouts had given him a full report of how Lee was setting up his defenses. They had estimated the Confederate force to be around forty thousand.

McClellan felt jubilant. He had the Confederates more than doubled in troops and pushed up against the Potomac.

He took a small unit of cavalrymen close to where the Confederates were positioned along Antietam Creek and scanned the area with his binoculars, then rode back to the camp and called a meeting with his division commanders.

As he stood in the long shadows of the tall trees, he drew a map of the Confederate stronghold in the dirt. After explaining how Lee had positioned his troops, he used the tree limb as a pointer and said, "My plan, gentlemen, is to make the main attack on the enemy's left. My decision to do so is dictated largely by the Confederate defenses at the two bridges that span the creek. We'll come at them with the bulk of our army from this third bridge, which they're not protecting.

"Now, while we're putting this major effort on Johnny Reb's left, we'll launch a diversionary attack against his right with a separate Corps. I'll watch how both attacks go. If either shows good success, we'll strike the center with reserves."

McClellan spoke to his generals one by one and laid out their particular positions. The key division would be that of "Fighting Joe" Hooker. He would lead the attack on Lee's left.

General Hooker was to move his division west toward Sharpsburg to a point where a country lane called Smoketown Road joined the turnpike. To the west, just across the turnpike, was a landmark by which Hooker would guide his advance: a one-story whitewashed brick building that stood out sharply against the green backdrop of the woods. The building was often taken for a schoolhouse, but it was the house of worship for a congregation of German Baptist Brethren, referred to by the locals as the Dunker church.

The Dunker church marked the southern boundary of the field where the first attack would be launched against the Rebels. The field of battle was rectangular-shaped, about a mile long and half as wide, and flanked by woods on the east, west, and north.

Even as McClellan was giving the other division commanders

their battle orders, people of the community were leaving the area along the turnpike on foot and in wagons and carriages. Others were moving across the fields.

Sharpsburg and its quiet countryside had been settled mainly by people of German and Dutch descent. They had been untouched by the Civil War until Lee's invasion.

Many of Sharpsburg's thirteen hundred citizens refused to leave their homes, taking refuge in their cellars. A few hundred townspeople and farmers sought shelter in a large cave near the Potomac River. Before leaving for the cave, the farmers over whose ground the battle would rage did what they could to safeguard their livestock by closing them up in barns and sheds.

One farmer hid his team of horses in his cellar and muffled their hooves in gunny sacks.

Rain came with the darkness.

In a wooded area along the west bank of Antietam Creek, Dr. Hunter McGuire and his staff labored in four hospital tents to care for the men wounded at South Mountain. Six more had died since noon.

Hunter was on his knees, tending a soldier whose arm he had amputated three hours earlier. The young sergeant was barely conscious, but was moaning incoherently.

Hunter did all he could to bring the man's fever down. While he bathed the wounded man with cool water from the creek, he heard footsteps at the tent opening and turned to see his old friend Tom Jackson enter.

"Hello, Doc."

"Hello, General."

Jackson's eyes roamed the interior of the fifteen-by-twenty-five-foot tent, observing the men who lay on its grassy floor. Most were either unconscious or sleeping. Two of them looked up at him with languid eyes.

"Where you going to put all your patients by this time tomorrow, Doc?"

"It's going to be a big one, isn't it?"

"'Fraid so."

Hunter sighed. "I don't know what we'll do with the wounded tomorrow. The other two tents are as packed as this one. Guess we'll have to lay them on the ground outside the tent. I wish we had a hundred doctors and two hundred nurses."

Stonewall was quiet for a moment as Hunter continued to bathe the fevered sergeant. Then he said, "If you could choose just one nurse to be by your side, do I have to guess who it would be?"

Hunter looked over his shoulder and grinned. "If you had to guess, I'd say you either don't know me like I think you know me, or you've lost your mind."

SEVENTEEN

The rain continued to fall until about an hour after midnight. Few men in either camp slept well. Stretched nerves grew more taut with every noise. Jumpy pickets punctuated the night with bursts of gunfire, waking those few men who were fortunate enough to have dropped off to sleep.

Near the upper bridge, a soldier of the 103rd New York Regiment nearly set off a panic in the Federal line when he stumbled into a stack of muskets and knocked them down.

Even the animals seemed to feel the tension.

In both camps, whispers of a great battle to be fought grew louder, and men shuddered at the prospect of the wounds and death that awaited them.

Inside his tent, Stonewall Jackson could hear the sibilant whispers of the men in their bedrolls. He too was sleepless and rose from his cot to turn up the lantern wick. He reached for his Bible and silently read from Psalm 91:

> He that dwelleth in the secret place of the most High shall abide under the shadow of the Almighty. I will say of the LORD, He is my refuge and my fortress: my God; in him

will I trust. Surely he shall deliver thee from the snare of the fowler, and from the noisome pestilence. He shall cover thee with his feathers, and under his wings shalt thou trust: his truth shall be thy shield and buckler.

Thou shalt not be afraid for the terror by night; nor for the arrow that flieth by day; nor for the pestilence that walketh in darkness; nor for the destruction that wasteth at noonday. A thousand shall fall at thy side, and ten thousand at thy right hand; but it shall not come nigh thee.

"General Jackson, sir…" The voice came from outside.

Jackson laid his Bible on the small folding table and pushed aside the tent flap. He squinted into the darkness and saw a young soldier, perhaps no older than seventeen.

"Yes, soldier?"

"Sir, I…I need to talk to you. I hate to bother you but… would you have a moment?"

"Sure. Come in. What's your name, soldier?"

"Bradley Akins, sir. I'm from General McLaw's division, General Kershaw's brigade."

Jackson indicated the extra chair beside the table. "Sit down, Bradley. What can I do for you, son?"

"Well, sir, I know you're a man of faith. And…well, sir, to tell you the truth, I'm scared. Really scared. I saw plenty of blood and death at South Mountain on Sunday. It was my first battle. That was enough to really put the fear into me."

"Fear of being wounded?"

"Well, nobody likes to think of having his body ripped up, General. But it's more the fear of dying. I'm a Christian, sir…I think. But—"

"Wait a minute. You're a Christian you *think?*"

"Yes, sir, I—"

"If a man's really a Christian, Bradley, he knows it. Being saved isn't something God wants you to wonder about. Tell me why you think you might be a Christian."

"I was christened when I was a baby, sir. My parents said that means I'm a Christian."

Jackson leaned forward and looked into the young soldier's eyes. "Bradley, with all due respect to your parents, nobody goes to heaven because of any kind of religious ceremony. What makes you a Christian, according to God's Word, is faith in the Lord Jesus Christ as your personal Saviour.

"Like the rest of the human race, Bradley, you came into the world with a sinful nature that goes in the wrong direction—away from God. We have to turn from the direction we're going, acknowledge to Him that we are guilty, hell-deserving sinners, and receive Him into our hearts."

Young Akins nodded, the truth sinking in.

"Jesus went to the cross and died for us because there is no other way of salvation, son. You do believe He shed His blood on the cross and died for you, don't you?"

"Yes, sir."

Jackson flipped the pages of his Bible to Romans 10:9. "Here, read that to me," he said.

Young Akins cleared his throat. "That if thou shalt confess with thy mouth the Lord Jesus, and shalt believe in thine heart that God hath raised him from the dead, thou shalt be saved."

"Where does it say you must believe it, Bradley?"

"In my heart."

"That's right. You can believe the facts of Calvary in your mind, Bradley, but that won't save you. Believing in your heart is when you call on Him yourself. Look at verse 13 and read it to me."

Bradley cleared his throat again. "For whosoever shall call upon the name of the Lord shall be saved."

"Understand?"

"Yes, sir."

"Then, since you believe everything a man has to believe to be saved, what do you have to do to settle it?"

Without hesitation Bradley said, "Call on Jesus in repentance of my sin and receive Him into my heart as my Saviour. And I'm going to do that right now, sir."

After Bradley Akins had opened his heart to the Lord, Stonewall Jackson showed him a few verses of assurance, then said, "Bradley, none of us know whether we'll be alive after the battle tomorrow. But whether it's me or you or both of us who is taken out of this life, we'll meet in heaven one day. God bless you, son."

The Federals had seven hospital tents set up along the east side of the creek in a forest of oak and walnut trees. Dr. Bernard Vanderkieft was in charge, assisted by Doctors William Child and William Ely, as well as several other war surgeons who were busy preparing for the battle.

Vanderkieft, Child, and Ely were in the main hospital tent, discussing the use of anesthetics, when Brigadier General George Meade, commander of Third Division, I Corps, appeared at the wide opening. A young woman, her dark hair parted in the middle and swept back into a bun, was with him.

"Gentlemen," Meade said, "you don't know this lady by sight, but you do know her name."

"Don't tell me!" Dr. Child said. "Is this Miss Clara Barton?"

Clara smiled as Meade said, "Your guess is correct, Doctor."

"And how did you know?" the lady asked.

"You've been at other battles to nurse the wounded, and I just had a feeling you might show up here. Thank you for coming."

Meade introduced the doctors to Miss Barton, saying she had already seen General McClellan. Clara then said with a smile, "Gentlemen, you will also be glad to know that before sundown I did a little recruiting in Sharpsburg. I have eight women who will come here at sunrise to help. They are not trained nurses, but they will be a tremendous help when the wounded are brought in."

Dr. Vanderkieft was a tall, dignified man of sixty. "Miss Barton," he said, "I want to add to Dr. Child's thanks, and tell you how much your being here is appreciated. And so is your recruiting work. I know those ladies will be a wonderful boon to us."

"Thank you, Doctor. I will be sleeping in the home of one of the women who will help us tomorrow. I came tonight because I wanted to know how you have things set up."

"Well, let me show you," Vanderkieft said.

As the first hint of dawn lighted the cloudless Maryland sky on Wednesday, September 17, 1862, ground fog hugged the hollows and moved on the surface of Antietam Creek. Countless misty tendrils danced over the fields, driven by a slight breeze.

On both sides, men rose from their bedrolls and prepared for battle.

Even the birds seemed to know what was coming. Instead of the usual dawn chirping and chattering and flitting from tree to tree, there was silence.

Hunter McGuire and his staff of surgeons ate a breakfast of hardtack, beef jerky, and water, then saw to their patients.

Hunter made his patients as comfortable as possible, then stepped outside. The morning light came slowly, putting an ominous spectral glow on the mists that enshrouded the towering trees.

Hunter had expected the Federals to attack at first light, but all was still. He looked at his pocket watch—5:51. He walked out onto the dew-laden, grassy field until he could see the creek winding its way toward the Potomac and the open fields toward Sharpsburg and the turnpike.

There was a sudden roar, like a clap of thunder. Seconds

passed, and there was another roar, followed by two more, widely spaced. Hunter couldn't see anything yet. Then there was a long silence.

He looked back toward the hospital tents nestled with the medical supply wagons in the trees. All of his doctors and some of the wounded men were standing in a tight cluster, looking at him. He pointed eastward, where the cannon shots and shell explosions had come from, then shrugged his shoulders. White clouds of smoke now drifted skyward near the upper bridge almost two miles away.

The silence was suddenly broken with the crash of musketry and the roll of cannons. In fields much closer than the upper bridge, Hunter saw thousands of Federals fanning out as they came his direction like a blue river spreading across the land.

Abruptly, a gray wave came from the forest to Hunter's right. Muskets barked, cannons boomed, and the Union soldiers shouted. But the high-pitched, bloodcurdling Rebel yell transcended it all as the two opposing forces swept toward each other in a race of death and destruction.

Hunter looked on, fascinated and horrified by the sight. Through blue-white wispy smoke and yellow streaks of the rising sun, he saw the two armies collide.

The Battle of Antietam had begun.

Suddenly, both armies' artilleries blasted away, shaking the very ground where Hunter stood. He wheeled and ran toward the men who stood within the shelter of the trees. A cannon shell burst in the air near the hospital tents. The concussion of it popped McGuire's ears as another shell exploded near the first one, blasting a tree into smithereens and raining fragments of bark and shredded wet leaves.

"I thought we were safe here, Dr. McGuire!" Dr. Wesley Jensen shouted.

"Only safer, Doctor," Hunter said. He looked back to the spot where he had been standing. "That field right there will be full of soldiers and guns before long."

As the battle spread wider along the four-mile stretch of creek bank, the Confederate artillery, firing from elevated positions, blasted Union soldiers with one shell after another. Bodies were blown twenty and thirty feet from where they had stood.

General Stuart had assembled eight cannons from his own horse artillery and a dozen of Stonewall Jackson's guns on high ground across the turnpike from the Dunker church.

General Hooker's nine batteries opened up on them from a ridge on a nearby farm.

In Sharpsburg, the citizens crouched in their cellars, listening to the growing sounds of the battle—sudden roars, mysterious hums, then shrieking shells followed by explosions. Their cellars shook, raining dirt on them as they huddled and prayed.

At the upper bridge, which was out of Confederate artillery range, McClellan had four brigades swarming over it to gain better positions against the enemy.

Lee, however, had his eye on the area from his lofty position behind Antietam Creek. His troops were ready. As soon as the blue uniforms began running across the bridge, they were met with a long line of gray-clad infantry, charging at them and shouting the Rebel yell.

Men in blue toppled off the bridge into the creek, while the hail of fire ripping into the Confederate lines was devastating. But the Rebels' conduct was worthy of their leader's trust—they continued to run over the rough and stony field with their comrades dropping all around them.

The outnumbered Rebels fought with a tenacity seldom seen on a battlefield. Within minutes, the Federals were off the bridge and the Rebels waved their muskets in the air and jeered. They had won the first round.

There were three heavily wooded areas north of Sharpsburg that both armies wanted to possess. The East and West Woods were directly parallel with a half mile of open fields and the Hagerstown Turnpike between them. The North Woods made a natural border for the open fields about a quarter-mile from the end of the other two woods, and was bisected by the turnpike. The battle was barely more than an hour old when heavy fighting broke out in all three wooded areas.

The Dunker church sat next to the turnpike with the West Woods just behind it. Along the eastern edge of the turnpike, between the woods, was a twenty-acre cornfield owned by farmer David Miller. Southeast of the Dunker church, about two miles, was the Sunken Road, which lay between two fields of battle.

The Dunker church became the eye of the storm. McClellan, with his huge army spreading north, west, and south, concentrated his heaviest forces on Lee's troops set to defend the area around the church.

Joseph Hooker's I Corps infantry came in a long row, firing on the run. Stonewall Jackson's troops formed a line with John Bell Hood's brigade positioned in the center, Jubal Early's brigade on the left, and Daniel Hill's entire division on the right.

James Longstreet's II Corps was spread south and west of Sharpsburg to meet Federals coming by the thousands against them.

The hot pulse of battle sent quivering waves over the countryside, each cannon shot and shell explosion sending ear-splitting concussions over the land. Musket fire added to the din, and amidst it all were the repeated Rebel yells and Yankee shouts…and now the wailing, crying, and moaning of the wounded.

Clouds of powder smoke thickened and at times blotted out the sun. As men were cut down by the hundreds, fresh troops took their places.

***

Stretcher-bearers on both sides were already leg-weary from carrying wounded men to the hospital tents. East of Antietam, Clara Barton labored to keep some kind of order as men were brought in by the hundreds. Her eight female companions proved to be of great value to the Union doctors and to Miss Barton herself.

At the Confederate medical facility, Dr. Hunter McGuire and his staff of doctors labored to keep up with the numbers of wounded being brought in. The men wounded at South Mountain were moved outside to make room. Soon the tents were full, and even the newly wounded had to lie on the ground outside and wait until the doctors could get to them.

Hunter was digging shrapnel out of a young lieutenant when a Union shell struck the creek bank directly behind the tents. It splintered tree limbs, raining branches and dirt clods on the roof.

Hunter glanced up and saw that one tree limb was pressing deeply into the canvas. There was no one to remove it but Dr. Jensen.

When Jensen returned, McGuire shook his head despairingly. "I sure wish we had some help."

"I guess we could ask General Jackson to take some men off the fields to give us a hand," Jensen said.

Hunter shook his head. "They need every able-bodied man out there in the battle."

A hundred and fifty yards from the Confederate tents, a South Carolina battery was moving to a new position when a Union shell hit a caisson loaded with gunpowder.

The caisson blew apart as the doctors turned to look, and they could see nothing but torn and lifeless bodies where once the battery stood. "None of those men will need our attention," Hunter said in a tight voice.

He finished working on the young lieutenant and Jensen carried him outside.

The next patient was a private whose left arm was seriously damaged at the shoulder. Hunter went to the man's head, leaving his feet for Jensen. Very carefully, Hunter gripped the man's shirt by the right sleeve and collar and hoisted him onto the table.

"This one probably won't need much chloroform," Hunter said. "He's pretty well out of it."

"I hope he stays that way," Jensen said. "You want me to handle him…take off the arm?"

"Let me get a closer look before we decide to amputate," Hunter said, as he picked up a pair of scissors.

As he cut away the blood-soaked shirt, Hunter said, "I'm a little slower to amputate than most army doctors. When it's plain to see there's no use to try resection, I'll proceed in a hurry. But if I feel there's any chance I can save a limb, I'll do the resection."

Hunter sleeved sweat from his face and carefully examined the shoulder.

"I think I can save it," he said. "A resection it is."

When he was finished with the surgery, a young private with a damaged leg was laid on the table. Jensen was putting him under with chloroform while Hunter examined the leg.

"What do you think?" Jensen asked.

"I've saved a few legs with resection, but many more arms. Can't save this one."

While Hunter waited for the chloroform to take full effect on the soldier, he stepped to the tent opening and ran his gaze over the mounting number of wounded men on the ground. He wished he had a force of surgeons ten times larger than the one he had. And nurses, too.

He lifted his eyes to the battlefield and saw riderless horses, and some lying dead on the ground. Exploding shells scattered men in every direction. Long lines of infantry—gray and blue—swayed to and fro, with puffs of blue-white smoke rising from their muskets.

The roar of it all was more than noise. It was a savage, continual thunder that resounded over the fields and hills—a death knell for thousands of gallant men.

EIGHTEEN

More troops entered the fray a few dozen yards west of the Confederate hospital tents. A double tide of blue and gray swept onto the blood-soaked field, guns blazing, bayonets fixed. There was no flinching or dropping to the rear. Both sides fought heroically under murderous fire.

Hunter had just finished amputating the soldier's leg and needed a breath of air. He asked two stretcher-bearers who had recently come in to carry the man outside. Now he followed them and watched as they eased the soldier down among the other wounded men.

"Dr. McGuire," one of the stretcher-bearers said, "I think those two men over there are dead."

Hunter followed the private's glance and moved among the men to kneel down. "You're right, Private. What's your name?"

"Rick Acheson, Doctor. My partner here is Randy Williams."

Hunter nodded. "Would you men mind while you're here re-moving those two bodies?"

"Be glad to, Doctor," Acheson asked. "We'll put 'em back here among the trees where we've already laid a good number."

Hunter glanced at Wes Jensen, who stood in the opening of the tent, mopping his brow. "Want me to do the next two or three, Doctor?" Jensen asked.

"What do we have in there?"

"Well, we had another probable amputation, but he just died. Next one is the one brought in about an hour ago with a chunk of shrapnel in his chest."

"Okay. We'll have Rick and Randy carry the dead man out. Let's get the next one on the table and—"

Hunter stopped speaking as he saw a man—a Union officer—not more than fifty yards out on the battlefield, stumbling blindly in wide circles. Even at that distance he could see blood streaming down the man's face blackened by gunpowder. The man was groping with extended hands as bullets buzzed around him.

"Be right back!" Hunter called over his shoulder.

Bullets zipped and thudded on all sides of Hunter as he ran in a zig-zag pattern toward the man. He felt a bullet pluck at his shirt-sleeve and another buzz by his head like an angry hornet. He could now see the insignias on the Union man's collar and shoulders that indicated he was a major.

Hunter brought the man down with a flying tackle. The major swung blindly, trying to lay hold on whoever had attacked him.

"Listen to me, Major!" Hunter shouted. "I'm a Confederate doctor. You've wandered close to our hospital tents. If we don't get out of here fast, we'll both die! Do you understand what I'm saying?"

"My eyes! I can't see!"

"I know, sir. I'll do my best to get you to safety if you'll let me."

"Yes! Please!"

"All right. Now, I want you to relax. Don't stiffen on me. I'm going to drape you over my shoulder and run for cover as fast as I can."

"Why would a Rebel doctor do this for a Union soldier?"

"I'll answer that later. Here we go!"

Hunter lifted the tall, lanky major onto his shoulder while he was still on his knees. "Lord," he said, as he rose to his feet, "only You can make those bullets miss the two of us."

Hunter had just started to run when a shell struck behind him. The concussion knocked him down, and the major rolled eight or ten feet. Hunter saw two Union officers coming toward him on the run. They opened fire with their revolvers, cursing him.

"I'm a doctor!" Hunter shouted.

The men kept firing and didn't even break stride. Hunter made a dive for the major's belt and whipped the revolver from his holster. He hadn't fired a handgun for years, but it felt as if it had been only yesterday. He dropped the hammer and the nearest soldier went down. The other soldier fired again, his bullet plowing sod within a foot of Hunter. The doctor fired a second time, and the charging Union officer hit the ground and lay still.

Hunter was breathing hard as he picked up the major and made a dash for the trees and the tents. The angry zip and hiss of bullets did not let up.

Hunter recognized two of his other Corps doctors standing with Jensen and the two stretcher-bearers. There was someone else standing next to Jensen—a dark-haired young woman in a light-blue cotton dress with white pinafore.

Jodie!

Hunter's breath came in short gasps as he drew near the Confederate tents. Jodie met him as he staggered in with the Union major on his shoulder.

"Hello, Jodie," he gasped. "Busy day."

"Oh, Hunter! You took an awful chance!"

"Had to keep this man from getting himself killed. But speaking of taking chances, what are you doing here?"

"I came to help."

Hunter turned to the other doctors. "See what you can do for this man, while I catch my breath."

"He's unconscious, Doctor," Jensen said, lifting the man from Hunter's shoulder.

Randy Williams stepped in. "Let me help you, Dr. Jensen."

Jodie walked to a water barrel that hung on the side of a nearby medical supply wagon, filled a tin cup, and handed it to Hunter. When Hunter put the cup to his lips, Jodie noticed the rip in his shirtsleeve.

"Hunter, was this sleeve torn before you went out there?"

"I don't know. I don't think so."

"Then it must've been a bullet. Hunter, you nearly got shot!"

Private Rick Acheson looked at Hunter and said, "Why didn't you leave him, Doctor? A bullet would've ended it for him sooner or later. Then there'd be one less blue-belly officer."

Jodie looked at Acheson with piercing eyes as Hunter regarded him steadily and said, "When I became a medical doctor, I took an oath to do all in my power to relieve human suffering and preserve life. I saw a human being out there, blinded and dazed, with death hissing all around him. I did what I said I would do when I took that oath."

"But he's our enemy," Acheson said. "He's killed our men, and he'll do it again if he gets the chance."

"A wounded and helpless enemy is not our foe, Private. And this man will never fight in another battle. His eyes are gone."

Hunter handed the cup back to Jodie and turned to see about the Union major. Doctors Jensen and Paymer were bent over him.

"What do you think?" Hunter asked.

"The eyeballs are burned out," Paymer said, "but he should live. The bleeding has almost stopped. It's strange how the powder could strike him square in the face but no shrapnel hit him."

"Stranger things have happened," Hunter said. "I know you and Dr. Bowman have plenty to do in your tents. You'd better get on back. I'll have Jodie clean him up, then see what I can do for him."

"Sure," Paymer said, rising to his feet. "We saw you out there with bullets buzzing all around you and had to see if you made it back."

"Well, thank the Lord I did. And I appreciate your concern."

"Don't want to lose our boss man," Bowman said.

"Tell you what, fellows. I can let Dr. Jensen come and help you and the other surgeons, since I have Jodie now. Oh, I didn't introduce you."

"It's all right," Jensen said. "We introduced ourselves. She told us the two of you are engaged."

Hunter glanced at Jodie and smiled. "That we are."

As the three physicians headed toward the other tents, Jensen called over his shoulder, "Holler if you need me."

"Will do."

Hunter turned to look at Jodie. "Well, sweetheart, the next patient has shrapnel in his shoulder. Let's get it out."

Private Williams tapped his partner on the shoulder. "C'mon, Rick. There are more wounded men out there."

"Just a minute," Acheson said, lifting a hand. "Doctor…"

"Yes, Private?"

"Sir, I…I was out of line. I shouldn't have talked to you the way I did. I just saw that man as the enemy and…well, my nerves are a little uptight and—"

"It's all right, soldier. I understand. This war has us all uptight."

"Thank you, sir."

Hunter cuffed him playfully. "Go bring in some more of our wounded men, Private."

"Yes, sir."

When the stretcher-bearers were gone, Hunter lifted the next patient onto the table. The soldier was conscious but made no cry, in spite of his pain. "We'll get you fixed up, soldier," Hunter said. Then to Jodie, "The chloroform is on that small table. If you'll put him under, I'll go to work."

It took only two minutes for the chloroform to take effect. Above the sounds of battle, a cry for water was heard from outside.

"Can you take care of him, Jodie? Our man here is pretty well under."

"Of course."

"Tell you what, Jodie. They all need water. Take care of several, come back in and pour some more chloroform on the cloth, then take water to a few more. Okay?"

At the shriek of a cannon shell, Hunter dropped his scalpel and grabbed Jodie, pushing her to the grassy floor of the tent. The explosion rocked the ground and shook the tent, sending bits of hot shrapnel hissing through the canvas wall on the north side.

Hunter helped Jodie up, then turned to the other men who lay waiting for his attention. "Any of you fellows get hit?" Hunter asked.

The men shook their heads. Hunter quickly checked those who were unconscious and found they had not been hit either. He turned back to the operating table and discovered that the man was dead. Hunter sighed and lifted the dead soldier, cradling him in his arms. He stepped outside and saw Dr. Jensen running toward him, an expression of horror on his face.

"Doctor, that last shell nearly tore our tent apart! Dr. Paymer took a load of shrapnel in the chest. It's awfully close to his heart. We all agree we need your capable hands."

Jodie had come to stand by Hunter and heard what Jensen said. Hunter glanced down at her. "I'll need your help…"

"You've got it," she said.

Hunter looked back at Jensen. "Okay, Doctor. Jodie will show you who's next in our tent. The one after that is a Sergeant Hector Tannen. Part of his jaw is gone."

"What about the Union major?"

"He's been in and out of consciousness, Doctor," Jodie said. "He isn't bleeding any more, so you can leave him until the men in worse shape are tended to."

Jensen nodded. "You two know where to find me."

"Wish you had somebody to assist you," Hunter said. "I'd let Jodie stay with you but—"

"You just do everything you can for Doc Paymer."

The clouds of powder smoke above the valley allowed sunshine through only when a gust of wind parted it. Dead men sprawled over the ground from the Potomac to the Antietam, and to the east for a mile. Some were crumpled in hollows, and a few lay draped over a waist-high stone wall or split-rail fence.

The acrid odor of burnt gunpowder, hot metal, and spilled blood filled the air. The smell of burnt and splintered trees and blasted earth only intensified the stench of death.

There was wreckage everywhere. Fences torn apart, farm buildings destroyed, heaps of human limbs outside hospital tents, cornfields trampled, army horses and domestic farm animals lying lifeless among thousands of dead and dying soldiers, and naked tree stumps where unmerciful artillery had wreaked havoc.

It was only noon.

Across a half-mile of battlefield around the Dunker church, everything seemed to be happening at once. The fighting had died down and almost come to a halt as both sides reloaded their weapons. The silence lasted for nearly five minutes, punctuated with the cries and moans of the wounded.

Then, simultaneously, the hostile battle lines opened up a tremendous fire upon each other. Just north of the church a long line of men in gray charged toward Union infantrymen situated behind a split-rail fence. McClellan had sent reinforcements to that spot, and Federal fire ripped through the oncoming ranks of Confederates.

Rebels went down in heaps, but those who survived the first volley pushed on, loading and firing and shouting as they advanced. These were Stonewall Jackson's men, and there was something in them of hysterical excitement—an eagerness to take the battle to the enemy with a reckless disregard for everything but victory.

Those who reached the fence vaulted it with bayonets flashing.

In an open field just west of the church, which stood thirty feet away, Union troops charged Confederates. Empty muskets brought bayonets into play. Soon there were more Rebels lying on the ground than standing on their feet. Their lieutenant called for retreat, and they began to pull back.

The Federals refused to let up. They came on with a vengeance, taking time to reload and shoot most of the fleeing Rebels before they could reach the relative safety of the trees near the church.

Across the Hagerstown Turnpike, at the north end of a ten-acre pasture, the Confederates had rushed a unit of Union artillery and captured a cannon. The Union captain in charge shouted for his five other cannons to swing about and fire their big guns loaded with canister at the nearly two dozen Rebels.

The Confederates, rejoicing in the capture of the Federal cannon, suddenly realized what they had gotten themselves into. They tried to find shelter when they saw the five black muzzles aimed their direction and the gunners yanking the lanyards.

When the smoke blew away, the bodies of the Rebels had been shredded beyond recognition.

Just south of the Dunker church, General Jackson had watched the battle turn into a nightmare. Two of his divisions had come across the turnpike from the fields to the east, only to meet a swarm of Federals.

His solid lines began to come apart as they crossed the turnpike under heavy artillery and musket fire, breaking into scattered clots with a few flags still upright. As the hail of bullets and grapeshot assailed them, the flags began to disappear.

Jackson sent for Brigadier General John Bell Hood's division, which was resting in a wooded draw three hundred yards to the west. They had been outnumbered better than two-to-one, and what had been a division of thirty-five hundred was now down to twenty-three hundred.

Still astride his horse, Jackson waited for Hood's troops to emerge from the draw. Soon he saw a rider galloping toward him from the northwest where Jeb Stuart's cavalry was fighting.

The rider pulled up, sweat streaming down his face, and gasped, "General Jackson, sir! General Stuart asks that you send at least a brigade to the fields west of the West Woods! We're being whittled down!"

"Tell him I'll send reinforcements as soon as possible, Sergeant. That's going to be awhile. Our forces are being whittled down everywhere. He'll have to hold on till I can send help. But I've got to find them, first."

As the sergeant galloped away on his foam-flecked horse, Stonewall Jackson felt a coldness settle in his bones.

NINETEEN

General Lee had stayed near the battle front earlier in the day, but as afternoon came on, he moved to an abandoned barn in a wooded patch a quarter-mile west of Sharpsburg.

By two o'clock, the battle was breaking into four sections—the West Woods, the Miller cornfield across the turnpike, the Sunken Road northeast of town, and the lower bridge a mile south of the Sunken Road.

Lee called his two Corps leaders to the old barn. He assigned Jackson to the West Woods and Miller cornfield areas, and Longstreet was to concentrate his forces at the Sunken Road and the lower bridge, known as Rohrback's Bridge.

General McClellan had set up headquarters at a farmhouse on a hill more than a mile east of the fighting. He kept Major General Fitz-John Porter with him.

The generals had telescopes strapped atop stakes in the ground. While McClellan sent orders to his division leaders, Porter studied the field with unrelenting attention and had something new to tell McClellan every time the chief commander turned back to him.

At the Confederate medical facility, Hunter McGuire finished his delicate task of extracting chunks of shrapnel out of Paymer's chest. Paymer was breathing steadily when the last stitch was taken. "You did a beautiful job, Doctor," Jodie said. "I'm proud of you."

"I'm just thankful you were here to help me." He picked up a towel, wiping blood from his hands, and moved toward her. "I sure could use one good solid kiss."

"I think that could be arranged."

"Oh, excuse me!" the couple heard Dr. Jensen say.

Hunter released Jodie and turned.

"I just wanted to see how you were doing with Doc Paymer," Jensen continued.

"Just finished. Look for yourself."

Jensen moved close to the operating table and looked at the unconscious man's features. "He's going to be okay?"

"Far as I can tell. The shrapnel was dangerously close to his heart but didn't touch it. How are things going at tent number one?"

"Good and bad. Did well with the man with the severed ear. The sergeant with the ripped-off jaw will live, but he's going to be disfigured for the rest of his life. Had two others die on the table, I'm sorry to say. Have one I'd like you to look at. Maybe you'll want to do the surgery."

"All right. How about the Union major?"

"Haven't gotten to him yet. I gave him some laudanum about half an hour ago. He's in quite a bit of pain."

Hunter turned to Jodie. "Honey, why don't you take a little rest?"

"No time for that, dear Doctor," she said. "Let's go see about those men."

Stonewall Jackson was positioned on a brush-covered knoll in the West Woods with one of his aides, Private Henry Kyd Douglas, at his side.

His troops were situated in the woods with artillery along the edge of the trees and infantry spaced intermittently between the cannons.

McClellan's infantry came across the open fields in seemingly interminable columns of blue flanked by artillery batteries. Jackson's artillery cut loose and the infantry followed suit. Cannon and musket belched their volleys with telling accuracy. Casualties in the Union ranks were appalling, but on they came with a flash of bayonets and flutter of flags, halting the lines only long enough to readjust themselves.

Stonewall Jackson stood fearlessly on the very edge of the terrible battle, observing it through his binoculars. The enemy was showing himself to be indomitable. No matter how many the Confederate guns cut down, there were always more to take their places. Not so with the men in gray. They started short in number and were becoming fewer.

There was one bit of encouragement. When Jackson had left Major General A. P. Hill's division in charge of the Union prisoners at Harper's Ferry and Martinsburg, he had told Hill to secure the prisoners so he could leave two brigades with them and bring the other two to Sharpsburg.

Hill and his two brigades had arrived at the Antietam battle at midmorning. Jackson had placed them with the Branch and Gregg brigades, letting Hill resume charge over them. They were now part of the fighting forces in the Miller cornfield.

Jackson swung his binoculars from the battle at the West Woods to see what was happening there.

General Hooker's compact columns of infantry had swept into the cornfield with the crushing weight of a landslide. The outmanned Rebels were pushed back at first, but fought back tenaciously.

Even as Jackson observed the battle from his lofty position, great patches of corn were blasted by artillery, and most of the field looked as if it had been struck by a storm of bloody hail.

At the north end of the cornfield, in the heat of the action, was the 18th North Carolina Infantry Regiment, commanded by Major Rance Dayton. Dayton had his regiment hunkered down in the corn, where some of it still stood seven feet tall. They had met a fierce onslaught from the enemy infantry and repulsed it with musketry fire so rapid and well-aimed that the Federals had backed off to regroup.

Now the Federals were coming again.

Dayton looked around at his weary, hollow-eyed men. They had fought for over nine hours. Since their meager breakfast, they'd had nothing to eat but the corn they were munching on now, while their dead and wounded comrades lay around them.

A sergeant appeared from the rear and knelt beside Dayton. "Major, we're runnin' mighty low on ammunition."

The blazing sun beat down mercilessly, and Dayton licked his parched lips. "Get to General Branch and tell him we need more."

"That's where I just came from, sir. He said there isn't much more left in the caissons."

"Then we'll have to throw rocks till they close in, then we'll go to bayonets, fists, and teeth," Dayton said. "Has General Branch sent word to General Jackson that we're low?"

"I don't know, sir."

"Go find out."

When the sergeant had disappeared, Dayton ran his gaze over the dirty faces of his men. "We're low on ammunition, boys. Gather the cartridge boxes off the dead and wounded. We're going to need all we can get!"

In a few minutes, the heavy lines of Union troops were closing in again. "All right, men, listen to me!" Dayton called. "Hold your fire until I give the word! I want them so close you can tell the color of their eyes!"

When the first line of Federals drew close enough, Dayton took a deep breath and shouted, *"Fire!"*

Muskets roared and flamed in the Federals' faces like a blaze of lightning. The entire front line, with few exceptions, went down. Those who were not hit wheeled and ran back toward the next wave, which halted under their commander's orders.

While the Federals regrouped, Dayton shouted, "Take the guns and ammunition off those dead Yankees, boys!"

As Dayton's men scurried to gather the guns and ammunition, he saw a fresh horde of Yankees. McClellan had sent reinforcements.

"Get ready, men! This'll be a big one! Don't fire till I say so!"

While the major waited, his mind flashed back to his latest talk with Stonewall Jackson about life, death, heaven, and hell. Jackson's words echoed in his mind: *Are you ready to die?*

No, he was not ready to die and face God. He had never come to Jesus in repentance of sin and asked Him for salvation. He watched the Federals close in, shouting curses.

"Fire!"

The whole world seemed to explode as guns on both sides belched flame. The air filled with dust and smoke and the cries of wounded men. Dayton saw the Yankee leader go down—a young major.

The wall of fire thrown up by the Confederates and the heaps of blue-uniformed bodies on the ground had the Yankees in disarray. They pulled back, looking for their leader. When they couldn't find him, they pivoted and headed back across the field.

"After 'em, men!" Dayton shouted, and led the charge.

They were about two hundred yards out from the cornfield, firing at the retreating Federals, when Dayton saw Yankee reinforcements forming at the far end of the field.

"Back!" Dayton shouted. "Back to the cornfield! Re-form the lines!"

As the 18th North Carolina wheeled at their leader's command, the retreating Yankees stopped to allow reinforcements to pass them. When the space between blue and gray widened, Union artillery opened up fire.

Cannon shells shrieked their high-pitched song of death,

exploding in yellow flame. The roar was deafening as shell after shell rained down. The double shriek of a pair of Union shells sounded close behind.

"Get down!" Dayton shouted.

The men dropped, hugging the ground as tightly as possible. As soon as shrapnel stopped hissing through the air, Dayton looked up and saw that his men in the front had taken a direct hit.

"Get up and run!" he shouted, scrambling to his feet. "The cornfield will be out of their range!"

It was every man for himself. Dayton bolted with them, but when he drew near the men who had been hit, he saw movement. It was Sergeant Buster Camden.

Dayton halted and knelt by the wounded man. "I'll carry you, Buster."

Camden's face was a mass of blood. "No, Major. Go on. I'm done for anyway."

"No way I'm leaving you here." Dayton heard the whine of another shell and felt something tug at his pantleg. "Okay," he said, running his hands under Camden's body, "here we go."

When he stood, his leg gave way. He cushioned Buster from falling and looked down to see torn flesh and a piece of jagged black metal embedded in his thigh. His pantleg was soaked in blood.

"Major, go on! They're coming!"

Dayton looked over his shoulder. The Union infantry was coming like a deluge. He gritted his teeth against the pain and struggled to lift Camden.

"Can't leave you, Buster."

The men of the Eighteenth staggered to a halt at the edge of the cornfield and looked back for the first time.

Billy Dean Baxter was the first to speak. "It's the major and—I can't tell who the other man is! The major's been hit, too!"

"I'm going after them!" Everett Nichols shouted, and broke into a run. "Cover me!"

Four more men ran after him—Billy Dean Baxter, Buford Hall, Hank Upchurch, and Chuck Carney.

"Cover us!" they yelled.

Captain Jack Fleming, who was next in command, gave the order. "Load up, men! We'll have to run out there a ways to be effective! Shoot around the men and over their heads! They'll stay low!"

Rance Dayton saw his five friends running toward him, and he glanced back at the oncoming horde of blue uniforms.

"Back! Go back!" he shouted. "There's no chance!"

The fearless five came on. Billy Dean and Everett lifted Dayton. The other three hoisted Camden and took off running as fast as they could. The Federals were now within range, and bullets began to zip and whistle around the rescuers.

Billy Dean grunted and went down, and Everett stumbled. The other three men paused.

"Go on!" Dayton shouted, gritting his teeth in pain.

"Billy Dean's dead, Major," Everett said.

"So's Buster," Hank said.

"You guys carry the major," Chuck Carney said. "I'll be a shield."

The other three men quickly had the major off the ground and were running toward their comrades. Suddenly the meaning of Carney's words sunk into Dayton's brain. Carney had positioned himself to take any bullets!

"Look over there!" Carney shouted with a whoop. Rebels were charging the Federals, taking them by surprise. The Federals left off their pursuit of Dayton and his gallant men, and braced themselves for the fresh onslaught.

It was Stonewall Jackson's doing. When he had seen what was happening in the cornfield, he'd sent two regiments of General Early's brigade to intervene for the Eighteenth North Carolina.

Jodie watched Hunter lift his latest patient off the operating table and carry him outside. She glanced through the tent opening and could see bodies strewn so thickly on the field that there was hardly a place for the stretcher-bearers to walk. The moans and cries of wounded men could be heard above the nearby sounds of battle.

As Hunter re-entered the tent and laid the blinded Union man on the table, Jodie moved up next to him. Hunter glanced at her, and a warmth reached out from her dark-brown eyes and touched him. He silently mouthed, *I love you.*

Jodie set a pan of fresh water on the table next to the operating table, picked up a clean cloth, and began to gently wash the major's face. The major was conscious, though laudanum had eased his pain. A slight smile curved his lips. "I thought I heard a woman's voice from out there. Those are female hands, aren't they?"

"You're very perceptive, Major," Hunter said. "What you don't know is that those hands and that voice belong to the most beautiful woman in the world. Her name is Jodie Lockwood. She's a Certified Medical Nurse and Surgeon's Assistant. But even more important, she's my fiancée."

The major was about to say that Jodie had to be the second most beautiful woman in the world, when it struck him that he would never again look upon the face of his wife. He kept his reply to himself, and said instead, "I think your last name is McGuire, Doctor. Correct?"

"Yes. *Hunter* McGuire. And we don't know your name, Major."

"Jim Halstead, II Corps, Third Division, under Brigadier General William French."

"Yes, sir."

"How can I ever thank you for what you did? You risked your life to save mine. I remember asking you why you would do such a thing. You said you'd tell me later."

"I did it, Major Halstead, on impulse. I saw another human

being about to get killed, and I ran out there to try to save his life."

"But did you stop to think the effort might cost you your own life?"

"It crossed my mind, but I couldn't let it stop me. Besides, I've taken an oath as a medical doctor to save lives. But there was a stronger force than my oath. I'm a Christian, Major. My faith is in the Lord Jesus Christ for the forgiveness of my sins and the salvation of my soul. When I saw you stumbling about out there, I didn't see an enemy in a blue uniform. I saw another human being on the edge of death. I had to save your life if I could."

A wan smile spread over the blind man's lips. "Well, bless the Lord! I'm a born-again, blood-washed man myself. It's wonderful to know I'm in the hands of a Christian doctor."

"Major, we can fellowship and talk a little later, but right now I've got to work on those eye sockets. There are burnt powder crystals in there that can cause infection. Jodie's going to put you under with chloroform. It'll take awhile, and I don't want you in any more pain than necessary."

"Thank you—both of you," Halstead said.

The sounds of battle were still thundering across the valley when Hunter and Jodie finished their work on Major Halstead.

Shuffling footsteps outside caught their attention, and they turned to see two exhausted, panting men carrying Major Rance Dayton. Hunter focused on Dayton's pale features, then recognized the two men as Everett Nichols and Chuck Carney. Hunter noted the makeshift tourniquet on Dayton's leg. "Looks like you took a bullet, my friend," he said.

"Shrapnel," Dayton replied.

"He asked us to bring him to you, Dr. McGuire," Carney said.

"All right. I've got some other men in worse shape, Major, but I'll get to you as quick as I can."

"That's fine, Doctor. I'll wait."

"This is Nurse Jodie Lockwood, Major. She'll check the tourniquet and give you some laudanum."

It wasn't until sunset that Hunter was free to work on Rance Dayton's leg. Rance told Hunter how his five friends had saved his life, risking their own to do so, and how Billy Dean Baxter had been killed while doing his part.

Jodie smiled at Hunter, who had shown the same kind of bravery that day. But she knew there would be no medals for saving the life of an enemy officer.

The battle raged on at the West Woods, the Miller cornfield, and Sunken Road.

Major General Ambrose E. Burnside's four divisions made a heroic stand at Rohrback's Bridge. Though they lost hundreds of men, they held onto the bridge. By dusk, the weary men on both sides were giving up the fight in sheer exhaustion, and the surviving men of IX Corps were calling it "Burnside's Bridge."

Generals Lee, Jackson, and Longstreet were glad for the Union army's weariness, for their own ammunition was almost gone.

TWENTY

As the sun buried itself below the western horizon, George McClellan withdrew his army across Antietam Creek to the east, and Robert E. Lee's army collected on the west side.

Battle-jaded men on both sides looked out over the smoldering fields where tiny flames still licked the bark of trees and the evening breeze carried wisps of smoke across the valley. After twelve horrible hours, the battle was over.

Bodies were everywhere…buckled, crumpled, sprawled, and in many places, heaped. The movement of the wounded in their torment gave the field a crawling effect.

Truce flags were raised to allow the long, tedious job of picking up the wounded. Night, when it came in its fullness, carried a mournful chorus of misery and suffering from the pitch-black hollows, woods, and fields. It would be days before doctors on both sides would be able to care for all the wounded. Many would die while waiting. Hundreds more would die from their wounds in the days and weeks to come.

Generals Jackson and Longstreet were busy with their division leaders, doing what they could to encourage and comfort them.

General Lee sat alone in his tent, his head bent low. Depression, like the hot wind that had blown through the valley that afternoon, descended on his mind. He had led his men into a horrendous battle they could not have won.

The odds were against them at the start, but he had felt there was a slim chance to chalk up a victory on Northern soil, and his men had willingly followed him.

Now, thousands of faithful soldiers were dead. Other thousands would be crippled and maimed for the rest of their lives.

Tears flowed down the general's cheeks as he prayed for God to take the moans of the men from inside his head.

Hunter and Jodie worked as fast as possible to care for as many wounded men as they could.

It was nearly midnight when Jodie asked, "Did you bring enough medical supplies? I mean, from what the stretcher-bearers are saying, we've got several thousand wounded men still lying out there."

"I don't think we've got nearly enough supplies. When this battle is over, I'll cross the creek and talk to the Union medical director over there. Maybe he'll give us what we need."

Jodie's eyes widened. "You mean they might start fighting again in the morning?"

Hunter was about to nod when a familiar voice came from the tent opening, "It's not likely, Miss Jodie."

Hunter looked over his shoulder. "Hello, Tom. I inquired about you earlier and the stretcher-bearers told me you were all right. Thank the Lord for that."

Jodie smiled at Jackson as Hunter said to her, "I guess you know who that is."

"Yes. I saw you in Frederick, General, when the boy was hit with a rock."

"I saw you too, Miss Jodie, but it was not the opportune moment to ask Hunter for an introduction."

"General," Jodie asked, "why isn't it likely there'll be more fighting tomorrow?"

"The Yankees fought as hard as we did today. They need rest as badly as we do. And if George McClellan stays true to form, it'll take him a day to get his troops ready to fight again."

"I hope you're right, Tom," Hunter said. "We're going to be a long time getting to all the wounded men as it is. Another day like today, and we'll bury more than we carry away."

"But what if they go back to fighting on Friday?" Jodie asked. "It'll be the same thing then."

Jackson nodded. "General Lee knows that. I've got a hunch he'll pull us out of here before Friday."

"Be foolish not to," Hunter said, keeping his attention on what his hands were doing.

"I agree," Jackson said. "Hunter, I was told that Rance Dayton was brought to you with a hunk of shrapnel in his leg. He doing all right?"

"Yes. He's out there on the south side of the tent. There's a lantern in the corner not being used. Light it and go see if he's awake."

"I'm glad you didn't have to take the leg," Jackson said.

"So am I. He'll be fine in a few weeks…won't even walk with a limp once it's completely healed."

Minutes later, Jackson made his way among the wounded men. Most were asleep. He spotted Dayton and knelt beside him. The major blinked at the lantern light, then focused on the face of his old professor.

"Hello, General. I sure am glad to see you."

"Same here, Rance. I saw what you did out there today. You're a brave man."

"How'd you see that?"

"Binoculars. I also saw what those five men in your regiment did."

"Yes, sir. I was going to talk to you about them, sir. I sure would like to see them get some kind of commendation from General Lee."

Jackson grinned. "I've already got that in mind," he said, pulling a slip of paper out of his shirt pocket. "Got it down right here, with all their names. I talked to some of the men in the regiment."

"Thank you, sir. They deserve to be honored for it."

"I've got a meeting with General Lee and General Longstreet in a few minutes, Rance. But one more thing before I go…"

"I took care of it, sir."

Jackson eyebrows came up. "You did? When?"

"When I came to, lying right here. I've been such a fool to put it off, General. When my mind came clear, it hit me that if I'd been killed out there today, I'd be in hell right now. What a fool I've been. The Lord was so good to me. Men dying all around me. Even—even Billy Dean. I'm saved now, General. Thanks to you. If you hadn't pressed the gospel to me over and over, well…I know you've prayed for me all this time, too."

"You're right about that," Jackson said, brushing tears from his eyes. "I'm so glad you opened your heart to Jesus."

"Best thing I ever did, sir. There's nothing like the peace I have in my heart right now. But then you know that, don't you?"

"I sure do, Rance. Glad you know it now, too. I have to get going. I'll check on you again tomorrow."

Jackson returned the lantern to the tent and doused its flame. "Well, Doc, when are you and Miss Jodie going to get some sleep? You can't work all night, you know."

Hunter, without looking up, said, "We've got two more men who need attention real bad, Tom. After we take care of them, we'll get some sleep. When will you know if General Lee is going to pull out?"

"Maybe tonight. I'm due at his tent in about ten minutes."

"Let us know, will you?"

Hunter and Jodie bid him goodnight and were finishing up with their present patient when two stretcher-bearers appeared.

"Dr. McGuire," one of them said, "we have a man here who needs attention right now. We took him to the tent next door, but when Dr. Jensen examined him, he said you were the man to handle this one."

"All right. Just hold on for a minute. We're about done here."

It took Hunter thirty seconds to finish up, and then he nodded toward the man on the stretcher. "Put him on the table. I'll be right back." He carried the last patient outside as Jodie began preparations for the new one.

As the stretcher-bearers lifted the man onto the table, what Jodie saw took her breath. The man's midsection was a bloody mass.

One of the stretcher-bearers saw her flinch. "Grapeshot, ma'am. He's lost a lot of blood."

The wounded soldier was conscious. He looked at Jodie through droop-lidded eyes. She judged him not more than twenty years old.

Hunter returned and the stretcher-bearers disappeared back onto the field of dead and wounded.

Jodie watched Hunter's face when he took his first look at the young private. He winced and shook his head. The grapeshot had done too much damage.

Hunter kept his voice to a whisper as he said, "All we can do is try to alleviate his pain."

Jodie nodded. "He's awake enough to take laudanum. I'll get some."

A sound came from the soldier's quivering lips. "Doc—Dr. McGuire…"

"Yes, soldier?"

"I'm not gonna make it…am I?"

"Well, I—"

"I heard what you said. There's no…chance, is there?"

Hunter bit his lower lip. "No, soldier, there isn't. You've been lying out there on the battlefield for hours. You've lost a lot of blood. It's a wonder you're still alive."

"I've been told you're a…a Christian."

"That's right."

"Doctor, I was raised in a God-fearing home, but I'm not a Christian. I don't want to go to hell. Please…help me."

"You come from a Christian home?"

"Yes. I went through a prayer once…when I was nine. But it was just to please Mama. By the time I was twelve, Mama… Mama knew I hadn't meant it. I lived and acted like the devil. Broke her heart."

"What's your name, soldier?"

"Eddie. Eddie Watkins. There's a letter from Mama…in my hip pocket. Has her address in Memphis."

"Listen to me, Eddie."

"Yes?"

"Do you understand who Jesus Christ is?"

"God's Son."

"Virgin-born and sinless…"

"Yes."

"Died on the cross for your sins, as well as the sins of the rest of humanity…"

"Yes."

"You know you're a guilty sinner before God?"

"The worst."

Jodie prayed silently as Hunter quoted Scripture, making sure Eddie Watkins understood the way of salvation.

When Eddie had finished asking the Lord to save him, he gritted his teeth in pain, and said, "Dr. McGuire…would you see that my mama knows I got saved…before…before I died? Her name and address—"

"Is in the letter in your hip pocket," Hunter said, pulling the letter from the pocket. "Yes, I'll write to her."

Eddie's eyes were turning glassy. "Tell Mama I'll…I'll meet her in heaven."

"I'll tell her, Eddie."

Hunter and Jodie continued to work, trying to save more lives. It was 3:20 A.M. when they heard footsteps outside.

"Doc…Miss Jodie…" It was General Jackson. "I thought you were going to get some sleep."

Both of them were so exhausted they could hardly stand. Hunter turned bleary eyes on Jackson. "After this one, Tom."

"You wanted me to let you know what General Lee decided about pulling his army out of here."

"Yes?"

"He's a very discouraged man right now. Blaming himself for the whipping we've taken…the men who died. But his thinking is clear. He sees no reason to keep us here. We'll pull out sometime late tomorrow. Probably be after dark."

"He doesn't think McClellan will attack today?"

"No. We've taken a pretty good toll on them. Of course, he could wipe us out if he had a mind to. We're out of ammunition, but McClellan doesn't know that. If he came at us, it wouldn't take him long to find out. We'll be gone by sunup on Friday."

"There's no way you can take the wounded men with you, is there?"

"No."

"Then Jodie and I, and all the Confederate doctors will stay until we've done all we can."

After less than three hours of sleep, Hunter and Jodie, who had slept on the floor amid the wounded, were fed a meager breakfast by the army cooks and went back to work.

Piteous moans and cries for water were still coming from the battlefields.

Stonewall Jackson was returning from the Sunken Road and heading toward the patch of woods that sheltered the Confederate medical facility. He was sickened as he let his gaze roam the valley. Like pages of a book, the battlefields told their story. Churned earth where cannon shells had exploded and blackened patches where they had burned the grass told of death, terrible and swift. The grass wore a garish red stain and quivered in the morning breeze. All around were the bloating bodies of dead horses and the broken, shattered artifacts of war.

The opposing armies—still under their truce—gathered their wounded who had survived the long night.

The general thought of home and his sweet wife, Mary Anna. He longed to hold her in his arms and feel her sweet warmth.

When he reached the hospital, he found Hunter and Jodie cleaning the operating table. They greeted Jackson and told him they felt refreshed after a brief sleep.

"Hunter, could I have a few minutes of your time?"

"Certainly, Tom. What can I do for you?"

"I need you to go for a little walk with me. I hate to take you away from your work, but this is important."

"Hunter," Jodie said, "I can go to the next tent and ask Dr. Jensen if he'll work in your place till you get back. He's got another doctor working with him at the moment."

"Go see if he can come right away. I'll put the next man on the table."

The general led Hunter to a long split-rail fence that bordered what the soldiers had dubbed "Bloody Lane" at sundown yesterday. His attention was drawn to a Confederate soldier at the fence on his knees with his rifle aimed across the road.

Hunter gave Jackson a quizzical look, then walked toward the man in tattered gray. The soldier wasn't moving a muscle as he stared along the barrel of his rifle with both eyes open. As Hunter bent low, he realized the man was not breathing. Then he saw the single bullet hole centered in the man's forehead beneath the brim of his ragged gray hat.

"What do you think of that?" Jackson asked.

"Death attitude."

"Death *what?*"

"Death attitude. Maybe more often called attitude of death."

"You know about this, Hunter?"

"It's rare, but not unheard of. Medical science hasn't been able to explain it, they just know that it happens. A doctor I graduated with at Harvard has done an intense study and written a journal article about it. Name's John Brinton. I read in the *American Medical Association Journal* that he's one of Lincoln's Corps Medical Directors."

"You say medical science hasn't been able to explain it?"

"Well, we know the preservation of these attitudes of death is not caused by rigor mortis. Dr. Brinton has determined that an unconscious muscle contraction at the instant of death can freeze a person's body position and facial expression. Look at this man's face. See how intense it is?"

"Yes…"

"Usually death relaxes the body muscles, and they go limp. But when this phenomenon happens, it freezes everything. See if you can take the musket from his hands."

Jackson took hold of the weapon, but the dead man's hands were unmovable. "Hunter, it's like his hands are made of steel. Come with me. We've got some more death attitudes yonder. General Colquitt told me about them. He's waiting there now."

As they drew near the place where Sunken Road took its famous dip, Hunter saw bodies strung out for more than a half-mile. Most of them were Confederates, but there were a few blue uniforms. Many of the bodies were heaped three and four deep.

Brigadier General Colquitt and his aides were standing nearby, talking with three Union soldiers. When Hunter drew closer, he saw that two of the Union men were officers, and the other was a doctor.

"Tom! It's my old college friend, John Brinton!"

Brinton had been told that General Jackson was bringing Hunter to the scene. When he saw the man who had led him to Christ, he hurried to meet him. The two men embraced as Union Generals Fitz-John Porter and George Meade looked on with General Colquitt and his aides.

Hunter kept a hand on John's shoulder as they turned their attention to the other men.

"Maybe we can talk later," John whispered.

"Yes," Hunter said. "I've read what you've written about death attitudes, John. Interesting."

"Well, I was sent here by General Halleck when we knew the battle would take place." As he spoke, Brinton pointed up the road. "Some stretcher-bearers told me there are some more death attitudes up there. We'll have to walk on the high edge of the bank to get around the bodies here. I'll lead the way."

Within ten feet of each other they found three bodies in the attitude of death. One was on his knees, as if he had died while trying to get up. The other two were in almost the same position. They lay on their backs, heads slightly lifted, arms raised rigidly in the air, as if reaching toward heaven.

"What you see here, gentlemen," Brinton said, "is reaction when the bullets struck their hearts. Both men apparently lived a few seconds and reached for heaven. There was a final muscular action at the last instant of life, in which the muscles set and remained rigid and inflexible."

Brinton then told Jackson and Hunter about the Confederate captain who had been shot while mounting his horse at South Mountain. He died sitting straight up in the saddle.

Jackson had heard about Captain Errol Taylor's strange behavior and apparent capture by General Jeb Stuart. It looked like they could finally clear up that puzzle.

As the men were about to depart Bloody Lane, Brinton said that earlier that morning, Battery B of the 4th U.S. Artillery had found a Union horse in death attitude. The animal had taken a bullet in the brain while apparently in the act of rising from the ground. Its head was held proudly aloft, and its forelegs set firmly forward in a lifelike pose.

This amazed them all.

Later that afternoon, Hunter and Jodie crossed the creek on the middle bridge and visited the Union medical facility at Dr. John Brinton's invitation. Jodie was glad to meet Hunter's old college friend and was elated to meet Clara Barton. The two camps agreed that in the next few days the Union and Confederate doctors and nurses would work together to take care of the wounded.

TWENTY-ONE

Hunter was carrying a man outside who had just died on the operating table when General Jackson appeared in the lantern light.

"Lost another one?" Jackson asked.

"Yes," Hunter said, placing the body tenderly on the ground.

There was more room in and around the facilities since the wounded men who were able to travel had been picked up and placed in wagons for the trip home.

The general followed Hunter inside and nodded at Jodie, then said, "Well, we're ready to pull out. How long do you think you'll stay, Doc?"

"Probably three or four more days—till we've saved the last life we can."

"Well, you're a volunteer, Doctor. You don't have to report back until you want to. I doubt there'll be any big battles in Virginia for a while. You need a good rest. Take it. When you're ready to come back, they can tell you at C.S.A. headquarters in Richmond where I am."

"All right. I think I'll take a room at the same boarding house where Jodie lives in Frederick and spend at least a week there."

"Good idea. After I get my Corps settled back on Southern ground, I'm going home for a while, myself. If you contact Richmond and I'm not there, they'll tell you where to report in."

"Good enough, Tom," Hunter said, giving his friend a hug.

Jackson then turned to Jodie. "You take care of this good man while he's with you, honey."

"I will, General." Jodie raised up on tiptoe to plant a quick kiss on his cheek. "I'll see you sometime down the line."

"Well, if I'm not tied up in a battle when you two get married, I'll be there to kiss the bride."

Jodie laughed and thought how good it felt. There had been so much sorrow all around her for two days.

Robert E. Lee took his army back into Virginia without opposition from McClellan. Little Mac wired General Halleck in Washington, saying, "Our victory is complete. The enemy is driven back into Virginia. Maryland and Pennsylvania are now safe."

Tactically, the battle at Antietam had been a draw. The Federals had gained ground, but they had failed to dislodge the Confederate army from Sharpsburg. The Confederate withdrawal transformed a tactical stalemate into strategic victory for the North.

President Lincoln seized the opportunity to issue a document that would lend a new and deeper meaning to the bloodiest day in American history—the Emancipation Proclamation, which decreed freedom for the Confederacy's three-and-a-half million slaves. Within a short time this action would incite the Confederates to fight even harder against the Northerners.

In spite of the Union's victory at Antietam, Lincoln was angry with McClellan. In his eyes, Little Mac had once again failed to vanquish the enemy when he'd had the opportunity.

Seven days after the battle, Hunter and Jodie returned to Frederick, having done all they could for the survivors of Antietam.

One of the first things Hunter did was write a letter to Mrs. Emily Watkins in Memphis, Tennessee. At least he could tell her that Eddie had opened his heart to Jesus before he died.

After a day of resting at the boarding house, Hunter and Jodie took a long walk on Friday afternoon, September 26. As they entered the woods, the lowering sun cast long shadows across the forest floor. A breeze began to stir the leaves and its invisible fingers fluffed Jodie's long silken tresses.

Hunter pointed to a fallen tree. "Let's sit down for a moment, sweetheart. I've been thinking."

"About what?"

"Our wedding. How about a December date? A little earlier than we had discussed before."

"Sounds good to me. Any special day?"

"Haven't gotten that far. I thought if you agreed on December we'd come up with the exact day together."

"Fine," she said, and smiled. "December it is."

Hunter pulled her close and kissed her tenderly. They sat together in silence, enjoying the sounds of the forest and each other's presence.

After several minutes, Jodie squeezed Hunter's hand. "You know what, Dr. Hunter McGuire?"

"What, Nurse Jodie Lockwood?"

"Do you realize how little we know about each other? At Lexington we had only a few days together. And the time was so short at Frederick…then at Sharpsburg there was hardly time to talk."

"I know all I need to know about you to be absolutely positive I want to spend the rest of my life with you. The rest I'll learn as time goes by."

"I don't have any doubts about marrying you either…but some things I want to know *now.*"

"Like what?"

"How about your middle name for starters."

Hunter laughed. "That's an easy one. It's Newman. I've told you about being adopted by Jason and Ellie McGuire when I was five."

"Yes."

"When they took me before the county magistrate to adopt me, they suggested that I carry the family n— Oh! I never even told you what my last name was before I was adopted."

"See what I mean? We need to learn some of the important things like that about each other."

"Well, I was Hunter Newman Jr. My mother's name was Florence, and I already told you my baby sister's name was Lizzie. When the McGuires took me before the county magistrate, they suggested I carry the family name as a middle name in honor of my real parents. So I became Hunter Newman McGuire. Now, Miss Jodie Lockwood…I don't know *your* middle name either."

"It's Elizabeth. My parents used to call me Jodie Beth when I was little. My Aunt Bertha—Mom's sister—still does."

"My baby sister's middle name was Elizabeth. That's why my parents called her Lizzie. So your name is Jodie Elizabeth?"

Jodie shook her head and brushed a lock of hair from her forehead. "No. Jodie is just a nickname. My name is actually Joan Elizabeth."

Hunter's smile faded. "Really? That's quite a coincidence. Lizzie's real name is Joan Elizabeth."

"You're kidding!" Jodie noticed a strange look in his eyes. "Hunter, what's the matter?"

He chuckled hollowly and ran shaky fingers through his hair. "Well, that you and my sister have the exact same first and middle name is really something. But…"

"But *what?*"

"I hadn't thought about it till now, but Lizzie's hair was black like yours, and her eyes chocolate-brown just like yours. And… and the two of you have to be very close to the same age. She was three years younger than me, the same as you."

"When is Lizzie's birthday? Do you remember?"

"I was only five when Mom died, and Lizzie and I were separated. It's in February, I think. Yes…February. But I don't remember what day."

Jodie raised a trembling hand to her mouth. "Mine's February 19. I was born in 1838. I assume Lizzie was too."

"I was born in '35, so Lizzie would've been born in '38. February '38." Hunter's chest felt tight. "But you were born in Tennessee. She was born in Virginia."

"Hunter, are…are we really thinking that I could be your long lost sister? I mean, this can't be, can it?"

"Jodie." Hunter tried to keep his voice steady. "These coincidences are really astounding, but that's where it ends. Like I said, you were born in Tennessee; Lizzie was born in Virginia." Hunter forced a laugh. "Besides, little Lizzie had a burn scar on her upper left arm. Mom accidentally spilled boiling water on her when she was about a year-and-a-half old."

The blood drained from Jodie's face and she began to unbutton her left sleeve at the cuff, methodically rolling it up. Her lips quivered as she said, "Was Lizzie's scar shaped like this?"

Hunter's eyes glazed with tears as he nodded.

"Hunter," Jodie whispered, squeezing his hand, "tell me I'm going to wake up and all of this will be gone."

"I don't understand…" was all Hunter could say. Then, "But you said you were born and raised in Tennessee."

"That's what I've always thought," Jodie said, looking at the scar on her arm. "But how do we explain this?"

"No, Jodie. This just has to be the strangest set of coincidences that has ever happened in all human history. The Lord would never let a thing like this happen to us. Weren't we just saying a little while ago how He so wonderfully kept us for each other for over seven years, then used the War to bring us together?"

"Hunter, didn't you tell me you've always wanted to find Lizzie, and have prayed that you would?"

"Yes."

"Well, I can't say I understand all that the Lord has done in our lives, but if I *am* Lizzie, at least God has brought us to each other."

Hunter stubbornly shook his head. "No. I'm *in love* with you, Jodie. How could I ever just love you as a brother loves his sister? And how about you? Could you just love me as your big brother?"

Jodie's tears began to spill over, and she couldn't speak.

Hunter folded her into his arms. "Sweetheart, we must believe that the circumstances are not what they appear to be. Somehow we've got to find a way to clear all of this up."

Jodie pushed back enough to look into his eyes. "Hunter, there *is* a way to clear it up. My Aunt Bertha can do it for us. We'll go to Athens, Tennessee. That's where she lives. I remember her telling me many, many times about being right there at our house when I was born. She can settle it for us, once and for all!"

Fifty-four-year-old Bertha Pittman, a widow for several years, hurried through the parlor to see who was knocking at her door. She peered through the heavy curtain and saw a tall, sandy-haired man with a small woman at his side. She opened the door a crack.

"Yes?"

A face appeared, exactly Bertha's height. "Hello, Aunt Bertha."

"Jodie Beth! Come in this house!"

They embraced for a long moment, then Bertha looked the handsome man up and down. "Jodie, you didn't go and get yourself married without writing to your Auntie, did you?"

"Not yet, but I want you to meet my fiancé, Dr. Hunter McGuire."

"I always knew that when my Jodie Beth found herself a man, he'd be as good-looking as she is beautiful!"

Bertha tugged at Jodie's hand. "Well, come in and sit down. I want to hear all about your nursing…and how you met this handsome doctor."

"Our time is a little limited, Auntie, so we'll have to tell it in brief. Actually we're here because we need your help."

Bertha guided them to a love seat in the parlor and took a chair facing them. "I can't imagine how you would need my help, honey, but I'm listening."

Together, Jodie and Hunter told their story.

"So…" Jodie said, "this is why we're here. I remember you telling me many times when I was growing up how you were right there in the house when I was born."

Bertha remained silent. Then her lips quivered and tears began to spill down her cheeks.

Jodie leaned forward. "Auntie, you were there when I was born, weren't you?"

Bertha left her chair and picked up a hanky from a small table. "Honey, I once swore to my sister and brother-in-law that I would never tell this, but now I have no choice."

The portly woman wept as she explained that back in the late spring of 1840, her sister, Bettieann, and brother-in-law, Jubal Lockwood, were on a trip to North Carolina in their wagon. They had gone to visit some of their old high school friends who had moved to Reidsville, some fifteen miles north of Greensboro. When they returned, Jubal and Bettieann had a two-year-old girl with them.

During their trip they came upon a wagon in the woods a few miles outside Reidsville. Apparently robbers had murdered the young couple they found, since there was no money on either person. In the back of the wagon, Jubal and Bettieann found the little girl. They also found papers showing that the couple had just adopted her in Virginia.

When Hunter and Jodie heard this, a hopeless feeling washed over them. Bertha saw it, but continued.

"Bettieann and Jubal had been married for nine years and hadn't been able to have children, so they took the little girl and the papers and headed back home to Tennessee. When they arrived home, Jodie Beth, they told me and your Uncle Harold what had happened. They figured they hadn't done anything wrong. After all, you needed a home."

Jodie leaned over and put her head in her hands.

"Jubal and my sister made Harold and me swear never to tell anyone about it, honey. They simply told folks hereabouts they had gone to North Carolina and adopted little Jodie Beth, which is what they called you right from the start. They liked the name Joan Elizabeth, which of course was on the papers, so they decided to let you keep it. No one ever questioned it, since they had often talked about adoption."

Hunter's voice had a dull tone as he asked, "Mrs. Pittman, did you ever actually see the adoption papers?"

"Yes, I did."

"Can you remember the name of the adoptive parents? The ones who were robbed and killed?"

Bertha put a hand to her temple, looking at the floor. "No, Doctor, it was just too long ago. I should be able to remember the name, but it just won't come to me."

"If you heard the name, would you know it?"

"Yes, I think I would."

"Was it William and Bessie Caterson?"

Bertha's eyes lit up. She snapped her fingers and said, "Yes, that's it! Caterson!"

"And Jodie Beth's original name, ma'am. Would you know it if you heard it?"

"I'm sure I would. I recall it had the word 'new' in it. Like Newcomb, or Newberry, or something like that."

"Newman?"

"Yes! Little Jodie Beth's name had been Joan Elizabeth Newman!"

***

Hunter drove the rented buggy through Athens toward the railroad station, keeping an arm around Jodie as she stared vacantly ahead.

Numb of soul, Hunter felt his world slipping through his fingers like grains of sand. All the dreams he had for a future with Jodie were gone. He knew the precious young woman by his side was suffering the same feeling of loss.

"Jodie…"

"Yes?"

"At least I'm glad to know that my little Lizzie's all right. I do have to say it's good to have found her."

Jodie squeezed his hand. "And I didn't even know I had a big brother."

"But, Jodie, what do I do with my love for you? It isn't proper that I should feel this way toward my sister."

"Nor for me to feel this way toward my brother. I don't understand, dar—Hunter. I don't understand why the Lord would let it happen in a way that has so torn our lives apart."

"I don't either. But we'll just have to trust Him. Our God does no wrong. We'll have to cling to that. I'll take you back to Frederick so you can resume your nursing career. We'll keep in touch. The Lord has somebody for you, I'm sure. One day he'll walk into your life."

Jodie knew she could never love a man like she had loved Hunter. She would just bury herself in her career.

At the depot Hunter bought tickets for Richmond, then on to Frederick. Now that the battle at Antietam was over, the Maryland trains were running pretty much on schedule again.

"Once we're over the initial shock of all this, little sister, we'll get together now and then. One day I want you to meet my adoptive parents. They've heard a lot about Lizzie."

"Oh, Hunter!" Jodie buried her face in her hands and sobbed.

Hunter folded her in his arms and wept with her.

The railroad car rocked and the steel wheels clicked rhythmically as Hunter and Jodie sat side by side watching the Tennessee countryside. Neither had spoken a word since the train pulled out of Athens. Now Hunter turned toward Jodie.

"I just thought of something," he said. "Tom Jackson was going to spend some time at home. He's probably still there. We could change trains at Knoxville and go to Lexington. Would you mind?"

"Of course not. General Jackson is your closest friend, and he will need to know, sooner or later, what's happened. Anyhow, I know it would be a comfort for you to see him."

Jodie loved Mary Anna Jackson immediately upon meeting her.

As they sat in the Jackson parlor, the general said, "I'm glad you caught me home. I'm heading back for duty day after tomorrow. Now, just what brought you two to Lexington? This is a long way from Frederick."

"Well, Tom," Hunter said, sighing, "Jodie and I have something to tell you and Mrs. Jackson."

Mary Anna waggled a finger at Hunter as she said, "Now, now, Doctor. I'm not 'Mrs. Jackson' to you. I want both you and Jodie to call me Mary Anna."

Hunter smiled and proceeded to explain the recent development in Jodie and his life. When he'd finished, Tom began rubbing the back of his neck and shaking his head. Finally he looked straight at his old friend and said softly, "Hunter, you need to go to Smithburg."

"Excuse me?"

"You need to go to Smithburg."

"Why, pray tell?"

"See if old Dr. Chet Riley is still alive. Tell him your story and ask him if it all makes sense."

"Why wouldn't it make sense?"

"I...I remember that when your mother gave birth to Lizzie—I was about thirteen years old—I overheard my Uncle Cummins and Aunt Ophelia talking about the Newmans' baby girl. There was a name brought into the conversation, and the only reason I can remember it is because it was the name of a teenage girl who used to live on a farm near McCann's Run, and then suddenly she wasn't living with her parents anymore. She had gone up north to live with some relatives. Her name was Elaine Worley. If Dr. Riley is still alive, ask him about Elaine Worley."

"But what can this Elaine Worley have to do with us?"

"I don't know. There's just something scratching at the back of my mind about her. Maybe it's the Lord talking to me, I'm not sure. All I can say is go ask Dr. Riley."

TWENTY-TWO

H unter rented a buggy for the ride from Parkersburg to Smithburg. When he and Jodie arrived at the small town, Hunter was surprised that it actually looked familiar to him. But where was Dr. Riley's office?

The next corner looked very familiar. Instinct told him to turn and follow that street. When he rounded another corner, there it was, a half-block away. Dr. Chet Riley's office.

"You drive like you know where you're going," Jodie said.

"I didn't at first, but it kind of came back to me. The office is right up here."

The small building was still a doctor's office, but the sign read:

GERALD BISHOP, M.D.
PHYSICIAN AND SURGEON

"Well, let's see if maybe they know where Dr. Riley might be," Hunter said.

Moments later, Hunter and Jodie entered the doctor's office to find the nurse-receptionist at the front desk.

"Good morning, folks. Which one is to see the doctor?"

"Neither of us, ma'am. I'm Dr. Hunter McGuire, and this young lady is Miss Lockwood."

"I'm Harriet Mulford. Is this a professional visit to Dr. Bishop?"

"No, ma'am. Actually, I came here to see Dr. Chet Riley."

"Oh, I'm sorry. Dr. and Mrs. Riley have both passed on. Both of them died in 1859, just two months apart. Dr. Bishop took over the clinic about five months before Dr. Riley died. Is there something I can do for you?"

"Well, ma'am," Hunter said, pulling at an ear, "I had hoped Dr. Riley could help me with a problem Miss Lockwood and I are facing. I don't think there's anything you could do."

"The problem," Jodie said, "involves some information Dr. Riley very possibly could have provided that affects both of our lives."

"Would there be anyone else in the community who might be able to help you? I know just about everybody. I was raised on a farm near here."

"I don't know who it would be, ma'am, but thank you just the same," Hunter said.

Harriet's heart went out to the couple. She could see they were quite distressed. "This information you were hoping to obtain from Dr. Riley…does it involve patients of his, or something like that?"

Hunter and Jodie exchanged glances again.

"I think so, ma'am," Hunter said. "Since you were raised around here, does the name Elaine Worley mean anything to you?"

Harriet blinked and thought for a moment, then said, "No, sir. Doesn't ring any bells. Was she a patient of Dr. Riley's?"

"I'm not really sure, but I assume so."

"Dr. McGuire, I don't mean to pry, but perhaps if I knew exactly what it was you were expecting to learn from Dr. Riley, I could help after all."

"Well, let me explain it, ma'am, and we'll soon see."

Harriet invited the couple to sit down, and they told her the whole story as briefly but thoroughly as they could.

When they had finished, Harriet said, "Well, bless your hearts.

What a horrible thing to have happen. You know what? Dr. Riley's long-time nurse, Linna Bittner, may be able to furnish the same information. Linna's retired now, but lives here in town."

Hunter helped Jodie out of the buggy in front of Linna Bittner's small house and continued to hold her hand as they approached the porch.

"Oh, Hunter," Jodie said, "if this lady has no idea what General Jackson was referring to by naming Elaine Worley, we're at a dead end."

"I know, honey. But the Lord is with us. It's all in His hands. We've trusted Him with our souls for eternity. We've got to trust him with our lives for our time here on earth."

Hunter knocked on the door. There were instant footsteps, and the door opened to a bright-eyed woman with snow-white hair and a pleasant smile.

"Yes?" she said. "Is there something I can do for you?"

"Mrs. Bittner, I'm Dr. Hunter McGuire, and—"

"Little Hunter Newman? The boy adopted by Dr. and Mrs. Jason McGuire years ago?"

"Yes, ma'am."

"Please, come in. And this young lady is your wife?"

"Well…ah…no, ma'am." Hunter allowed Jodie to enter ahead of him. "Since you remember me, do you remember my little sister?"

Linna's eyes widened as she closed the door behind them. "Lizzie?"

Hunter smiled. "You have a terrific memory, ma'am. Yes. This is my little sister, Lizzie. Only she goes by Jodie now."

Linna looked stunned. "Well, isn't this wonderful? When did you find her?"

"You knew about the Catersons disappearing?"

Linna nodded. "Please," she said, gesturing toward an over-stuffed couch, "sit down."

Linna sat in a chair across from them. "I know about the disappearance of the Catersons and little Lizzie because your adoptive father came here looking for them—what was it?—maybe a year or so after they had taken you to Boston."

"Oh, yes. I hadn't thought about that."

"My, both of you children grew up to be very good-looking. Of course, you were awfully cute when you were little. So when did you find her, Hunter?"

"On September 14, ma'am."

"*This* September 14?"

"Yes. I'm a volunteer surgeon for the Confederate army, and I was with General Stonewall Jackson at the Antietam battle. I'm his Corps Medical Director."

"Really! Well, how is Tommy?"

"He's just fine, ma'am. Well, anyway, Jodie—Lizzie to you—was in Frederick, Maryland. She's Dr. Harvey Roberts's nurse at the clinic there."

Linna's eyes brightened. "A nurse! That's wonderful, dear."

Jodie smiled.

"General Lee passed his army through Frederick on Sunday, before the battle at Sharpsburg. There was Jodie—Lizzie—on the street. We hadn't seen each other for—well, I started to say twenty-two years. But we had met in Lexington seven years ago for a brief time, and then I lost track of her."

"Which brings us to why we're here, Mrs. Bittner," Jodie said. "We're facing a serious crisis in our lives. Because Hunter and General Jackson are very close friends, we talked to him about it. Not knowing that Dr. Riley had died, General Jackson sent us here to ask him a question. The nurse at Dr. Bishop's office thought you might be able to help us."

"I'll certainly try. Exactly what is this crisis?"

Jodie remained silent as Hunter told Linna Bittner the story. When he brought up the name of Elaine Worley, Linna looked as if she would cry.

"I see you know her name," Jodie said. "What can you tell us about her? General Jackson seemed to think that Elaine would be the key to our dilemma."

Linna pulled out a hanky and dabbed at her tears. "I was sworn to secrecy on this, children. But after hearing your story, I can't keep it from you. Bless your hearts. What a horrible experience for you."

Linna wiped tears again. "The Worley family lived on a farm near McCann's Run. One day Ralph and Edna Worley brought sixteen-year-old Elaine to Dr. Riley. I'll never forget the look on their faces. Elaine was so pale and just stared at the floor. She was pregnant out of wedlock. Ralph and Edna were terribly devastated and ashamed. They couldn't bear to face the community with such a scandal hanging over them. The boy who fathered the baby had left Virginia. His name was Bobby Henderson. No one knew where he had gone.

"The Worleys told Dr. Riley in my presence that they would keep Elaine inside the house until she gave birth to the baby. In the meantime, they wanted Dr. Riley to help them find someone in a distant town or city who would adopt the baby.

"Dr. Riley agreed to help them. Ralph and Edna told him they would tell the community that Elaine was staying with relatives up north for a few months. Now, children, I want you to understand that I heard all of this with my own ears."

Hunter and Jodie nodded, listening with rapt attention.

"At that time, Hunter, your mother was carrying her second child. You were three years old."

"Yes'm."

"Florence—your mother—was having complications with the pregnancy. Dr. Riley was making house calls almost every day. Of course, you were too young to understand what was going on, Hunter."

"Yes'm."

"When Florence's time to deliver drew near, Dr. Riley brought her to the clinic so he could keep an eye on her. During the nights, either he, Mrs. Riley, or I stayed with her. Some nights, your father was there, too. Thora Kemp was keeping you at her house. You probably remember Thora."

"Yes."

"Well, your father was there at the clinic when your mother delivered."

Jodie and Hunter hung on Linna's next words.

"The baby was stillborn."

Hunter's mouth went dry.

Jodie's heart thumped against her ribs as tears filled her eyes, and she scooted forward on the couch. "Mrs. Bittner, I'm Elaine Worley's daughter, aren't I? I'm Elaine Worley's daughter!"

"Yes."

Jodie flung herself into Hunter's arms, sobbing, "O Hunter, I'm not your sister! I'm not your sister! You're not my brother! You're my precious husband-to-be!"

Linna cried with them as she watched Hunter and Jodie weeping for joy and praising the Lord. Finally, the overjoyed couple settled down enough to listen to the rest of the story.

"Elaine gave birth to her baby girl at the Worley home that same night. Dr. Riley left Florence and Hunter Sr. with me at the clinic.

"When Dr. Riley returned, he told the Newmans that since their baby—a girl—had been born dead, he had a newborn baby girl they could adopt if they wanted her.

"Dr. Riley made them promise to keep secret what he was about to tell them, even if they decided they didn't want to adopt the baby. When they were told about Elaine, and that she had given birth to a healthy girl just an hour before, the Newmans were elated, saying they would take her.

"Dr. Riley told them everyone must believe the little girl was the baby Florence had brought into the world. They could never tell a single soul, not even you, Hunter. They made the promise and took the little black-haired, brown-eyed baby girl home the next night.

"Of course, I was sworn to secrecy too. Say! It just struck me why Tommy Jackson would bring up Elaine to you, though he didn't really know why."

"We'd be interested to know that," Hunter said.

"Well, one day a few months later, Tommy's Aunt Ophelia Jackson came to the clinic for some medicine. We were alone while I was filling the bottle. Ophelia said she and Cummins suspected that Elaine Worley's real reason for dropping out of sight was that she was pregnant by the Henderson boy she'd been running around with. She asked if it was so.

"I tried to lie about it, but Ophelia saw through me. In order to keep it from going any further, I told her the whole thing. I knew she would have to tell Cummins, but I asked her never to let it go beyond that. She promised she wouldn't, and as far as I know, it never did. From what you told me, Tommy must have overheard part of the conversation when Ophelia told Cummins."

"God let him overhear it," Jodie said. "He knows the end from the beginning. And way back there He was working all of this out."

"No reasonable person could deny that," Hunter said. "Well, we'd better be going." Hunter rose to his feet and helped Jodie up.

On the porch, Linna put her hand on Jodie's arm. "Is it going to bother you, honey? Knowing that you're Elaine Worley's daughter?"

Jodie looked into Hunter's eyes as she replied, "Not in the least. I'm just so happy to know that I'm going to become Mrs. Hunter McGuire!"

Jodie clung to Hunter's arm as they drove out of Smithburg and headed north for Parkersburg. When they reached a wooded area, he tugged at the reins and pulled off the road onto a grassy spot.

"What are you doing, darling?" she asked.

Hunter turned on the seat and took Jodie into his arms. "I know at times my faith grew a little weak, sweetheart, but down deep I just knew the Lord wouldn't do a thing like that to us."

"I did too, but my faith wavered sometimes, just the same."

"You know what?"

"What?"

"On that windy day in Frederick, the Lord really brought *two* people to me on the wings of the wind—the woman I love and my sweet little Lizzie!"

EPILOGUE

The Federal Sanitary Commission in Washington, D. C., re-acted to the horrible carnage of the Antietam battle by bringing in supplies and materials, as well as food, to treat the wounded men on both sides. Before the last hospital barn, house, or tent was closed, and the last wounded man sent from the Sharpsburg area, the Commission had distributed over twenty-eight thousand pieces of dry goods, shirts, towels, bed ticking, pillows, and other ne-cessities; thirty barrels of bandage for dressing of wounds; some thirty-two hundred pounds of farina; twenty-six hundred pounds of condensed milk; five thousand pounds of beef stock and canned meats; four thousand sets of hospital clothing; several tons of fruit, plus crackers, tea, sugar, coffee, and tin cups. They provided medical supplies such as opium, chloroform, and surgical instruments.

All of these supplies were donated by volunteers in the Northern communities or bought with money donated by people of the North.

On October 26, 1862, nearly six weeks after the Battle of Antietam, General McClellan finally set his army in motion. President Lincoln had visited him in the field on October 4, expressing his displeasure that McClellan had not vanquished the Confederate Army of Northern Virginia when he had the opportunity. McClellan gave his reasons for not doing so, but Lincoln was not convinced they were valid. However, he decided to give McClellan one more chance.

His army reinforced to 110,000 men, McClellan sent his vanguard across the Potomac five miles south of Harper's Ferry. He would pursue Lee and annihilate his army.

General Lee was still suffering from chest pains but had recovered from his depression over the devastating loss of men at Antietam. He moved to thwart McClellan's advance by once again dividing his army. On October 28, he left Stonewall Jackson's Corps, including Dr. Hunter McGuire, in the Shenandoah Valley and took the other half of his army on a swift sixty-mile march southeast through the passes of the Blue Ridge Mountains.

By the time the Federal vanguard had reached Warrenton, Virginia, Lee had established himself at Culpepper Courthouse, twenty miles to the southwest. From this position, he could oppose a Federal march on Richmond.

To Abraham Lincoln, this meant that McClellan's slows had allowed the enemy to get away again. McClellan had failed the final test.

On November 5, Lincoln had papers drawn up relieving McClellan of his command and replacing him with Major General Ambrose E. Burnside. McClellan was instructed by Lincoln to return immediately to his home in Trenton, New Jersey, where he was to await "further orders"—orders which would never come. George B. McClellan had fought his last battle.

On November 11, 1862, McClellan boarded a train at Warrenton Junction. Thousands of weeping Union soldiers were there to see him off. The general stepped onto the rear platform of his coach and calmed the distraught soldiers by saying, "Stand by General Burnside as you have stood by me, and all will be well. Good-bye, lads."

The train steamed out of the station, carrying the beloved McClellan away from the War. Later, Colonel Edward Cross of the 5th New Hampshire wrote, "A shade of sadness crossed his face. He carried the hearts of the army with him."

BOOK EIGHT

TURN OF GLORY

BATTLE OF CHANCELLORSVILLE

To Mike O'Donell,

Christian brother, loyal fan, dear friend,

and insurance agent supreme.

God bless you, Mike.

1 Thessalonians 5:16

✳ ✳ ✳

PROLOGUE

For more than a century and a quarter, in the minds of Civil War buffs like myself, the Battle of Chancellorsville—May 1–4, 1863—has remained the ultimate campaign of General Robert E. Lee's Army of Northern Virginia.

I have never picked a side to favor in the Civil War. I see gallantry and heroism on both sides. I understand the cause of both sides. President Abraham Lincoln was against slavery. I am against slavery. As a Bible-believing, born-again child of God, I do not believe that my heavenly Father wants one human being to own as chattel another human being, regardless of the color of his skin.

But the issue that sparked the flame for the War between the States was not slavery, it was states' rights. The Southern states resisted the intent of the Northern states to force the abolition of slavery upon them. They felt they had the right to make their own decision in the matter. And I generally agree with that principle too.

People have asked me if I have a favorite character on each side of the War. I do. Though many soldiers on both sides have caught my attention as I've studied the War, two stand out in my mind. Both of them were Christian men with positive testimonies of having trusted the Lord Jesus Christ and His shed blood, death, burial, and glorious resurrection for their salvation.

Those men are Major General Joshua L. Chamberlain, the shining hero of the Battle of Gettysburg, and Lieutenant General Thomas J. "Stonewall" Jackson, the hero of numerous battles, and certainly the shining star in the Battle of Chancellorsville.

My faithful readers know that I have already written a novel on the Gettysburg battle, *Season of Valor*.

Though in the Battles of Destiny series I have not written the novels in chronological order, I am following the previous novel, *Wings of the Wind*, with the book you now hold in your hands. I want to pick up the story where *Wings of the Wind* left off after the Battle of Antietam, where much of the spotlight was on Thomas "Stonewall" Jackson. I not only want to proceed with Jackson's part in the War, but with the life of his longtime friend and personal physician, Dr. Hunter McGuire. This, of course, will also throw the spotlight on McGuire's lovely fiancée, Jodie Lockwood, who ultimately becomes his wife.

Also, in chapter 5 you will meet Chaplain B. Tucker Lacy, who is not a fictional character. Although his last name is the same as mine, I did not create Chaplain Lacy for the story; I have simply followed history. Lacy was a close friend of General Stonewall Jackson and was appointed Chaplain General to II Corps by Jackson himself.

Several years ago, after casually reading a brief historical sketch about the Chancellorsville campaign, I picked up a modern road atlas and tried to find the city of Chancellorsville on the Virginia map. When I couldn't locate it, and it was not listed in the directory of Virginia cities, towns, and villages, I figured the city of Chancellorsville must have either had a name change since the Civil War or died out.

Further study showed me that Chancellorsville never was a city, town, or village, but simply a mansion two and a half stories high, built in 1816 by wealthy George Chancellor. It stood at the intersection of the newly built Orange Turnpike and Ely's Ford Road. Chancellor built it large enough to provide a sufficient home for his large family, plus bed-and-breakfast rooms to provide accommodations for turnpike travelers. He gave the place its name—Chancellorsville.

The famous battle took place around the huge estate, and the mansion itself was severely damaged by cannonade.

General Lee's army was outnumbered more than two to one. They faced a foe better equipped and better supplied and lacked the presence of one of their two corps commanders, yet they were able to crush and demoralize the federal Army of the Potomac in one of the most daring engagements in military history.

The Chancellorsville battle forever solidified the lasting fame of the wise and gallant General Thomas J. "Stonewall" Jackson.

This fact, however, belongs at the end of the story. Let's go back to September 17, 1862, at the Battle of Antietam, where our story really began....

ONE

On the winding banks of Antietam Creek, near Sharpsburg, Maryland, a raging titanic combat had begun just after the break of dawn. It was now midafternoon, and the heat was almost unbearable as powder smoke hung densely above the valley. The sun's rays shone through only when a gust of wind parted the veil of smoke.

Men went down by the dozens as the hostile battle lines of both Union and Confederate armies unleashed fire without letup. In spite of the carnage, there was an air of excitement. Both sides eagerly pressed the battle to the enemy—an almost reckless disregard for life in a wild quest for victory.

Dead men sprawled over the ground from the Potomac River to Antietam Creek, and to the east for a mile. Some were crumpled in hollows, and a few lay draped over waist-high stone walls and split-rail fences.

The acrid odor of gunpowder, hot metal, and blood filled the hot September air. The smell of burnt and splintered trees and blasted earth only intensified the stench of death.

Unmerciful artillery had wreaked havoc—fences torn apart, farm buildings destroyed, cornfields trampled, trees reduced to naked stumps. Human limbs were heaped beside hospital tents, and army horses and domestic animals lay lifeless among thousands of dead and dying soldiers.

The Confederate II Corps's commander, Major General Thomas J. "Stonewall" Jackson, stood on a brush-covered knoll in the west woods with one of his aides, Private Henry Kyd Douglas. Jackson's artillery troops were situated in the woods along the edge of the trees, and infantry were spaced intermittently among the cannons.

Major General George B. McClellan's Union infantry came across the open fields in seemingly interminable columns of blue, flanked by artillery batteries. Jackson's artillery cut loose, and the infantry followed suit, ejecting the wild, bloodcurdling Rebel yell. Cannon and musket belched their volleys with telling accuracy.

Casualties in the Union ranks were appalling, but on they came with a flash of bayonets and flutter of flags, halting the lines only long enough to readjust for their fallen comrades.

Stonewall Jackson stood fearlessly on the very edge of the terrible battle, observing it through binoculars. The enemy was showing itself indomitable. No matter how many Yankees the Confederate guns cut down, there were always more to take their place. Not so with the men in gray. They had started short in number and were becoming even fewer.

Suddenly a fierce battle opened up in a cornfield owned by a farmer named Miller. Jackson swung his binoculars there and focused on the action.

Major General Joseph Hooker's Union infantry swept into the cornfield with the crushing weight of a landslide. The Rebels were grossly outnumbered but fought back valiantly.

Even as Jackson watched the battle from his position on the knoll, great patches of corn were blasted by artillery, and most of the field looked as if it had been struck by a hailstorm.

At the north end of the cornfield, in the heat of the action, was the Eighteenth North Carolina Infantry Regiment commanded by Major Rance Dayton. The Eighteenth was part of Jackson's II Corps.

Jackson caught a glimpse of Major Dayton and briefly thought of their time together at the Virginia Military Institute, where Jackson had been a professor. Each time Jackson had talked with Dayton about the Lord Jesus, the young cadet had listened politely, but that was all. Then, a few days ago, the general had talked with Dayton again about his need to know the Lord. But all Rance would say was that he would think about it. Jackson's last words to him had been: "Just don't die while you're thinking about it."

Now Jackson prayed silently, *Dear God, don't let Rance get killed down there. Please don't let him die lost.*

Major Rance Dayton hunkered down with his regiment amongst the cornstalks. Most of the field was flattened, but some of it still stood almost seven feet high. They had met a fierce onslaught from the enemy infantry and repulsed it with musket fire so rapid and well aimed that the Yankees had backed off to regroup.

Flanking Major Dayton were Privates Chad Lynch and Bo Gentry. Lynch peered through the thick stand of corn toward the ravine where the Yankees had retreated and said, "How long you think it'll take 'em to regroup, Major?"

Dayton removed his campaign hat and paused to sleeve sweat from his brow before saying, "Not long. Ten minutes, maybe."

"Sir," said Gentry, "aren't those Yankees gonna run out of men pretty soon? How many do we have to kill before they decide that taking this cornfield isn't worth it?"

Dayton grinned. "I think they grow new Yankees instantly when they pull back to regroup. I declare, I'm sure I've shot some of the same Yankees every time they've come at us."

Both privates chuckled nervously.

Major Dayton ran his gaze over the men he could see. They looked weary and hollow-eyed as they crouched among the cornstalks. They had already fought for over nine hours. Since their meager breakfast of dried beef, two-day-old biscuits, and water from the creek, they'd had nothing to eat but the corn they were munching on now, while their dead and wounded comrades lay around them. Some were helping the wounded drink from canteens.

A sergeant appeared from the rear and knelt beside Dayton. "Major, we're runnin' mighty low on ammunition."

"Get to General Branch and tell him we need more."

"That's where I just came from, sir. He said there isn't much more left in the caissons."

"Then we'll have to throw rocks till they close in. Then we'll go to bayonets, fists, and teeth. Has General Branch sent word to General Jackson that we're low?"

"I don't know, sir."

"Go find out."

When the sergeant had disappeared, Dayton let his eyes move over the dirty faces of his men. "We're low on ammunition, boys," he said. "Pass the word to gather the cartridge boxes off the dead and wounded. We'll need all we can get!"

"Major!" shouted one of the lieutenants. "Here they come!"

Every eye fastened on the heavy lines of men in blue who came out of the ravine like a swarm of insects.

"All right, men, listen to me!" Dayton called loudly so that all could hear. "Hold your fire until I give the word! We're hard to see in this corn! I want them so close you can tell the color of their eyes before you fire!"

The men's nerves were strung tight, and sweat poured down their faces as they watched the blue lines coming toward them. Soon the first line of Federals drew dangerously close. Suddenly Dayton shouted, "Fire!"

Muskets roared and flamed in the Federals' faces like a blaze of lightning. The entire front line, with few exceptions, went down in a virtual wall of hot lead. Those who were not hit wheeled and ran back toward the next wave, which halted under their stunned commander's orders.

While the Federals regrouped, Dayton shouted, "Take the guns and ammunition off those dead Yankees, boys!"

As the men of the Eighteenth North Carolina Regiment scurried to gather the guns and ammunition, Dayton saw a fresh horde of Yankees swarm out of the ravine.

"Get ready, men!" shouted the major. "This'll be a big one! Don't fire till I say so!"

The Federals were closing in. Rance could hear them shouting curses. He waited until they were almost upon the Eighteenth, then gave the order: "Fire!"

Suddenly the whole world seemed to explode as guns on both sides belched flame. The air filled with dust and smoke and the cries of wounded men. Dayton saw the Yankee leader—a young major— go down.

The volley of fire by the Confederates and the heaps of blue-uni- formed bodies on the ground had the Yankees in disarray. They pulled back, looking for their leader. When they couldn't find him amidst the dust and smoke, they pivoted and headed back across the field.

"After 'em, men!" Dayton shouted, and led the charge.

They were some two hundred yards out from the cornfield, fir- ing at the retreating Federals, when Dayton saw more Yankee reinforcements forming at the far end of the field.

"Back!" Dayton shouted. "Back to the cornfield! Re-form the lines!"

The Eighteenth North Carolina wheeled at their leader's com- mand and ran for the cornfield. As the space between blue and gray widened, Union artillery opened fire.

Cannon shells shrieked their high-pitched song of death, striking the ground and exploding in orange and yellow flame. The roar was deafening as shell after shell rained down on the Eighteenth. Suddenly the double shriek of a pair of Union shells sounded in a deadly arc close behind them.

"Get down!" Dayton shouted at the top of his lungs.

Every man in the regiment dropped, hugging the ground as

tightly as he could. The earth shook as the cannonballs struck and exploded. As soon as shrapnel stopped hissing through the air, Dayton looked up and saw that some of his men up front had taken a direct hit. They were sprawled and crumpled like broken dolls.

"Get up and run!" shouted the major, scrambling to his feet. "The cornfield is out of their range!"

It was every man for himself. Dayton bolted with them, but when he drew near the men who had been hit, he saw movement. Sergeant Buster Camden was still alive!

Dayton halted and knelt by the wounded man while the Union artillery continued to bombard the fleeing Rebels. "I'll carry you, Buster," he said.

"No, Major. Go on. I'm done for anyway."

"No way I'm leaving you here."

Dayton heard the whine of another shell, sensed the concussion as it struck and exploded to his left. He felt something tug at his pant leg but paid it no mind. "Okay," he said, his hands running under Camden's body, "here we go."

When Dayton stood, his leg gave way. He cushioned Buster from the fall and looked down to see torn flesh and a piece of jagged black metal embedded in his thigh.

"Major!" gasped Camden. "Go on! The Yankees…"

Dayton looked over his shoulder. The Union infantry was coming like a deluge. "Can't leave you, Buster." He gritted his teeth against the pain and struggled to lift Camden.

The men of the Eighteenth staggered to a halt at the edge of the cornfield and looked back for the first time. Private Billy Dean Baxter's eyes bulged when he saw Dayton's predicament.

"It's the major," Baxter said. "I can't tell who the other man is.… The major's been hit too!"

"I'm going after them!" Everett Nichols shouted as he broke into a run. "Cover me!"

Four other men ran after him—Billy Dean Baxter, Buford Hall, Hank Upchurch, and Chuck Carney. "Cover us!" Upchurch shouted as they bent low, darting toward Dayton and the man he was trying vainly to lift.

The five running men now had the attention of Captain Jack Fleming, who was next in command. "Load up, men!" Fleming shouted. "Shoot around them and over their heads! They'll stay low!"

Rance Dayton saw his men running toward him and glanced back at the oncoming horde of blue uniforms.

"Go back! Go back!" he shouted. "There's no chance!"

The fearless five came on, bent low and zigzagging their way across the field. Billy Dean and Everett lifted the major as the other three hoisted Camden and took off running as fast as they could go. The Federals were now within range, and bullets began to zip and whistle around the rescuers.

Billy Dean grunted and went down, causing Everett to stumble and drop Dayton, who grimaced as his body struck the ground.

The men who were carrying Buster Camden paused.

"Go on!" shouted Dayton, gritting his teeth in pain.

"Billy Dean's dead, Major," Everett said.

"So's Buster," called Hank Upchurch.

"You guys carry the major; I'll be a shield," Carney said.

The other three men quickly had Dayton off the ground and were running toward their regiment, who were cheering them on.

"Look over there!" Carney shouted with a whoop.

A horde of Rebels were charging the Federals from the side, guns blazing. The Yankees left off their pursuit of Dayton and his gallant men and braced themselves for the fresh onslaught.

While the sounds of Union and Confederate guns thundered across the valley, Nurse Jodie Lockwood stood in a hospital tent on the edge of the battlefield and watched Dr. Hunter McGuire lift a patient off the operating table. Dr. McGuire, who was a childhood friend of

Stonewall Jackson's, was also his personal physician, as well as head physician of Jackson's II Corps.

What few hospital tents there were, on either side of the battle, didn't have sufficient doctors and nurses to keep up with the number of wounded men. Many died before they could be attended to.

Jodie cleaned the operating table quickly. As soon as the doctor laid the latest surgery patient on the ground outside, he would return with another wounded soldier. She glanced through the tent opening and could see bodies strewn so thickly on the field that there was hardly a place for the stretcher bearers to walk. Moans and cries could be heard above the nearby sounds of battle.

Jodie watched Dr. McGuire as he walked back to the tent, carrying his next patient as tenderly as he would a child. In spite of the tension in the air and the smell of blood, Jodie felt her heart grow warm at the sight of the handsome man she loved. His wavy, thick sand-colored hair fell across his forehead as he walked, and she longed to brush it back and smooth the furrow from between his eyes.

He entered the tent and gently laid the wounded man on the table. When Jodie moved up beside him, Hunter glanced at her and felt the warmth in her eyes and silently mouthed, *I love you.*

A slight smile curved her lips as she held his gaze.

Hunter McGuire had fallen in love with Jodie while doing intern work at a clinic in Lexington, Virginia, where Jodie worked as a nurse. Though Hunter didn't know it, Jodie had fallen in love with him, too, but circumstances separated them before they could tell one another how they felt.

Seven long years passed as Hunter searched for Jodie, praying earnestly that the Lord wouldn't let her marry another man before he found her.

It had taken the War for them to find each other. Both were working in the medical corps and had been assigned to Antietam. As grounds were being laid for battle along Antietam Creek, Hunter and Jodie had stumbled onto each other. They professed their love for each other, and Hunter had wasted no time proposing marriage. Now they were engaged.

Hunter and Jodie had just finished working on a patient when they heard shuffling footsteps outside the tent. They turned to see two exhausted, panting men carry Major Rance Dayton through the tent opening. Hunter focused on Dayton's pale features and the makeshift tourniquet on the major's leg. "Looks like you took a bullet, my friend," he said.

"Shrapnel," Dayton replied through clenched teeth.

"He asked us to bring him to you, Dr. McGuire," Chuck Carney said.

"All right," McGuire said, nodding. Then to Dayton, "I've got some other men in worse shape, Major, but I'll get to you as quickly as I can."

"That's fine, Doctor. I can wait."

Hunter turned toward Jodie and said, "This is Nurse Jodie Lockwood, Major. She'll check the tourniquet and give you some laudanum to ease the pain."

"Take good care of him, Doctor," Nichols said, as he and Carney headed for the tent flap. "We need him back to lead our regiment as soon as possible."

"Jodie and I will do our best," said McGuire. "You can bank on that."

It was almost sunset before doctor and nurse were able to put their full attention on Major Rance Dayton.

McGuire eased him onto the table, and Jodie removed the tourniquet. While the doctor scrutinized the chunk of shrapnel embedded in the major's leg, Dayton said, "Doc, you know the five men in my regiment from Fayetteville?"

McGuire nodded, noting how much flesh he would have to cut to get the shrapnel out.

"Those wonderful men risked their lives to rescue me."

"God bless them," said Jodie.

"Those boys are heroes, Doc. I've never seen such courage on a battlefield."

Jodie placed a flat tin plate that bore medical instruments beside Dayton's head. "Major," she said softly, "such love as those men showed you is a wonderful thing."

Tears welled up in Dayton's eyes, and he managed a slight smile as he said, "And don't I know it, ma'am. If ever I was called upon to hazard my life to save theirs, I'd do it without batting an eye."

"I'm sure you would," she said.

The tears spilled down Dayton's cheeks. "I...I only wish there was some way I could thank Billy Dean for giving his life to save mine."

It was a few minutes to midnight, and weary medical personnel on both sides of the Antietam battle were still working on wounded soldiers, doing all they could to save lives.

On the Confederate side, nurses dashed from tent to tent, seeking supplies their doctors had exhausted. Jodie had just given a portion of her laudanum to a nurse when she saw the tall, broad-shouldered form of General Jackson pass through the tent opening. He smiled and spoke to her.

Hunter McGuire, who was bent over a patient, looked over his shoulder and said, "Hello, Tom. I inquired about you earlier and the stretcher bearers told me you were all right. Thank the Lord for that."

Jackson smiled. "Hunter, I was told that Rance Dayton was brought to you with a hunk of shrapnel in his leg. They said you got it out without any trouble. He doing all right?"

"Yes. He's on the south side of the tent. There's a lantern in the corner not being used. Light it and go see if he's awake."

"I'm glad you didn't have to take the leg," Jackson said quietly.

"So am I. He'll be fine in a few weeks...won't even walk with a limp once it's completely healed."

Minutes later, Stonewall Jackson made his way among the wounded men. Most were asleep. He spotted Dayton and knelt beside him. The major turned his head, blinked at the lantern light, then focused his gaze on the face of the man who had taught him so well at V.M.I.

"Hello, General. I sure am glad to see you."

"Same here, Rance. I saw what you did out there today, risking yourself for Sergeant Camden. You're a brave man."

Dayton batted his eyelids. "How'd you see that?"

"Binoculars."

"So that's how you got two regiments of General Jubal Early's Brigade to intervene just in time!"

"Yes. And I also saw what those five men in your regiment did."

"Yes, sir. I was going to talk to you about them, sir. I sure would like to see them get some kind of commendation from General Lee."

Jackson grinned, rubbing his bearded chin. "I've already got that in mind," he said, pulling a slip of paper out of his shirt pocket. "Got it down right here, with all their names. I talked to some of the men in the regiment."

"Thank you, sir. They deserve to be honored."

"I've got a meeting with General Lee and General Longstreet in a few minutes, Rance. But one thing before I go…"

"I took care of it, sir."

Jackson's eyebrows arched in surprise. "You did? When?"

"When I came to, lying right here. I've been such a fool to put it off, General. When my mind came clear, it hit me that if I'd been killed out there today, I'd be in hell right now. The Lord was so good to me. Men dying all around. Even—even Billy Dean. I called on Jesus to save me, just like you've told me I should. I'm saved now, General. Thanks to you. If you hadn't pressed the gospel to me over and over—well…I know you've prayed for me all this time too."

"You're right about that," Jackson said, brushing tears from his eyes. "I'm so glad you opened your heart to Jesus."

"Best thing I ever did, sir. There's nothing like the peace I have in my heart right now. But then, you know about that, don't you?"

"There's a deep settled peace in my heart, put there by the Lord Himself the day He saved me as a boy. If in God's plan there should be an enemy bullet or cannonball out there with my name on it, I can die in peace, knowing that all is well between Tom Jackson and the One who died for him on Calvary's cross. I'm glad you know it now too."

"Yes, sir. I sure do."

"I have to get going," said the general, patting Dayton's shoulder as he rose to his feet. "I'll check on you again tomorrow."

TWO

During the night of September 18, 1862, General Robert E. Lee led his battered Army of Northern Virginia to the banks of the moon-dappled Potomac River at Shepardstown, Maryland. Heavy of heart, the silver-haired Confederate leader guided Traveler, his horse, into the river and halted in the four-foot water midway. From there he watched his troops move past him and touch ground on the opposite bank in the Old Dominion.

Soon Major General Stonewall Jackson appeared in front of his II Corps, rode to the middle of the river, and drew up beside Lee. The general's shadowed face beneath the brim of his hat showed the deep distress he was feeling. He was only fifty-five years old, but tonight he looked twenty years older.

Jackson was trying to think of something to say when Lee spoke in a broken voice. "Well, so ends our Maryland campaign."

"Yes, sir," said the younger man, who would be thirty-nine in four months. "I know you're feeling the weight of our losses, but please don't punish yourself."

Lee sighed. "This battle will go down in history as the bloodiest day in this War, Thomas J." He paused, then added, "That is, unless we have a worse one later. I figure we lost over three thousand men today. We've got better than seven thousand wounded…and a great many of *them* will die."

"I realize that, sir, but—"

"Don't use a soft cushion on me, General Jackson. If a military leader is willing to accept the glory when he's been victorious, he must be willing to take the blame when he's not."

"But we probably killed and wounded just as many Yankees, sir. It was more like a draw than a victory for either side."

"It isn't a draw when one army turns tail and runs back home," Lee said.

"But you're leading us back into Virginia because we're nearly out of ammunition, sir. You have no choice."

"I know, Thomas J., but it was yours truly who made the choice to invade Yankee territory. There was no decided victory in this campaign for the Confederacy. The blame lies with the man who walks under Robert Edward Lee's hat." He choked and swallowed hard. "So many men dead. So many wounded…"

Jackson hipped around in the saddle and watched the troops as they forded the river. They were coming through slowly: caissons, howitzers, cavalrymen on horseback, infantry. At the end of the line were the ambulances and wagons carrying the wounded.

Some of the Confederate medical staff rode along to care for them. The rest of the medical staff had stayed behind to care for the vast number of wounded men who were in no condition to travel. Lee had left enough men, mules, ambulances, and wagons behind to transport the wounded back to Virginia when they were well enough to withstand the long hours on rough roads. Many of those left behind would have to be buried before the last wagons and ambulances headed south.

Jackson thought of his medical chief of staff, Dr. Hunter McGuire. Hunter and Jodie had asked to remain behind where they could do the most good. "Bless 'em, Lord," he said aloud.

Lee turned and looked at his right-hand man. "What say, General?"

"Oh, just something between me and the Lord, sir."

Lee nodded and turned his tired eyes to the lines of men and equipment making their way onto friendly soil.

When the last wagon had crossed the river, Lee left General William Pendleton and his artillery on a bluff above the Potomac in case the Yankees decided to follow. Lee and Jackson then trotted ahead of the lines and called for them to haul up deep in the Virginia woods about five miles south of the Potomac.

"We'll make camp here, men," said Lee, riding amongst them with Jackson at his side. "We'll rest here tonight and hope Little Mac doesn't decide to come after us first thing in the morning."

"Do you think he will, General Lee?" called out a young sergeant.

"He might. Abe Lincoln's going to chew him up and spit him out if he doesn't."

"But what will we fight them with, General?" came another voice. "Aren't we out of ammunition?"

"Almost," said Lee. "But we've reserved enough for rifles and howitzers to give them a fight if they come after us. If we run out, we'll do as General Jackson has taught II Corps—we'll throw rocks, use our fists, and gnash on them with our teeth!"

A rousing cheer went up.

Jackson leaned close to Lee and said, "They don't sound like defeated men, General. I still say you're too hard on yourself."

Lee nodded and managed a tight grin.

When the battered army had eaten their rations, what few military band members there were among them took their instruments out of the wagons. They huddled close beneath the trees, and one of them said, "We've got some Marylanders among us who fought the Yankees with everything they had—on their own soil. How about we show them our appreciation by playing a little of 'Maryland, My Maryland'?"

The others agreed and struck up the band with the familiar song. They weren't more than five or six bars into it when there were loud boos and hisses while angry voices shouted for them to stop.

"All we want to hear is 'Dixie'!" came a loud voice.

When the band played "Dixie," the boos and hisses turned to shouts, cheers, and whistles of approval.

General Lee quietly made his way to a solitary spot in the shadows and sat down on a fallen tree, then bent his head and wept. Over and over he half-whispered, "So many men...so many dead. So many wounded...so many more will die..."

Stonewall Jackson's aide, Private Henry Kyd Douglas, had stayed behind to help bring the wounded along when they were able to travel. Another aide, Private Jim Lewis, drew up to Jackson as he was removing Little Sorrel's bridle and said, "Let me do that, sir. I'll take care of your horse. You go get some rest."

At the same moment, Jackson saw Major Rance Dayton hobbling toward him on the two broken tree branches he was using for crutches.

"Sir," Dayton said, "could we go talk to General Lee? He's sitting alone over there behind those trees."

"Sure," said Jackson, handing the bridle to Lewis. "Thanks, Jim."

"It's my job, sir. And my pleasure."

General Lee heard the snap of twigs on the forest floor. He lifted his head as the two officers drew up, and started to rise.

"Oh, no, sir," said Jackson. "Don't get up. We'll sit down with you."

Jackson helped the major ease onto another fallen log and then sat down beside him.

In the moonlight, Lee's drawn features showed the strain he was under as he said, "I'm sorry about your wound, Major Dayton."

"I'll be fine, sir, thanks to the skilled hands of Dr. Hunter McGuire. He says I'll not even limp once the wound heals."

"There's none better than Dr. McGuire, that's for sure," said Lee. "What can I do for you gentlemen?"

"We wanted to tell you about the young men of the Eighteenth North Carolina who rescued Major Dayton, sir," said Jackson.

"Ah, yes. General Jackson told me about the incident while we were making preparations to pull out awhile ago, Major Dayton. Four young heroes rescued you from certain death, at the risk of their own lives. And he told me about—" Lee pulled a crumpled slip of paper from his shirt pocket and held it toward a patch of moonlight "—Private Billy Dean Baxter being killed in the rescue attempt."

"Yes, sir," Dayton said quietly, adjusting his position to make his wounded leg more comfortable.

Lee cleared his throat and said, "I was deeply touched by the story when General Jackson related it to me. I agree with him that the men who rescued you are to be commended."

Rance's face brightened.

Lee rubbed his chin thoughtfully. "Major Dayton, General Jackson also told me these were the same men, along with yourself, that I commended in person for going above and beyond the call of duty at Harper's Ferry."

"Yes, sir."

"Well, I'd like those men brought to me immediately."

Dayton's eyes lit up. "Yes, *sir!*"

"Stay where you are, Major," said Jackson, rising to his feet. "I'll bring them."

When Jackson returned in less than five minutes, General Lee and Major Dayton were standing.

Lee smiled as he watched the eager young faces draw near. When the men were shoulder to shoulder in front of the Confederate leader, they saluted and stood at attention.

"General Lee, sir," Chuck Carney said, "General Jackson informed us you wanted to see us immediately. Privates Everett Nichols, Buford Hall, Hank Upchurch, and Chuck Carney at your service, sir. You met us after the Harper's Ferry incident, sir, but I wasn't sure if you would remember our names."

Lee smiled. "To be honest, Private Carney, I wouldn't have

recalled your names. Thank you for giving them to me."

"Yes, sir."

Lee took a deep breath. "Let me say first, gentlemen, that I am deeply sorry about the loss of your friend, Billy Dean Baxter."

"Thank you, sir," the four said nearly in unison.

"You young men went much further today than your gallantry at Harper's Ferry. General Jackson has told me what *he* saw, and filled me in on what Major Dayton told him. What you men—and your friend Baxter—did on that battlefield today is of the utmost valor. To risk your lives to save the life of Major Dayton without the least reservation tells me you men are the backbone and fiber of what the Confederate army is all about. My only regret is that I come up short for words. I cannot express myself fully as I say that I commend you from the depths of this soldier's heart. You are fine, brave young men. I am proud to be in the same army with you, and I salute you!"

The privates flushed with mixed pleasure and embarrassment as the commander of the Army of Northern Virginia snapped them a salute.

"And furthermore, gentlemen," said Lee, "I am making plans to have you honored by President Jefferson Davis and myself at a public ceremony held for this singular purpose at the Confederate capitol in Richmond. This is the kind of heroism that needs to be instilled in all the men of the Confederacy who wear the gray uniform."

Everett Nichols cleared his throat and said, "May I say something, General Lee?"

"Of course."

Nichols licked his lips nervously. "Sir, I'm sure I speak for my comrades here. We're pleasantly stunned that what we did on the battlefield today has gained such recognition from you, but we don't really deserve the public recognition you have planned. We…we're honored, but we're just plain Southern boys who simply did what we could to keep our major from getting killed."

Buford Hall and Chuck Carney nodded their agreement as Hank Upchurch said, "That's right, General. We're really not worthy. We—"

"Nonsense," cut in Lee. "You gentlemen are perfect examples of what Confederate soldiers ought to be. You *will* be honored with public recognition. You've earned it. When President Davis and I present you to the crowd of soldiers and civilians, you are going to have your moment of glory. I appreciate your humility, and I know it's genuine, but my mind is made up. And General Jackson knows that when I make up my mind to do something, there's no deterring me. Right, General?"

"Right, sir," said Jackson, smiling.

"I will set the date for the ceremony when I arrive in Richmond," said Lee. "I'll get in touch with you through Major Dayton. Now, you gentlemen go get yourselves some much needed and deserved rest."

The six men bade Lee good night and walked away slowly to accommodate Rance Dayton, who hobbled on his makeshift crutches. As they moved through camp, weaving around the men, animals, and equipment, Buford Hall said, "Major Dayton, we appreciate your bringing about this commendation."

"Fellas," Dayton said, "it would never have been done without General Jackson telling General Lee about it."

"General, sir," said Chuck Carney, "as Everett has already stated, we really don't deserve this public commendation. But it will mean more to us than anything that has ever happened in our lives."

It was after midnight, and Stonewall Jackson was inside his tent, on his knees in prayer, when he heard the sounds of pounding horse's hooves and voices. Seconds later, a sentry stood outside his tent and said, "General Jackson, sir..."

"Yes," called the commander of II Corps, opening the flap.

"It's General Pendleton, sir," said the sentry. "He needs to see you."

Jackson looked past him and saw Pendleton's vague form in the shadows. "Come in, General."

When Pendleton stepped inside, he was out of breath. His words came in fits and starts.

"McClellan...the river...blue-clads got over..."

Not only had Major General McClellan crossed the Potomac to pursue the battered Confederates, he had been successful in capturing all of Pendleton's big guns. And he was heading toward the very spot where the Rebels had camped for the night.

Jackson's first thought was for General A. P. Hill and the Light Division. He hurried to find Hill, and within twenty minutes the Light Division was on its way to confront the Union soldiers.

Hill's rugged troops raced into withering, shattering artillery fire, but they kept moving forward, blasting away with their guns, determined to stop McClellan.

Before the sun appeared on the horizon, Hill's division had the Federals in the Potomac, scrambling for the other bank. The Confederates fired their muskets without mercy, downing one Yankee after another, and soon the Potomac was clogged with blue-clad bodies.

The Confederates recaptured all but four cannons, lost 261 men, but saved their army. It was near total disaster for the Yankees.

McClellan didn't try it again.

Abraham Lincoln's private secretary, John Hay, entered his White House office early on Monday morning, September 22. He was at his desk at 7:50 when the door to the Oval Office opened, and the tall, gangly Lincoln appeared.

"Good morning, John," said the president, looking very tired. "Bring your note pad and come in."

Hay followed the president toward his desk and sat down in his usual chair. "Are you all right, Mr. President?" he asked. "You look as if you haven't slept."

"I didn't get much sleep last night, John, but I'm ready for you to make the announcement to the press."

"All right, sir," said the secretary, poising his pencil above the pad. "Which newspapers?"

"Both Washington papers, Baltimore's, New York's, Chicago's, and Boston's. Once they have it, the rest will pick it up, and the Southern newspapers will have it by Wednesday."

"All right, sir," Hay said with a nod, writing fast.

"And John, make sure they all understand that the Emancipation Proclamation comes on the heels of our Union victory on the banks of Antietam Creek last Wednesday, and that it's to take effect January 1."

"Yes, sir."

"And be sure the newspapers understand that the Proclamation is a fit and necessary war measure designed to suppress the Southern rebellion. My purpose is to deplete the Southern manpower reserve in slaves. And you can add that I believe it will enhance the Union cause abroad. Especially in Great Britain."

"I'll get it right on the wire, Mr. President," said Hay, rising.

"Good. September 23 will be the big day for the newspapers to announce it all over the North." Lincoln glanced at the grandfather clock in the corner. "Now, General Halleck ought to be out there in your office waiting to see me."

Hay hastened to open the door and peer into the outer office. "Yes, sir. General Halleck is here."

Henry W. Halleck was Lincoln's general-in-chief of all the Union forces. Tough as harness leather and bullheaded, he was a short, stout man in his mid-fifties, with a built-in scowl. His coarse gray hair was always tousled. As soon as the door opened, he rushed through it and said, "Good morning, Mr. President. I appreciate your giving me a few minutes on this busy Monday."

Lincoln was already on his feet behind the desk. "Good morning to *you*, General. My time is your time when it comes to war matters. And I assume it is a war matter this morning."

Halleck took the chair John Hay had vacated and said, "I hope, sir, you have decided to put the Emancipation Proclamation on hold until you replace McClellan with a good man and we win us a decided victory."

Lincoln's lips pulled into a thin line as he sat down, resting his bony elbows on top of the desk. "As a matter of fact, General, I have Mr. Hay contacting the major Northern newspapers right now to let them know that as of tomorrow, I am announcing that the Proclamation will take effect January 1."

Halleck's face darkened. "Pardon me, Mr. President, but I think the announcement that you're going to free all the slaves would give a much stronger moral weight to the Union war effort if it came on the heels of a victorious battle. It would show we have the power to back it up."

"We *did* just have a victorious battle, General," said the president. "A week ago today."

Halleck snorted, running his hand over his mouth and nose. "Sir, I don't know how you can call what happened at Sharpsburg a victory. Tactically, at best, it was a stalemate."

"Not so in my estimation, General Halleck. Lee's withdrawal across the Potomac into Virginia transformed your tactical stalemate into a strategic victory for our side."

Halleck, who had been trying to talk the president into replacing McClellan for months, spoke bluntly. "You say that, even if that pint-sized would-be Napoleon couldn't so much as hold on to Pendleton's big guns, and he let Ambrose Hill's little handful drive him back into the river like a whipped dog with his tail between his legs?"

Lincoln eased back in his chair and rubbed his deep-set eyelids. "It was still a decided victory for the Union, because Robert E. Lee invaded Northern territory and was driven back to where he came from. Now, I didn't say I was happy with General McClellan's performance. As far as I'm concerned, he could've repelled Lee had he arrived at Sharpsburg earlier, before Lee had fortified his troops on the banks of the Antietam. General McClellan has once again demonstrated his lack of aggressiveness toward the enemy. If he hadn't been so slow getting his army to Sharpsburg, Lee's forces could have been vanquished once and for all right there."

"Well, sir," said the general-in-chief, "you've accused General McClellan of the 'slows' numerous times already. In my position, I have to know if you're going to keep putting up with it or are you going to do something about it?"

"You are aware, my friend," said Lincoln, "as are other men in high places in the United States government, that I'm having serious thoughts about relieving General McClellan of his command. I haven't been hasty to do so because I must choose wisely the man to replace him. The wrong choice could make things worse than they already are. At least General McClellan has the love and respect of his men, in spite of his 'slows.'"

Halleck ran stubby fingers through his tousled gray hair. "Yes, sir. I understand. But may I say with all due respect to you...while General McClellan is in command of the Army of the Potomac, we're wasting valuable time. If we don't hurry up and wipe the Rebel armies out, they'll wipe *us* out. I'm in no position to tell you what to do, but I certainly hope you make a decision soon."

On the same day the Emancipation Proclamation hit the headlines of the Northern newspapers, Dr. Hunter McGuire and Nurse Jodie Lockwood left Sharpsburg, Maryland, and went to Frederick, where Jodie had been working. There, they agreed on a December wedding.

Since General Stonewall Jackson had told McGuire to go to Richmond and meet him there, or learn where to find him, Jodie quit her job and went with Hunter. She would probably have lost her job anyway when it came out that she'd aided a Confederate doctor at the Antietam battle.

Hunter and Jodie made some visits south of the Mason-Dixon

line, including a quick stop at the Jackson home in Lexington. They found the general at home and enjoyed meeting Mary Anna, who was expecting their first baby. General Jackson said he would be home a little while longer, then would go to Richmond. Hunter should wait for him at the army camp outside the city. If for some reason General Lee sent him elsewhere, he would wire Hunter at the camp and tell him where to join him.

Hunter and Jodie arrived in Richmond on September 29. Using his medical influence as chief physician of Stonewall Jackson's II Corps, Hunter was able to get Jodie a job at the large hospital in Richmond.

With this settled, he took her to a boardinghouse a block from the hospital, where many of the single nurses resided. She obtained a room, and Hunter carried up her little bit of luggage.

As he placed the luggage on the sofa, he said, "I've got to get myself to the army camp outside of town."

"You'll come and see me every opportunity you get, won't you?" she asked, walking him toward the door.

"I'll even *make* opportunities." Hunter took Jodie in his arms and kissed her tenderly. "I love you, Jodie."

"I love you too."

They kissed again, then Hunter stepped into the hallway. "I'll have to stick pretty close to the camp until Tom either shows up or I receive a wire telling me where to meet him. I'll visit you as much as I can, but I may have to go in a hurry. But before I leave Richmond, I'll let you know where I'm going."

Tears misted Jodie's eyes. "Oh, Hunter, I'll be so glad when this horrible war is over. When we get married I want us to be able to live a normal life."

He grinned. "I know what you mean, but a doctor who has his own practice doesn't exactly live a normal life."

Jodie stood on tiptoe, kissed him again, and said, "At least when you've got your own practice, we won't have to worry about cannon-balls crashing through the roof."

THREE

On Wednesday evening, October 1, Pastor John Griffin of Richmond's First Baptist Church smiled as he looked across his desk at Hunter McGuire and Jodie Lockwood.

"Because of your positive testimonies as believers," he said, "it will be my pleasure to perform your marriage ceremony."

Hunter clasped Jodie's hand as he said, "This church comes highly recommended by many of the men at the army camp outside of town, Pastor. And if the kind of preaching we heard in the service tonight is any indication of what the folks hear around here on Sundays, we're going to feel right at home."

Griffin's smiled broadened. "Well, I preach the same truth whether it's the midweek service, Sunday morning, or Sunday night. I hope the Lord will lead you to put your membership here. I know that with this war going on, and your lives being so chaotic, it's hard to settle on anything. But we sure would love to have you be a part of us."

"Thank you, Pastor," said Hunter. "You're our kind of preacher, I'll tell you that." He glanced at Jodie and she nodded.

"We were both brought up on old-fashioned straight-from-the-shoulder Bible preaching, Pastor Griffin," said Jodie. "And I really liked what I heard tonight too. I love the way you exalted the Lord Jesus Christ."

"He deserves all the glory we can give Him, and a whole lot more, Miss Lockwood," said Griffin.

"Amen," said Hunter, rising from his chair and gently tugging Jodie's hand.

The preacher stood up with them and said, "I'll be willing to work with you on whatever date you set for the wedding. I realize your plans could be interrupted, no matter what date you set. But if that happens, we'll just make the necessary adjustments."

As he walked them to the door, the pastor said, "You might think about a date sometime near Christmas. Maybe both sides will decide not to fight at Christmastime."

"Thank you, Pastor," said Hunter. "We'll see you Sunday morning, Lord willing."

Late on Friday afternoon, Jodie walked past the receptionist's desk at Richmond's hospital after a hard day's work and told the girl at the desk that she would see her the next day. She was almost to the front door when it opened and the man she loved appeared.

"Hello, gorgeous," said Hunter with a big smile. "Busy day?"

Jodie let out a sigh. "Yes…but I feel refreshed now just seeing you."

"Aren't you sweet," he said, taking her hand and leading her toward the army wagon he'd borrowed at the camp.

"Is this visit an indication that you're about to leave Richmond?" Jodie asked. "Did you get a wire from General Jackson?"

"Yes. About an hour ago."

"Oh? Where will you meet him?"

"A place that will surprise you."

"Well, smarty, out with it. When are you leaving?"

"Depends on you."

Jodie looked perplexed. "Me? I don't understand."

"It all depends on whether you want to go with me or not. Because I'm not going unless you go with me."

They had reached the wagon, and as Hunter helped Jodie board, she said, "But you have to go wherever the general orders you to go. You've got me confused, Dr. McGuire."

"It's quite simple, really. You and I have received an invitation to the Jackson home."

"Really? Right away?"

"Yes," Hunter said, rounding the back side of the wagon. As he climbed aboard and took the reins, he said, "Tom's going to be home until a week from Monday, as far as he knows at this time. He and Mary Anna want us to come for whatever time we can between now and then. You start the midnight shift this Sunday night, if I remember correctly."

"Yes…"

"And you have Tuesday and Wednesday off?"

"Well, I don't actually go to work till midnight on Thursday."

Hunter put the horses in motion. "So, would you like to go stay with the Jacksons a couple of days?"

"Oh, I'd love it, Hunter! I really fell in love with Mary Anna when we were there before. Did the general say anything in the wire about how she's feeling?"

"No, but I'm sure that if she was having any trouble with her pregnancy, he wouldn't have invited us. He said in the wire that *they* wanted us to come."

"Wonderful! So what do we do next?"

"We'll go right now to the railroad station and get our tickets. Then I'll wire Tom and let him know the arrival time, and how long we can stay."

Jodie chuckled. "You know, I still have a hard time adjusting to you calling him Tom."

Hunter grinned as he guided the team around a corner and headed for the depot. "Well, honey, even though I address him as General when we're in the presence of anyone other than Mary Anna or you, he's been Tom to me ever since I can remember. Though he's a few years older than I, we were the best of friends as boys. We did a lot of growing up together until the McGuires adopted me and took me to Boston."

"Yes. But he's such a great man, Hunter, and a magnificent soldier. I understand about you, but I could never call him by his first name."

Hunter chuckled. "Want to hear something?"

"What?"

"He told me outside the hospital tent at Sharpsburg that he hoped you would call him Tom whenever we were alone with him."

"He did?"

"Yes'm. He sure did."

Jodie blushed. "Hunter, I could never do it."

"Why not? We hadn't been at their house ten minutes the other time when Mary Anna told you not to call her Mrs. Jackson. You started calling her Mary Anna immediately."

"I know, but it's different with him. His position as major general, and the…well, the dignity he carries. I couldn't do it."

"It'll make him happy."

"And it'll make me uncomfortable."

Hunter purchased their tickets at the depot then drove her to the army camp, where he sent a wire to Stonewall Jackson to advise him they would arrive in Lexington at midafternoon on Tuesday and leave on Thursday morning.

Then they went for supper at the Capitol Café. They hadn't been seated long before they began to talk again about the Jacksons.

"Let's see now…Mary Anna's baby is due in December, isn't it?" Hunter asked.

"Yes. Unless her doctor has changed his mind about the due date, it's to be the first week of December."

"Well, then, if we took Pastor Griffin's advice and set the wedding close to Christmas, she would no doubt be up to being your matron of honor."

"Mm-hmm. I was thinking the same thing. What about December 20? We agreed we should get married on a Saturday, and the twentieth is the last Saturday before Christmas."

"Strange how great minds run on the same track," he said, chuckling. "I was going to suggest the same thing to you. I was studying a calendar just this morning at the camp."

"Then December 20 it is," said Jodie, her eyes glistening with joy.

The waitress came and took their order and filled two cups with steaming coffee.

"On Sunday we'll talk to Pastor Griffin and tell him the date," Hunter said.

Jodie's smile reflected the joy she felt as she said, "The Lord has been so good to me, Hunter. All those years we were apart I kept praying that in His own way and in His own time He would let us find each other. Of course, I had to pray that He wouldn't let you fall in love with someone else, since you didn't even know how I felt about you."

"It was the same with me," Hunter said. "The Lord made you for me as sure as he made Eve for Adam. He already had it worked out. How would either of us have guessed He would use this awful war to bring us together?"

"We couldn't have guessed that, darling. But isn't it wonderful to serve the great God of the universe? He not only loved us enough to send His Son, but He also loves His children so much that He plans out their lives."

Hunter nodded. "That's why it behooves us to walk close to Him so we don't mess up His plans with some of our own. No Christian will ever go wrong if they walk close to Him."

Just then the waitress came with their food. As she was placing it on the table, Hunter said, "I'm so hungry I could eat a bear!"

"Sorry to disappoint you, sir," said the waitress, "but all you get in this place is the fried chicken you ordered. We don't cook bears here."

Hunter and Jodie laughed out of all proportion to the waitress's quip. It felt so good to let go after all the pain, misery, and death they had seen on the Antietam battlefield.

A storm was rolling in from the west, and it was beginning to rain in Richmond as Hunter and Jodie boarded the train for Lexington. Masses of inky clouds boiled overhead, driven by high winds, and a fork of white lightning flashed. Thunder followed like the booming of cannons.

Far to the east the sky was still clear, with shafts of orange light shooting up from the rising sun to touch the dark, encroaching clouds.

Inside their coach, Hunter guided his fiancée to a seat near the front and said, "There you go, sweetheart. You sit next to the window."

"I won't argue about that," said Jodie. "I want to get a good look at the Blue Ridge Mountains in this storm."

Hunter placed their hand luggage in the rack overhead and was just sitting down beside her when she pointed out the window at the Rebel soldiers boarding the train. Some were climbing on top of the cars. "I'm glad they always have soldiers on these trains, Hunter."

"Me too."

"But those poor men riding on top are going to get soaked."

"I guess that's part of the Jefferson Davis Protection Program," Hunter said, chuckling. "If these trains are going to be safe for civilians to ride, the army has to guard them, no matter what the weather."

Jodie nodded. Then, after a moment, she said, "I just wish the Yankees would all go back north where they belong and leave the Southerners alone. This war isn't accomplishing anything but getting a lot of good men on both sides killed or maimed. I don't believe the Southern plantation owners should be into slavery...not for a minute. But getting thousands and thousands of men killed over it isn't the answer. War is such a horrible thing."

"Can't argue with that," said Hunter. "War has been a blight on the human race ever since Cain declared war on Abel."

"Thank the Lord the day is coming when Jesus will return to earth and set up His kingdom and put an end to war," said Jodie.

"Won't that be wonderful! When the Prince of Peace reigns on earth, this battle-scarred old world will finally know real peace."

Jodie and Hunter noticed an elderly man being helped into the coach by the conductor and another man. The two men guided him to the seat across the aisle from them.

The old gentleman thanked the conductor, then the man with him said, "Now Grandpa, when you arrive in Amherst, Paul and Della will be there to meet you. Don't try to get off the train by yourself. Let Paul and this nice conductor help you, okay?"

"All right, Ronald," said the old man, whom Hunter guessed was somewhere in his late eighties.

"I'll look after him, sir," the conductor said.

Ronald thanked the conductor and left the coach. After a few seconds, the conductor exited the coach at the opposite end. The engine whistle blew.

Hunter crossed the aisle and leaned over the old gentleman. "Hello, sir," he said. "My name is Hunter McGuire. I'm a medical doctor."

The elderly man smiled and raised a shaky hand. As Hunter shook his hand, the old man said with quavering voice, "Are you the Dr. Hunter McGuire who heads up the medical staff for Stonewall Jackson's II Corps?"

Hunter nodded.

"Well, I'm proud to make your acquaintance, young man. My name is Grover Maddox. You know my grandson, Dr. Wayne Maddox."

"I sure do! He's one of my staff physicians in II Corps."

"Well, let me tell you, Wayne thinks the world of you. He's written home about you several times. In fact, I got a letter from him just a few days ago. He was telling me about the horror of that battle near Sharpsburg, Maryland. Pretty bloody, eh?"

"Yes, sir," said Hunter. "Well, I just wanted to let you know who I am, so that if you should need me on the trip, I'm right here to help."

"Thank you, Doctor." Grover Maddox glanced past Hunter. "This lovely lady your wife?"

"Not yet, sir. Her name is Jodie Lockwood. She's a certified medical nurse. We're getting married in December."

"Well, congratulations to both of you!"

"Thank you, sir," said Jodie, smiling at him warmly.

The train lurched, and Hunter grabbed the edge of the old man's seat. "So you're going to Amherst, Mr. Maddox?"

"Going to visit one of my granddaughters and her husband. I'll stay about a month. My wife, Sadie, died two years ago. Since I'm getting up in years, some of my family members take me into their homes for a month or so to spend some time with me."

"That's nice of them."

The train was rolling out of the station now, and as the conductor came through the front door, ready to punch tickets, two Confederate soldiers could be seen, rifles in hand, standing on the platform between cars.

Hunter sat down beside Jodie just as stark white lightning cracked through the black clouds. A roar of thunder vibrated the coach, and rain splattered the window, sending tiny rivulets down the panes.

The conductor walked to the rear of the coach, wheeled about, and worked his way forward. "Tickets, please!" he said. "Have your tickets ready!"

The train was at full speed by the time the conductor reached Grover Maddox. The old gentleman handed him his ticket with shaky fingers and then replaced it in his coat pocket after it was punched.

Jodie peered through the window, trying to see the beautiful Virginia countryside through the rain. Hunter watched her and then took her hand and leaned close, saying, "I love you."

She turned and met his gaze and whispered a response.

When Hunter glanced across the aisle toward Grover Maddox, then looked back to Jodie, she said, "Go ahead, darling. If you weren't here to do it, I would."

"The Holy Spirit's really running wild in my heart," he said.

"I'll be praying."

Hunter squeezed her hand and slipped across the aisle to sit next to Grover Maddox.

The old man turned to Hunter with a smile. "Some storm, eh?"

Hunter nodded. "Sure is. Mr. Maddox…you mentioned a few minutes ago that your wife died."

"That's right."

"I'd like to ask you a question, if I may?"

"Certainly."

"Mr. Maddox, when your time comes to die, do you know that you'll go to heaven?"

"Can't say that I do, son. Nobody can know for certain."

"Oh, but they can, sir. God says so in His Word."

Maddox licked his wrinkled lips. "You sound just like Sadie and some of my relatives, Doctor. Sadie was always telling me about Jesus being in her heart, and begging me to believe on Him. I believe in Jesus Christ, Doctor, but not like Sadie did. She was consumed with Him. Just like some of the other relatives…even the two I'm going to visit in Amherst—my granddaughter, Della, and her husband, Paul."

"What do you mean by *consumed*, Mr. Maddox?"

"Well, always going to church, and having friends in from the church for a hymn sing…talking about how wonderful it is to be saved and know you're going to heaven. That's just a crutch, Doctor. A shaky crutch. I say nobody can know whether they're going to heaven or hell until they die and stand before God at the judgment and find out if their good deeds outweigh the bad."

Hunter nodded. "Well, when you say you believe in Jesus, but not like your wife and some family members…what do you mean?"

"I believe He was a good man and did a lot of good for people when He was here on earth…and He looks down on us from heaven right now. But every person has to prove to Him that they deserve heaven in order to get in."

"So you do believe that Jesus rose from the dead after He was crucified, and He's in heaven right now?"

"Oh, sure."

"And you believe that He's more than just a good man. You believe that He's the virgin-born Son of God?"

"Sure. That's what the Bible says, doesn't it?"

"Yes, sir, it does. And it also says that Jesus came into the world for one purpose: to save sinners from hell. In order to do that He had to pay the price that God's holiness and justice demanded—a blood-shedding death as the sacrificial Lamb of God. Do you believe that?"

"Well-l-l…yes."

"And the same Bible says that you can know you're going to heaven when you die. You don't have to guess or wonder about it."

"Sadie did show me something about that, Doctor, but it just didn't fit with the way I believe it."

"Well, sir, what your wife believed is based on God's Word. On what do you base your belief?"

"On what I feel in my heart."

"Just a minute," Hunter said and stepped across the aisle to get his Bible out of a small overnight bag. He sat back down beside the older man and flipped some pages as he said, "Let me show you what God says about the human heart, Mr. Maddox, including yours."

Hunter turned to Jeremiah 17 and placed the Bible in the old gentleman's hands. "Can you read the print, sir?"

"Hold on," said Maddox, reaching in his shirt pocket. He took out a pair of half-moon spectacles, placed them on his nose, and hooked the wires behind his ears. "Now I can."

"All right. Read me verse 9, right there. This is what God says about the human heart."

Grover read the verse silently at first, then aloud, "'The heart is deceitful above all things, and desperately wicked: who can know it?'"

"All right, sir. According to the next verse, who does search the heart and know it?"

"God does."

"Since your heart, like mine, is deceitful above all things, is it capable of deceiving you?"

Maddox thought on it briefly, then said, "I suppose so."

"Will God deceive you, Mr. Maddox?"

"Well, of course not."

"Then, rather than listen to your heart, you ought to listen to God's Word. Shouldn't you?"

Another pause. "Ah…well, yes."

"That's what Sadie did, sir. Am I right?"

"Yes, she did."

"Then she did the right thing, didn't she?"

"Yes. I see that now."

"And I know for a fact that your grandson, Wayne, does the same thing, sir. He and I have talked about it. He's a fine Christian man."

"That he is, Doctor."

Hunter flipped back to the book of 1 John, chapter 5. "I want you to see what God says about those who have believed on the name of His Son. Read me verse 13, Mr. Maddox. When God speaks of these things that have been written, He's talking about the Scriptures."

The old man read aloud: "'These things have I written unto you that believe on the name of the Son of God; that ye may know that ye have eternal life, and that ye may believe on the name of the Son of God.'"

"Do you understand, sir?" Hunter asked. "God says that He gave us the Scriptures so that we could learn of salvation in His Son and believe on His name. If we believe on His name the Bible way, He saves us, and we can know—not hope or think or wish—but *know* that we have eternal life while we're right here on earth."

The old man shook his head. "Why have I been so blind, Doctor? Sadie and many of my family tried to tell me this, but I just couldn't see it."

Hunter nodded encouragingly and said, "The Lord has to open our eyes to see the truth, Mr. Maddox. The psalmist wrote in Psalm 119, 'The entrance of thy words giveth light; it giveth understanding unto the simple.'"

Grover Maddox looked at Hunter with a new light in his eyes as he said, "Well, I see the light, and I've sure been simple. Now it comes back to me what Sadie and the others told me. To believe on the name of Jesus Christ is to believe that He is the one and only Saviour who does all the saving all by Himself, without human works or religious deeds, and to turn in repentance of my sin and un-belief and call on Him to save me."

"They've taught you well, sir. That's it!"

"I'm ready, Doctor. Will you help me?"

Jodie had been watching the scene as she prayed. Now she was wiping tears and thanking the Holy Spirit for working in Grover Maddox's heart.

When the old gentleman had finished calling on Jesus, Hunter prayed and asked the Lord to help him grow in his new Christian life.

Maddox, wiping tears from his cheeks, said, "What a fool I've been all these years, Dr. McGuire. If I had died as a fool, I would have gone to hell...and I would never have seen my precious Sadie again."

"That's right."

"But now that I'm saved, when I die I'll go to be with her in heaven! I'll see her and hold her again, Doctor!"

"That you will, sir," said Hunter, patting his arm.

"Thank you for talking to me, Dr. McGuire. Thank you!"

"It was my honor and pleasure, sir."

"I'm so happy for you, Mr. Maddox," came Jodie's voice nearby. Both men looked up to see her standing beside them.

The train rolled westward, making a few stops along the way. Each depot had its share of gray-clad Rebel soldiers who stood sharp-eyed and alert.

The storm moved further eastward, and soon the rain stopped and the clouds broke up, letting the sun's rays shine through.

Jodie pressed her cheek to the window, trying to see if the rugged line of the Blue Ridge was in view yet.

"You should be able to see them pretty soon," Hunter said, "but instead of the storm, you'll see those mountains in sunshine."

"Either way is fine," she replied, glancing past him to Grover Maddox, whose head was cushioned by a pillow as he leaned against the window with eyes closed. "Mr. Grover's had quite a nap."

Hunter glanced at the older man and nodded.

"Where is Amherst, Hunter? Will Mr. Maddox be getting off soon?"

"It's about ten miles this side of the Blue Ridge. Last depot before we enter the mountains and come out at Lexington on the other side. We should be in Amherst in about an hour and a half."

Jodie nodded and laid her head on his shoulder. "Wake me when we can see the mountains, will you, darling?"

"Sure."

Jodie was dreaming about their wedding when she felt Hunter's shoulder move and heard his voice. "Honey, I'm sorry to disturb you, but—"

"Oh, can we see the mountains now?" she asked, straightening on the seat and brushing stray locks of hair from her forehead. She pressed her cheek to the window.

"You'll be able to in a few minutes, but that's not why I woke you. I'm concerned about Mr. Maddox." Hunter stood up as he spoke. "His color doesn't look right."

Some of the passengers watched as Hunter eased onto the seat next to Grover Maddox and studied the elderly gentleman. He pressed his fingertips against the side of Maddox's neck. Jodie got up to stand beside him.

"Hunter, is he…?"

"Yes," Hunter said in a low tone. "He's dead."

FOUR

few passengers heard Hunter McGuire's words. Some gasped, while others stared silently in shock.

"It appears to be heart failure," said Hunter, reaching for one of the blankets in the overhead rack. He quickly covered Maddox's head and face.

Jodie's eyes misted as she said, "I understand now why the Holy Spirit was pressing you so strongly, Hunter. He knew it was almost time for this dear old man to die, and He wanted you to talk with him before it was too late."

"Yes," said Hunter, fighting his own tears. "The message was clear to me to get to him right away." He drew a deep breath. "Well, bless his heart, he and Sadie are in each other's arms now and looking into the face of Jesus."

"Oh, yes. Thank the Lord!"

"Looks like we'll be the bearers of good news along with the bad," Hunter said. "Mr. Maddox said his granddaughter and her husband in Amherst are Christians. They tried to lead him to the Lord. At least we can tell them that before he took his last breath he called on Jesus to save him."

Someone had gone after the conductor, who drew up beside

Grover Maddox's seat, his eyes wide. He looked at Hunter and said, "I'm told Mr. Maddox just died, sir."

Hunter smiled as he replied, "Not really...he's just begun to live."

Mary Anna Jackson looked up at her tall, broad-shouldered husband as the train from Richmond chugged into the Lexington station. Her dark eyes flashed as she said, "It will be so good to see Hunter and Jodie again!"

"Yes. I'm glad for this respite in the fighting so that we could have them come."

The engine bell clanged as the big locomotive rolled to a halt and ejected a blast of steam. A moment later, passengers began to alight from the three cars. While the Jacksons watched for Hunter and Jodie to appear, the soldiers atop the cars stood up. One of them spotted the general and called out, "Hey, look! It's General Stonewall Jackson! Hello, General!"

Passengers who had stepped onto the platform smiled at the sight of the famous general waving at the soldiers.

"There they are, Tom!" exclaimed Mary Anna.

Stonewall saw Hunter and Jodie at the same time and took Mary Anna's hand, leading her toward them.

Hunter had jumped off the train and turned to help Jodie down the steps when Jodie spotted the Jacksons. The instant her feet touched the platform, she hurried to meet Mary Anna, whose arms were open wide. The two women embraced for a long moment, then Mary Anna embraced Hunter.

General Jackson grinned down at Jodie and said, "Well, if that quack doctor can hug my wife, I guess I can hug his wife-to-be!"

The four got into the Jacksons' buggy, and as they rode across town Jodie told them of Hunter leading Grover Maddox to the Lord and of Maddox's death shortly thereafter. Both of the Jacksons marveled at the way God had orchestrated the event and praised the

Lord that the old man became a Christian before going into eternity.

"Maddox…" said Jackson thoughtfully, as he held the reins. "Hunter, do you suppose he was any kin to Dr. Wayne Maddox?"

"He sure was, Tom. He was Wayne's grandfather."

"Well, what do you know! Wayne'll be plenty glad to learn that his granddaddy got saved, won't he."

Thomas and Mary Anna Jackson lived in a large two-story white frame house in Lexington near the Virginia Military Institute. Hunter was assigned a bedroom on the second floor, and Jodie's room was on the ground floor at the rear of the house.

After Hunter and Jodie had been given time to unpack their luggage, Mary Anna served coffee in the parlor. The couples sat on love seats that faced each other over a large oak coffee table.

"Does your doctor still say the baby is due the first week of December, Mary Anna?" asked Hunter.

"Yes, and I can hardly wait!"

"And I'm praying hard there will be no complications," said the general.

Mary Anna smiled at her husband and took his hand. To Hunter, she said, "I imagine Tom told you about Ellie."

"Yes," Hunter said, nodding, "but Jodie doesn't know."

"What's that?" asked Jodie. "Who's Ellie?"

"Tom's first wife," said Mary Anna.

"Oh. I wasn't aware…"

"Ellie died in childbirth," said Mary Anna. "And the baby—a boy—was stillborn. That's why Tom's a bit on edge with me having a baby."

"I can understand that," said Jodie.

"I've been taking it to the Lord in prayer," Jackson said.

"There's another similarity in the story, Jodie," said Mary Anna. "Ellie was the daughter of a Presbyterian preacher, as I am. I think in the back of Tom's mind he fears that the loss of his preacher's-daughter wife and their baby will be repeated with this preacher's-daughter wife and *our* baby."

Hunter looked at his lifelong friend. "What are you hoping for, Tom? A boy or a girl?"

"It really doesn't matter. I just want Mary Anna and the baby to come through the birth with no complications."

Jodie sipped her coffee, then said, "Have you picked out names?"

Mary Anna glanced at her husband and smiled. "Yes, we have. We've agreed that if it's a boy, we'll name him after Tom's father, whose name was Jonathan."

"I know that Jonathan is your middle name, General," said Jodie. "So, of course, you were named after your father."

"Not in the usual sense," said Jackson. "Actually, my parents didn't give me a middle name. I gave it to myself a few years ago in honor of my father. He died back in 1836."

"Oh. That was a beautiful thing to do, General."

"He was a great man, Jodie. And while I'm thinking of it, I told Hunter to tell you to call me Tom."

Jodie's features tinted as she flicked a sidelong glance at Hunter and saw him grin. She cleared her throat. "Umm…General Jackson, sir, I really don't think I can do that. I hold you in the highest esteem. And…you being a major general and all, I'd feel that I was being audacious to call you by your first name."

Jackson studied her for a moment. "Even if I say I would *like* for you to call me Tom? That since you're engaged to marry the best friend I have in this world, it gives you a special place in my life, and I *want* us to be on a first-name basis?"

Jodie glanced at her fiancé again. Hunter appeared to be enjoying the moment.

"I know, sir. But…well, you've been called General Robert E. Lee's right arm. By the general himself. Such dignity behooves me to call you *General.*" After a few seconds' pause, she said, "I know! How about when I become your best friend's wife, and my name is Jodie

McGuire? I'll start calling you by your first name then."

"Promise?" said Jackson, grinning broadly.

Jodie smiled and said, "Let's just say it's a pending possibility."

The general shrugged. "Well, I guess that's better than a flat no."

Mary Anna and Hunter laughed, then Mary Anna said, "Anyway…if our baby should be a girl, Tom and I have agreed to name her after his mother—Julia—who died in 1831."

"I like that name," said Jodie. "It's beautiful, and so feminine."

The general rose and poured more coffee around. Mary Anna watched him for a moment then said, "Have you two set a date for the wedding?"

"Indeed, we have," replied Hunter. "Saturday, December 20, unless the war interferes."

"Will it be in Richmond?"

"Yes, ma'am. At First Baptist Church."

"First Baptist?" said Jackson. "I knew Hunter's adoptive parents were Baptists and they would raise him to be Baptist. Is that your case too, Jodie?"

"Yes, sir," said Jodie, catching the impish gleam in the general's eye. "The people who raised me were also Baptists."

The general shook his head. "What a shame. You two ought to straighten up and become Presbyterians. At the very least you should get married in a Presbyterian church."

Jodie flipped her hair back with a toss of her head and said, "But General, our new pastor's name is John Griffin. Hunter and I will be married by John the Baptist."

Mary Anna giggled, and Jackson laughed heartily and came back with, "Well, *our* pastor's name is John—John Brooks."

Jodie crinkled her nose and said, "But where in the Bible did you ever read of John the Presbyterian?"

Hunter guffawed as Jackson's smile disappeared.

Mary Anna laughed and clapped her hands together. "Tom, you may be the Presbyterian deacon here, and you may be the Army of Northern Virginia's general most famous for maneuvering forces in combat, but this little Baptist nurse just outmaneuvered you!"

"Jodie, I could use you at my side on the battlefield!" the general said.

"If they'd let women do that, Tom," said Mary Anna, "we'd whip the socks off those Yankees in no time and end the war!"

When the laughter subsided, Hunter said, "Tom, I have an important question to ask you."

"Sure," said the general, draining his coffee cup and setting it back in the saucer.

Hunter scooted to the edge of his seat and rested his elbows on his knees. With a gleam in his eyes, he said, "I want you to be best man in the wedding."

"I'm deeply honored, my friend," Tom said. "I…I'm at a loss for words."

"How about, 'Yes, Hunter, I'll be best man in your wedding'?"

The general got an impish look in his eyes again and said, "I'll be happy to be your best man, Hunter *if* they'll allow a Presbyterian deacon inside a Baptist church!"

"I hadn't thought of that, Tom. Guess I'll have to check with John the Baptist Griffin and see if he'll let Thomas the Presbyterian Jackson stand on his platform!"

"Well, he'd better!" Jodie said. "Because the lady I want to be my matron of honor is not only a Presbyterian preacher's daughter, but she's married to a Presbyterian deacon named Stonewall Jackson!"

Mary Anna blinked hard. "Jodie! Really? You want *me* to be your matron of honor?"

Jodie rose from the love seat and leaned over to hug Mary Anna. "I sure do! *Will* you?"

"Oh, yes! I'm thrilled and honored! The baby's due at least two weeks before the wedding date. I should be back to full strength by then."

Jodie gave her another squeeze. "Thank you," she said softly, and kissed Mary Anna's temple.

Hunter watched Jodie return to sit beside him, and said to the

Jacksons, "Of course, like I said, it'll be December 20 unless the war interferes."

"Never know about the Yankees," said Jackson, "but if they're willing to ease off fighting at Christmastime, we certainly will too. Even if you have to postpone it until we have another break in fighting, like we're enjoying right now, Mary Anna and I will very happily take part in your wedding."

"It's all in the Lord's hands," said Jodie. "We'll leave it there and trust Him to work it according to His plan."

"Amen," said the general.

"I've written my adoptive parents in Boston," Hunter said. "I told them I finally found Jodie and that we're getting married on December 20, the Lord willing. There hasn't been time enough to hear back from them—*if* the letter even got through—but I'm sure if it did, they'll come unless travel into the South is restricted from Northern civilians."

"That changes on both sides quite often," said Jackson. "Just like getting the mail through. Depends on how things are going for either side at the time. I sure would enjoy seeing the McGuires again."

"And I'd love to meet them," said Mary Anna.

"Me too," Jodie said with a chuckle, "since they're going to be my in-laws!"

Tom Jackson leaned back and looked up at the ceiling. "I'll never forget the day Dr. Jason McGuire and his wife showed up in our little town," he said.

"Nor will I," said Hunter. "They were willing to take this poor little orphan boy, raise him, educate him, and give him a happy life. They're wonderful people."

"So you became a medical doctor because your adoptive father was one, is that it?" asked Mary Anna.

"Yes, ma'am. He's the best. I had the greatest example to follow."

"And I'm sure he's proud of you."

"Yes, ma'am. That he is. And so's Mom."

"We had some marvelous times as boys," said Tom. "Even

though I was a few years older than Hunter, we were great friends."

Hunter laughed. "Except when I sneaked up on you a couple times when you thought you were alone with your girlfriend. What was that one girl's name?"

"Cancel that memory," Tom said, chuckling.

Mary Anna gave a mock scowl, and Jodie laughed.

"Okay. New subject," said Hunter. "Tom…any ideas on what the Yankees are going to do next? Now that they've driven us out of Northern territory?"

"General Lee wired me yesterday. Word from Confederate spies in Washington is that Lincoln's about to send McClellan's army on a march toward Richmond. General Lee has beefed up security around the city, and he has scouts on alert. I was already scheduled to go there on Friday, but General Lee especially wants me there with my Corps in case McClellan shows his face on the Virginia border. He also wants me there because on Saturday he and President Davis are having that special public meeting at the army camp to honor the four young heroes of the Eighteenth North Carolina."

Jodie nodded her approval as Hunter said, "Ah, yes. The men from Major Rance Dayton's hometown who so gallantly saved his life at Sharpsburg."

"Tell me about it," said Mary Anna.

Some of the liveliness went out of Mary Anna's face as she listened to her husband tell of the young men from North Carolina who saved their wounded major. Her voice quavered slightly as she said, "And President Davis and General Lee are going to have a special public meeting to honor them?"

"That's right, honey. Of course there will be a posthumous commendation for Billy Dean Baxter."

"I think that's wonderful. Those have to be very brave young men."

"That they are. President Davis and General Lee want to honor them in front of as many military personnel and civilians as they can muster for the occasion…to let our men in uniform know what kind of soldiers they should strive to be."

"I'll be working the midnight shift," said Jodie to Hunter, "so I'll be free to attend the ceremony. I really would like to see it."

"Me too," said Hunter. "This should bolster the morale of the entire Army of Northern Virginia. I expect President Davis and General Lee hope it will instill a greater desire in the hearts of all our men to redouble their efforts to win this war."

Tom let out a huge sigh, then said, "The Lord knows we need something to help us overcome the horrible losses we suffered at Sharpsburg. I don't know where the next big battle will take place, but we'd better win it decisively. Even the morale building can't carry us if we have the kind of losses we experienced in Maryland."

Mary Anna gave her shoulders a small shake, as if shrugging off a weight, then said, "Won't it be wonderful when Jesus comes back to earth to establish His kingdom? Just think of it. No more war!"

Jodie glanced at Hunter and then back at the Jacksons and said, "We were saying the same thing on the trip over here."

"Well, amen," the general said. "I'll say it with the apostle John at Patmos…'even so, come, Lord Jesus!'"

General McClellan's diminutive form was highly recognizable as he rode up Pennsylvania Avenue toward the White House, flanked by eight cavalrymen. One of the riders was Brigadier General Alfred Pleasonton, commander of the Cavalry Division of the Union Army of the Potomac.

At the entrance to the White House grounds, the guards saluted and swung open the gate. The guard in charge said, "Welcome, General McClellan, sir! President Lincoln advised us through his personal secretary that you would be arriving at 9:45 this morning." He smiled as he said, "You are precisely on time, sir. Welcome to the White House."

"Thank you, Corporal," said McClellan.

"I'll lead you to the front door, sir. Mr. Hay didn't tell me these other men would be seeing the president."

"No…and they won't. General Pleasonton and his men have come along as my escorts. Never know when some Confederate spy might decide to do a little sniping."

"You can't be too careful, sir," responded the guard. "If you'll follow me…"

McClellan and the others stayed in their saddles until they reached the front portico of the White House. When two stern-faced guards stepped forward from their posts at the door, the gate guard said to them, "Only General McClellan is to see Mr. Lincoln. General Pleasonton and his men will be seated in the reception room to await the general's return."

As McClellan and the others dismounted, the guard who had escorted them said, "Your horses will wait in the barn across the street, General McClellan. It will only take a few minutes for us to return them to you when you're finished."

McClellan thanked the man, and one of the door guards opened the front door to allow them inside. The other door guard stepped in behind the group and pointed out presidential secretary John Hay, who was coming across the vestibule.

"Mr. Hay is here to escort you to the president's office, General McClellan," he said. "General Pleasonton, sir, if you and your men will follow me…"

John Hay drew up to General McClellan and shook his hand. "Mr. Lincoln appreciates promptness, General. He'll be glad to see you even a few minutes before ten o'clock."

Moments later, Secretary Hay ushered General McClellan into the Oval Office.

Lincoln rose from behind his desk, his gaunt figure reminding the general of some of the Union men he'd seen who had spent time in Southern prison camps. The president's deep-set eyes seemed even deeper than before, and his cheeks a little more sunken.

McClellan held his campaign hat under his left arm and

saluted. "Good morning, Mr. President."

"Good morning, General. Please sit down."

When both men were seated, Lincoln said, "General McClellan, I won't spend a lot of time rehashing my disappointment when you didn't pursue General Lee and his army as they ran back to Virginia."

"Yes, sir," said Little Mac, his features stoic.

"I sent for you because I believe—as does General Halleck—that we need to strike hard and fast at Lee's army before they can rebuild their forces. My spies below the Mason-Dixon line tell me that Lee is running low on ammunition as well as morale. We must hit them full force before they replenish their ammunition supply, and before they get over the losses they incurred at Antietam."

"I agree, sir," said McClellan.

"Good. Then this meeting will be quite brief. To put it succinctly, General, I want you to take your army across the Potomac as soon as possible and give battle to the enemy. I want Richmond captured. That will end the war. Let's get it done. We outnumber Johnny Reb almost two to one. We have more horses, mules, wagons, guns, ammunition, and experienced army officers. Win the war for the North, General."

At the tone of finality in Lincoln's voice, McClellan rose from his chair, saluted the president, and said, "It's been nice to see you, sir."

Lincoln rounded the desk, towering over the general by twelve inches. As they walked toward the door, he laid a hand on McClellan's shoulder and said, "Now, General, this time I want action. No more slows. Understood?"

As the president opened the door for him, McClellan nodded his assent, passed through the outer office, and disappeared into the hallway.

Abraham Lincoln drew in a deep breath and let it out slowly through his nostrils. As John Hay stepped up beside him, he said, "I don't know, John. Somehow I don't think I've gotten the message across to him yet."

FIVE

Southern newspapers had announced the commendation ceremonies several days in advance, and loyal Southerners came from miles around to honor the five young privates of the Eighteenth North Carolina Regiment.

The Virginia countryside looked golden beneath the sun's bright rays as thousands of people gathered at the army camp a mile north of the Confederacy's capital city. White cottony clouds, rambunctious in a light westerly wind, made a drifting patchwork of light and shadow over the land.

Near the grassy spot where a portable wooden platform was set up, a creek meandered among towering oaks, elms, and evergreens, its dappled surface sparkling in the bright sunlight.

The ceremony was scheduled to begin at 2:00 P.M. sharp. At 1:50, a military band next to the platform began playing rousing Southern songs while soldiers and civilians gathered, most of them sitting on the grass.

The newly designed Confederate flag—one flag at each corner of the platform—flapped in the wind.

Most of the high-ranking officers of the Confederate Army of Northern Virginia were in attendance. On the platform with

President Jefferson Davis were Generals Robert E. Lee, Thomas J. Jackson, James Lane (commander of the North Carolina Brigade within II Corps), and James Longstreet (commander of I Corps), along with Major Rance Dayton and the four young privates to be honored.

Also on the platform—at Stonewall Jackson's request—was his close friend, Presbyterian evangelist B. Tucker Lacy, whom Jackson had appointed Chaplain General of II Corps.

A delegation from Fayetteville, North Carolina, including family members of the honorees, was seated on the ground directly in front of the platform.

At precisely 2:00 P.M., under the eyes of some twenty thousand spectators, President Davis stepped to the center of the platform. The band was just finishing a snappy song, and when the music faded, Davis raised his hands to quiet the crowd and gave a few opening remarks.

This was followed by cheers and applause, but when the band struck up Daniel D. Emmett's "Dixie," the crowd came to its feet. When the song ended, everyone cheered, prodding the band to play the song again. They remained on their feet as the band played out the last notes, and President Davis called Chaplain Lacy forward to open the meeting in prayer.

Lacy's voice carried strongly as he thanked God for the reason they were assembled. He asked the Lord to give special comfort to the Baxter family, who had lost their loved one during the gallant rescue.

After the amen, Lacy returned to his seat, and President Davis introduced Major General Thomas J. "Stonewall" Jackson, who gave testimony of what he had seen on September 17 on the battlefield near Sharpsburg, Maryland. When Jackson was finished, he called Rance Dayton to address the crowd. The soldiers and civilians applauded and cheered as Dayton limped to the center of the platform.

"Mr. President, General Robert E. Lee, honored military leaders...I thank you for making this day possible. And ladies and gentleman, I thank you for honoring, by your presence, five of the bravest young men you will ever meet. In a moment, we'll introduce them to you. But first let me say that I would not be here today if it weren't for these men who put their lives on the line…and one of those men gave up his life. I count it an honor to command these men in battle, and I count it the highest honor to also call them friends."

Dayton proceeded to tell in graphic detail the story, holding the crowd spellbound. When he came to the part about Private Billy Dean Baxter's death, his composure faltered. As he spoke in a broken voice of the fine young soldier Baxter had been, and that he would never forget Billy Dean's willing sacrifice, all eyes went to the Baxter family. They wept openly, flooded by pride and sorrow.

When Dayton finished the story, he turned to the four young heroes and said, "Ladies and gentlemen, it is now my privilege to introduce to you Privates Everett Nichols, Hank Upchurch, Buford Hall, and Chuck Carney. Come forward, gentlemen!"

The young men, somewhat embarrassed by all the attention, made their way to the center of the platform and stood with their commander.

The crowd rose to its feet as one, and the roar of voices and applause, along with the blaring horns of the band, grew deafening. The "fearless four," as they had been dubbed by their fellow soldiers, humbly accepted the glory showered on them.

Then Dayton introduced Brigadier General James Lane, who eloquently praised the courage of the five young privates. "The gallantry of these men is a supreme example to all the soldiers in the Confederate armies. I am proud to wear the same gray as Privates Everett Nichols, Hank Upchurch, Buford Hall, Chuck Carney, and Billy Dean Baxter."

As soon as Lane sat down, General Robert E. Lee gave a speech about heroism, explaining that what the five young soldiers had done, in his estimation, was the epitome of courage and self-sacrifice.

President Davis joined Lee as the general called for Billy Dean's father to come to the platform. Together, Davis and Lee presented Baxter a written posthumous commendation for Billy Dean.

Jodie clung to Hunter's arm as tears rolled down her cheeks, and the sound of weeping could be heard all through the crowd.

As soon as President Davis and General Lee presented written commendations to the four other young men, General Stonewall Jackson came forward again. The crowd grew momentarily quiet as Jackson told the honorees that each was being promoted to corporal. Then turning to the crowd, he said, "Ladies and gentlemen, I present to you the South's four 'lions of notability'!"

When Jackson started to follow the newly promoted corporals to their seats, General Lee said, "Wait a moment, General Jackson. While these other gentlemen take their seats, I want you to remain." He then called for President Davis and General Longstreet to join them.

"Ladies and gentlemen," said President Davis, "as you are about to see, this meeting actually has a double purpose. I have asked General Robert E. Lee to explain."

Lee smiled at his two generals, then turned to the crowd and said, "As all of you know, Major General James Longstreet and Major General Thomas Jackson are two of the finest men who ever wore a Confederate uniform. They are heroes themselves, in every sense of the word. What I'm about to say will take these two fine gentlemen by surprise. President Davis and I have created a new rank for these two generals. They have both been major generals for some time, but they're now being promoted to the rank of lieutenant general.

"The word *lieutenant* has several meanings. One of those meanings is 'representative' or 'aide-de-camp.' In this sense, President Davis and I are promoting these fine soldiers to lieutenant general as aide-de-camps to myself and as my personal representatives before the Confederate states and the Confederate armies."

As the zealous throng lifted its loudest ovation yet, the band once again played "Dixie." This time it could hardly be heard for the tumult of the crowd.

When the crowd began to disperse, General Lee slipped up to Longstreet and Jackson and told them to come meet with him immediately.

Minutes later, when they were seated in his tent, Lee said, "Gentlemen, just before noon I received word from our leading spy in the capitol in Washington. He tells me that Lincoln has given McClellan strict orders to begin a move on Richmond."

"Do you suppose the move will actually begin immediately, sir?" asked Longstreet.

Lee chuckled. "Well, not unless old Abe has somehow been able to change Little Mac's philosophy of warfare. However, since there's no way to know that, we will proceed with maneuvers to block the attempt to move on our capitol. I jotted down a few notes right after receiving the message. Here's what we'll do...."

On Wednesday morning, October 15, John Hay was at his desk in the White House, writing letters for the president, when General-in-Chief Henry Halleck came through the doorway from the hall.

"Good morning, General Halleck," said Hay.

Halleck's scowl showed that it was anything but a good morning as far as he was concerned. "Unh," he grunted. "Mr. Lincoln is expecting me."

"Yes, sir," said Hay, rising from his chair.

Halleck followed Hay to the Oval Office door and waited for the secretary to announce his presence.

Lincoln stood up behind his desk as Halleck entered, took one look at his face and said, "General, you look like I feel."

"Good," said Halleck. "Maybe if both of us get angry at the same time, we'll get something done about little molasses-blood McClellan. Sir, I have never known a man to be so slow."

Lincoln shook his head and sat down. "I haven't either, General. It was a week ago today that I told him to move his army toward Richmond *immediately*. Instead of offering battle, he's offering excuses."

"Such as?"

"I sent him a message on Monday, asking what was delaying him moving across the Potomac." Lincoln picked up a wrinkled sheet of paper and scooted it across the desk to Halleck. "Look at his reply."

Halleck read the message, raised his bushy eyebrows, and met Lincoln's gaze. "His horses are fatigued and must rest before crossing the Potomac to move on Richmond? Mr. President, this is absurd."

Lincoln nodded and handed him a slip of paper. "This is my reply, General. It's going to him by messenger in about thirty minutes."

Halleck smiled as he read the president's words:

Major General George B. McClellan, Field Commander
Camp Headquarters, Union Army of the Potomac

My dear sir, will you pardon me for asking what the horses of your army have done since the Battle of Antietam that fatigues anything?

A. Lincoln

Halleck chuckled. "I'd like to see the general's reply, sir."

"You shall. That is, if I get one."

At the federal camp on the north bank of the Potomac River, a few miles outside of Washington, Major General McClellan was standing outside his tent in conversation with Major Generals John Sedgwick and George G. Meade when a messenger galloped in and slid from his saddle.

"General McClellan, sir," the messenger said as he saluted, "I'm sorry to disturb you, but I have a message for you from President Lincoln."

"Excuse me, gentlemen," said McClellan, turning slightly to look the messenger in the eye. "No disturbance, Corporal. You're just doing your duty."

"Yes, sir." He handed McClellan a sealed envelope. "I've been instructed to await your reply in writing, sir."

"Of course," said McClellan with a smile, ripping open the envelope. "You wait right here."

McClellan turned to Sedgwick and Meade. "We'll take up the subject at another time, gentlemen. Right now, I must attend to the president's message."

McClellan entered his tent and scanned the piece of paper. As he read, his face paled. Then he quickly turned to his crude, portable desk, took out a sheet of paper, and dipped a pen in the inkwell to write:

President Abraham Lincoln
White House
Washington D.C.

My dear Mr. President,

Our horses are doing better, and I am now beginning preparations to make a sustained march on Richmond. We should have an unconditional surrender from the enemy within a few weeks.

Respectfully,
Maj. Gen. George B. McClellan
Field Commander, Union Army of the Potomac

President Lincoln and General Halleck waited in Washington for news of McClellan's move across the Potomac River into Virginia. Finally, at dawn on Sunday morning, October 26, the Army of the Potomac began the crossing.

By nightfall, all the troops, guns, and wagons were across, and they camped on the south bank.

McClellan was eating breakfast in his tent at dawn when his aide, Corporal Leonard Smith, called from outside, "General McClellan, sir. I have Lieutenant Roger Malloy from General Alfred Pleasonton's First Cavalry Division out here. General Pleasonton asked that you see the lieutenant immediately upon his arrival."

The previous night, just after midnight, McClellan had sent Pleasonton's division of the cavalry corps farther south as scouts.

McClellan greeted Malloy and said, "I assume no campfires were seen, or I would have heard last night."

Malloy saluted. "We saw no campfire, General, but at first light we caught sight of a massive force of Rebels spread across what would be our path to Richmond. General Pleasonton asked that you ride down immediately and take a look for yourself."

An hour later, McClellan returned to the Union camp and called all of his Corps commanders together. Standing before them, he said, "Gentlemen, south of here, about four miles, is a massive force of Rebels ready to greet us with heavy artillery and a well-fortified infantry. I saw it with my own eyes."

Major General Oliver Howard, commander of XI Corps, voiced the question that was in everyone's mind. "We *are* going to meet them head-on, whip them, and go on to Richmond, aren't we, sir?"

McClellan rubbed his jaw nervously. "No, we're not, General Howard. Bobby Lee has quite strongly interposed his army between us and Richmond, and I'm fearful that our men are still so low in morale from our devastating losses at Antietam that they're not ready to attack such a well-situated bastion. It is my decision that at this time we must pull back across the Potomac."

"What?" Abraham Lincoln gasped as he read a message handed to him by John Hay. "This is preposterous! Get General Halleck over here right away!"

In less than twenty minutes, General Halleck stood in Lincoln's office reading the message from General McClellan.

"So Little Napoleon figures his men are too low in morale, eh?" Halleck said. "Maybe. Or is it, Mr. President, that General McClellan is too low in courage to charge into the jaws of enemy artillery?"

Lincoln ran splayed fingers through his hair. "I don't understand it, General. When General McClellan has a mind to fight, he is unequaled in leading an army into battle. But this— I'm at a loss for words."

"Well, sir," said Halleck, "since I'm being paid to serve as your number-one military advisor, my advice is: Get rid of McClellan. If you don't, we're going to lose this war."

On November 5, 1862, Abraham Lincoln issued orders for Major General George Brinson McClellan to be relieved of his command. Much to the surprise of General-in-Chief Henry Halleck and the men of the Union Army of the Potomac, Lincoln appointed Major General Ambrose E. Burnside in his place.

Two days later, Halleck appeared in John Hay's office, asking for a meeting with the president.

"I'm sorry, General Halleck," said Hay, "but the president isn't in his office at this time."

"I see. All right, when will he be in so I can see him?"

"Probably not until tomorrow morning, sir. Mrs. Lincoln is quite ill with influenza, and the president is at her bedside."

"Oh. Well, I'm sorry to hear that," said Halleck.

"I will let Mr. Lincoln know you want to see him, General, and unless you hear differently, you will have the first appointment tomorrow morning."

The next morning, Halleck was ushered into the Oval Office by Hay, and a weary Abraham Lincoln said, "Sorry I couldn't see you yesterday, General, but Mary really needed me. I consider myself a husband and a father before I am president of the United States."

Halleck managed a tight smile. "I can appreciate that, sir. Is Mrs. Lincoln doing better?"

"Yes. Her fever has come down, and she's much better today."

"I'm glad to hear it."

Lincoln leaned forward, placed his elbows on the desk, and asked, "What did you need to see me about?"

"We've got a real problem, sir—your appointment of General Burnside in McClellan's stead. There is an undercurrent of dissatisfaction among our military leaders over it. As you well know, Mr. President, none will dare openly question your wisdom in this, but the man is a known loser. Our military leaders feel that we're worse off now than with McClellan. And I have to be honest, sir. I agree with them."

Lincoln eased back in his chair but didn't reply.

Taking advantage of the silence, Halleck said, "Word is, sir, that General Burnside told you he's incapable of leading an army the size of ours. Is this true?"

Lincoln nodded. "Yes, it's true."

"And you still made him field commander?"

"Yes. General Burnside is a good man, General Halleck…and a bit humble."

"But sir, if he doesn't even have confidence in himself to command the Army of the Potomac, how can *you* have confidence in him?"

"Like I said, he's a good man. And you must admit that everybody likes him."

"Yes, General Burnside is a kindly, unselfish man with a gentle nature, and he definitely is liked amongst his peers. But his fellow officers cringe at the thought of him in charge of their army. Are you aware, Mr. President, that when traveling to the war in Mexico, General Burnside lost his traveling money to a Mississippi riverboat gambler? Do you know that after the Mexican War, he lost his entire fortune in a financial venture, which to any thinking man had the marks of failure from the beginning?"

"No. I had not heard these things," said Lincoln.

Halleck inched closer to the edge of his chair. "The crowning embarrassment was his wedding ceremony. When the minister asked the bride, 'Do you take this man to be your lawfully wedded husband,' she said 'No' and walked out of the church, leaving him standing there in front of hundreds of people. Mr. President, the man is a born loser. And you know that while serving under McClellan at South Mountain and Antietam, he made some inexcusable blunders."

Lincoln sighed. "Yes, I know that. But he's the best man I have to replace McClellan."

"But sir, what about General Porter? Or General Sumner? Or General Meade?"

"I considered them…along with Generals Franklin and Hooker."

"General Franklin would be good, sir…or Sumner, Meade, or Porter. I would suggest you consider one of them."

Lincoln shook his head. "No, General. My decision has been made, and I am sticking to it unless and until General Burnside actually proves himself incapable. I can't change horses in midstream, as they say. General Burnside has already begun preparing his army to launch an offensive that both he and I believe will ultimately take us to victory at Richmond."

SIX

At the camp near the Rappahannock River, where General Lee had established his bastion against encroachment by the Federal troops, revival spirit was in progress. Dr. Joseph C. Stiles, chaplain of I Corps, had been invited by Lieutenant General "Stonewall" Jackson and Chaplain Lacy to preach an old-fashioned camp meeting to the entire Army of Northern Virginia. Though attendance at the preaching services was not mandated by General Lee, most of the men attended faithfully.

Jackson, Lacy, and Dr. Hunter McGuire served as counselors at the close of the sermon each night and had the joy of leading a great number of soldiers to Jesus Christ.

After one such service, Stonewall Jackson was sitting on a chair near the altar. He had his Bible open, and by the light of a nearby campfire he was writing notes from Stiles's sermon in the margins.

Nearby, a cluster of infantrymen stood around a young sergeant named Ryan Colston, who was known to be a blatant unbeliever.

Something Colston had just said caught Stonewall's attention, and he rose from the chair, Bible in hand, and headed toward the group.

With a sneering laugh, Colston said, "What kind of a God

would put people in hell? Huh? Can you guys tell me that?"

The others saw Jackson's approach but didn't let on.

Suddenly, from behind the mocker, came the general's strong, deep voice: "The kind who hates sin and will not have it in His presence in heaven, Sergeant."

Colston whirled around at the sound of the familiar voice. He had the grace to blush as he stammered, "Wh-what's that, sir?"

"You just asked a question—what kind of a God would put people in hell. I answered your question. The kind of God who hates sin and will not let it into heaven."

Colston felt a trickle of sweat start to roll down his forehead. "Well, no offense, General," he said, "but I don't believe in hell. Nobody can convince me that such a place exists."

"God will convince you."

"What's that, sir?"

"I said God will convince you. The choice of how He does it is up to you. You can allow Him to convince you by His Word…or when you die and wake up in the flames of hell. Problem with the latter is it's too late to do anything about it."

"Again, no offense intended toward you personally, General," said Colston, "but it's my belief that God is going to take everybody into heaven."

"Based on what?"

Colston thought on it, then replied, "Based on my belief that God is good, kind, and loving."

"Mm-hmm. What would you think about a judge who has a convicted murderer standing before him. The judge's duty is to pass sentence on the man for his vile crime. But the judge smiles sweetly and says, 'Mr. Jones, I know you've been convicted of murdering your neighbor's three children, but I'm going to release you. You see, Mr. Jones, I am a good, kind, and loving judge, and I just couldn't be so unkind as to send you to the gallows for your crimes. When you go back out there in society, you try to be a better man.' What about that judge, Sergeant? What would you think of him, turning the killer loose so he could snuff out more innocent lives?"

Colston licked his lips. "I...uh...well—"

"Would the judge be right to endanger other lives by turning the cold-blooded killer loose on them, just because he's a good, kind, and loving judge?"

Colston cleared his throat. "Well, uh...no, sir. No, that wouldn't be right."

"But you think God—the righteous Judge—is going to let wicked, unregenerate sinners into heaven. What kind of heaven would that be?"

"Well, they'll be good after they die. They won't be bad anymore."

"Your theory won't hold scriptural water, son," said Jackson. "God points to eternity in Revelation 22:11 and says, 'He that is unjust, let him be unjust still: and he which is filthy, let him be filthy still.' Dying doesn't change a sinner's nature. Only being born again by the Spirit of God can do that."

Colston shook his head. "I still don't believe in hell."

"But you do believe in heaven?"

"That's right."

"Why?"

"Well, we have to go somewhere when we die. So I believe we all go to heaven."

The general's voice remained quiet as he said, "Are you aware, Sergeant Colston, that you wouldn't know there was a heaven except that you learned it from the Bible? That's our only source for the knowledge that there's a place called heaven."

Colston shrugged. "That's good enough for me."

"I see. So you're willing to take the Bible's word for the fact that heaven exists."

"Sure."

"Well, son, the same Bible says hell exists. What about that?"

There were snickers among the small group when Sergeant Colston found himself without a sensible reply.

Jackson opened his Bible, flipped to Matthew 23, and said, "Look at what Jesus Christ said to unbelievers, Sergeant—here in verse 33: 'Ye serpents, ye generation of vipers, how can ye escape the damnation of hell?'"

Flipping back a few pages to Matthew 13, Jackson said, "In this chapter, Jesus twice calls hell a furnace of fire. Look at verse 42: 'And shall cast them into a furnace of fire: there shall be wailing and gnashing of teeth.' Verse 50: 'And shall cast them into the furnace of fire: there shall be wailing and gnashing of teeth.' Sergeant, are you so bold as to call Jesus Christ a liar?"

While Colston was trying to come up with a reply, Jackson flipped forward to Luke 16. Look, here, Sergeant. This is a true story told by Jesus about a man who went to hell. See? In verse 23 Jesus says the man lifted up his eyes in hell, being in torments. What was causing the torments? Next verse. The man in hell says he is tormented in 'this flame.' Hell is real fire. The man in hell said so. Jesus said so."

Colston licked his lips nervously.

"I'll ask you again, Sergeant," said Jackson, "are you going to call Jesus Christ a liar?"

"Well, I—"

"Do you think Jesus came from heaven, shed His blood on the cross, and died to save you from nothing, Sergeant? If there was no hell to save you from…why did He go to the cross? And if there was no hell to save you from, why did He lie and say there was?"

Sergeant Ryan Colston's eyes filmed with moisture, and his lower lip quivered slightly. "General, sir, I…I've been wrong. I'm lost. Would you help me? I want to be saved."

Jackson quickly showed Colston that Jesus demanded repentance of sin, and faith in Him alone, before He would save a sinner from hell. He then showed him Romans 10:13: "Whosoever shall call upon the name of the Lord shall be saved."

The Spirit of God had done His supernatural work. Where previously a cynical scoffer had stood, now a humbled and convicted young man called on the Lord Jesus Christ to save him.

* * *

While General Lee and his army waited on the banks of the Rappahannock for news from Confederate intelligence, Jodie Lockwood climbed aboard a train in Richmond and headed for Lexington, early on Tuesday morning, December 2.

It was midafternoon when Jodie alighted from the hired buggy with her small overnight bag in hand, paid the driver, and stepped onto the front porch of the Jackson house.

Before she could knock, the door opened, and a middle-aged woman greeted her with a warm smile, saying, "Miss Lockwood?"

Jodie smiled back and said, "Yes…and you're Mrs. Zimmer."

"Come in, child," said the chubby woman. "And you can call me Gertie. Short for Gertrude May."

"All right, Gertie." Jodie followed her inside. "And you can call me Jodie. Short for Joan Elizabeth. How's Mary Anna?"

"She's doing fine. Taking her nap right now."

"No, I'm not," came a voice from down the hall. Mary Anna suddenly appeared, waddling uncomfortably toward them in a bulging robe and slippers. "Jodie! I'm so glad you're here!"

"You look like you could blossom any time," Jodie said as the two women embraced.

"Oh, I'd love to have the baby while you're here, Jodie. I guess you met Gertie. She's a member of our church, and she's been such a good friend to me."

Jodie nodded. "Yes, we met, and I like her very much already."

"Same here, Jodie," said Gertie.

"Gertie has been with me day and night for over a week. She won't leave me for a minute."

"That's awfully sweet of you, Gertie," said Jodie. "Since I'll be here tonight, would you like to go home and sleep in your own bed?"

"No need. I'm a widow, so there's nobody at home to take care of. And the bed I've been sleeping in is very comfortable. Besides…I want to be here when that baby comes."

"Well, I can tell you right now," said Mary Anna, smoothing some loose strands of hair from her forehead, "it's mighty close to time."

Jodie took Mary Anna by the arm and said, "All right, little lady, as your visiting nurse I want you to go back to bed and lie down. You look very tired."

"I am a little fatigued. Didn't sleep well last night. Backache."

"Well, the cause of the backache will soon keep you awake in another way," giggled Jodie. "You know…wa-a-ah, wa-a-ah, wa-a-ah!"

Mary Anna rolled her eyes and Gertie burst into laughter.

As Jodie started to guide Mary Anna down the hall, Gertie took the expectant mother's other arm. "Come on, honey," she said. "Do like your nurse has told you…back to bed."

When Jodie and Gertie had tucked the covers around Mary Anna, Jodie said, "You close your eyes, now. Sleep if you can. We'll be right here."

Mary Anna pulled the covers up under her chin. "What do you hear from Hunter, Jodie?"

"Same thing you hear from the general. Everybody's waiting for the Yankees to make their move."

"Oh, I'll be so glad when this war is over! It will be wonderful to have Tom home for good. I'd love to have him teaching at the institute and home with the baby and me every night."

"Maybe that isn't so far off," spoke up Gertie. "The kind of trouble Abe Lincoln is having with his army…he just might decide to call the war off and let us all settle down to a normal life again."

"I'd love to believe that," said Jodie.

Mary Anna fell asleep while both women sat by the bed, chatting quietly.

Gertie finally stood up and whispered, "I need to go to the market and buy some groceries, Jodie. Usually I have to call in a neighbor to stay with Mary Anna while I shop, but since you're here, I'll leave you in charge. I'll be back in an hour."

Jodie nodded. "How far away is her doctor…just in case she should start labor?"

"He's about four blocks from here. Name's Dr. Harvey Roberts. If that should happen, the neighbors next door to the west will fetch him for you. Their name is Nelson. Just give them a holler, and stay close to Mary Anna."

When Gertie left, Jodie stood over her sleeping friend for a few moments, smiling down at her, then adjusted the covers and eased back onto the chair.

Gertie had been gone just over an hour when she arrived back at the Jackson home and pushed the little cart up the walk and alongside the house to the back porch. As she picked up a grocery bag, she heard a sharp cry from inside the house.

"Mary Anna!" she gasped, dropping the bag into the cart and bounding up the steps and through the kitchen door. She heard another cry and hurried toward Mary Anna's bedroom.

She could hear Jodie speaking in low tones. When she entered the room, Jodie was bent over Mary Anna with her hands on Mary Anna's knees, saying, "Take a deep breath, honey, and push!"

Mary Anna's face was shiny with perspiration, and her eyes were closed.

When Jodie sensed movement behind her, she turned in relief and said, "Her water broke right after you left! The baby's head is showing! I ran over to the neighbors like you said, but they aren't home. I tried two other houses. They're not home either. Would you go bring the doctor?"

Gertie nodded and dashed out the door.

When Gertie Zimmer arrived at Dr. Harvey Roberts's office, his nurse informed Gertie that he had been called to a farm outside of town to deliver a baby, and she had no idea when he might return.

* * *

Gertie had been gone about an hour and a half when she returned to the Jackson house. Puffing from exertion, she mounted the steps, bustled through the door, and forced her weary legs to hurry down the hall.

When she stepped into the bedroom, Mary Anna was sitting up in bed, holding a small bundle in a blanket, a smile of contented joy on her face. Jodie, who was seated next to her on a wooden chair, looked exultant from the miracle she had just witnessed. Gertie just stood there like a statue, eyes wide, mouth gaping.

"Come, Gertie," said Mary Anna. "I want you to meet Julia."

On Saturday morning, December 6, Dr. Hunter McGuire had already attended to several minor medical problems inside the hospital tent on the east bank of the Rappahannock. As he applied salve to a soldier's back, the tent flap parted.

"Hello, General," said Hunter, looking up to see his lifelong friend.

"Hello, yourself," said Stonewall. "How long you going to be tied up here?"

"Just about done. I think this man is my last patient."

"I'll wait outside…I've got some good news."

Hunter grinned. "The baby?"

Stonewall tried to cover a smile as he said, "I'll see you outside when you're finished."

"It's a girl, isn't it?"

Jackson gave him a mock scowl. "I said I'll see you outside when you're finished."

Five minutes later the soldier Hunter had been treating emerged from the tent, slipping on his coat. The December air was quite nippy. "General Jackson…?"

"Yes, Private?"

"Did your wife just give birth?"

The general took him by the arm and led him a safe distance from the hospital tent. "Yes!" he said in a low voice. "I just wanted to tell Dr. McGuire first."

"Is Dr. McGuire right, sir?" asked the private in a whisper. "Is it a girl?"

"Yes! But I don't want him to know it yet."

"Could I spread the word? We've all been waiting for your baby to be born, sir."

Jackson laid a hand on his shoulder. "Give it a few minutes, will you, Private? Then you can spread the word."

"Sure, General. Is Mrs. Jackson all right?"

"Yes. Mother and baby came through it just fine."

"Oh, that's good, sir." The private started to walk away, then turned back. "Oh! What's the baby's name, General?"

"Julia. After my mother."

The private nodded, and hurried away. Jackson returned to the tent and waited near the opening.

Seconds later, Hunter came out, smiling from ear to ear. "Okay, General Jackson," he said, looking the man in the eye, "Was I right? Is it a girl?"

Jackson smiled broadly. "How'd you know?"

"By the way Mary Anna was carrying the baby. I'm a medical doctor, remember?"

"Oh, yeah! I almost forgot!"

Hunter laughed. "Sometimes I can be fooled…but most of the time, I'm right. So when was little Julia Jackson born?"

"Tuesday. Mary Anna wrote me a long letter about it."

"Mama and baby all right?"

"Fine."

"Praise the Lord!"

"Amen. But there's something else, Hu—" The general looked around to see if anyone was within earshot then continued. "There's something else I want to tell you."

"Yes?"

"It was Jodie who delivered Julia."

"Jodie! How did that happen?"

"She used her two days off this week to visit Mary Anna, and the baby decided to come while she was there. Our doctor was out in the country delivering another baby, so Jodie did it all by herself."

"Well, what do you know!" said Hunter. "I knew from her last letter that she was planning to visit Mary Anna, but she hadn't settled on when." Hunter scratched his chin. "Tom, since Jodie delivered your daughter, and Jodie's going to be my wife...doesn't that make you and me some kind of relatives or something?"

Jackson chuckled. "I guess we're in-laws of some kind!"

"Did Mary Anna say if Julia looks like either of you?"

"She has lots of dark hair, like I used to have before it started thinning, but she strongly resembles her mother."

Hunter chuckled. "Well, little Julia can be thankful for that!"

Suddenly the general and the doctor were surrounded by soldiers who had come to congratulate the new father. After a few minutes, when most of men had gone, Rance Dayton and the four Antietam heroes walked up.

They congratulated Jackson on the birth of his baby girl, then Dayton said, "General, sir, these men and I took up a little collection among us. We'd like you to send it to Mrs. Jackson to buy your little girl something she might need."

As he spoke, Dayton handed the general a wad of Confederate bills. "It's ah...twenty-three dollars, sir. Actually, it was Corporal Carney's idea."

"Aw, Major, it wasn't either," said Carney. "It was Buford's idea. I'm just the one who brought it up to you."

Jackson was touched by the gesture and said, "Thank you...all of you. I'm sure Mary Anna will find something real nice for Julia with all this money. Your kindness means a lot to me."

"General Jackson," said Hank Upchurch, "we just wanted you to know how much we look up to you and respect you, sir."

"And we mean it from the bottom of our hearts, sir," said Everett Nichols. "We're proud to serve in II Corps, because you're our commander."

"Thank you," said Jackson. "You men are very kind."

"Just truthful, sir," said Carney.

Jackson ran his gaze over their fresh young faces. "I've not had the opportunity to ask you gentlemen about your spiritual state. Are you Christians? Do you know the Lord?"

Everett Nichols cleared his throat lightly and said, "We…ah…we're not like you and the major, General. We have our own ideas about religion, but we appreciate your concern for us."

"Major Dayton has talked to us about his newfound faith, General," said Chuck Carney. "But we're just not ready to get that involved with religion."

"It isn't religion, men," Dayton said. "I've told you before, there's a difference between religion and salvation—"

"Excuse me, gentlemen," said Lieutenant General James Longstreet, drawing near the small group. "General Lee asked to meet with us, General Jackson. He just received news from intelligence."

Rance Dayton and the young heroes excused themselves, and Jackson headed toward Lee's tent with Longstreet.

"Do you know what it's about?" asked Jackson.

"No. I just happened to be passing by his tent when a messenger handed him an envelope. He saw me and asked me to find you. Said the message was from intelligence, and he needed to talk to both of us."

Lee was standing in the opening of his tent as the two lieutenant generals drew up. "Come in, gentlemen," he said, gesturing them inside.

Lee waited until the two men had sat down, then said, "It's been a month since Lincoln replaced McClellan with Ambrose Burnside."

Longstreet and Jackson nodded.

"I figured things would begin to move," said Lee. "The message

I just received from Confederate intelligence is that Burnside is gathering his troops in preparation to cross the Potomac and head for Fredericksburg on a planned march to capture Richmond. Burnside wants to capture Fredericksburg first, which would serve as a stronghold for his rear flank as he marches to Richmond."

"So he'll be coming down the Rappahannock, right at us," said Longstreet.

"That's it. So, gentlemen…we're going to move on down to Fredericksburg and be there to meet Ambrose and his boys."

That night, before retiring, General Stonewall Jackson sat at his portable desk and took out pen, ink, and paper.

> December 6, 1862
> My sweet Mary Anna,
>
> Oh, how thankful I am to our kind heavenly Father for having spared my precious wife and given us a little daughter! I cannot tell you how gratified I am, nor how much I wish I could be with you and see my two darlings!
>
> You will be happy to hear that we have had revival here in the camp. Dr. Stiles did the preaching, and several hundred men have come to the Saviour! We are now about to engage the enemy once again. Thank you for praying for your husband.
>
> Tell my little Julia that Papa loves her. And never forget that I love her mother with all my heart!
>
> I will see you both when God wills.
>
> Your loving Tom

On December 10, General Burnside began laying pontoons across the Rappahannock River just north of Fredericksburg, Virginia. His plan to take Fredericksburg would leave him a direct, unhindered route to march his army fifty-seven miles due south to the Confederate capital.

General Lee was ready for him, having devised a plan using the ingenuity of his "right arm," Stonewall Jackson.

While the pontoon project was under way, Lee had the town evacuated on December 11. Once the people were out of Fredericksburg, Lee's Confederate sharpshooters were stationed in the trees along the river's banks and started picking off Union soldiers who were assembling the pontoon bridge. Dozens of bluecoats dropped dead in the water.

Angered at the Rebel guns, Burnside commanded his artillery to bombard the town. By December 12, the battle was in full array. Stonewall Jackson's II Corps distinguished itself in the battle along the river while I Corps, under General Longstreet's command, unleashed a bloody horror on the Yankees from atop a hill called Marye's Heights. General Lee was on the hill with Longstreet, looking on.

By darkness on December 13, the Union forces—though outnumbering the Confederate forces nearly two to one—had been soundly whipped by Lee, with losses mounting to over six thousand.

The discouraged and beaten Yankees pulled back to Falmouth, taking as many wounded with them as possible. Burnside's tactical blunder had cost the Union Army of the Potomac dearly.

On December 14, presidential secretary Hay knocked on the door of the Oval Office.

"Yes, John?" came the president's voice.

"A wire just came for you, sir."

Lincoln extended his bony hand to receive a white envelope. Hay waited while Lincoln read the message, and saw his countenance fall.

"Bad news, sir?"

Lincoln crumpled the paper in his hand. The permanent furrows in his brow deepened. "Yes. General Burnside has been defeated at Fredericksburg. Six thousand casualties. They've retreated back to Falmouth."

Hay bit his lower lip. "General Halleck will say he told you so, sir…as will many others."

Lincoln nodded. "I'm going to try to give General Burnside the benefit of the doubt, John. Some other general might not have done any better, given the same circumstances and an already discouraged army to lead."

"Yes, sir."

"Send for General Halleck, now, so I can talk to him."

When Hay was gone, Lincoln pressed stiff fingertips to his temples. He was close to letting down, but he couldn't let on to anyone how he really felt about having chosen Burnside to follow McClellan. In spite of everything, he still couldn't come up with another man he would have picked instead.

SEVEN

On Monday, December 15, Jodie Lockwood was back on the day shift at the Richmond hospital. As she washed up after assisting in surgery, Nurse Nan Fenton joined her and plunged her hands into the bowl of lye soap.

"I haven't talked to you in a couple of days, Jodie," she said. "Is Dr. McGuire still at Fredericksburg?"

"Yes," said Jodie, scrubbing her hands with vigor. "His wire yesterday said it's going to take quite some time to do the surgeries and patch up all the men who were wounded in the battle. General Lee is trying to get some more doctors there to help. Besides Hunter, there are only three other doctors. He says some of the wounded have died because they can't get to the men soon enough. They're working day and night as it is."

"Hmm. What about your wedding plans for Saturday?"

"I'm doing a lot of praying about it, I'll tell you that much."

"I sure hope you don't have to postpone the wedding."

"It's in the Lord's hands, Nan. Pastor Griffin says if Hunter can't get loose to come home, we'll have the wedding within a few days after he does get here. We have to give everybody who's invited a little bit of notice so they can attend."

"Well, I'll be there with bells on," said Nan, scrubbing her hands vigorously. "One thing about being a child of God…we know He has His powerful hand on our lives, and He cares about what's important to us. If next Saturday is His choice for your wedding day, Dr. McGuire will be back in time."

Jodie gave her friend a sunny smile and picked up a towel. "That's right, Nan. And Hunter and I only want His will in our lives. So…I'm praying that Hunter will be here in time, since the Lord says for us to pray; but whatever our heavenly Father chooses for us, we're willing to accept it."

On Wednesday morning, Jodie had her time of prayer and Bible reading, then went to breakfast in the dining room of her boarding-house. She had just returned to her room when someone knocked at the door.

Outside was a young corporal, who grinned at her and said, "Another wire for you, Miss Lockwood. It came to the camp from Fredericksburg about fifteen minutes ago."

"Thank you, Corporal."

As soon as Jodie closed the door, she ripped open the envelope and quickly read the message. "Oh, thank You, Lord Jesus!" she said. "Thank You!"

The wire from Hunter told her that extra help had come, and he and the other doctors were wrapping things up at Fredericksburg. He would be home late tomorrow afternoon.

When Jodie arrived at the hospital to begin her shift, Nan Fenton met her in the hall. One glance at Jodie's face and Nan said, "Did you get some good news?"

"Hunter will be home tomorrow! I stopped by the parsonage on the way to work and told Pastor Griffin."

"Oh, Jodie, that's wonderful! Guess I'd better get my bells ready!"

Jodie sighed. "I wish bells were all I had to get ready! Hunter and

I will have only one day to wrap up what we don't already have done."

"Is there anything I can do?"

"No, but thank you. What's left are things that only Hunter and I can do. We've already paid a month on our new apartment, so it stands ready. Looks like everything's going to go as planned."

"Miss Lockwood!" came the voice of the corporal who had delivered the wire at the boardinghouse.

Jodie turned and saw an envelope in his hand and giggled. "More?" she said.

"Yes, ma'am. This one's from Mrs. Stonewall Jackson."

"Oh, yes. Probably advising me of her and baby Julia's arrival on Friday."

Moments later, Jodie stepped into the ladies' powder room and opened the envelope. Her smile faded as she read the message.

At the same time Jodie was reading the wire from Mary Anna, Stonewall Jackson stood inside General Lee's tent at the army camp near Richmond.

As soon as they finished the meeting, Lee said, "Are Mary Anna and the baby still due to arrive Friday?"

Jackson smiled broadly. "Yes, sir! I can hardly wait to see both of them, but it will be especially sweet to see my little Julia for the first time."

"I assume, then, that Dr. McGuire's wedding is still on for Saturday?"

"It must be, sir. I'm sure that either Hunter or Jodie would have let me know by now if it wasn't. Last word I had from Hunter was, the doctors you sent had been such a big help that everything was under control."

"Good!" said Lee. "I'm looking forward to attending the doctor's wedding myself."

"Doc and Jodie make a beautiful couple."

When Longstreet and Jackson stepped outside the tent, the same corporal who had delivered the wire to Jodie Lockwood stood before them. He saluted and said, "General Jackson, I have a wire here from Mrs. Jackson. I would have had it in your hands sooner, but I didn't want to intrude on your meeting."

"That's all right, Corporal. Thank you."

The corporal and Longstreet walked away together, and Jackson opened the envelope. As he began reading the message, a deep frown penciled itself across his brow, and his shoulders slumped.

"General," came Lee's voice from behind him. "Something wrong?"

Jackson turned slowly, lifting his eyes from the paper. "Yes. Mary Anna's having some complications from the birth…some slight hemorrhaging. The doctor says she'll be all right, but she can't travel. I won't get to see her and my little Julia this weekend after all. She says she wired Jodie to let her know she can't be in the wedding."

When Hunter McGuire arrived in Richmond, late in the afternoon on Thursday, Jodie told him about Mary Anna and that she had chosen Nan Fenton to be her matron of honor. Hunter knew Nan and liked her. If Mary Anna couldn't be there, Nan was a fine replacement. Nan's husband was in the Confederate navy and was somewhere on the Gulf of Mexico.

The wedding practice on Friday night went well, though Stonewall Jackson couldn't hide his sadness at Mary Anna and baby Julia's absence.

Hunter and Jodie were also saddened to learn that Hunter's adoptive parents would not be able to attend. All passenger trains heading south out of Union territory had been halted for the time being.

Saturday evening came, and the wedding moved with precision.

The newlyweds had only two days for a honeymoon, which they spent in a small cabin in the Blue Ridge Mountains.

On Monday, December 22, Gertie Zimmer thanked the messenger who had brought a telegram and then headed for the parlor. Mary Anna, looking a bit pale, had just finished feeding little Julia. She looked up quickly as Gertie entered the room.

"Is it a wire from Tom?"

"Yes," said Gertie. "Let me take the baby so you can read it."

As Mary Anna read the message, a distressed expression captured her wan features and her lower lip began to tremble.

"He won't be coming home for Christmas, will he?" Gertie said levelly.

"No. General Lee is keeping his entire army right where they are. Tom says General Lee fears the Yankees might try to take them off guard because it's holiday time. They must be prepared."

"Well, even though I was going to go home in another day or two," said Gertie, "I'll just stay right here. I don't want you alone on Christmas."

Mary Anna pressed fingertips to her lips and blinked against the tears that had surfaced. "I was alone last Christmas, too, because of the War. Maybe…maybe by next Christmas, this will all be over and Tom can be here with us."

"I sure hope so, honey."

Mary Anna looked up at her loyal friend and said, "You can come and spend Christmas with us, Gertie. I don't want you alone on Christmas either."

"I'll take you up on it," Gertie said, kissing little Julia's chubby cheek. "I'll look forward to it."

On Christmas day, General Burnside's army was still camped at Falmouth, Virginia.

Late in the afternoon on the following Monday, December 29, word came to President Lincoln and military officials in Washington that General Burnside was preparing to lead his troops south. The message contained no details, but Lincoln and the officials with him realized this would mean another crossing of the Rappahannock, and another battle at or near Fredericksburg.

Shortly after the president had learned of Burnside's intentions, presidential secretary John Hay looked up from his desk to see a crimson-faced General Halleck stomp through the door.

"I want to see the president...now!" Halleck said.

Hay laid down his writing instrument and spoke quietly as he said, "President Lincoln anticipated your arrival, General, and is also expecting Mr. Stanton. He told me to tell both of you gentlemen that he's trying to make contact with General Burnside, and that it would be better if he met with the two of you after he learns some details from him."

Halleck's face grew darker, and his breathing sounded ragged.

"The president said I was to tell both you and Mr. Stanton to be here at ten o'clock tomorrow morning. He will discuss the situa-tion with you then."

Halleck exhaled gustily and said, "I want to talk to the president right now!"

Hay let a smile tug at the corners of his mouth and said firmly, "I have given you Mr. Lincoln's message, General. Your meeting with him is tomorrow morning at ten o'clock. Therefore, I will not ven-ture to knock on his door and tell him you demand to see him right now. However, if you wish to barge through the door on your own and make your demand, there it is."

Halleck stood, clenching and unclenching his hands. He stared for a moment at the door that led to the Oval Office, then pivoted and walked away, mumbling curses at Burnside.

On Tuesday morning at 8:30, John Hay was filing papers in the cab-inet behind his desk when Secretary of State William Seward entered.

"Good morning, Mr. Seward," Hay said with a smile.

"And good morning to you, John. Is Mr. Lincoln in his office?"

"Yes, sir."

"I have Brigadier Generals John Newton and John Cochrane in the hall. They've just arrived from Falmouth and would like to see the president. They said it's of the utmost importance and has to do with General Burnside's latest announcement."

"Mr. Lincoln has an appointment at ten o'clock with General Halleck and Secretary Stanton, Mr. Seward, but I think he'll have time to see the generals before then. Just a moment."

Hay entered the Oval Office and returned a minute later. "Yes, Mr. Seward, the president will see Generals Newton and Cochrane in a few minutes. Have them come in."

Seward ushered the generals into Hay's office and introduced them, then excused himself. Hay took their hats and coats and invited Newton and Cochrane to sit down, saying that Mr. Lincoln would see them shortly. Then he returned to his work at the filing cabinet.

Some three or four minutes had passed when the hall door opened and a nine-year-old boy entered.

"Hello, Tad," said Hay as the boy approached him.

"Hello, Mr. Hay. I need to see my father."

The generals looked on in bewilderment as Hay preceded the boy to the office door, knocked, and then stuck his head in to say, "Mr. President, Tad is here to see you."

"Send him in," came the familiar voice.

When Hay closed the door behind Tad, he turned to the generals and said, "I'm sorry, gentlemen, but you'll have to wait until Mr. Tad Lincoln has whatever time he needs with his father."

"I would think the boy could have waited until after we saw the president," Cochrane said.

John Hay smiled. "It doesn't work that way, sir. Mr. Lincoln considers himself a husband and father first, and president and military commander-in-chief second."

The generals exchanged glances again. Then Cochrane's frown disappeared as Newton said, "I'll say this, General Cochrane…the whole world would be in better shape if all husbands and fathers took the same philosophy!"

Cochrane nodded, and after a few seconds, replied, "Can't argue with that."

Almost ten minutes had passed before the door to the Oval Office finally swung open and the president appeared with his son.

"Thank you, Papa," said Tad, smiling up at his father.

"My pleasure, Tad. See you tonight."

"See you tonight, Papa," said Tad, heading toward the hall door. When he reached the door, he looked back and said, "I love you, Papa."

"I love you too, son."

When Tad was gone, Lincoln set his deep-set, tired gaze on Cochrane and Newton, and said, "Come in, gentlemen." He shook their hands, bid them sit down, and lowered himself to his chair with a sigh. "All right, gentlemen," he said, his voice revealing his weariness, "what can you tell me about the situation at Falmouth?"

With concern evident on his face, Brigadier General Newton said, "Mr. President, we've been sent here by Major Generals William B. Franklin and William F. Smith, who would have come themselves, but in their positions of command they don't dare leave Falmouth at this time."

Lincoln nodded. "All right."

"Sir," spoke up Cochrane, "Generals Franklin and Smith have asked us to inform you that all of the generals in the Army of the Potomac have lost faith in General Burnside, as have the other officers, and even the bulk of the troops." Cochrane paused, then said, "And I have to be honest with you, Mr. President. I didn't have faith in General Burnside from day one. He's a good man…but he isn't leadership material for an army the size of ours."

"I agree, sir," said Newton. "As we see it, this is an army scarred by repeated failures under George McClellan, and now a devastating defeat at Fredericksburg under Burnside. No failure under McClellan, however, has seemed so senseless and pointless to the men as the one under Burnside."

Lincoln scrubbed a bony hand across his mouth, blinking slowly to acknowledge that he understood what Newton was saying.

"Sir," said Cochrane, "Generals Franklin and Smith, as well as all the other generals, fear that the men are so demoralized that they might do the unthinkable if they have to enter another battle under Burnside—they might simply refuse to fight, and walk away."

Lincoln's jaw slacked in disbelief.

"Yes, sir," said Cochrane. "The officers have picked up an under-current of talk in that direction."

"I have a meeting at ten o'clock with General Halleck and Secretary Stanton," Lincoln said. "I will relay this information to them." He rose from his chair and shook their hands. "I want to thank you gentlemen for coming. And please express my apprecia-tion to Generals Franklin and Smith for sending you. Tell them I was not aware things had gotten this bad."

"We'll do that, sir," said Newton. "And thank you for giving us of your time."

"My pleasure. I assure you, gentlemen, that good will come from this interview. And please make sure Generals Franklin and Smith know that I said so."

"We will do that, sir," said Newton.

Lincoln followed them into the outer office, where John Hay gave them their hats and coats.

As soon as they had passed through the door, the president turned to Hay and said, "John, when General Halleck and Mr. Stanton arrive, bring them into my office without delay."

On Saturday afternoon, January 3, 1863, Confederate unit leaders were gathering their men at the campsite on the Rappahannock, some in the forest and others by the river.

Major Rance Dayton stood before the four hundred men of the Eighteenth North Carolina Regiment, who were seated on the river-bank. The air had a bite to it, and the men could see their breath as they huddled together and pulled up the collars of their overcoats.

The closest unit to them was some thirty yards downstream.

"Men," said Dayton, "as you know, all unit leaders had a meeting with Generals Lee, Jackson, and Longstreet a little while ago. Word has come from our Washington spies that there's serious trouble in the ranks of the Army of the Potomac."

There was a low murmur as the men smiled at each other. They listened closely as Dayton explained that General Burnside had been about to move his troops out of Falmouth and begin another offensive on Fredericksburg as a minor pause on his way to Richmond. However, the big brass put a stop to it.

A hoot of laughter went up.

"We understand," Dayton said, "that last Tuesday Abe Lincoln had a meeting with General Halleck, his general-in-chief, and Secretary of War Edwin Stanton. Lincoln had received word there was talk amongst the men of rebellion if they had to fight another battle under Ambrose Burnside."

More laughter.

"This rebellion, our spies tell us, is actually being led by some of the Yankee generals. They have no confidence in Burnside as a military leader. Word is that after Lincoln met with Halleck and Stanton, he sent a message to Burnside to scrap the idea of moving on Fredericksburg again, and to stay put, pending further orders. Lincoln now has the proverbial tiger by the tail. He's afraid to hang on and afraid to let go. General Lee believes Lincoln is probably losing sleep while he tries to come up with another general to take Burnside's place. No doubt this will give us a respite in fighting until he's got a new leader for his Army of the Potomac."

The men of the Eighteenth raised a cheer. Other cheers went up around the camp as the other groups of soldiers heard the news.

When Dayton had dismissed the men of the Eighteenth, he and the four corporals from his hometown huddled around a fire and talked about old times in Fayetteville. Dayton had no family there anymore, but the corporals shared news from letters they had received from family members.

Soon the conversation went to the War.

Buford Hall said, "Maybe ol' Abe Lincoln will just get so fed up tryin' to find a general who can lead his Army of the Potomac that he'll call the whole war off."

"Wouldn't that be wonderful?" said Dayton. "Then we could all go back home and try to put our lives together."

Chuck Carney held his cold hands over the fire as he glanced at Dayton and said, "Major, do you think you can get elected sheriff of Cumberland County again?"

"I'm not even going to try, Chuck."

"Why not? You've said plenty of times that you want to get back into law enforcement."

"I'll definitely do that, but not in Fayetteville. I guess a moment ago I should have said *you* can all go home and try to put your lives back together. Since my family has died off, Fayetteville isn't really home to me anymore."

"Where will you go, sir?" asked Hank Upchurch.

"When the War's over, I plan to go out West and start a new life on the frontier. I want to become marshal of one of those cattle towns, find the right woman, get married, and enjoy life."

Buford Hall grinned at the major and said, "A lot of women out there in the wild and woolly West don't want to marry a man who wears a badge, sir. I've read about it in some magazines. The women are afraid of becomin' widows too quick."

Dayton chuckled. "That's why I said I'd find the right woman, Buford. The Lord will cross my path with the one He has chosen for me. She'll be the right one, and she'll marry me in spite of my badge."

Everett Nichols went to the nearby pile of firewood and threw some more logs on the fire. As he sat down again, he said, "Major, you sure won't have any problem findin' a job as a lawman out there in the West. Not if those folks know about your fantastic record as a deputy sheriff and then as sheriff of Cumberland County."

"That's for sure," put in Chuck Carney. "I remember reading about that when you were running for sheriff. And you got a big write-up in newspapers all over the South when you resigned as sheriff to join the Confederate army."

"Yeah!" said Nichols. "Rance Dayton hunted down and brought to justice more criminals than any peace officer on record in the entire South!"

"How many murderers did you put on the gallows, Major?" asked Hall.

Dayton chuckled. "I really don't recall. I didn't keep a record book."

"I'd be safe in sayin' he put at least thirty coldblooded killers' necks in the noose," said Upchurch. "And probably sent better'n a hundred and fifty to prison for lesser crimes."

"Well, one thing's for sure," said Carney, "once people out West know his record, they'll be standing in line to pin a badge on him."

Hank Upchurch got misty-eyed as he realized that even if they all survived the War, life would never be the same. Maybe more of his boyhood friends would strike out for parts unknown. He felt sadness wash over him, but all he said was, "Major, Fayetteville sure won't be the same without you livin' there. We'll really miss you."

The others murmured agreement, and then a somber quiet settled over the small group.

It was Dayton who seemed to speak for everyone when he said, "Well, there are five marvelous men I'll never forget, I'll tell you that much. I wish Billy Dean were alive to hear me say it…but I want to thank you men one more time from the bottom of my heart for laying your lives on the line to save mine. You'll always be very special men in my memories, and in my life."

"The same goes for us, Major," said Hank.

Dayton smiled. "Fellas, if there's ever anything I can do for any of you…consider it done."

Chuck guffawed and said, "Who knows! Maybe someday we'll all need a favor!"

EIGHT

On Sunday morning, January 25, 1863, General-in-Chief Henry Halleck and Secretary of War Edwin Stanton walked down a long hall of the White House, greeting maids and janitors as they went. When they reached the east wing, they started up the winding staircase to the second floor.

"I sure hope he's going to tell us Burnside is out and General Meade is in," said Halleck. "And if not Meade...then Porter, Sumner, or Franklin."

"You're aware that he's also considered Hooker?" asked Stanton.

"Yes, and I've already expressed my opinion of Hooker to the president. I can't believe Mr. Lincoln would consider putting that man at the head of the Army of the Potomac."

At the top of the stairs they turned toward the open door of John Hay's office.

Hay stood and greeted them with a smile, saying, "Good morning, General Halleck, Secretary Stanton. Mr. Lincoln said to bring you in as soon as you arrived." He walked them to the door of the Oval Office and without knocking ushered them in.

Lincoln greeted the men and gestured for them to sit down before he eased into his own chair with a sigh. He looked at them with a steady gaze and said, "My decision has been made, gentlemen. As of today, I am relieving General Burnside of his command."

"This is good news, sir," said Stanton. "I was hoping the purpose of this meeting was to let General Halleck and me know that you had decided to replace him."

"Indeed it is good news, Mr. President," said Halleck almost boisterously. "And I trust you're appointing one of the generals we discussed earlier."

Lincoln nodded. "I'm appointing Major General Hooker in General Burnside's stead."

Both men looked as if they'd been slapped in the face.

Lincoln watched their expressions closely as he said, "General Hooker is the best qualified of any general I have."

"But, Mr. President," said Halleck, "what about General Meade?"

"He hasn't the combat experience of General Hooker," Lincoln said flatly. "Neither do Generals Sumner, Porter, or Franklin. Hooker has more experience than all of them."

"But, sir," said Stanton, "Hooker is a hard drinker. What if he gets drunk when it's time to lead his army?"

"He won't. He knows better than to do that."

Stanton frowned. "But he's also foul-mouthed, sir. I've heard many men who have served under him say they feel like they need to wash their ears out after having a conversation with him. I realize we can't change a man's speech habits, but as a leader of men, he should be an example as an officer and a gentleman. No gentleman uses his kind of language… especially in front of others."

Stanton looked toward General Halleck, silently urging him to support his comments.

"Mr. President," Halleck said, "the man's morals are corrupt. On many occasions when he's been camped somewhere between battles, he's brought prostitutes to his men."

"That's right," said Stanton. "The man is vulgar."

Lincoln bent his head and rubbed his tired eyes, then said,

"Gentlemen, I know General Hooker's character is far from what it ought to be. I abhor the prostitute thing and his foul mouth...but I've got a bloody war on my hands, and General Hooker's record as a leader of men in combat is extraordinary. That's why he's been dubbed Fighting Joe. Right now he's stronger in his military prowess than any other general in the eastern theater. And as I've already stated, he's the most experienced in battle leadership of all the leaders I have to pick from."

"But, sir," said Halleck, "I wish you would consider one of the other generals in spite of the experience element."

"He is the man I must appoint to lead the Army of the Potomac, General Halleck," said the president, "for he's the best choice there is. I'm convinced he's the right general to command this shaken army, which desperately needs its confidence restored."

Halleck and Stanton exchanged glances but could think of nothing more to say.

Lincoln leaned his bony elbows on the desktop and said, "If either of you gentlemen can suggest another man who has as much experience as General Hooker in combat leadership and the willingness to engage the enemy in battle, I'm ready to listen."

Halleck and Stanton were silent for a long moment, then Halleck chuckled. "There is one man, Mr. President. He has much more experience in combat leadership than Hooker, and he's never hesitated to lead his men into battle, no matter how fierce. And he's been the victor in battle after battle."

Stanton stared at Halleck, trying to think of whom he spoke.

Lincoln's heavy eyebrows arched. "Well, who is he?"

Halleck chuckled again. "That's the one hitch, sir. He isn't one of our generals. But if we could persuade Stonewall Jackson to switch sides and take over the Army of the Potomac, we'd see this war finished in a hurry."

Stanton chortled. "That's for sure! Think what that man has done with a much smaller number of troops than he would have if he was on our side. A shortage of guns, ammunition, and supplies, yet he's brought off victory after victory."

"Well, only in our dreams will we ever persuade General Jackson to become a Yankee," said Lincoln.

"How well I know," said Halleck. "But you can't fault me for wishing."

Lincoln managed a slight smile. "But since we must face reality, and between us we can't come up with a man from our army to match General Hooker's military experience…my decision to appoint him as field commander of the Union Army of the Potomac will stand."

On Monday afternoon, at his field tent on the Rappahannock, General Lee received a wire from Confederate intelligence and immediately called for his corps leaders. While he was waiting for them to arrive, the mail came, and in it a letter from Confederate Secretary of War James A. Seddon.

Lee had finished reading the wire and the letter by the time Lieutenant Generals Longstreet and Jackson entered his tent.

As soon as they were seated Lee said, "Gentlemen, I have a wire from intelligence and a letter from Mr. Seddon. The wire informs me that Mr. Lincoln has appointed Major General Joseph Hooker as new commander of the Union Army of the Potomac."

"Hmm," said Longstreet. "Ol' Fighting Joe, eh?"

Jackson rubbed the back of his neck. "Well, if they can keep Joe off the whiskey, he'll be leading his army this way once he can get it reorganized. We'll have some real war on our hands with him at the head of it."

"We will act accordingly," said Lee. "Now, for Secretary Seddon's letter. He says there is unusual activity at the southern tip of the Virginia Peninsula, which as you gentlemen know has long been held by the Yankees. Seddon fears they may be planning to launch an attack against Richmond from that direction, or they may even be preparing to open a new front in North Carolina."

"Either way, we need to get some manpower headed in that direction, sir," said Longstreet, tugging at his long beard.

"Correct," said Lee. "I was thinking about it while waiting for you gentlemen. We must not delay. I'm going to send two crack divisions out of your I Corps, General Longstreet—George Pickett's and John Bell Hood's."

"Yes, sir."

"And I'm going to send you with them, General," said Lee. "I'll feel better if you are leading them."

"If you say so, sir, it's all right with me."

"Good. I'll command I Corps here in northern Virginia myself."

Longstreet chuckled. "Once the men serve directly under you, sir, they'll see what a great soldier you are, and they won't want me back."

Lee grinned and said to Jackson, "The man's a flatterer."

"Yes, sir. But my mother used to say that flattery is only soft soap, and soap is 99 percent lye!"

The three men had a good laugh.

On February 2, Mary Anna Jackson was washing diapers in the kitchen when she heard a knock at the front door. She let the scrub board slide back into the tub of water and quickly dried her hands as she hurried to the door.

"Jodie!" she exclaimed when she opened the door, spreading her arms wide.

Jodie dropped her overnight bag on the porch and gave her friend a big hug. Mary Anna quickly pulled Jodie inside as she felt the cold air rushing past her into the parlor.

"Oh! It's so wonderful to see you, Jodie! To what do I owe this pleasant surprise?"

Smiling broadly, Jodie said, "To the fact that this is little Julia's two-month birthday!"

Mary Anna laughed and hugged her friend again. "Does this mean you'll come and see us every two months?"

"Can't guarantee that, but I just couldn't wait any longer to see both of you!"

"Julia's asleep in her crib right now, but we can go into my bedroom and sneak a look at her if you want to. I only put her down about twenty minutes ago. She usually sleeps a couple of hours."

"Let's go," Jodie whispered. "I can't wait to see how much she's grown!"

The women tiptoed into the bedroom, and tears came quickly to Jodie's eyes as she studied the chubby little face and marveled over how much the baby had changed already.

Mary Anna quietly placed another log on the fire, then led the way to the kitchen.

While Jodie pitched in to help with the washing, Mary Anna asked for all the details of the wedding. By the time the washing was done, they were talking about how the War was going in the western theater, and discussing the new developments to the east.

"With the way things are shaping up on the peninsula, and the threat of Hooker coming down the Rappahannock, I know Hunter has been tied to the camp," said Mary Anna. "Tom's letters keep me up on news of him."

"Yes," said Jodie. "I haven't seen much of him since we returned from the honeymoon. And according to Hunter's letters, General Jackson hasn't yet been home."

"You mean Tom, don't you?" said Mary Anna. "You did say you would consider calling him Tom after you and Hunter were married."

Jodie laughed. "Oh, I did, didn't I? Well, while I'm considering it, I'll still speak of him as the general."

Mary Anna shook her head in mock exasperation, then her expression sobered. "It's so sad that the baby is two months old and her papa has yet to lay eyes on her."

"It sure is," agreed Jodie. She paused for a moment and then asked, "In his letters, has the general described the winter quarters he and Hunter are sharing?"

"Oh, yes. Sounds pretty nice, doesn't it?"

Soon they were comparing notes on the way their husbands had described the English-style manor house on an estate called Moss Neck, which overlooked the Rappahannock River some eleven miles below Fredericksburg.

By the time they had the kitchen cleaned up, baby Julia's cry could be heard from down the hall, and Jodie rushed to pick her up. Mary Anna watched as Jodie lifted the baby out of the crib. Immediately Julia stopped crying.

Jodie kissed her soft little face and said, "I think we've got another dirty diaper to deal with."

After the infant had been changed and powdered, Jodie carried her into the parlor and Mary Anna followed. When they sat down, facing each other over the coffee table, Jodie cooed to Julia, and the baby smiled as Jodie jiggled her little fat cheeks.

From a small end table next to where she sat, Mary Anna lifted a magazine. "Have you seen this, Jodie?"

Focusing on the cover, Jodie saw that it was the January issue of the *Southern Literary Messenger*. She shook her head no.

"Well, you've heard of the well-known Rebel correspondent, Peter Alexander, haven't you?"

"Oh, yes. Quite a writer. I've seen his articles in other magazines and newspapers. Has he written something in that issue?"

"Yes, and it's about Tom!"

"Oh, really? Tell me about it! What does he say?"

Jodie kissed Julia's chubby cheeks again as Mary Anna opened the magazine and flashed the two-page article with a small photograph of the general. The headline read:

HERO OF THE WAR: LIEUTENANT GENERAL STONEWALL JACKSON

Mary Anna began reading the article aloud, which described Jackson's reputation as an outstanding military officer. The article also identified the many distinguished foreign visitors who had visited Stonewall at Moss Neck. He was greatly admired abroad as well as at home.

Jodie was touched by the article and smiled from ear to ear. "You must be very proud of your husband, Mary Anna," she said.

Mary Anna swiped at tears rolling down her cheeks and said, "Oh, I am very proud of him, Jodie, and I miss him so terribly!"

"Too bad nothing was said about the general's strong Christian character, his love for the Bible, and his love for the Lord."

Mary Anna nodded. "I guess Mr. Alexander wasn't interested in that side of my husband."

"Apparently not. He can't help but know that the general is a Christian, though. Too many people talk about his clear testimony of faith in Christ, and his eagerness to bring others to Him."

"Oh, Mr. Alexander knows what my husband is, all right, but this article was just to show him as the soldier. Plenty could be written of him as a Christian husband and his dedication to the Lord. And once he has a chance to be with his daughter, I know he'll shine as a father." Mary Anna suddenly looked stricken. "I just hope he can see little Julia soon."

Jodie stood up with the baby in her arms and said, "Honey, let's just talk to the Lord about that right now."

Jodie lay Julia on the sofa, and the two women knelt beside her and prayed together, asking the Lord to allow Tom to be able to see his little daughter soon. They also prayed that God would protect their husbands in the War.

As the weeks passed after his appointment as commander of the Union Army of the Potomac, Major General Joseph Hooker gained popularity in the North in spite of his dissolute character.

Given to arrogant pretension, Hooker was quoted in the Northern newspapers as saying, "My battle plans are perfect. May God have mercy on Bobby Lee, for I will have none."

Such a positive note, though edged with self-boasting, was enough to give hope to the people of the North that they could yet be victorious in the War between the States.

Songs were written about 'Fighting Joe' Hooker, and balladeers sang them in theaters, drinking establishments, and even on street corners. One song, which became popular quickly, had a line that proclaimed: "Joe Hooker is our leader; he takes his whiskey strong!"

Spirits rose in the Union camps along the Rappahannock as Hooker continued to form his battle plans. With his blessing, a number of officers sent for their wives and children to join them in their quarters, lightening everyone's mood.

As far as many of the men in his army were concerned, Fighting Joe's stock was rising fast. And by early April, the Union Army of the Potomac, in Hooker's words, was "in condition to inspire the highest expectations."

Those expectations, however, were diminished by two things—relentless rain, and the fact that nearly a third of Hooker's infantrymen were scheduled to leave the army in the next three months. They had signed up for two years early in the War and would be discharged by the end of June.

Hooker announced that he would do all in his power to convince them to reenlist. But they were tired of fighting, and many were still not convinced that the Union could be victorious over the Confederacy and its doggedly stubborn leaders and fighting men. Unsure of his success in getting them to reenlist, Hooker planned to move his campaign ahead as soon as the rains let up.

During the rainy season in Virginia, even the best-equipped and best-prepared army would be hostage to the inclement weather. This was the case as one hard rain after another turned Virginia roads to bottomless mud, transformed small creeks and brooks into raging rivers, and made rivers like the Rappahannock too deep and swift for even cavalry to ford safely.

***

At the Confederate capitol in Richmond, on a rainy day during the first week of April, General Robert E. Lee and President Jefferson Davis stood together, looking through a rain-splattered window at the storm. With lightning flashing, thunder rolling, and trees limbs cracking in the wind, Lee said, "Hooker offers me no more to worry about than any of his predecessors, sir."

"Well, I'm glad to hear that, General," said Davis.

"I hold very little respect for the man."

"Are you referring to his low morals?"

"Well, I didn't have that in mind, although it certainly disgusts me. What I meant was, as a soldier I hold very little respect for him. His arrogance and constant bragging about what he's going to do to me is a bunch of hot air as far as I'm concerned."

"He does blow hard, doesn't he?"

"Yes. Now, George McClellan is one Yankee leader I did respect—both as an officer and a gentleman. His timidity, however, made him relatively easy to predict. I have only contempt for General John Pope. He blundered the Union's chances of victory in the second battle at Bull Run, and certainly General Burnside's floundering at Fredericksburg drew him no respect from this Southern boy."

Davis had to raise his voice above the rumble of thunder as he said, "So what do you think of all this talk by Hooker of a master battle plan?"

"Hot air, sir. I don't expect any surprises from him. If the commander of an army really has something big to spring on his enemy, he doesn't blow off about it. He implements it quietly. All this loud talk doesn't impress me, even though Hooker will command an army twice the size of mine when we go to battle."

"What about that latest quote of his that he commands the finest army on planet earth?"

"More of the same old stuff. His army is untested under his command. Such a statement is meant to intimidate us. Well, Mr. President, we will not be intimidated, but we *will* meet Mr. Hooker on the field of battle and let him see what a small army of determined, courageous men can do." Lee paused, then said, "Only don't tell him I said so. I don't want to sound like a braggart."

Davis uttered an appreciative laugh.

The heavy rains continued almost daily, keeping the land soft and the roads virtually impassable.

On April 17, Stonewall Jackson met with General Lee at Lee's headquarters in an old farmhouse near the raging Rappahannock.

"Well, of course I don't mind, General," said Lee. "It's past time for you to see your little daughter and to be with Mary Anna. Exactly where is William Yerby's farm?"

"Only three miles due north of the Moss Neck place, sir…but it would give us some privacy that we wouldn't enjoy at Moss Neck. Too many other officers and medical personnel have moved in there."

"Will Dr. McGuire remain at Moss Neck?"

"He feels it best to let me have all the privacy I can get when my family comes."

"You know this Yerby family well, do you?"

"Not real well, but they are admirers of mine and made the offer so I could have a place to spend time with Mary Anna and the baby."

"You had better move fast on it, then," said Lee. "The rains will begin letting up as we get closer to May, and when those roads start drying out, ol' Joe Hooker will be moving this way."

"I'll send Mary Anna a wire and get her here with the baby as soon as possible," said Jackson. "Thank you for understanding, sir."

"I'm a family man too," said Lee with a smile. "It's just that my children are all grown. I miss my Mary like you miss your Mary Anna, but it's got to be eating your heart out that you haven't held that baby in your arms."

"Yes, sir, it is."

"Well, keep me posted as to when you're going to move to the Yerby place, and be sure to greet Mary Anna for me."

"I'll do that, sir." Jackson headed toward the door.

"Oh, and General…give little Julia a hug from Robert E. Lee, would you?"

"As soon as I give her a hundred from her father, sir."

Lee was still grinning as Jackson left him.

On April 18, Stonewall Jackson was in the room he shared with Hunter McGuire at the Moss Neck estate when there was a knock at the door. McGuire was cleaning his medical instruments at a table, and Jackson was sitting in a chair in a far corner, polishing his boots.

"I'll get it, Tom," said Hunter, heading toward the door.

"Wire for General Jackson, Doctor," said a corporal as he handed an envelope to Hunter. "It's from Mrs. Jackson."

"Thanks, Corporal!" called Jackson, waving at him.

Hunter closed the door and turned to face his friend. "Want me to read it to you, Tom?"

"Sure," Jackson said, rubbing a boot with a soft cloth to bring out the shine. "Since it's a wire, there won't be any mushy stuff, which would be none of your business!"

Hunter laughed and tore open the envelope. After reading the brief message, he said, "Well, it's going to happen, Tom. Mary Anna is bringing your daughter on the train from Lexington on Tuesday. They will arrive at Guiney's Station at ten-thirty that morning."

"Hallelujah!" Jackson shouted.

The rain had fallen all day on Monday and was still falling on Tuesday morning, April 21, when Stonewall Jackson's aide, Corporal Jim Lewis, drove him in a borrowed carriage to the depot.

"Since this carriage has a roof on it, sir," said Lewis, "I'll wait here for you and your family."

"Fine, Jim," said Jackson, picking up an umbrella at his feet. "See you in a few minutes."

Even as the general spoke, the sound of the train whistle filled the air, and he jumped down from the carriage and dashed to the depot.

A few people waited inside for the arrival of passengers. The general recognized two lieutenants from Longstreet's I Corps and nodded at them.

As the train chugged in and stopped, Jackson scanned the three coaches, trying to see inside, but the windows were covered with rain and filmed with moisture on the inside.

Suddenly Stonewall's eyes locked on the small dark-haired woman who was stepping off the rear platform of the second car. She was cradling a small bundle in her arms.

When Mary Anna's eyes found Tom's, his heart leaped in his chest.

NINE

In no more than a few seconds, Tom had enfolded Mary Anna, with the baby between them, in his arms.

His face and hat brim dripped rainwater as he bent his head to kiss her. "I hope you don't mind getting a little wet."

Mary Anna let him know how little the rain mattered as her tears mingled with the raindrops and she returned his kiss.

Easing back after a prolonged kiss, Jackson eagerly reached toward the covering blanket and said, "Let me see her!"

"Excuse me, Mrs. Jackson," came the voice of the conductor beside them. "Here's your luggage."

"Oh, yes," said Mary Anna. "Thank you, Mr. Compton."

"I'll take it, sir," said Jackson. "Thank you."

"You are most welcome, General," said the conductor, admiration showing in his eyes. "God bless you, sir."

"And may the Lord bless you too, Mr. Compton," Jackson said with feeling. As the conductor walked away, Stonewall turned back for the first look at his baby daughter.

Mary Anna lifted the blanket from Julia's face, and Jackson smiled broadly as he said, "Oh, sweetheart, she's beautiful! I…I want to hold her, but this slicker is sopping. I don't want to get her wet."

The sound of his strong, deep voice drew little Julia's attention. She set her eyes on him and released a toothless grin.

"Look, Mary Anna, she's smiling at me! She knows me! Hello, precious darling. You know I'm your papa, don't you?"

Julia made a cooing sound.

"Did you hear that, Mary Anna? She said yes!"

By this time, a small crowd had collected to take in the rare scene of the rugged military leader reduced to mush.

A middle-aged woman said to her husband, "That's the way you acted the first time you saw your little Harriet, Ralph."

"Hey, General Jackson!" came the voice of a Confederate soldier with sergeant's stripes on his arm. "Congratulations, sir! We heard you'd had a baby. I…I mean that your wife had a baby."

The other soldiers with him laughed.

Stonewall looked up and smiled, then said, "Let's go, sweetheart. Jim Lewis is waiting in the carriage. I'll hold my little darling when I can get out of this slicker."

Rain was still pouring down as Stonewall Jackson picked up Mary Anna's small piece of luggage and held the umbrella over her and the baby as they hurried to the carriage.

Jackson quickly introduced Mary Anna to Jim Lewis and helped her into the carriage, then placed the suitcase and umbrella on the floor behind the second seat and peeled out of his slicker. He laid it on the third seat and tossed his hat on top of it, then jumped in beside Mary Anna and closed the door.

He held his arms open, and Mary Anna gently laid the baby in her husband's hands.

"Jim," said the general, "this is absolutely the most beautiful baby girl the Lord ever made!"

Lewis twisted on the seat and glanced at the dark-haired infant. "Well, I declare, sir, you're right! She sure is!"

"And what if Jim had not agreed with you?" said Mary Anna.

Stonewall chuckled. "He'd be lying out there in the road with a broken neck!"

Lewis laughed. "Sure am glad I have good eyesight, sir!"

The general took hold of Mary Anna's graceful chin and kissed her softly, then said, "Thank you for giving me such a precious little daughter!"

Stonewall caressed little Julia's tiny cheeks, speaking words of love to her, and every few seconds he kissed her face. Mary Anna felt a warmth flood her heart at the sight of how much her husband loved and delighted in the baby.

The drive to the Yerby farm was less than four miles. When they arrived, Corporal Lewis drove them to the front porch, and General Jackson thanked his aide for driving the carriage and all that entailed—taking the carriage to the barn and unhitching the horses, then riding his own horse back to the Moss Neck estate, where he had a room.

Inside, Jackson introduced Mary Anna to William and Frances Yerby. Though Jackson had already been occupying the large guest room at the rear of the house, the Yerbys led them upstairs and down the hall to the room. Frances Yerby wanted to explain to Mary Anna where everything was kept.

The room was beautifully furnished, and Frances had made sure Mary Anna had everything she needed to care for the baby. Little Julia even had her own crib, which stood near the large canopied bed.

When they were finally alone, Tom Jackson laid the baby on the bed, kissed her cheeks some more, then took Mary Anna in his arms. When they had held each other for some time, the baby began to fuss.

"She's just jealous," said the general.

Mary Anna put her hands on her hips and laughed. "Oh, so that's it. I almost forgot I was married to quite a ladies' man."

"Wasn't that why you fell for me? Because I'm so handsome and irresistible?"

"Why, of course. I just couldn't help myself."

"Well, neither can Julia. She's crazy about me and jealous when I hold another woman." He stooped over to pick up the baby. As soon as he did, she stopped fussing. "See? What did I tell you? She was jealous."

"My eyes tell me you're right," said Mary Anna contentedly as she sat down in an overstuffed chair.

Jackson carried little Julia to a large full-length mirror that stood near the door. Placing her tiny face next to his own, he studied their images in the glass. "You know what, Mary Anna?"

"What?"

"Julia really does look a lot like you."

"That's what most people say."

"Of course, as I look closely, I can see that she does have my nose."

"I've noticed that myself. But I'm sure her nose will get prettier as she grows older."

Jackson laughed. "How could something so perfect get prettier?"

Julia began to fuss again and Mary Anna got up from the chair and held out her arms. "She's hungry and no doubt needs a diaper change." Grinning slyly, she added, "Tell you what. Why don't you change her diaper while I get ready to feed her?"

II Corps's brave and dauntless commander turned pale. "Me? Change her diaper? But, honey, I…well, I've never changed a diaper in my whole life! I—"

Mary Anna burst into laughter. "I was just kidding! You sit down and rest your bones, O fearless Stonewall. I'll take care of it."

Later, when little Julia was in her crib asleep, the Jacksons sat down together on a love seat and settled comfortably against each other.

As they gazed out the nearby window and watched the storm clouds break up, they talked about Julia's birth. Tom told her how very much he appreciated Jodie's being there to deliver the baby, and that she had shown up at the house for Julia's two-month birthday.

"Jodie's very special, darling," said Mary Anna. "I believe I'd have to say that just as Hunter is your best friend in all the world…Jodie has become mine. I can't wait to see her again."

The general squeezed her hand. "Well, I did a little something toward that."

"What do you mean?"

"Hunter went home to spend some time with Jodie right after I came here. When I moved in, the Yerbys asked about Hunter. They know about him being chief physician of II Corps, and that he and I are close friends. They also were aware of Hunter's marriage to Jodie, so they asked if possibly the McGuires could come and spend some time with us while we're here."

Mary Anna's eyes were dancing as she said, "Are you telling me they're coming here?"

"Yes, ma'am! I wired them…explained that the Yerbys had offered them a nice room to stay in if they could come, and they're coming."

"Oh, when?"

Mary Anna forgot to keep her voice low, and Julia began to stir. Mary Anna covered her mouth and looked toward the crib. The baby made a few grunting sounds and was soon quiet again.

Whispering, Stonewall said, "They'll be here Saturday. The train arrives at Guiney's Station at noon."

"Oh, wonderful!" whispered Mary Anna. "It will be good to see them again. And I'm anxious for Hunter to see our baby!"

The Virginia sky was cloudless, and the sun's single eye watched as the Jacksons met the McGuires at Guiney's Station on Saturday noon. After they had greeted each other, Jodie took the baby from Mary Anna and held her up so Hunter could see her.

"Look, honey! Isn't she the most beautiful baby girl you've ever seen?"

Hunter took the baby from Jodie and scrutinized her carefully.

He shook his head in wonderment, saying, "You're right, she is. I've never seen such a beautiful baby girl."

Stonewall Jackson's chest puffed out, and a wide grin spread over his face. "Now that's the smartest thing I've ever heard you say, Doctor!"

The women just smiled at one other.

"She really is, Tom," Hunter said. "Of course that will all change when Jodie and I have our first girl."

Jackson squared his jaw and narrowed his eyes into slits. "Only if she looks exactly like Jodie and nothing like you!"

The two couples had a good laugh together as they left the depot.

As the Jacksons and McGuires neared the Yerby farm in the carriage, Stonewall turned to Jodie and said, "I want to thank you for delivering our little Julia, and for being such a good friend to my Mary Anna."

"For both, General," she said softly, "the pleasure was and is mine."

"Tom," Mary Anna said, "you haven't told them about the services tomorrow."

"Oh, that's right. We're going to have an open-air meeting tomorrow with probably two thousand soldiers in attendance, plus locals. Chaplain Tucker Lacy is preaching."

"He's Chaplain General of II Corps, isn't he?" Jodie said.

"That's right," Jackson said.

"General..." Jodie said.

"Yes?"

"It is my duty to warn you that Chaplain Lacy is not a Presbyterian. He's a Baptist spy!"

Stonewall Jackson threw back his head and laughed as he pulled the carriage to a stop in front of the Yerby house. "Baptist spy! That's a good one, Jodie!"

Sunday, April 26, was a sunny day, and nearly twenty-five hundred Confederate soldiers, along with well over three hundred local farmers and townsfolk, were gathering for the preaching service, which would begin at ten o'clock.

The site was an open field next to the Confederate camp some five miles south of Fredericksburg, on the west bank of the Rappahannock River. Everyone knew Joe Hooker's Army of the Potomac was camped barely eight miles north on the other side of Fredericksburg, but General Lee's scouts were keeping a sharp eye on the Yankee camp. Any suspicious move would be spotted, and there were some sixty-three thousand Rebel troops in the camp who were not attending the preaching service.

Next to the hastily built speaker's platform, Stonewall Jackson was showing off his new daughter.

Nearby, Hunter McGuire made it a point to introduce Jodie to Chaplain B. Tucker Lacy. She found the preacher warm and delightful.

Before the McGuires walked away to find a place to sit down, Jodie glanced toward Stonewall and said, "Chaplain Lacy, would you do me a favor?"

"Sure," he said. "What is it?"

Stonewall Jackson was on the platform, sitting beside his chaplain general, as a young lieutenant stood before the crowd seated on the grass and led them in several hymns and gospel songs. The final song was John Newton's "Amazing Grace." When the last note faded, the song leader sat down and General Stonewall Jackson stepped forward. He led the crowd in prayer, asking the Lord to shine His gospel light into hearts during the preaching, then introduced Tucker Lacy as his good friend and "one of the greatest Presbyterian evangelists of the nineteenth century." Jackson shook hands with Lacy and returned to his chair beside the song leader.

When Lacy stepped to the crude wooden pulpit and laid his Bible down, he ran his gaze over the crowd and said, "My good friend General Stonewall Jackson just introduced me as a Presbyterian evangelist. Well, folks, I suppose I really ought to make a confession here in front of all of you. Actually, I am a Baptist spy!"

A roar of laughter spread over the crowd. Jackson first covered his face in mock embarrassment, then settled his eyes on Jodie McGuire and shook his fist at her. Jodie turned palms up and shrugged her shoulders.

When the laughter drained away, Lacy said, "We've had a little fun here. Now I want to speak to you from the gospel of Luke, the sixteenth chapter, on a very serious subject."

Tucker Lacy preached his heart out about the rich man and Lazarus, warning those in the crowd who had never been saved that they would spend eternity in hell with the rich man unless they repented of their sin and opened their hearts to Jesus Christ, trusting in Him and Him alone to save them.

As many of the soldiers and some local men and women responded to the invitation, the Christians in attendance were elated, and for a little while the War seemed far away.

The next day, there was indication at the Union camp that General Hooker was getting ready to move at least some of his troops from the camp near Falmouth. Confederate scouts reported it to General Lee, and Lee called for a conference with Stonewall Jackson and all brigade and regiment leaders.

When the conference was over, Jackson returned to the Yerby farm and told Mary Anna and the McGuires that the entire Army of Northern Virginia was on alert. Once Hooker had declared his intentions, the Confederates would need to be prepared to meet him. Because fighting could break out on short notice, it was imperative that Hunter stay with the troops.

The general looked at Mary Anna's distressed face and said, "Sweetheart, I wish you and Julia didn't have to be in Lexington, so far away."

"They could stay with me in Richmond…for as long as Mary Anna wants to," said Jodie.

Mary Anna's expression brightened immediately, and the general smiled as Mary Anna clapped her hands and said, "Oh, Jodie! I accept."

The husbands kissed their wives as they put them on a train to Richmond. Thomas J. Jackson shed tears as he hugged and kissed his baby daughter last of all.

Shortly after daybreak on Wednesday, April 29, General Lee was awakened by a knock at his door in the farmhouse near the Rappahannock.

"Just a moment!" he called, rolling out of bed and hurrying into his uniform.

When he opened the door, hair tousled and eyes still fighting sleep, he found Lieutenant James P. Smith of Stonewall Jackson's staff looking at him with solemn eyes.

Smith saluted and said, "Sorry to bother you, General, but General Jackson wants you to know that Joe Hooker is moving part of his army due west across the Rappahannock from Falmouth under cover of fog."

"All right," said Lee, "tell your good general that I will meet him at the front shortly. If Hooker's troops keep moving west, they'll be in the Spotsylvania Wilderness by midmorning. Old Joe just might want to fight us there. Tell General Jackson to keep his scouts alert. I'll grab a little breakfast, and when I get to the front, I'll want to know exactly where those Yankees are."

"Yes, sir," said Smith, hurrying toward the front door where two sentries looked on. "I'll tell him."

*** *** ***

The wilderness of Spotsylvania was a distinctive stretch of Virginia woodland of some seventy square miles. North to south it ran from the Rappahannock and Rapidan Rivers to three or four miles south of Chancellorsville, which was simply a rural crossroads marked by a large red-brick, white-columned mansion that had once been a bed-and-breakfast stopover for travelers, as well as the home of the wealthy George Chancellor family.

Just west of the Rappahannock, a group of investors had financed construction of the Orange Turnpike in 1812. The turnpike connected Fredericksburg with Orange Courthouse thirty-six miles to the west. In late 1816, George Chancellor opened his "overnight stopover" to cater to traffic on the Orange Turnpike where it intersected the busy Ely's Ford Road.

Chancellorsville, as George had dubbed it, was exactly ten miles due west of Fredericksburg, and sat on seventy acres of open land that edged the dense forest of the wilderness. George's dream was that his roadstop would evolve into a settlement, then a town. Though his dream was never realized, his mansion at the crossroads became the most prominent landmark in Spotsylvania County.

When George Chancellor died in 1836, his widow carried on with the overnight stopover until she died in 1860. At that time, the mansion was inherited by George's brother, Stanford, who died shortly thereafter, leaving it to his widow, Fannie Pound Chancellor, and their nine children.

In 1863, Fannie had seven of her children in the mansion with her—two sons and five daughters, all unmarried. Since the War's beginning, troops had marched along the turnpike, and the Chancellor girls had become the apples of many a Rebel soldier's eye.

For the most part, the Spotsylvania Wilderness was rugged, uneven ground, much of it marshland. A series of boggy watercourses cut ravines across it to empty into the Rapidan and Rappahannock, or the Ny River to the south. The low ridge lines between the watercourses ran generally north and south, and there were scattered marshes and sloughs, one of them extensive enough to be called Big Meadow Swamp. What cleared ground there was in the wilderness was mostly along the turnpike and a road called the Plank Road. The largest clearing was the seventy acres at Chancellorsville.

Fannie Pound Chancellor and her seven children were just finishing breakfast when they heard the sound of horses blowing and the tinkle of harness.

Twenty-year-old Matthew shoved back his chair and moved to a side window. He could see Union soldiers on horseback, in wagons, and on foot drawing up to the front of the house. Sixteen-year-old Malachi was just getting up from the table when Matthew said, "Mama! It's Yankees!"

Fannie Chancellor feared for her daughters. The oldest was nineteen, and the youngest was thirteen. Rising from her chair, she said, "Upstairs, girls! Now! Hide under the beds!"

The girls headed for the front of the house where they would mount the winding staircase, and Fannie called after them, "Don't make a sound, and don't come out until one of the boys or myself tells you it's safe!"

Fannie and her sons moved toward the front door to face the enemy soldiers.

"Should we get our guns, Mama?" asked Matthew.

"No! We cannot fight them, boys. All we can do is try to stay calm and see what they want."

They could hear heavy footsteps on the front porch and could make out men in dark uniforms through the lace curtains that covered the door windows. Suddenly there was a loud knock on the door.

Matthew hurried ahead of his mother to unlatch the door and swing it open.

A tall, husky man with a handlebar mustache speckled with gray stood in the doorway. Four stern-looking men in blue flanked him. His mouth was a thin, grim line as he said, without bothering to touch his hat brim, "Mrs. Chancellor, I presume."

"Yes," Fannie said nervously.

"I am Major General George Meade, commander of V Corps, Union Army of the Potomac."

Fannie's sons kept themselves a half-step ahead of their mother. Their eyes never left Meade's.

"I am here to tell you that Major General Joseph Hooker has chosen your house for his headquarters until the Rebel Army of Northern Virginia and their Bobby Lee have been vanquished."

Fannie's back arched, but before she could speak, Matthew moved closer to Meade and said, "No army can whip General Robert E. Lee's army! And this house is not for rent!"

Meade took a step through the door, and men with bayoneted rifles followed. "We're not asking to rent it, son," Meade said evenly. "We're telling your mother that General Hooker is taking it over until further notice."

Matthew moved up to meet Meade nose to nose, his face set in rigid lines. "Your General Hooker has no right to move in here, and it's not going to happen, General Meade!"

One of the soldiers swung the butt of his rifle at Matthew's jaw and knocked him to the floor. Fannie's hands trembled as she fell to her knees beside him. He was out cold, and there was a gash on his jaw.

Malachi looked at the Yankee soldier, his eyes glowing with hatred, as Fannie screamed, "Look what you've done!"

The soldier who had hit Matthew nodded and said, "Your son needs to learn some manners, ma'am."

"Now, as I was saying," said Meade, "we're taking over this house as headquarters for General Hooker. Any more arguments?"

TEN

Fannie Chancellor ignored General Meade's question as she cupped Matthew's face in her hands and said, "Malachi, get me a wet towel."

Meade hunkered down beside her and said, "General Hooker wants the largest downstairs bedroom for his office, Mrs. Chancellor."

Fannie continued to caress her son's head. Matthew's eyes began to flutter, and he ejected a moan.

"Did you hear what I said, woman?" Meade said.

"I'm not deaf, General," she said without looking at him. "But right now I'm concerned about my son."

Malachi came running back with a dripping wet towel in his hands. Fannie took it and began dabbing at Matthew's face, then pressed the towel to the cut on his jaw. Holding it there while Matthew's eyes cleared, she looked at Meade with undisguised wrath, then turned her gaze on the soldier who had struck Matthew. "If I were a man, I'd take that gun away from you and put that bayonet through your belly!"

The soldier just smirked at her.

Matthew shook his head, winced, and let his eyes run past his mother to Meade, then to the other Yankee soldiers.

"You're cut, honey," said Fannie. "Let's get you to the kitchen so I can put a bandage on it."

"Mrs. Chancellor," said Meade, as Fannie and Malachi helped Matthew to his feet, "we want the largest bedroom on this floor as an office for General Hooker. Now where is it?"

"That's my room, but you're not welcome to it," Matthew said, blinking.

Meade drew in a deep breath, let it out slowly, and said, "Mrs. Chancellor, I would suggest you explain to your son that we are in control here, and if he gives us any more trouble, he'll get more of what he just got. Cooperate, and no harm will come to you or your children. If any of you refuse to obey us, you will suffer the consequences."

Fannie stared at him icily but nodded her acquiescence.

"Now, where are your daughters?" asked Meade.

Fannie's face paled.

"We won't harm them, ma'am. But we want the whole family together. My men will be stationed throughout the house so we can keep an eye on all of you."

Fannie blinked in bewilderment. "You mean you want us to stay here in the house? I thought—"

"That we'd throw you out? Oh, no, ma'am. We want all of you to stay right here. We can't have you running around out there, now, can we?"

Fannie's pallor became a red flush of anger. "So we're your prisoners, is that it?"

"That's it. But let me say it again, ma'am. None of you will be harmed in any way if you cooperate with us."

"You're telling me that my daughters are safe with Hooker in the house? I know about that lecher, General."

Meade's jaw stiffened. "Ma'am, I assure you...there won't be a hand laid on you or your daughters by General Hooker or anyone else in this army. And I repeat, if all of you cooperate with us, there won't be any more incidents like what just happened to your son."

"All right, General Meade, we'll cooperate because I believe you are a man of your word." Then to her younger son she said, "Malachi, bring your sisters downstairs to the kitchen."

As Malachi headed up the winding staircase, Meade called after him, "Don't get any ideas about trying to escape, son. We've got men surrounding the house."

Malachi looked back over his shoulder but didn't reply.

Fannie was about to guide Matthew toward the kitchen when the soldier who had struck him moved close and said, "How come you're not in a gray uniform, fella? You afraid to leave mama?"

Fannie gave the man a cold, level stare and said, "Matthew was born with a defective heart. He's not supposed to exert himself."

The soldier looked chagrined. "Oh."

General Meade turned to a corporal who was standing on the porch just outside the door and said, "Corporal Wingate, ride to General Hooker and tell him the Chancellor mansion is now secured for his occupancy."

It was midmorning when Major General Joseph Hooker arrived on the seventy-acre clearing that made up the Chancellor estate. He was on horseback and accompanied by some two dozen cavalrymen from First Division, including Brigadier General Alfred Pleasonton.

At forty-nine years of age, Joseph Hooker had puffy sacks under his pale blue eyes from many years of heavy drinking. An 1837 graduate of West Point, he was rawboned and stood three inches under six feet. He was the only officer to be breveted three times during the Mexican War, and this due to the frightening ruthlessness he displayed in battling the enemy. Thus he was dubbed "Fighting Joe" before he entered the Civil War.

Hooker let his gaze take in the tents outside the Chancellor mansion and the men in blue who stood on the wide porch and at each corner of the house. "Looks like we have it secured for sure," he said to Pleasonton.

"I'll be glad when we have the entire South secured as well, sir," said the brigadier general.

"Well, I'm expecting the battle we're about to enter with Bobby Lee will be the beginning of that."

They drew up to the front porch and General Meade came out the door.

"Good job, General," Hooker said to Meade as he dismounted. "Looks like everything is under control here."

"Yes, sir," said Meade. "We've got the largest bedroom on the ground floor set up for you, desk and all. We borrowed the desk from the library."

"Good. Any problems from the widow Chancellor or her off-spring?"

"A little at first from the oldest son, but we've got him under control. You'll see a bandage on his face. Corporal Tedderman had to clobber him. Cut his jaw."

"I'm sorry to hear that. I don't want civilians hurt unless they force us to do it."

"Matthew forced us, sir."

"How old is he?"

"I'd say nineteen or twenty."

"Oh? Wonder why he isn't in the Rebel army."

"Has a bad heart, according to Mrs. Chancellor."

"I see. Well, I hope we won't see any more resistance out of him or any of the others. If I recall correctly, there are five teenage girls."

"Yes. And a teenage boy about fifteen or sixteen."

"And you've assured the widow that if they cooperate, no harm will come them?"

"Yes, sir."

Hooker dismissed General Pleasonton and his cavalrymen to return to the Falmouth camp and entered the mansion to find that

Meade had Fannie and her children seated in the parlor. Three soldiers stood guard.

Meade led Hooker into the room and said, "General, this is Mrs. Chancellor and her children."

When none of the family stood up, Meade said, "It is customary that when the field commander enters a room, civilians rise to their feet."

"I don't want to sound uncooperative, General Meade," said Fannie, "but that would be true only north of the Mason-Dixon line, wouldn't it?"

Meade's features stiffened. "Now, see here—"

"Well, if you were a civilian up in the North, and General Robert E. Lee or General Stonewall Jackson entered the room…would you stand up to honor him?"

Joe Hooker laughed. "I like this lady, General Meade. She's got spunk." He addressed his next remark to Fannie. "I'm sure he wouldn't stand for either of those men, ma'am…and neither would I. You and your children stay seated."

"Thank you, General," said Fannie, giving Meade a cool glance.

"Well!" said Hooker. "I'd like to see my quarters."

"It's my bedroom, General Hooker," Matthew said. "I would appreciate it if you'd take good care of it."

"I will, son," replied Hooker. "When we've conquered Lee, we'll pull out for Washington with the stars and stripes waving the victory sign, and the South will once again be part of the Union. And your room will be intact, I assure you."

Meade said, "I'll take you to your quarters, sir."

They started toward the hall, then Hooker paused and looked back at Fannie. "Did General Meade tell you we will cook our own food outdoors, the same as we do when camped?"

"I hadn't brought that up, yet, sir," said Meade.

"Is that because you don't wish to impose on me, General?" asked Fannie, who at forty-one was still quite attractive. "Or because you're afraid I might poison you?"

"Definitely the latter, ma'am," said Hooker with a smile.

Fannie smiled cryptically. "And you are right, General."

More Union army personnel arrived during the afternoon, and that evening General Hooker sat down in his new office with Major Generals John Sedgwick, John Reynolds, Daniel Sickles, and John Gibbon.

Fannie and her daughters were on the second floor in a sitting room, and Matthew and Malachi were in Malachi's bedroom, which was next door to Hooker's office.

Upstairs, Fannie told her girls she had learned that the only soldier who would sleep in the house was Hooker, who would use Matthew's bed. There would be night sentries inside and outside the house, but all others would sleep in the tents they had pitched around the house.

In Malachi's bedroom, the Chancellor brothers pressed their ears to a weak spot on the wall, which they had discovered a few months earlier. They could easily hear every word spoken in the next room.

Hooker looked at his generals and said, "I have devised a series of deceptions that, if executed properly, will bring about swift victory over Bobby Lee."

In the next room, Matthew whispered, "Malachi, get me a pencil and some paper. I need to get this down!"

Hooker explained that on Friday, which was May 1, General Sedgwick would lead his VI Corps, and Reynolds his I Corps, across the Rappahannock below Fredericksburg to feign a major attack on Stonewall Jackson's II Corps. To confuse Lee's scouts even further, two other units—Sickles's III Corps and Gibbon's II Corps—would remain temporarily in the camp at Falmouth, but clearly visible to Confederate pickets.

In the adjoining room, Matthew wrote hurriedly as Malachi whispered, "Are you getting it?"

"I'll have to rewrite it so it's legible," Matthew said, "but I'm getting it."

"These deceptions will give the rest of our massive army a good edge to wipe out Bobby Lee."

"It's ingenious, sir!" said Reynolds. "Even using our units as decoys, you'll still have some ninety thousand men to swarm Lee's mere sixty-five thousand."

"Yes!" Hooker said, banging his fist on the desk. "We'll win this one, gentlemen. Bobby Lee is about to meet his Waterloo! God Almighty Himself couldn't keep me from victory!"

There was a sudden hush in the room as the generals exchanged fearful glances.

"What's the matter?" asked Hooker, frowning.

"Excuse me, General Hooker," John Sedgwick said, "but as God-fearing men, we respectfully request that you not speak in such bold terms concerning almighty God."

Hooker blinked as Daniel Sickles said, "I was named after the great prophet Daniel in the Bible, sir. In the book of Daniel, the story is told of King Belshazzar, who mocked God while banqueting with a thousand of his lords. During the banquet, God's own finger wrote a message on the wall to the brash king, saying he had been weighed in the balances and found wanting. That very night Belshazzar was slain by his enemies. If I were you, General Hooker, I wouldn't tempt God to show me that He could prevent me from a victory…and instead bring me defeat."

Joseph Hooker laughed. "I'll win this battle, General Sickles. You can bet your last dollar on it!"

In the next room, Matthew Chancellor was copying his hastily written notes to make it readable to other eyes. While the voices of the Union generals continued to come through the wall, he whispered, "It's dark now, Malachi. I wish I could be the one to deliver this, but you know I don't dare put that much strain on my heart."

"I'm glad to deliver it," whispered Malachi. "Should we talk to Mama about it first?"

"We can't. You know she wouldn't want either of us taking the risk. You'll have to do it without her knowing. I'm not sure where General Lee is, but I know General Jackson is just south of Fredericksburg, close to the river. You've got to get this information to him!"

With the folded slip of paper in his shirt pocket, Malachi Chancellor eased through the open window of his bedroom, with Matthew's help, and dropped quietly to the ground.

The night was a shroud of darkness as he pressed his back to the brick wall and inched toward the rear of the house. There was no moon, and the sky was partially covered with clouds, leaving little starlight to guide him.

Malachi hauled up as he reached the back porch. Two sentries were there, talking in low tones. He could barely make them out, but both had their backs to him.

The boy's heart pounded as he veered away from the house, moving from tree to tree, trying not to step on a twig or stumble on a stone and give himself away.

When he reached the last tree before the open stretch to the corral and barn, he paused, looked back, and saw the shadowed forms of the two sentries moving toward the other side of the house. Malachi knew there were at least four other sentries outside. Two of them were at the front, and he had no idea where the other two might be.

He made his way to the corral gate and cautiously slipped between the rails of the fence and moved toward the barn.

He decided to enter from the rear, rather than on the side where the sentries might be. It took Malachi three or four minutes to reach the back side of the barn by inching his way along the wall. He held his breath as he tripped the latch as quietly as possible and eased the door open. The hinges voiced their objection, but moving the door very slowly kept the sound to a minimum.

Two of the horses nickered at Malachi's presence. He paused to let them get used to his being there, then moved along the wall in the almost pitch-black gloom to where the saddles and bridles hung near the front of the barn. Soon he had the desired bridle in his hand, and peering into the inky blackness, he whispered, "Bucky! Bucky! Where are you?"

A familiar nicker came from a few feet away. Soon, Malachi had a hand on the muzzle of his horse and slipped the bridle on, gently pressing the bit into Bucky's mouth. He buckled the strap and whispered, "Okay, boy. We're going for a little bareback ride. Be real quiet."

Malachi wished the corral had a back gate, but there was only the gate at the front side of the barn. He led the horse out the rear door and walked him slowly along the wall. When they reached the front of the barn, Malachi paused, trying to see the sentries at the rear of the house. They were no doubt somewhere there in the shadows, but he couldn't make them out.

His eyes burned as he scanned the darkness near the gate and strained his ears for any telltale sounds of the enemy. There was nothing.

Holding one hand over Bucky's muzzle, he led him slowly across the corral. Once he was past the area where the tents had been pitched, he would ride to the edge of the woods, then put Bucky to a gallop and head for the Confederate camp on the Rappahannock.

Malachi reached the gate and eased the latch from its place. The latch made a clicking sound, and the boy froze, listening for the sentries. His muscles ached from the sheer fright that gripped him.

He heard only silence, but even that was like some great force squeezing his lungs.

He inched the gate open until there was room enough to lead Bucky through. The horse followed obediently, his hooves making soft muffled sounds on the spongy ground.

When Malachi had Bucky out of the corral, he held the reins at length while closing the gate. The latch dropped in place much quieter than it had come out. He raised the reins over the horse's head and swung up on his back.

Suddenly there was a rustling sound in the direction of the house, and a voice pierced the darkness. "Hey! Who goes there?"

Bucky nickered at the sound, and a cold, icy hand clutched Malachi's heart.

He could hear the sound of pounding footsteps as a soldier called out, "Rex, what's going on out there?"

"Got somebody on a horse, Sergeant!" came the quick reply. The next words came out harshly. "Identify yourself or die, mister!"

Malachi felt the muscular quivering of near panic as his breath came in jerky gasps. "It's…me. Malachi Chancellor."

In the sitting room on the second floor, Fannie Chancellor was playing a word game with her daughters. Suddenly they heard heavy footsteps in the hall, followed by a deafening knock on the door.

"Mrs. Chancellor!" boomed a heavy voice.

Wide-eyed, the girls watched their mother open the door. Two husky soldiers stood before her, their faces rigid.

"Ma'am," said the one who had knocked on the door, "we've got a problem downstairs. General Hooker wants you there immediately."

"Well, what is it?"

"Your sons are in trouble. Come with us."

Fannie looked over her shoulder and said, "Girls, you stay here. I'll be back shortly."

As the soldiers ushered Fannie toward the winding staircase, she said, "What did my boys do?"

"They overheard General Hooker's conversation with some of his generals and wrote down what was said. Your oldest addressed a note to Stonewall Jackson, telling him all about General Hooker's battle plans, and your other boy tried to ride to Jackson and give it to him. We caught him, ma'am. And General Hooker is very upset!"

When Fannie entered Hooker's office she found two pale and frightened boys standing before the commander.

Hooker wheeled as one of the sentries said, "Here's their mother, sir."

Fannie rushed to her sons, throwing an arm around each of them, and held them tight.

Hooker stepped up to her, and said, "Look at this!"

Fannie glanced down at the slip of paper and took it in her hand.

"Your sons were eavesdropping on a meeting I held with some of my unit leaders. We caught the youngest one about to ride to Stonewall Jackson to give him my strategy!"

Fannie nodded. "Your men told me about it, General."

Hooker's face was flushed and his eyes bulged as he said, "You'd better have a good long talk with these boys, lady! I'm not going to punish them this time, but if something like this happens again, you're not going to like what I do to the whole family!"

Fannie held his gaze for a long moment, then said in a low tone, "May we be excused, General?"

"Just make sure you get the message across to them."

"There won't be any more episodes like this one, General," she said, pushing her sons toward the door. When they reached it, Fannie stopped, looked over her shoulder, and said, "You have to admit it was pretty good thinking on their part. That information might have thwarted your battle plans. If you had been in their place, General, what would you have done?"

Hooker wiped a hand over his dissolute features. "I…well, I guess I have to say I'd have done exactly what they did."

Fannie smiled.

"But I'm telling you, lady…if they do anything akin to it again, the whole family's going to be sorry."

"As I've already told you, General, they won't."

Fannie took the boys into Malachi's room, closed the door, and keeping her voice low, said, "I'm proud of both of you! I'm glad you were willing to risk getting caught in order to get the message to General Jackson. But please, don't do anything like that again. Hooker means what he says. He'll punish all of us."

"We won't, Mama," said Matthew. "But I can't help wishing Malachi had been able to get through to General Jackson. He was so close!"

"Well," she breathed, "our army is going to whip them anyhow."

"I sure hope so," said Malachi. "I'd like to see Meade and Hooker eat dirt."

"Yeah," said Matthew, "and that guy that hit me with the rifle butt too."

On April 30, Jackson was up before dawn, ready to meet with General Lee and form battle plans. Lee was at the I Corps camp nearby. After breakfast, Jackson went back to his tent to await Lee's appearance for their meeting and fell on his knees to pray.

Corporal Lewis, who was the general's "shadow" and devoted aide, stationed himself near the opening of the tent to keep anyone from disturbing him.

Lee and Jackson met just after sunrise, and put their heads together to come up with a way of impeding, if not crushing, Hooker. They knew they were outnumbered far more than two to one, and in place of manpower they would have to come up with ingenuity. They would have to outguess Hooker and anticipate what he was going to do.

As they discussed the situation, Lee said, "General, I think the best plan for us is to fortify ourselves and simply let Hooker come to us."

"I don't think so, sir," said Jackson. "It's my opinion that we ought to go on the offensive and attack Hooker while we're trying to outguess him. Let's take the battle to him."

Lee scratched his beard. "Well, my friend, you know I have the utmost confidence in you. If this is how you feel, then make your plans and take the battle to ol' Fighting Joe!"

"As you know, sir, our scouts say Hooker has bivouacked some of his men in tents at Chancellorsville, and they think Hooker is staying inside the mansion. Unless there's some kind of major move today, I'd like to do a little reconnoitering after dark tonight. Should be a new moon. I need to take a look at the situation when no Yankee could possibly see me."

Lee nodded. "Whatever you say. In the meantime, if Hooker makes an aggressive move, we'll have to counter."

"Yes, sir. I have a feeling he's not quite ready. Let's hope we can beat him to the punch."

Lee chuckled. "Well, if it's good ol' Stonewall doing the punching, I'm all for it!"

ELEVEN

It was after ten o'clock that night when Lieutenant General Thomas J. Jackson mounted Little Sorrel.

"I appreciate your offer to ride with me, men," he said to the earnest faces looking up at him. "But this is something I must do alone. I can move much quieter by myself."

"But General, there could be Yankee snipers out there and—"

"I'll be very careful, Major Dayton," Jackson said with a smile.

The other men were Dayton's Antietam heroes, Corporals Everett Nichols, Hank Upchurch, Chuck Carney, and Buford Hall.

It was Hall who said, "Sir, what if we ride a half-mile or so behind you? At least then, if you got into trouble, we could help you."

A few other men of the North Carolina Regiments were starting to gather around the small group, curious as to why their commander was leaving camp at this hour.

"Men, I appreciate your concern, but this reconnaissance must be done by one man, and since General Lee has placed the responsibility of planning the battle strategy on me, I'm the one who has to look the situation over. See you at dawn, if not before."

The soldiers watched their leader trot away along the bank of the Rappahannock. Then Private Bo Gentry said, "He's the best, fellas.

I'd follow him into the devil's lair if he asked me to."

"Me too," said Private Chad Lynch. "The man's going down in history as a military leader the likes of Napoleon and Alexander the Great."

"Except Stonewall Jackson will be head and shoulders above them," said Corporal Ken Dykstra.

"You hit the nail on the head," agreed Corporal Myron Flynn. "I believe General Lee will be amongst them, too, but there's just something special about General Jackson."

"Hard to put it into words, isn't it?" said Rance Dayton. "I felt that way when he was my favorite professor at V.M.I., and I feel even stronger about him now that I've been on the battlefield with him." Dayton looked in the direction where Jackson had ridden, and said, "Take care of him, Lord."

Stonewall Jackson kept to the bank of the river and under the trees, all the way to the edge of the wilderness. The four-mile ride was uneventful, and the night air was peaceful and quiet as he guided Little Sorrel to a high knoll.

Before him lay the open fields that were part of the Chancellorsville estate, the Orange Turnpike, Ely's Ford Road, and the dark area, which was the Spotsylvania Wilderness.

The area ran north to south from the Rappahannock and Rapidan Rivers to some three miles south of Chancellorsville. East to west, it extended from Tabernacle Church to beyond Wilderness Tavern, a local hotel. Jackson could make out parts of the old plank road that wove its way through the wilderness, along with the turnpike. The only cleared ground was along the sides of the roads.

Jackson studied the wilderness—a dense forest of scrub oak, pine, hickory, and cedar. He had been told that no one left the roads to enter the woods. For there was nothing there but mucky marshes and sloughs in dark, eerie, impenetrable undergrowth.

Stonewall stroked his beard thoughtfully. "You know what, Little

Sorrel?" he said aloud. "I just got an idea. That wilderness would be a perfect place to hide my II Corps and pull a surprise on ol' Joe Hooker."

Little Sorrel nickered softly as if he understood and agreed.

Jackson left the knoll, riding slowly, and ventured closer to Chancellorsville, where he could make out the Yankee tents near the mansion. He dismounted and scanned the open fields that edged up to the dark forest. With his experienced eye he judged the artillery range from the edge of the wilderness and measured the ground his men would have to cross before meeting the enemy with bayonets.

Suddenly he gave a decisive nod and mounted up, putting Little Sorrel to a moderate gallop across the moon-sprayed land. If General Lee approved, Jackson would move his II Corps the four miles to the edge of Chancellorsville and position them in the dark shadows of the wilderness. Joe Hooker would never expect that.

Robert E. Lee sat in his tent after midnight, stifling a yawn as he listened to Jackson's plan. He liked it immediately and said, "Go to it, General. Move your men out as soon as you can. I will position I Corps accordingly. We'll give ol' Joe a little surprise."

"Surprise is half the victor's battle," said Stonewall. "But even then, sir, this will likely be a bloody fight. I suggest we move our medical staff close to Chancellorsville, which will no doubt be the field of battle. Wilderness Tavern would be the best spot."

"I agree," said Lee. "And the folks at the hotel will open their arms to them, I'm sure."

The generals concurred. Medical directors Dr. Jason Franks of I Corps and Dr. Hunter McGuire of II Corps, along with their staff and supply wagons, would move immediately to Wilderness Tavern.

The calm, resolute, sensitive, and scholarly Robert E. Lee, and his fiery but calculating Stonewall Jackson were ready to take on an army more than twice the size of their own.

In I Corps, under Lee, the divisions were commanded by Major

Generals Lafayette McLaws and R. H. "Dick" Anderson. The cavalry division was led by Major General J. E. B. "Jeb" Stuart.

In Jackson's II Corps, the division commanders were Major Generals A. P. Hill, Jubal Early, R. E. Colson, and D. H. Hill. The artillery was commanded by Colonel Stapleton Crutchfield, who had been trained with the big guns by Stonewall Jackson himself at Virginia Military Institute.

Within half an hour, Jackson and his II Corps were ready to leave the camp on the Rappahannock and march two hours northward to the wilderness.

By 4:30 A.M. Jackson had his men well situated in the marshes and sloughs of the dark forest.

At daylight, General Hooker set in motion the deceptive moves he had revealed to his men inside Matthew Chancellor's bedroom. However, Generals John Sedgwick and John Reynolds, who were to feign a major attack on Stonewall Jackson's II Corps on the Rappahannock, found the camp deserted.

There were a few skirmishes that day between small bands of troops, but as the sun ran its arc through the Virginia sky, it was evident there would be no major battle that day.

Inside the Chancellorsville mansion, Fannie and her children were gathered in the library with the door closed. The mother had spoken with General Hooker and convinced him that she and her family deserved some privacy. Two soldiers, however, stood guard outside in the hall.

Fannie's daughters were Naomi, nineteen, Ruth, seventeen, Sarah, fifteen, Martha, fourteen, and Rebecca, thirteen. While the family talked about what might have happened if Malachi had reached General Jackson with the information, the youngest of the siblings began to sniffle.

Matthew, who was sitting next to her, gently took her hand and said, "What's wrong, Rebecca?"

Her lips quivered as she spoke. "When General Jackson finds out the Yankees are staying in our house and in our yard, they'll start shooting their cannons. We'll all be killed by our own army."

"Our soldiers won't shoot at the house if they know we're in here," said Malachi.

"I'm sure you're right," said Naomi. "But since we're kept inside, and they can't see us, they might figure the Yankees have run us off. If that's what they think, they'll bombard the house for sure."

"Well, let's hope and pray that it never gets that far," said Fannie. "Maybe General Lee will outsmart Hooker and it will all be over before any guns are fired around here."

"Speaking of guns," said Matthew, "if those dirty Yankees hadn't taken ours, I'd break through my bedroom door and use one to shoot Hooker."

"Yeah, and I'd blast him too," put in Malachi. "I'd kill him deader'n a doornail."

The widow looked at her sons aghast and said, "Boys, you shouldn't want to kill anybody, not even Hooker."

"You told Hooker you'd poison him, Mama," spoke up Martha.

Fannie's face tinted. "Well, I didn't mean it. I couldn't really take anyone's life unless they were trying to kill one of you, or if I had to in self-defense."

"But this is war, Mama," said Matthew. "I'd poison any one of those dirty Yankee soldiers if I had the chance. Or I'd kill them any way I could…especially Hooker. If he didn't want to be in danger of being killed, he should've been a store clerk or a farmer instead of a general. Besides, I don't like the way he looks at you."

"I don't either," said Naomi. "He's got evil, shifty eyes."

"I don't have a gun," said Malachi, "but if he ever comes near you, Mama, I'll climb on his back and ram my fingers in his eyes."

"And I'll kick him in the shin," put in Ruth.

"And I'll kick him in the other shin," said Sarah.

"And I'll kick him in the stomach," Martha growled.

"Yeah, and I'll kick him where he sits down!" said Rebecca, who had long since stopped sniffling.

Fannie covered her mouth to hide her grin.

"And if there's anything left of him," said Matthew, "I'll finish him off!"

Fannie gave up trying to hide her amusement and laughed out loud.

That night, Stonewall Jackson, Rance Dayton, and Chaplain B. Tucker Lacy entered Jackson's tent to pray about the impending battle.

All the tents were set up deep in the wilderness along the edge of the old plank road. No lanterns or fires were allowed.

A dozen men of the Eighteenth North Carolina Regiment stood watch near the edge of the wilderness where II Corps was hiding. A buttermilk sky partially covered the moon, and the men peered into the gloom, watching for any kind of movement on the open field that lay between them and the Chancellor mansion a half-mile away.

All was still, except for a slight breeze that rustled the trees, and the repeated hoot of an owl somewhere deep in the dark regions of the forest.

Sentries Everett Nichols, Hank Upchurch, Buford Hall, and Chuck Carney were huddled together, with their friends Chad Lynch, Bo Gentry, Ken Dykstra, and Myron Flynn close by, watching the road.

Out of earshot from the others, the Fearless Four talked in low tones of the coming battle.

As he ran his gaze to the south, Upchurch said, "The artillery is ready for action. How I hate to see that beautiful Chancellor mansion get blasted. But with Hooker in there, I'm sure Colonel Crutchfield will unleash his guns on the house to flush Hooker into the open."

"I wonder where the family went?" said Carney.

Hall shrugged his shoulders. "Probably staying with a neighbor, I would imagine. Isn't that the way it usually is when the Yankees take over somebody's house as headquarters?"

There was silence for a moment, then Nichols said, "I've got a feeling this move to the wilderness is going to throw Hooker for a loop. Maybe the surprise will be all we need to catch him off guard."

"Yeah," put in Hall, "especially when General Lee hits him from the other side."

"You gotta hand it to General Jackson, fellas," said Carney. "He's one smart cookie, if you'll pardon the expression. I have no doubt his ingenuity will lead us to victory in this battle."

It was nine o'clock in the evening on May 1 when Jodie McGuire answered a knock at her apartment door. Mary Anna Jackson was in the spare bedroom, checking on little Julia. A neighbor had loaned Jodie a crib for the baby.

"Good evening, Mrs. McGuire," said a young soldier at the door. "I'm Corporal Justin Porter. I have a message for Mrs. Thomas Jackson from the general. He said she was staying here."

"Yes, Corporal," said Jodie. "Please come in. I'll get Mrs. Jackson."

Porter removed his cap and stepped just inside the door. "I'll wait right here, ma'am."

Seconds later, Mary Anna appeared alongside Jodie and said, "Good evening, corporal. Mrs. McGuire said you have a message?"

"Yes, ma'am. A messenger from II Corps arrived at our camp outside Richmond about an hour ago. General Jackson asked him to send someone to let you know the situation at this time."

The women exchanged glances, and Mary Anna said, "We've been wondering what's happening."

"General Jackson wants you and Mrs. McGuire to know that there will be a big battle tomorrow, and it's certain to take place at the crossroads of the Orange Turnpike and Ely's Ford Road."

"That would be near the Chancellor mansion, then," said Mary Anna.

"Yes, ma'am. General Jackson's corps is set up very close to Chancellorsville. And Mrs. McGuire, your husband and Dr. Franks of I Corps and their staffs are stationed at Wilderness Tavern to care for the wounded."

Mary Anna's brow furrowed. "Do you know how many men the Yankees have there?"

"I'm told about a hundred and forty thousand."

"And we have less than half that number," she said.

"Yes. About sixty-five thousand. But we still have the advantage, ma'am. We have General Stonewall Jackson's military skill to plan the strategy. The Yankees only have Joe Hooker."

"Of course," said Jodie. "So that gives us the edge, no matter how many troops the Yankees have!"

Porter nodded, bade the ladies good evening, and left the premises.

When Jodie closed the door, she turned and put a hand on Mary Anna's shoulder. "I know it's a scary thing to have your husband on the battlefield, no matter what the odds are, but our army has had to fight almost every battle outnumbered by the Yankees. And look how many we've won!"

"And we'll win this one too," said Mary Anna, forcing a note of confidence into her voice. "Of course, that doesn't mean there won't be casualties. Thank the Lord, when you're saved you know that all death can do is usher you into the arms of the Saviour."

"I wouldn't trade that precious truth for anything this world has to offer," said Jodie.

"That makes me think of the Scripture Tom always reads before he goes into battle." Mary Anna turned toward the spare bedroom. "I'll get my Bible and read it."

Moments later the women sat side-by-side at the kitchen table, and Mary Anna opened her Bible to 2 Corinthians 5:1-8.

"That's the passage where Paul deals with the Christian's earthly body compared to his or her heavenly, glorified body, isn't it?" asked Jodie.

Mary Anna nodded.

Jodie followed along, reading silently, while Mary Anna read the passage aloud. When she came to verse 4, she said, "Here is Tom's favorite verse. 'For we that are in this tabernacle do groan, being burdened: not for that we would be unclothed, but clothed upon, that mortality might be swallowed up of life.'"

Jodie nodded solemnly. "It's good that the general can face each battle with this passage firm in his heart. Think of all the men who go to the battlefield and have no such claim on heaven."

Tears misted Mary Anna's eyes. "I'm so glad that both of our husbands are saved, Jodie. If God should allow either or both of them to be taken from us, we know we'll meet them again in heaven."

Sudden tears sprang to Jodie's eyes. "Thank God for Calvary."

"Yes, thank God," said Mary Anna, closing her Bible.

Rising from her chair, Jodie said, "Well, prayer time, then bedtime."

To avoid disturbing little Julia, the two women went to Jodie's bedroom, knelt beside the bed, and asked the Lord to keep their husbands safe.

At the edge of the dark, shadowy Spotsylvania Wilderness, the clouds were drifting away from the moon, allowing its silver rays to shine down clear and bright. The Confederate sentries stood alert and still as they scanned the area for any sign of the enemy. Suddenly Chuck Carney stiffened and squinted.

"What's the matter?" Hank Upchurch asked, following his line of sight.

Carney raised his rifle and snapped the hammer into firing position. "Movement down there on the field at the edge of the woods, to the right."

From a few yards away, Bo Gentry whispered hoarsely, "What's up?"

"Down there!" Carney said, pointing with his rifle muzzle. "Riders!"

Other rifles cocked as three horsemen became visible, their horses hugging the edge of the woods.

Carney led the others out of the shadows to face the oncoming riders. At twenty yards out, the one in the lead saw them and pulled rein. "Hold it, men!" he said. "Don't fire! It's Jeb Stuart!"

"Come on in, sir," said Carney. "Who you got with you?"

"Couple of scouts. We need to see General Jackson."

Stonewall Jackson's prayer time with Rance Dayton and Tucker Lacy was over, and the three men now stood in front of Jackson's tent in the moonlight, speaking in low tones. The conversation stopped abruptly when they heard a tiny jingling sound and a metallic clank. They turned to see four men coming their way.

"What do you suppose this is, sir?" asked Lacy.

"Sounds like a cavalry officer in the bunch," said Jackson. "Only a saber on a man's side makes that kind of noise."

As they drew up, Corporal Chuck Carney said, "General Jackson, I have General Jeb Stuart here, along with a couple of scouts."

Stuart and Jackson greeted each other quietly, then Stuart said, "General, these men are scouts from Brigadier General Fitzhugh Lee's cavalry brigade. General Lee sent them with news you need to hear."

Jackson thanked Carney and sent him back to his post, then took Stuart and the scouts inside his tent.

"General, do you mind if Major Dayton and I listen in?" Lacy said through the tent wall.

"Not in the least. Whatever I'm about to be told, you'll know about it anyway."

The scouts told Jackson about General Hooker's series of planned deceptions, including his move on the spot where Jackson's II Corps had been camped on the bank of the Rappahannock.

When he had the entire picture, Stonewall said, "Thank you, men, and please take my thanks to your commander for sending you tonight. This information is invaluable."

Jeb Stuart chortled. "Looks like the mighty Joe Hooker is going to get the surprise of his life tomorrow!"

Lacy and Dayton shook hands as Lacy exclaimed, "Praise the Lord! He's already answering prayer!"

When Stuart and the scouts were at the edge of the forest, mounting up, Jackson held a sheet of paper on which he had drawn a crude map and marked the Union army's positions, according to the scouts. "I wish General Lee was still close by," he said to Dayton and Lacy.

Lee had gone to Fredericksburg to stay in the hotel and get a good night's rest. His heart was bothering him again, just as it had before the Antietam battle.

"It's too far to Fredericksburg," said Jackson. "I'll have to make the decision to counter Hooker's moves without General Lee's approval, then send a messenger to tell him what I've decided to do so he can maneuver I Corps accordingly."

Rance Dayton scrubbed a hand over his mustache. "I doubt General Lee would disagree with your strategy, sir, whatever it is."

"I appreciate your confidence, Major."

"You've got that a thousand percent, sir."

Lacy chuckled. "You've got that with all of your men, General."

Jackson smiled and looked at the slip of paper by moonlight. "I've got to figure the routes to send my corps to counteract Hooker's moves. Problem is, I'm not very familiar with the area."

"I can help you with that," said the chaplain. "I've preached in this area many times, and I know it well."

"Good. What we'll need to do is move on the Federal rear, and God willing, not be seen by them till it's too late for them to counter.

When I Corps joins us, the element of surprise in this entire operation will carry a heavy weight toward bringing off a victory against such great odds. Let's sit down in the tent and—" Jackson turned his head, covered his mouth, and sneezed. "Excuse me, gentlemen. I think I'm coming down with a cold."

"Maybe we should send for Dr. McGuire, General," said Dayton.

"You're probably right."

"I'll send one of my men for the doctor, sir," said Dayton, and hurried away.

Jackson pulled a handkerchief from his hip pocket, wiped his nose, and said, "As I was about to suggest, Chaplain, let's sit down in the tent and you tell me some things I need to know so I can get them down on this map."

TWELVE

Rance Dayton returned to Jackson's tent within a few minutes and informed him that a messenger was on his way to fetch Dr. McGuire. Jackson thanked the major and invited him to stay while he questioned Tucker Lacy about the lay of the area.

It was near midnight when Jackson finalized his strategy. In the morning I Corps would join II to launch an offensive on the Union forces. He sent a messenger to Fredericksburg to inform General Lee.

After the messenger had gone, Jackson leaned back and began rubbing his tired eyes.

"Sir," said Rance Dayton, "something's been on my mind since Hooker moved into the Chancellor mansion."

"What's that?"

"Where did the Chancellor family go?"

"Well, we've had no report of the family moving about the grounds. Certainly Hooker's aware of the great possibility of a battle right around the mansion. I would think the man has enough character and good sense to have allowed the Chancellor family to go elsewhere for safety's sake."

Lacy cleared his throat gently. "Ah…General, from what I've heard about Hooker, I doubt he has. He likes to bully people, and he doesn't care who it is. You're aware that there's no man of the house—that the widow Fannie Chancellor lives there with seven of her nine children?"

"Yes, I am aware of that," said Jackson. "But do you really think Hooker would hold them captive?"

"Yes, I do. Tell me…would turning your howitzers on the mansion be part of the plan?"

"Yes, if it comes to that."

"Then I want to go over there right now and ask the sentries if the family is still in the house. If they are, I'll demand to see Hooker and put pressure on him to let them go."

"You wouldn't get within thirty yards of the mansion, Chaplain," said Jackson. "They'd cut you down."

"Not if I go in carrying a lighted lantern."

"I don't know…they might shoot first and ask your dead body questions later."

"I'm willing to take the risk," said Lacy. "I must make sure Mrs. Chancellor and those children are safely placed elsewhere before the battle begins."

Jackson shook his head in wonder and glanced at Dayton, then said, "Too bad I don't have you in a uniform with a gun in your hand, Chaplain Lacy. You'd make a great soldier."

"I am a soldier, General. A soldier of the cross."

"You sure are, my friend, and God bless you for the way you preach the cross."

Lanterns burned late in Matthew Chancellor's bedroom as General Hooker stood before his seven corps leaders.

The Chancellor boys had been moved upstairs so they couldn't listen in on any more of Hooker's private conversations.

On the second floor, Fannie Chancellor lay awake, unable to get her mind off the pending battle.

Joe Hooker was lighthearted as he stood before his generals and said, "Gentlemen, we're ready to take on Bobby Lee and Stonehead Jackson in the morning. Some surprise we have in store for those boys!"

None of the generals seemed to share their leader's attitude. While Hooker waited for a show of enthusiasm from his generals, a knock at the door interrupted the silent tension.

A sentry looked around the door and said, "General Hooker, there's someone on the front porch who would like to speak to you."

Hooker scowled. "Who wants to see me at this time of the night?"

"A preacher."

"A preacher?"

"Yes, sir."

"Well, I don't need a sermon at this time of night! What's he want?"

"He asked the sentries on the porch if the Chancellor family was being held as captives. They didn't want to lie, so they told him they are. He wants to see you."

Hooker snorted in disgust and said, "Tell him I'm not seeing visitors tonight."

The disapproving frowns on the faces of his corps leaders made him lift a hand. "On second thought, Private Selby, bring the reverend in."

While Selby was gone, General Meade said, "General Hooker, I've been thinking about the Chancellor widow and her children. We told them no harm would come to them if they cooperated with us. But if the Rebels should shell this house, and any of them are injured or killed, that makes us liars. I'm sure this reverend, whoever he is, is going to ask you to release them. I, for one, think you should do it."

There was a rumble of agreement among the generals.

Hooker frowned. "But I had in mind that if we let it be known the family was here, the Rebels wouldn't turn their guns loose on the mansion."

Major General Darius Couch looked at his commander with

disdain. "You mean hide behind a woman and her children?"

Hooker saw the same look in the eyes of the other men. "Well, I—"

The sentry appeared at the door. "Chaplain Tucker Lacy of II Corps, Army of Northern Virginia, sir."

As the chaplain entered, Hooker moved toward him. "I'm Major General Joseph Hooker, Reverend."

"I know," said Lacy. "I've seen your photograph in the papers, sir."

"What is it you wish to see me about, Reverend?"

"I came here to see if Mrs. Chancellor and her children were being held captive in this house, sir, and your sentries outside confirmed that they are. I would like you to let me take them away from here until this conflict is over."

"Well, isn't that a coincidence?" Hooker said, smiling. "I was just talking to my corps commanders here about that very thing. We'd certainly like to get the lady and her children off our hands."

"May I talk to Mrs. Chancellor, please?" asked Lacy.

Fannie was awake when the knock came. She opened the door and clutched at the neck of her robe, glancing at Hooker and the sentries, and then at the man in their midst. Her gaze stayed riveted on the man, and she said, "I know you, sir. You're evangelist Tucker Lacy. I heard you preach when you were at Bonner Grove Presbyterian Church."

Lacy smiled. "That's right, Mrs. Chancellor. I am presently Chaplain General of II Corps, Army of Northern Virginia."

"That's General Jackson's Corps."

"Yes, ma'am. You are aware there could be a battle right here in this area…"

"Yes, I am."

"Well, I came to ask General Hooker to let me take you out of here."

Fannie's eyes flicked to Hooker's face.

"I've given permission," he said quickly.

"Do you and the children know somebody who would take you in, ma'am?" asked Lacy.

"We have some close friends who live just five miles down Ely's Ford Road. An elderly couple—Jack and Elsie Courtman. They have a large house, and I know they would welcome us."

"All right," said Lacy. "How long would it take you to get the children up and ready to go? I'm sure General Hooker will provide a wagon, and I'll go along to make sure the Courtmans are home."

"We can be ready in less than an hour," said Fannie.

"All right. We'll be waiting in the room General Hooker is occupying."

"I'll hurry," said Fannie. "And…and thank you, Reverend Lacy."

"My pleasure, ma'am."

She set her gaze on Hooker. "And thank you for allowing us to leave, General."

Hooker nodded silently.

Fannie had her children packed and ready to go in forty-five minutes. General Meade had appointed four men to ride as escorts, and since Chaplain Lacy wanted to go along, he was assigned to drive the wagon.

Captain Miles Carlton was in charge, accompanied by Lieutenant Errol Waters, a sergeant, and a corporal. Meade and Hooker stood on the porch of the mansion and watched them move away in the moonlight toward Ely's Ford Road.

Jack and Elsie Courtman were unruffled by being awakened after midnight. They welcomed Fannie and her children, glad to offer their home as a place of safety.

Fannie thanked Lacy again for risking himself on her and her children's behalf.

When the widow and her children had entered the Courtman

house, the Yankees mounted their horses and Lacy climbed back in the wagon.

"Chaplain," Captain Carlton said, "you go on and take the wagon back to General Hooker. I've heard a lot about the wilderness north of the mansion, and I'd like to take a look at it in the moonlight. If General Hooker is still up, tell him we'll be along in a few minutes."

"Will do," said Lacy, and put the wagon in motion.

"Come on, men," said Carlton, "let's take a little ride."

The captain left the road and guided his men toward the darkness of the wilderness. As they trotted along, Sergeant Mel Finch said, "Captain, what about the forest on the south side of the mansion? Is that part of the wilderness too?"

"No. That's just a normal forest. Lots of trees and brush, but not the sloughs and marshes that make the wilderness a spooky place. I'd just like to take a look at it while there's a chance. May not get another opportunity."

At the edge of camp, the Fearless Four continued their watch of the Chancellor mansion, wondering what was taking Chaplain Lacy so long to return.

Chad Lynch, Bo Gentry, Ken Dykstra, and Myron Flynn were still positioned nearby where they had kept watch since going on sentry duty. There would be a shift change at three o'clock.

Keeping his voice low, Buford Hall said to his three companions, "Maybe those Yankees took Lacy prisoner."

"Why would they do that?" asked Nichols. "He's no threat to them."

"Yeah, but from what I hear about Hooker, he's the kind that just might lock up a preacher."

Hank Upchurch chuckled. "I don't think there's anything that mean, lowdown Hooker wouldn't—"

"Sh-h-h!" came Chuck Carney's hiss. "Look!"

The other men followed the direction Carney pointed and saw four riders trotting along the edge of the wilderness.

"S-s-s-t!" came the sound from their friends nearby. "Riders coming!"

"They're Yankees!" Hank said. "Dark uniforms!"

"Yankees sure enough," said Everett, raising his rifle.

Bo Gentry held up his hand. "Wait a minute! If you fire, they'll hear it over at the mansion and it'll give away our position!"

"But what if they decide to ride the plank road in here?" said Buford. "They'll see the tents! Hooker'll find out anyhow!"

"Let's capture 'em," said Dykstra.

"We can try," said Chuck, "but if they make a break for it, we'll have to cut 'em down. We sure can't let 'em get back to Hooker. Better that Hooker hears a few shots and wonders what's going on than to have even one of 'em tell him we're in here!"

The riders were coming close now, and the sound of hoofbeats was getting louder.

"Okay, men," said Everett. "Guns ready?"

Each man cocked his rifle.

"Follow the leader," he said, and ran out of the shadows to intercept the riders.

Captain Miles Carlton saw the movement in the shadows first, drew rein, and shouted, "Rebels!" as he whipped out his revolver.

Lieutenant Errol Waters followed suit, and the other two soldiers brought up their rifles.

"Hold it right there!" shouted Nichols, the other seven men on his heels.

Carlton's horse was startled, and when he fired into the advancing group that had stepped into full view in the moonlight, the bullet went astray, plowing sod several feet from them.

The eight Rebels unleashed their rifles on the Yankees.

Moments later, as the Rebels stood over the dead Yankees, Flynn said, "We'd better get their horses. They couldn't have gone far."

When Chaplain Tucker Lacy arrived at the Chancellor mansion, he explained to a sentry why Captain Carlton and his men would be a few minutes behind him. The sentry, unwilling to believe that Carlton would want to investigate the wilderness so late at night, told Lacy he would have to stay until Carlton and his men returned.

General Jackson stood in the moonlight, looking down at the dead Union soldiers, whose bodies had been dragged into the wilderness to a spot near his tent.

"We can be sure they heard the gunfire at the mansion," he said to the eight sentries. Some of the men disturbed from their sleep by the gunshots had gathered around.

"We really had no choice, General," said Chuck Carney. "It was them or us."

"I know you had to defend yourselves," said Jackson, "but I sure wish these men hadn't come here. It could ruin part of our surprise. I wonder what they were doing, riding here at this time of night?"

"Who knows?" said Rance Dayton.

"Guess when it comes to Yankees riding around our camps at night, we should shoot first and ask questions later," said Buford Hall.

Stonewall Jackson was eating a cold breakfast in his tent about an hour before dawn when he heard the voice of General Robert E. Lee. He pulled back the tent flap as Lee drew near in the waning moonlight.

"Good morning, General Jackson," said Lee. "I received your message and thought it best that I cut my sleep a little shorter and join you."

"I'm glad you're here, sir, but I'm a bit surprised. How's the heart?"

Lee rubbed his chest as he sat down. "Better. Dr. Franks gave me some powders last night. The pain has eased up quite a bit."

"I'm glad. I prayed that it would," said Jackson, sitting down in a facing chair.

"Thank you. The sentries were telling me about the shooting incident."

Jackson shook his head. "I'm also praying about that. Hooker no doubt heard the gunfire, and by now he's wondering where his four men are."

"Well, at least he can't see you in here. He won't have any idea how many—"

"General Jackson…" came the voice of Corporal Jim Lewis.

"Excuse me, General." Stonewall got up and pulled back the flap. "Yes, Jim?"

"Just wanted to let you know that Chaplain Lacy is back. He'll explain it to you later, but he wanted me to tell you that Mrs. Chancellor and her children are safe with neighbors a few miles from here. The Yankees tried to hold him after the Chancellors were placed with the neighbors, but he managed to escape. Said to tell you that no one followed him."

"Good. Thank you for letting me know, Jim."

When Stonewall sat down again, Lee said, "Chaplain Lacy was able to get that dear widow and her offspring out of the mansion?"

"Sure enough. Don't know how he persuaded Hooker to let them go, but as you just heard, he did."

"I'm glad. Now, General, let's get down to business. I want to say that I concur with your battle strategy 100 percent. So you've already moved troops during the night?"

"Yes, sir. They're in position as I described in my message." As he spoke, Jackson pulled a handkerchief from his hip pocket and turned his head away to sneeze.

"You all right?" asked Lee.

"Yes, sir. Just a head cold."

"You doing something for it?"

Jackson nodded and slipped the handkerchief back in his pocket. "I sent for Dr. McGuire last night. He came over and gave me some medicine. Anyway, General, we're ready to give Hooker a big surprise on his rear flank."

"You sent twenty-eight thousand men to do that…and you've kept fifteen thousand here in the wilderness, right?"

"Right."

"Okay. This leaves me with twenty-two thousand embedded on two sides of the Chancellor estate, and we both have sufficient artillery. Do you still feel sure we've got our numbers placed correctly?"

"I do. As I told you in the message, sir, you are left with an actor's job. You will have to make Fighting Joe believe your troops make up the main army—the bulk of it embedded in the forest on the south side. And you'll have to convince him that your twenty-two thousand are actually sixty thousand."

"And how do you propose I do that?"

"I already explained it to Generals McLaws, Anderson, and Stuart, sir, just in case you weren't able to be with them."

"And what did you tell them?"

"You will have to have sharpshooters running back and forth in the trees, with men there to reload for them as they fire rapidly, making one man appear to be a company. It will take precision timing between firing and loading, but it can be done."

Lee nodded. "And the same thing, in essence, with those men in the low spots behind the hills to the west?"

"That's correct. You'll also have to shift the artillery batteries around on the fly, in the forest and the low spots in the fields, confusing the bluebellies about your positions. You have to hold Hooker's attention from those two sides so we can come at him from behind, and from right here in the wilderness."

Lee chuckled, shaking his head. "General Jackson, my friend, you are indeed a genius. I never thought of Robert E. Lee as an actor."

"You will when we win this battle, sir." Jackson whipped out his handkerchief just in time to sneeze into it again.

"You take care of that cold," said Lee.

"Yes, sir. And you take care of that heart."

Lee grinned. "Yes, sir."

As dawn broke over the Virginia countryside, General Joseph Hooker was astride his prancing horse, riding before his troops who were standing at attention. He tried not to show it but he was concerned about the gunshots he'd heard the night before, and the fact that his four men had not returned. To make it more annoying, the preacher had gotten away before he could get out of bed and question him.

Hooker looked his army over with pride. He was plagued with uncertainty as to where Stonewall Jackson had gone with his II Corps, but with more than twice as many men as Lee and Jackson, he would make short work of them. He figured Jackson had somehow covertly joined Lee near Fredericksburg and had been able to hide his army from Union scouts. Lee and Jackson would come marching toward Chancellorsville with their relatively small numbers and meet up with Joe Hooker's great Union Army of the Potomac for a final showdown. Soon this war would be over.

Hooker was the picture of a confident warrior chief: ramrod straight in the saddle, cheeks rosy, spiffily clad in tailored dark blue. When the inspection was over, he dismounted at the front porch of the Chancellor mansion, where Generals John Gibbon and Oliver Howard waited for him.

"Did you gentlemen get a good look at that marvelous army?" Hooker asked as he dismounted.

"We did, sir," said Howard.

"They seem more confident now, General," said Gibbon. "You've instilled it into them."

"Part of the reason President Lincoln gave me the job. Those are the finest troops in the world out there, and the best prepared. It's taken me some time, but I have no doubt I've gotten the job done."

Both generals nodded.

"Yes, sir," said Hooker, "those men out there are spick-and-span, healthy, alert, and ready to take on those slow-talking, laid-back Southerners. Bobby Lee will have to use every man, woman, child, dog, horse, and mule in Dixie to even make a dent in my army!"

When Hooker had gone inside the mansion, Gibbon and Howard walked toward the troops.

"I'm not exactly fond of the general's frequent gasconade," said Gibbon, "but his confidence is reassuring…far better than Ambrose Burnside's lack of it."

"I appreciate that, General. But his boasting that even God Almighty can't keep him from whipping the socks off Bobby Lee has me a bit disturbed."

"You figure God just might decide to show him?"

"Something like that."

THIRTEEN

General Robert E. Lee, escorted by a group of Jeb Stuart's cavalry, met up with the leaders of I Corps and explained the role they would play in the battle plan, then sent them to assemble their men accordingly.

At the same time, Stonewall Jackson was getting his II Corps ready, placing them strategically to launch the rear attack on Joe Hooker's much larger army.

Jackson could see only a small part of his corps where he sat his horse at the edge of the wilderness. But he knew that out there in the hills and forests were thousands of gray-clad men—some little more than boys—who were eager to attack the unsuspecting Union army. The general let his gaze take in the multiple guns, wagons, and animals close by as his men made last-minute preparations.

He guided Little Sorrel deeper into the trees to meet Brigadier General James H. Lane of the North Carolina Brigade, who was walking toward him from the deep shadows.

When they came together, Jackson dismounted. "Everything ready, General?"

"Yes, sir," replied Lane. "I just wanted to say, sir, that I like your battle plan. Even if it takes two or three days to whittle down

Hooker's massive numbers, I believe we will come out the victors. And when we do, it will be your ingenuity that did it."

Jackson shook his head. "Not without brave and dedicated men to execute the plan, General. And that victory will cost many of them their lives."

"I know that, sir," said Lane, "but I just wanted to express my deep appreciation to you for coming up with the plan, and to say how I admire you as a military leader."

Humbled by Lane's sincere words, Stonewall nodded and thanked him. He cast a glance toward the brightening eastern sky and said, "Well, General, the sun will be up shortly. It's time to take the battle to the enemy."

The sun's brilliant rays spread a fan-shaped light in the eastern sky as Stonewall Jackson waited in readiness to launch his surprise assault. As he stood by, a courier from General Lee came riding in with a dispatch, which read:

> Lieutenant General Thomas J. Jackson.
> Be assured that at the first sign of your engagement with the enemy from the wilderness in front of Chancellorsville, I will vigorously begin my actor's task with infantry and artillery from this position so as to make Hooker think the larger Confederate force is on this side. You then can surprise him by hitting him hard from the rear with your other forces. May God speed us the victory.
> Robert E. Lee

Jackson smiled as he stuffed the paper in his pocket and turned to the courier. "Corporal, tell General Lee I'll be expecting a full show, and that maybe someday he and I can do a Shakespeare play on some stage together."

The corporal cocked his head, his brow furrowed. "Pardon, sir?"

Jackson chuckled. "General Lee will understand. Just tell him what I said."

"Yes, sir," said the courier, and galloped away, keeping within the shadow of the trees.

Major General Joseph Hooker stepped out on the wide porch of the Chancellor mansion, attended by Captains Harry Russell, William Candler, and Delbert Binkley. Only two sentries were near the porch, and they vigilantly scanned the fields as the brilliant sun peeked over the eastern horizon.

Hooker leaned an arm against one of the massive white pillars and watched Major General Darius Couch's approach. Couch's II Corps was situated in the hills to the northeast.

Couch dismounted and was about to speak to Hooker when sudden rifle fire came from the northwest. There were more rifle shots, as if the firing were being answered.

Hooker squinted toward the sound then looked around at the others and said, "Skirmish somewhere beyond those hills."

"Appears to be, sir," said Couch, moving toward the porch steps. "Couple of things I need to ask you…"

In the forest about a half-mile to the south, General Lee was in conversation with Major Lafayette McLaws when the sound of rifle fire came rolling across the hills.

"General McLaws!" shouted one of his men, who thought the firing was coming from the wilderness. "Stonewall Jackson has started his assault!"

"Excuse me, General!" McLaws ran toward his brigade. "Open fire, men! Make it sound like there's a million of us! Yell, too! Yell your lungs out! Jackson is in their rear!"

The other brigade leaders gave the same command, and rifles and cannons cut loose amid the bloodcurdling sound of the Rebel yell.

In the deep shadows of the wilderness, General Stonewall Jackson was studying the sounds of the skirmishers when suddenly Lee's guns opened up and the men of I Corps were giving out the Rebel yell.

Jackson realized Lee had mistaken the skirmishers to be his corps opening up on Hooker. He looked through the dense trees where his artillery was hidden, with guns aimed toward the Chancellor house, and gave a hand signal.

Instantly, the cannons began to roar.

Joe Hooker and the men with him now had their attention on I Corps's guns to the south. By some mysterious fluke of acoustics, the roar of Jackson's assault did not meet their ears. Seemingly from out of nowhere, and without warning, a shell landed close by the Chancellor porch and exploded.

A rain of smoking shrapnel ripped into the house and the pillar where Hooker stood. Chunks of brick flew in every direction, one of them striking Hooker and knocking him down.

At the same instant, while the men were diving for cover, Captain Delbert Binkley took a hunk of shrapnel in the chest and went down with a grunt.

Cannon and rifle fire roared and rattled from the wilderness, shells exploding all across the front yard of the mansion. Bullets spent their force, ripping at foliage and crashing through trees as well as striking the big brick structure.

"Help me get the general inside the house!" Couch shouted at Russell and Candler as he bent over to grasp Hooker's arms.

The two sentries lay crumpled on the ground, and Captain Binkley was sprawled on the porch floor. All three had been killed instantly.

Sounds of Rebel guns seemed to be coming from every direction as Joe Hooker's men laid him on the bed in Matthew Chancellor's room. He was regaining consciousness and moaning as Couch examined the purple knot on his temple.

"One of you bring a wet towel," Couch said. "He's cut."

Candler disappeared into the hall, and Russell bent close to examine the wound.

The sounds of Confederate guns and exploding cannonballs were deafening.

When Hooker's eyelids began to flutter, Couch said, "General, sir! Can you hear me?"

Fighting Joe moaned and opened his eyes to give Couch a glassy look.

"Do you know where you are, sir?" asked Couch.

Hooker closed his eyes, then opened them again. "Mmm?"

"Do you know me, General?"

Hooker worked his mouth, trying to focus his eyes on Couch. "Y-you are Darius Couch."

"Yes, sir! You were just struck by a brick, sir. A Rebel cannonball hit the house. Lee's army is firing at us. We must counter-attack immediately. Do I have your permission to signal our army to counterattack?"

Still glassy-eyed, Hooker mumbled, "No. Have...to...ask President Linc— President Lincoln."

Captain William Candler rushed in with a wet towel, and Couch stepped back, allowing him to press the towel to the wound. Hooker jerked, swearing with a thick tongue.

To Russell, Couch said, "He's not coherent. I've got to order a counterattack. When his mind clears, tell him what I'm doing. I'll be back once I've got all units involved in the fight."

By eight o'clock that morning, the battle of Chancellorsville was in full swing. The battle area, covering sixteen square miles, shook with the heavy fire of artillery punctuated with musketry. The shrill whistling of cannonballs and bullets gave an adrenaline rush through soldiers' veins on both sides of the conflict.

The hostile artillery batteries of the Confederates blasted away from the wilderness, and the Federals' big guns were masked in ravines and small patches of dense thicket as they answered with deep-throated roars.

White sulfurous clouds rose slowly in the air from every spot where artillery fired.

So far, Stonewall Jackson's surprise attack on the Union rear had not been activated. Jackson would wait till the enemy grew complacent, thinking that the heaviest fire was coming from Lee's I Corps. Then he would unleash his deadly artillery on them.

The din of battle reached the people of Fredericksburg and the small villages and settlements that surrounded the Chancellorsville area. People stood on their porches and in their yards, and many farmers had even climbed on their barn roofs to get a glimpse of the battle.

The rising smoke from cannons and rifles filled the sky and could be seen for miles around.

At the Jack Courtman place, a worried Fannie Pound Chancellor stood with her children and the Courtmans on their front porch. She and the girls wept, while Matthew and Malachi gazed in the direction of the mansion, their faces stiff and pale.

Elsie Courtman draped her arm around Fannie's shoulders, trying to give her strength.

"Oh, Elsie," Fannie sobbed, "I just know our house is going to be destroyed, if it isn't already."

"Maybe not, honey," said the elderly woman. "Maybe our men won't fire on it."

Fannie sucked in a sharp breath and swallowed hard. "They'll have to, Elsie. Getting Hooker will be at the top of the list."

Silver-haired Jack comforted Rebecca and Martha, while Naomi,

Ruth, and Sarah huddled together in a tight knot, weeping as if their hearts would break. Their brothers stood next to them, wordlessly patting their shoulders.

"We've lost it all!" sobbed Sarah. "Everything is probably blown to bits by now!"

"The horses will be killed or stolen by those horrible Yankees!" wailed Naomi. "Oh, why does there have to be war? Why? Why? Why?"

The weather was warm that spring morning as twenty-eight thousand Confederate men lay low in the woods at the rear flank of Hooker's army. Stonewall Jackson was there with his unit leaders, who were prepared on a moment's notice to move the infantry out, as well as the cavalry and artillery.

Jackson stood near the edge of the woods, listening to the battle as it grew more fierce by the moment. With him stood cavalry division commander Major General Jeb Stuart and one of Stuart's aides, Corporal Richard Austin. Both men knew Jackson was biding his time, waiting for the proper moment to pull off his surprise. He had just sent four scouts to appraise the situation and bring him word as to all enemy positions.

Jeb Stuart knew Stonewall well and could feel the fire building in him as water builds behind a dam. Thomas Jackson was eager to hit the Yankees with his surprise, but it had to come at just the right time.

"I'd say Hooker's got most of his troops in the battle now, sir," said the cavalry leader.

"Most, but not all," replied Jackson, his eyes fixed on the smoke of battle to the south. "He'll keep some reserves. And, of course, we'll have them to contend with once this bunch gets into the fight."

Stuart grinned. "I like your plan, General. Gonna be a real shocker."

"General Jackson," Corporal Austin said, "there's some kind of fancy word for what you're doing. I can't remember it right now. Know what I mean?"

The general smiled and said, "It's called *en échelon.*"

"That's it! My father fought in the Mexican War, and I remember him using that description."

"It means 'in steps' or something planned or arranged in continuous order."

"Yes, sir. I remember now. Do we have time for you to explain the strategy in more detail?"

Jackson nodded. "You begin on one side…like I had planned to do from the wilderness, until General Lee was confused by the skirmish that broke out unexpectedly. Turns out it still worked pretty well. Anyway, when you set up en échelon, the enemy sees you coming at him from one side. He naturally begins to move his troops there to meet you. At the right moment, your attack opens in another place.

"The enemy leaders don't know where to move their troops next, or if they should move any at all. They'll usually delay because of the uncertainty of it. What you hope they will do is go on the move. That's the best way to catch them—on the move. They aren't situated for battle then.

"But while the enemy is delaying and trying to decide what to do, your own situation strengthens. He doesn't know the attack is en échelon. He just might figure you're throwing a diversion at him, and you'll hit him at another flank. If he decides that indeed it could be a diversion, he waits till he can find out for sure. In the meantime, you've surrounded him where he stands. You look for where his line is the weakest and hit him hard and fast. If you've executed your plan correctly, you've got him."

Austin looked admiringly at Lieutenant General Jackson, who had the air of a man who knew what he was doing. It was no wonder General Lee had so much confidence in him.

***

At the Chancellor mansion, no more bombardment had rained down since the initial one that killed three men and rendered General Hooker unconscious. The Confederate troops were now occupied with a swarm of Yankees advancing across the open field, guns blazing.

By nine o' clock Hooker was clear-minded, and he stood at a window on the third floor, observing what portion of the battle he could see. Captains Russell and Candler had wrapped a makeshift bandage around his head to stay the flow of blood.

Hooker rubbed his head and swore vehemently. "I wish General Couch would show up!"

"He said he would be back as soon as he could, sir," said Russell.

"Well, it's not soon enough. We've got to change our tactics out there."

"Should I see if I can find some powders downstairs for your headache, sir?" asked Candler.

"Forget the powders. There's a bottle of whiskey in my saddlebags down in the kid's bedroom. Bring it to me."

"But, sir," said Candler, "President Lincoln—"

"I know, I know! I'm not gonna get drunk! I just need something to ease the pain of this headache. Get the whiskey for me. That's an order!"

Moments later, Captain Candler returned with the bottle. Hooker downed several big gulps, then smacked his lips and belched. As he replaced the cork, he saw a small group of Union men on horseback gallop by and quickly vanish from sight.

"Sir," said Candler, who was standing at Hooker's shoulder, "wasn't that General Sickles?"

Hooker nodded. "Yes, and I don't understand what he's doing this close to the mansion." He swore again and growled, "Where is that Couch?"

The sounds of battle continued to roll across the Virginia countryside as Russell moved up to Hooker's other side. "Sir, could you clear something up about General Sickles?"

"What's that?"

"I've heard he killed Francis Scott Key's son."

Hooker pulled the cork on the bottle, took a short swig, and said, "That was back a few years…when Dan Sickles was a U.S. congressman from New York. He was well known for his explosive temper, just as he is now. He found out Mrs. Sickles and Key's son were having an affair, and he shot and killed the man. Sickles pleaded temporary insanity and was acquitted."

"So that's it," said Russell. "I'd heard bits and pieces, but never had the whole—"

"General Hooker!" a sentry called from the bottom floor. "General Couch is here, sir!"

Hooker rubbed his head as he went to the door and called back, "I'll see him in my office! Be right down!"

Hooker's line, at present, formed an arc that ran southwestward from the Rappahannock River, curved around Chancellorsville, then jutted northwestward to its terminus along the Orange Turnpike, just beyond Wilderness Chapel—a small settlement centered by an old stone church building. Meade's V Corps, anchored on the Rappahannock about a mile downstream from a crossing called United States Ford, held the left. Howard's XI Corps manned the right, with the corps of Sickles, Couch, and Major General Henry Slocum deployed in the immediate area of the Chancellorsville cross-roads.

Major General Daniel Sickles had his First Division brigade commander, Brigadier General David Birney, at his side as they galloped past the Chancellor mansion and veered off to the left into a part of the wilderness where there were no Confederates.

Three other officers were with them, Major Eli Worth, Captain Eldridge Buckman, and Lieutenant Milo Dartt.

Birney had spotted Stonewall Jackson's twenty-eight thousand troops as they swarmed out of the forest like a horde of insects coming for the kill and had told Sickles, but the general had to see for himself.

Pointing to the southwest, Birney said, "Look right there, sir!"

Sickles's eyes bulged and his jaw slacked. "Lieutenant Dartt, get to the mansion as fast as you can and tell General Hooker we're being flanked on the rear! Hurry! We'll get back to the men. I need to know the general's orders…fast!"

Dartt gouged his horse's sides and headed for the mansion. Sickles led the others back toward their position at a gallop.

As General Couch sat down in Matthew Chancellor's bedroom, Hooker took another swig of whiskey. When he saw Couch frown, he grinned and said, "Medicinal purposes, General. I've got a whopper of a headache."

Couch eyed the bottle, noting it was half full. He wondered how much of it Hooker had consumed since the bandage had been put on his head.

"All right," said Hooker, "what can you tell me?"

"Thus far, we have suffered comparatively little damage anywhere, sir. Our officers responded quickly when the attacks came, and we've gained some strong positions on high ground. We're ready to—"

Couch was interrupted by a loud knock at the door.

"Come in!" called Hooker.

A young private appeared at the door, opening it just wide enough to stick his head in. "General Hooker, I have Lieutenant Milo Dartt of II Corps out here. General Sickles sent him, and the lieutenant said his message is urgent."

"Tell him to hold on a few minutes," said Hooker, clipping his words. "I've got General Couch in here, and I can only talk to one man at a time."

Suddenly the door flew open all the way, and Lieutenant Dartt plunged into the room. "General, we're being flanked from the rear by a massive force of troops! General Sickles wants to know how to react, immediately!"

General Couch banged his fist into the palm of his hand, swearing angrily. "I should have known it! That's Jackson's troops! Hid those men and their equipment somewhere after pulling them away from the Rappahannock, and now, after decoying us with the other troops, he's coming in on our rear flank!"

Joe Hooker's face was pallid as he opened a map of the area and spread it out on the desk. "Show me, Lieutenant! Where are those troops, exactly?"

When Hooker saw the position of Jackson's twenty-eight thousand, he quickly sent a courier to General Oliver Howard, whose XI Corps was deployed to the south. He sent Dartt with orders for Sickles, then said to Couch, "Take your corps and join Howard. Do it fast!"

Couriers from unit leaders all over the area came to the Chancellor mansion, reporting on Jackson's massive force and their move on the rear flank. And the battle raged on as the hours passed.

Lieutenant Dartt returned to the mansion with a message from his commanding general. General Sickles was asking Hooker for permission to swing around on Jackson's rear flank and attack him. Hooker's reply was for Sickles to stay close to General Howard's corps and fight alongside them.

Sickles knew from Lieutenant Dartt that Hooker had been drinking and figured his mind was muddled. Leaving one of his three divisions to fight alongside Howard, he took the other two and assaulted the rear of Jackson's Confederate force. The Union attackers overwhelmed the Twenty-Third Georgia Regiment, inflicting some three hundred casualties in a matter of minutes.

Like snarling dogs who had been bitten on their tails, regiments from Major General Robert Anderson's division and from Major General A. P. Hill's division turned on Sickles's troops and drove them off, killing dozens before they could get away.

As noon came and went, reports came to General Hooker in rapid succession that the assault by Jackson's troops out of the south was taking a horrible toll. Hooker's army was being whittled down by the smaller number of Rebels.

Joe Hooker was taking a swallow of whiskey when Captains Harry Russell and William Candler entered the office. He looked up at them and said, "This stuff isn't helping my headache at all."

"Be best if you threw the rest of it away, sir," said Candler.

Hooker gave him a look of disdain, then said, "Because of the reports I've been getting, I've decided to make a rash change in this battle. I want you two to send my couriers to every corps leader and tell them to abandon whatever ground they hold and to return to the positions they occupied last night around Chancellorsville."

"Are you sure, sir?" asked Russell. "That wouldn't be a wise thing to do. It—"

"Don't tell me what's wise!" said Hooker, the whiskey making his eyes watery. "Just do what I tell you!"

It was almost three o'clock when Major General George Meade received his orders. He was among a stand of trees on the ridge he had gained in the battle that morning. Glancing up at the courier who had handed him the written order, he swore and spit on the ground. "Has Hooker lost his mind? If we can't hold the top of the hill, what makes him think we can hold the bottom of it?"

The courier shrugged. "Sorry, General. I'm only delivering the message. I have nothing to do with its contents."

***

Major General Darius Couch was so angry when he received his orders to retreat to Chancellorsville that he left his corps in charge of Major General Winfield Hancock and rode his horse across the battlefield, dodging bullets and shrapnel amid thick clouds of gun smoke.

Joe Hooker was alone in his office when the door burst open and Couch barged in.

"General Hooker, what on earth has happened to your mind?" he fumed. "Why are you ordering us to retreat to Chancellorsville? Sure, we've been taken by surprise, and we're having ourselves a tough fight, but what can we gain by falling back here? You're taking us completely off the offensive and putting us totally on the defensive! You don't win battles by fighting defensively!"

Hooker wiped a hand across his face and said, "You don't understand, General. I'll have Lee and Jackson just where I want them. By pulling my army back here, I'll make them fight me on my own ground."

"Is that you talking, or is it the whiskey? If you do this, General Hooker, we're going to lose the battle…and it'll be all your fault!"

Hooker rose to his feet. His voice was ragged as he snapped, "You just do what I tell you, Couch!"

The commander of II Corps clamped his mouth shut, pivoted, and stormed across the room, slamming the door behind him.

FOURTEEN

As the afternoon wore on, Stonewall Jackson rode Little Sorrel up and down the ranks, shouting encouragement to his men. One of his main objectives was to take the high ground at a farm owned by a family named Taylor and situated a thousand yards down the Orange Turnpike from the Chancellor estate.

About the time Darius Couch was slamming the door of General Hooker's office, Brigadier General James Lane and his North Carolina brigade positioned themselves in the forest just east of the Taylor farm.

A brigade of General John Sedgwick's VI Corps under Union Colonel Hiram Burnham was occupying the farm's high ground.

The North Carolina men stayed far enough in the forest to remain unseen and watched General Lane as he met with his regiment leaders.

They could see that the Yankees who had taken possession of the farm were facing an angry farmer and his family. The farmer was waving his arms and apparently telling Burnham and his troops to get off his property.

Keeping his eyes on the scene, Lane said, "Seems a shame those Yankees can just take the place over and give those nice people a hard time. Since General Jackson told us to take it and secure it for the Confederate cause, I think we'd best do it."

"I agree," said Major Rance Dayton, who stood next to him. "We need that high ground right now…and those nice Southern people need to be shed of those bluebellies."

Seconds later the North Carolina Brigade rushed through the trees with the bloodcurdling Rebel yell reverberating through the dense woods. The attackers ran forward, ignoring the underbrush that tugged and ripped at their clothes and flesh, as the surprised Federals turned to meet the onslaught.

The farmer and his wife made a mad dash for the house.

Occupying the farm was the First Division of Major General Oliver O. Howard's XI Corps. Spread around the area was the rest of XI Corps in fields, ditches, gullies, and small wooded patches. Jackson's charging Rebels drove brigade after brigade of Yankees into hasty retreat.

When the fleeing men descended on the astonished men of the One Hundred Fifty-third Pennsylvania and Fifty-fourth New York— the two regiments on Howard's flank that were facing west—they formed ranks and were able to fire three volleys, momentarily checking the Confederate advance before giving ground. They were hit by a murderous volley, then broke for the rear without firing another shot.

Another unit in the Union XI Corps, the Seventy-fifth Ohio Regiment, commanded by Colonel Robert Reilly, opened fire when the oncoming Confederates were only thirty yards away and kept at it until they were overwhelmed by the Rebels, who were bearing down on them like an avalanche. In a matter of minutes, Colonel Reilly was killed, and 150 other officers and men were killed or wounded. The rest of the regiment was swept away in retreat.

General Howard waited nearby in his headquarters at Dowdall's Tavern on the plank road. When he heard the firing, he leaped on his horse with two aides following and rode to the top of a nearby hill. At first he saw only rabbits, foxes, and deer tearing through the woods toward him. But then came the panic-stricken men of his entire First Division.

Howard and his aides sat their horses, observing the rush of men in blue and the swarm of gray coming at them like quick lightning. The roar was doubled in volume by the echoes through the forest.

The general felt sick to his stomach observing the panic of his men as bullets and shrapnel ripped into them, the dead and dying crumpled and sprawled on the ground, and the wounded straggled along—the frantic efforts of a surprised corps attempting to flee an angry Rebel storm.

"General!" gasped Lieutenant Michael Davenport, one of the aides. "They mustn't retreat from Jackson's troops! They're whipped unless they stand and fight!"

His features resolute, Howard said, "You have a flag in your saddlebags, don't you, Lieutenant?"

"No, sir," said Davenport. "I gave mine to one of the regiments who lost theirs."

"I have one, sir," said the other aide, a sergeant named Bill Kopatich. He pulled the flag from his saddlebag and handed it to Howard. The general clutched it under the stump of his right arm, which he had lost in the Battle of Fair Oaks ten months before, and galloped down the slope until he was within thirty yards of his retreating troops. Dropping the reins, he raised the flag high with his left hand, waved it, and shouted, "Halt! Don't run! Turn and fight them! Turn and fight them!"

Most of the frenzied men didn't see their leader, but Colonel Adolphus Buschbeck, commander of a Second Division brigade, saw the fluttering flag in the hand of General Howard and called for his men to turn and make a stand.

Buschbeck's brigade had been deployed in reserve in a line of rifle pits at right angles to the plank road near Dowdall's Tavern. They halted at the colonel's command and managed to produce enough fire power to delay the Confederate onslaught for a brief moment, cutting many of the Rebels down with musket fire and canister fired by their artillery.

But Stonewall Jackson's men would not be denied their victory. With a yell, they kept coming, and closed in, blasting away with a deadly series of volleys. The blue line gave way, and the Rebels continued their attack.

As the Confederate tide swept past the spot where General Oliver Howard sat his horse, waving the flag and calling for the fleeing soldiers to turn and fight, General Daniel Sickles and his III Corps, on the opposite side of Chancellorsville, were unaware of the dis-aster befalling Howard's XI Corps.

Distracted by a demonstration mounted by General Lee's I Corps at a small settlement called Catherine Furnace, Sickles doubted the word of an aide sent by General Howard to get help. It took the aide a few moments to convince Sickles that such havoc and loss could come from the enemy's smaller army. When the truth of it took hold in his mind, Sickles ordered a cavalry regiment—the Eighth Pennsylvania under Major Pennock Huey—to ride to Howard's assistance.

Huey and his regiment galloped down a country lane toward the area where Howard's XI Corps was under siege. They topped a gentle rise and skidded to a sudden halt as they ran head-on into Brigadier General R. E. Rodes's brigade, who were in battle position in a half circle, waiting for them.

Although his cavalry unit was vastly outnumbered, Huey gallantly shouted for his men to charge and led them into the teeth of Rodes's guns.

A deadly Confederate volley halted the cavalry unit in its tracks. Major Peter Keenan, commander of Huey's First Battalion, went down in a hail of enemy fire, along with the regimental adjutant, thirty men, and eighty horses.

Caught in the same volley, Union Sergeant John Collins had his horse shot out from under him. He leaped to his feet amid gunfire and smoke and dashed away through the woods as fast as he could run. Gaining the plank road, he found himself in a scene of terror and confusion like he had never experienced in any battle before. Panting for breath, Collins crossed the road and made for the woods on the opposite side.

Men and animals were dashing against one another in wild dismay before the line of assault that came crackling and crashing after them. The smoke was so thick in the forest that Collins wondered if it was on fire. The thunderous roar of exploding cannonballs seemed to come from every direction, and he was confused as to which way was safety.

When a shell struck a few feet to his left, Collins felt something claw at his left leg as the concussion of the explosion knocked him down. Stunned, he lay there until his head cleared. He could hear wild screaming above the crackle of flames devouring trees. The forest was aflame, and through the smoke Collins could make out his Union comrades dashing about in frenzied terror, stumbling, falling, and screaming—their clothing on fire.

Collins struggled to his feet. It was then that he looked down and saw a dark chunk of metal embedded in his left thigh, and blood soaking his pant leg. He took a halting step forward; he had to get out of the woods before the fire consumed him!

His eyes smarted from the smoke, and the heat of the flames scorched his uniform. He looked around in confusion. Which way had he come into the woods? Which way was closest to the edge of the woods and safety—at least safety from the blazing forest?

With the screams piercing his eardrums, Collins chose a direction and limped as fast as his wounded leg would let him. He gripped his thigh just above the place where the shrapnel was embedded and stumbled in the direction where there seemed to be the fewest flames.

Some twenty yards outside the forest to the west, Brigadier General James Lane had his North Carolina Brigade in position to unleash artillery and musketry on the Yankees who came along the old plank road. Lane's artillery had been shelling the woods for an hour, mercilessly killing the Yankees still in there and capturing those who came running out to escape the shelling. Twenty-nine Federals were already held as prisoners in a nearby gully.

A few yards down the infantry line from Lane were Major Rance Dayton and his Eighteenth North Carolina Regiment. Flanked on each side by his hometown friends, Corporals Everett Nichols, Hank Upchurch, Buford Hall, and Chuck Carney, Dayton was concentrating on the road, waiting for more Yankee troops.

The nearby forest was ablaze, and the men could feel the heat from it where they hunkered down. Massive billows of black smoke boiled toward the sky, darkening the sun.

Suddenly, a dark clot of blue uniforms appeared on the plank road, and General Lane shouted for his brigade to open fire. The Yankees were part of General Howard's routed XI Corps and were seeking another place to take cover since the woods were aflame.

Lane's order brought a thundering roll of musketry, and an increase of noise that was almost deafening. Shouts and loud commands were drowned out in the awful noise as the Yankees dashed to the opposite side of the road to take what cover they could find and return fire. Many of them didn't make it across the road.

While muskets barked and bullets whizzed through the air, sounding like angry hornets, the screams from the blazing forest were heard above it all.

As he knelt to reload his musket, Corporal Upchurch let his gaze swing toward the nearby forest where wounded Yankees were burning to death. Amid the smoke and flames, he caught sight of a stumbling human form at the edge of the woods.

Sergeant John Collins was in severe pain from the hunk of shrapnel in his thigh, but he limped as fast as he could toward the edge of the forest. Just a few more steps and he would be out of the blazing woods!

Collins staggered forward, gripping his leg and trying to keep his senses. His brain felt as if it were on fire. Suddenly the wounded leg gave way, and Collins fell to the ground amid burning leaves. He rolled to escape the flames, but his pants began to smoke.

Struggling to rise, Collins beat at the hot spots on his trousers. He made it to his feet and stumbled toward the edge of the forest, where he could see Rebel troops dug in and firing toward Yankees on the road. Two more steps and he fell again. A wild cry forced itself from his lips as he slapped at the flames taking hold of his uniform.

Hank Upchurch watched the man in the blue uniform stumble and fall. Dropping his musket, he said to Dayton, "Major, there's a wounded Yankee over there in the woods about to burn to death! I'm going after him!"

Before Dayton could respond, Hank was dashing across the open field toward Collins.

"Hank! Come back here!" Dayton shouted. "You'll get yourself killed!"

But if Upchurch heard the major, he didn't show it.

Chuck Carney, who had just emptied his rifle at Yankees on the road, bent down to reload. When he heard Hank's words, he let his musket fall and sprang to his feet.

"Chuck!" said Dayton, grabbing his arm. "Don't try it!"

"Have to, Major!" said Carney. "Hank might need help, and I can't let that Yankee burn to death either!"

Hank was aware of someone on his heels as he reached the edge of the burning forest. He paused briefly, trying to pick the best route to the fallen man.

Chuck drew up beside him. "This way!" he cried, and took off, zigzagging around burning trees and grass.

When Chuck reached Collins, he saw the bloody pant leg and realized the man was seriously wounded. Collins was trying as best he could to put out the flames. Chuck pounced on him, smothering the flames with his own body, and when Hank knelt beside him, he used his hands to beat out the flames.

Sergeant Collins thought he must be dreaming. He blinked against the smoke and squinted to make sure he was seeing correctly. Two Rebel soldiers had come to his aid!

"Let's get him out of here!" yelled Chuck above the din of battle and the roar of the fire.

Together, they lifted the wounded Yankee into their arms.

"What are you doing?" gasped Collins.

"We're taking you to a safe place, Sergeant," said Chuck. "This whole forest is going to be a hot box in a few minutes!"

"Are…are you taking me prisoner?" asked Collins.

"You might say that," said Hank. "But if we don't take you out of here, you're going to be burned meat! Would you rather stay?"

"No! Let's go!"

The battle raged on as the two men from Fayetteville, North Carolina, carried their wounded enemy across the field. They saw their regiment commander watching them, along with Everett Nichols and Buford Hall.

Bullets hissed and zipped about them as Upchurch and Carney hurried to relative safety with their prisoner. When they eased him down next to a huge bush behind the firing line, Major Dayton appeared beside them. He looked at the shrapnel in the Yankee sergeant's thigh and thought of the similar wound he had suffered at Antietam.

Running his gaze between the two men, Dayton said, "You boys did a very humane thing. Even though you disobeyed me when I told you not to do it, I won't report you."

Hank hunched his shoulders. "I didn't hear any command not to do it, Major."

Dayton grinned. "I'll never know whether you're telling me the truth or not, will I?"

Hank grinned back at him.

The major knelt beside the wounded Yankee and said, "I guess you know these two brave soldiers saved your life, Sergeant."

Gritting his teeth, Collins said, "Yes, sir. I know that. I don't understand why, but…" He looked up at Carney and Upchurch. "But I sure do thank you."

"It's something our major has taught us, Sergeant," said Hank. "When an enemy soldier is wounded and out of the battle, he's no longer our enemy. He's a human being in need of help."

"What's your name, Sergeant?" asked Dayton.

"Collins, sir. John L. Collins."

"Well, Sergeant John L. Collins, I hereby declare you a prisoner of the Confederate States of America. And since you are our prisoner, you will now be taken to our corps medical staff so they can get that shrapnel out of your leg and patch you up. Did you suffer any burns?"

"Must not have, sir. I don't have any pain except in my thigh. These men must've put the flames out before they burned through my clothing."

"Good. Well, we'll get you to our medical people right away."

"I appreciate that, Major," said Collins. Then he looked at Upchurch and Carney. "I am forever in your debt, gentlemen. You risked your lives to save mine. I wish there was some way I could express my gratitude."

"Well," said Chuck, "maybe someday, when this crazy war is over, we can meet together somewhere at the Mason-Dixon line and talk about what happened here today."

Collins managed a grin. "Hey, that would be great. I…I don't know your names."

"Hank Upchurch."

"Chuck Carney."

"Well, Corporal Upchurch…Corporal Carney, I owe my life to you."

Moments later, Sergeant Collins was carried away on a stretcher by a pair of Rebel soldiers who made it plain they were taking him to Dr. Hunter McGuire and his staff only because Major Rance Dayton was ordering them to do so.

Soon the Yankees either lay dead on the plank road or had retreated far enough to get out of the line of fire. General Lane's North Carolina Brigade was able to pull back from the road for a brief respite in the fighting.

The sounds of fierce battle on the other side of Chancellorsville still rode the air.

After a few minutes, General Lane approached Lance Dayton and said, "Well, Major, our rest period is about up. We've got to head down the plank road and find more Yankees to fight. We'll pull out in five minutes. I'll go pass the word along to the other regiments."

Dayton hurriedly moved among his men, telling them General Lane wanted to pull out in five minutes.

The Fearless Four were gulping water from their canteens when a half-dozen infantrymen of the Twentieth North Carolina drew up. One of them had a sneer on his face as he looked at Upchurch and Carney and said, "Big heroes, aren't you? Went to the trouble to save that stinkin' bluebelly so he can fight us again…maybe even kill some of us."

"Yeah," said another, "you glory boys sure did us a bad turn today."

Buford Hall's face went a deep crimson. "What's the matter with you guys? I suppose you'd have let that Yankee burn to death!"

"You bet! And why not? If he could've done it, he would've killed us. Why should we lift a finger for him? We're here to kill 'em, ain't we?"

"Killing them in battle is one thing," said Chuck Carney, "but letting a man die a horrible, agonizing death when you can prevent it is another."

"Bah! You fools should've let him die! War is war!"

When the six soldiers were gone, Everett said, "Don't let 'em bother you. You did the right thing."

Chuck Carney spit on the ground and said bitterly, "Too bad when your fellow soldiers have to upbraid you for saving a human life."

"Don't let a few soreheads get to you," came the voice of Corporal Ken Dykstra.

They looked around to see Dykstra standing close with Corporal Myron Flynn and Privates Chad Lynch and Bo Gentry. As the four stepped closer, Gentry said, "That sergeant isn't going to be killing any of us. He'll be a prisoner till the end of the war."

The North Carolina Brigade was back in the thick of the battle when Dr. Hunter McGuire stood over Sergeant John Collins at Wilderness Tavern after examining the man's wound.

"I'll have to put you under with ether, Sergeant," McGuire said. "There'll be quite a bit of cutting to do to get that metal out of your leg."

Collins nodded. "Whatever you say, Doctor."

McGuire nodded to the middle-aged nurse who stood on the other side of the table. As she turned away to get the ether, he looked down at his patient and said, "According to the men who carried you in here, it was a couple of soldiers of the North Carolina Brigade who pulled you out of the burning woods."

"Yes, Doctor. Couple of corporals. Names are Hank Upchurch and Chuck Carney."

"Doesn't surprise me," McGuire said with a chuckle.

"What do you mean?"

"They are two of a group of five who won themselves presidential commendations for saving their major's life on the battlefield at Antietam."

"That I can understand, but I'm still having a hard time believing they hazarded themselves to save me."

"They're great men," said the doctor as the nurse moved up to the table with the bottle of ether in one hand and a folded white cloth in the other.

Forty minutes had passed when Dr. McGuire and an assistant, Dr. Floyd Vickers, carefully lifted the Yankee sergeant from the table and laid him on a cot across the hotel conference room where the medical staff was set up to do their work.

McGuire turned to the nurse, who was coming through the door, and said, "Who's next, Hilda?"

"We were to work on a lieutenant who had a finger blown off, Doctor, but they just brought in a young sergeant who has a bullet lodged next to his heart."

"Bring him in!"

When the sergeant was laid on the table, he was conscious, though his face was sheet-white. Sweat beads covered his brow. Doctor McGuire pulled the shirt open to expose the wound, examined it carefully, and said to Hilda, "Laudanum."

While Hilda was preparing the pain medication, McGuire looked down at the wounded soldier, who said weakly, "It's bad…isn't it, Dr. McGuire?"

Hunter nodded. "Yes, I won't try to kid you, Sergeant. The bullet's dangerously close to your heart."

"Sir…?"

"Yes?"

"If I don't make it…would you tell General Jackson something for me?"

"Sure, but don't give up. I—"

"Doctor. Please. My name is Ryan Colston."

"Yes."

"Please...tell General Jackson that if he had not cared for my soul...and led me to Jesus—" He choked, swallowed with difficulty, and his eyes began glazing over. "Tell General Jackson...I will meet him...in heaven."

Ryan Colston's eyes closed. His head rolled to one side and his breathing stopped.

Hilda stepped up with the laudanum, took one look at the doctor's face, and halted. "Is he...?"

"Yes." Hunter looked down at Colston and said, "I'll tell General Jackson for you, Sergeant. And...I'll meet you there too."

As darkness fell over Chancellorsville, General Hooker paced the floor in his office. Major General John Sedgwick and Captains Harry Russell and William Chandler were in the room with him. Sedgwick had come to tell Hooker that the First and Second Divisions of his VI Corps had been cut to shreds.

Hooker had been given similar information from a good number of his corps leaders.

Hooker still wore the head bandage, and there was despair in his voice as he said, "We've lost the battle. We're beaten. Lee and Jackson beat us. They beat us."

General Sedgwick sat in silence, his head bowed and resting in his hands.

"We can't give up yet, General Hooker," said Russell. "We still have almost twice as many men as Lee and Jackson do."

"It doesn't seem to matter," said Hooker. "Oh, we won't surrender. We'll keep on fighting...but there's no way around it. We're whipped, I tell you. This battle is lost."

A haggard-looking John Sedgwick rose from his chair and quietly headed for the door. Hooker stopped pacing, looked toward him, and said, "Where are you going, General Sedgwick?"

The commander of VI Corps stopped, turned, and said, "Back to my men. But before I go, let me remind you of what you said in my hearing—that even God Almighty couldn't keep you from winning the victory in this battle. Maybe you'd better apologize to Him."

With that, Sedgwick passed through the door and closed it behind him.

Hooker stood mute, staring at the door.

FIFTEEN

The Union Army of the Potomac was being routed on all fronts around Chancellorsville when twilight finally gave way to darkness. The fighting dwindled, and soon all was still across the valley.

Stonewall Jackson, who could taste victory, met with his division leaders: Major Generals A. P. Hill and Jubal Early, Brigadier General R. E. Rodes, Colonel Stapleton Crutchfield, Brigadier General William Pendleton, and Major General Jeb Stuart.

"Gentlemen," he said, "I know that night fighting is almost unheard of in this war, but I believe if we keep up our attack tonight, we'll finish Hooker off by morning. The moon will be up shortly and give us some light. We've got those bluebellies just about whipped. We need to stay after them."

"General Jackson," said Hill, "I noticed some clouds in the west just before the last glimmer of sunlight, and the breeze is coming from the west. In two to three hours the winds could drive those clouds this way and cover the moon. We'll lose most of our light if they do."

"Well," said Jackson, "we just might have this battle won in two or three hours. The quicker we get after it, the quicker we can finish it. Now, here's the plan...."

Twenty minutes after Jackson's meeting with his division leaders, the Yankees were settled down in their camps for the night, expecting to get some rest.

Major General Hooker stood on the wide porch of the Chancellor mansion in conversation with his corps leaders, Major Generals John Reynolds, Darius Couch, Daniel Sickles, George Meade, John Sedgwick, Oliver Howard, Henry Slocum, and Brigadier General George Stoneman.

Though the generals could barely see their leader in the darkness, they knew by the sound of his voice that he was a whipped man.

"Gentlemen," Hooker said, "I know there's plenty of fight left in you in spite of the heavy losses we've incurred, and I'm not going to tell you to pull out and retreat back to Washington. But after we give Bobby Lee and Stonehead Jackson everything we've got in the morning, if we don't put a dent in their army we won't have any choice but to turn and run for home.

"It hurts me to even have to say this, but Jackson's surprise attack on our rear flank was a staggering blow. Are you willing—after a good night's rest—to meet Johnny Reb with everything you've got?"

There was an affirmative rumble of voices.

Darius Couch, who was still upset at Hooker for calling the troops back to Chancellorsville and giving up ground they had gained, said, "General Hooker, are we going to just sit and wait for the Rebels to come at us, or are we going to launch an attack?"

"We'll get us a good night's rest, General Couch, and take the battle to the enemy. Let's put our heads together now and work out a plan."

Suddenly the sharp blast of a bugle cut through the soft evening air. Every head whipped around toward the sound. A series of bugle calls came from brigade after brigade, left and right. Then an etched moment of pure silence.

"They're going to attack us!" Couch gasped.

Joe Hooker glanced at the rising moon in the east. "I can't believe this! Are Lee and Jackson so foolish as to attempt a night battle?"

"If I read those bugle signals correctly," Meade said, "that's exactly what they're doing!"

"We'd better get to our men!" said Oliver Howard.

"Do it!" Hooker said, almost in a daze. "Give those Rebels a reason to be sorry they've been so foolish!"

The moon was spreading its silver beams across the Virginia countryside as the Confederates attacked. All around Chancellorsville, Union soldiers were in a state of confusion as Rebel skirmishers came at them, guns blazing. Then came the solid battle lines on the run, determined men in gray, surging forward like ocean waves in a storm. They held their red battle flags out front and unleashed their high and eerie Rebel yell.

Frightened deer and rabbits scattered before the Rebels as they kept coming, their bayonets flashing in the moonlight and rifles spitting fire.

In several places, the startled Yankees became as wild as the deer and rabbits. Many stumbled and fell in their rush to get away. Some took time to drop their knapsacks and gear so they could run faster.

Stonewall Jackson was with General Early's division a few hundred yards east of the Chancellor mansion. In the moonlight, hundreds of Yankees could be seen running ahead of the Rebel lines, many dropping to earth as bullets tore into them.

As the troops swept by him, Stonewall cried, "Press on, men! Press on! Don't let them get away!"

Wild cries of victory resounded across the fields and through the wooded areas. Little Sorrell snorted and danced in the excitement. "Whoa, boy," said Jackson, tightening the reins. "You can't chase those bluebellies. You have to stay here."

Abruptly, a young lieutenant drew up beside Jackson on his horse and said, "They're running too fast for us, General! We can't keep up with them!"

Stonewall turned a stern gaze on the young man and said, "They never run too fast for me! Press them! Press them!"

High, thin clouds were floating eastward, carried by the wind, as General Hooker stood on the porch of the mansion with his two aides. He paced, swearing and muttering, with the near-empty whiskey bottle in his hand. He had heard nothing from his corps leaders since they'd gone to join their troops.

The heavy brush and trees in the surrounding forests muffled the firing and the cries of the combatants. Hooker paced for over an hour before Harry Russell pointed to the south side of the mansion and shouted, "General! Here they come!"

Hooker cursed when he saw a swarm of Rebels charging across the open fields from the south, chasing a wild mob of crazy-eyed Yankees. As the Rebel guns spit fire, Yankees fell, and many were trampled by their comrades. The closer they came, the louder the din of booming guns and the bloodcurdling Rebel yells.

It was Brigadier General R. E. Rodes and his brigade chasing the fleeing Federals.

Joe Hooker swore again, popped the cork of the bottle, and drained its contents. He threw the bottle away, pulled his saber from its sheath, and headed for the porch steps.

Captain Candler watched his leader, aghast. "General! Where are you going? What are you doing?"

Hooker didn't reply. Down the steps he went toward the running troops. As he drew near his fleeing soldiers, he swung the saber to get their attention and shouted as loud as he could, "Halt! Halt! Turn around and give them the bayonet! Do you hear me? Halt! Turn around! Give them the bayonet!"

It was as if Major General Joseph Hooker did not exist. Not one man even showed that he saw or heard him. This infuriated Hooker, and he continued to shout commands.

Captains Russell and Candler looked on, wide-eyed, as the rushing Confederates closed in on the spot where Hooker stood and swallowed him up in the melee.

Amazingly, the rout passed right by Fighting Joe. Not one Yankee had stopped for him, and he became so engulfed in the mob of Rebels chasing the Yankees that no one noticed him. Indeed, it was as if he didn't exist.

When the swarm of Confederates had passed, Hooker stared after them and raised his saber, swearing at the top of his lungs.

The Rebels chased the scurrying Federals until they reached the woods, where the dense trees engulfed them. The moon was still clear in the sky, but Rodes's men had sprinted for miles and were exhausted. Unwilling to let the Yankees go without further pursuit, Rodes called for General A. P. Hill's fresh troops, who had taken a breather. Hill sent his men into the woods, shouting commands to press the battle to the Yankees.

At his position to the east, Stonewall Jackson decided now was his opportunity to claim full victory. He was not going to let it slip by. As he watched A. P. Hill's division thunder into the woods after the Yankees, he made a decision.

Next to Jackson sat his brother-in-law, Lieutenant Joseph G. Morrison, who was in Jubal Early's division and had come to make a report. Jackson had hardly laid eyes on Mary Anna's brother since they'd arrived at Chancellorsville.

With Jackson and Morrison was Captain Keith Boswell, whom Jackson knew had grown up in the area. Corporal Jim Lewis was nearby, talking to a small group of men.

"Captain, you know the countryside around here pretty well, don't you?" Stonewall said to Boswell.

"Yes, sir."

"I want to find the enemy's stronghold and demolish them. The last concentrated firing from the Yankees came from over in that direction." He pointed southwest.

"Yes, sir."

"I want you to pick the best route and guide me over there. I want to get a look at their position."

"I can do that, General," Boswell said.

Jackson hipped around in the saddle. Speaking to the small group, he said, "Captain Boswell's going to lead me to where the Yankees are concentrated the heaviest. I'd like you men to ride with us."

General Hill rode up, having sent his men into the forest in pursuit of wild-eyed Yankees. Jackson explained to Hill what he was doing, and Hill said he wanted to ride along too.

Brigadier General James Lane and his North Carolina Brigade chased Union troops until they spread out and disappeared in the deep shadows of the woods on the west side of the Chancellor estate. When it became obvious they were wasting their time to pursue any farther, Lane took his brigade back to the main Confederate camp at the edge of the wilderness, which was settled deep in the trees along the plank road.

Upon arriving at the camp, Lane found others coming in from different units, and there were little pockets of excited conversation as the men talked of the rout they were giving the Yankees.

General Lane and Major Rance Dayton dismounted near a spot where several of the Eighteenth were collected, including the Fearless Four and some of their closest comrades.

Lane looked back toward the open fields and said, "Major, did you notice there are no sentries guarding this position out there?"

"Yes, I did," said Dayton. "I guess nobody's thought to set them up since we're routing the Yankees."

"Probably so, but those bluebellies might have a few brave ones who'd like to come charging in here and see how many of us they can kill."

"I agree, General," spoke up Everett Nichols, moving toward the officers with his friends following. "Who knows what those four who rode in here last night had in mind? Never know what those Yankees might do."

"Yeah," said Ken Dykstra. "Maybe those guys last night were on a suicide mission. I wouldn't put it past them."

"Be even more likely for them to do it tonight," said Chuck Carney. "Since they're being routed, they're probably pretty desperate by now."

Dayton nodded and said, "We'd best keep a sharp eye."

"How about us volunteering to do the sentry duty tonight, men?" said Myron Flynn, looking around at the others.

"I'm in," said Buford Hall.

The rest volunteered quickly.

"All right," Dayton said. "Let's see…there are eight of you. Should be enough. Take your usual places along the side of the road."

"And thanks," said General Lane.

Lane and Dayton headed for the tents on the back side of the camp, and the sentries checked their weapons in preparation to take their posts.

They were about to head toward the edge of the wilderness when some unidentified Rebel deeper in the woods called out, "Hey, Barney! Is General Jackson in camp?"

"I think so!" Barney called back. "But I don't know where he is at the moment!"

"Okay! I'll find him!"

The sentries eyed each other.

"I wasn't aware the general had returned," said Everett Nichols.

"Me neither," said Chad Lynch. "Guess he got in ahead of us."

* * *

Captain Keith Boswell led the small group along the old plank road in the moonlight. General Jackson noted that all gunfire had ceased; there weren't even any sounds from I Corps some five miles to the southeast. He hoped General Lee's heart wasn't acting up.

Riding next to Jim Lewis in the group was Sergeant Bill Cunliffe, who was in the signal corps. "General Jackson," he said, "if you find the stronghold out here as you suspect, are you going to wait till dawn to hit them?"

"No, Sergeant. We're going to hit them tonight. I want this battle settled and won as soon as possible."

"I like your style, General," said Cunliffe, chuckling.

"We all do," said Hill.

"What's this up here, Captain?" Stonewall pointed with his chin to a small building a few yards off the road.

"Schoolhouse, sir," replied Boswell. "Colonel Crutchfield has an artillery battery set up here. He wanted to make sure any Federals who might come along this road got a taste of Southern hospitality."

Major Sandie Pendleton of Early's division rode next to General Hill. Pendleton, a brilliant young man who had not yet reached his twenty-second birthday, let his eyes roam the moonlit fields on both sides of the road. There were grassy patches and dark spots where ditches threaded their way across the fields. Such places would be excellent spots for snipers, he thought.

They could see sentries standing at the corner of the old school-house, watching their approach.

General Hill pulled his horse up a step or two ahead of Little Sorrel and called out, "I'm General Ambrose P. Hill! General Jackson is with us!"

"Come in slowly!" came the reply, as the sentries stood, guns ready.

Jackson and his companions knew that somewhere in the deep

shadows around the schoolhouse were howitzers. No doubt some were trained on them.

Seconds later, the group hauled up and one of the sentries said, "Welcome, General Jackson! And all of you."

"Thank you," said Stonewall. "I'm looking for a Yankee stronghold in this direction."

"Yes, sir," said the sentry. "They came in late this afternoon and set up their guns about a mile and a half down the road. We watched them battling with some of our troops until it got dark. They didn't come by here, or we'd have blasted 'em."

Jackson smiled. "I'm sure of that. Thank you. We'll be moving on."

The general led the group another mile or so down the road, then halted and looked at the Union camp laid out on both sides of the road.

Sandie Pendleton scanned the moonlit fields and noted all the dark spots. "General Jackson," he said softly, "don't you think this is the wrong place for you?"

Jackson glanced at him and smiled. "The danger's over, Major. The enemy is routed." Then to A. P. Hill: "General Hill, let's go back to camp, gather our forces, and attack Hooker's last stronghold while they're licking their wounds. Let's finish it for good ol' Dixie tonight."

"We'll all be happy when it's done," said Hill.

Jackson turned to his aide and said, "Jim, by now news has reached Richmond that there's been a lot of fighting going on around Chancellorsville today. I'd like for you to ride to Fredericksburg and have them send a wire to Mary Anna. Let her know I'm all right."

"Certainly, sir. I'll be back as soon as possible."

With that, Jim Lewis galloped away, angling in the direction of the Rappahannock River, whose west bank he would ride to Fredericksburg.

The group wheeled about and headed back up the plank road.

They were within three hundred yards of the wilderness camp when a single rifle shot shattered the stillness of the night. Jackson raised a hand, signaling for the group to stop.

Lieutenant Joe Morrison turned to his brother-in-law and said, "Sir, that might be a Yankee sniper out there somewhere."

"We need to get the general to camp as fast as possible!" Pendleton said.

At that instant, there was a second shot, a third, then a smattering of shots. Bullets were buzzing through the air, but they couldn't tell from which direction they were coming.

"Let's go, General!" Morrison said.

Stonewall Jackson gouged Little Sorrel's sides, and the others surrounded him as they galloped toward the camp. A few clouds were drifting overhead, covering the moon and cutting down its light.

At the Confederate camp, Rance Dayton's sentries were firing at what they believed were Union skirmishers along the plank road, though they couldn't see them. Others joined them quickly, firing blindly.

The firing kept up for several minutes, then Major Dayton appeared and said, "Hold it! Nobody's firing back! Don't waste your ammunition."

There was a period of silence. When it remained so, Dayton said, "Keep your eyes open, but don't shoot unless you can see what you're shooting at."

The major moved back into the trees, followed by the men who had jumped in to help.

Chuck Carney looked around at the other seven men, and said, "Okay. Load your guns and stay sharp."

The muskets were reloaded and the sentries hunkered down in silence.

Not long after, they heard a rumble of hooves coming from the same direction where the gunfire had been moments before. They raised their rifles and waited, squinting past the dark shadows cast by the trees to the open field.

"Riders!" said Buford Hall.

They could all see the vague figures in the flat white light of the moon. The horses were trotting straight toward them on the plank road. When the horses reached the dark shadows beneath the trees, Hank Upchurch—skittish from the experience with the four Yankee riders the night before—raised up, put his musket to his shoulder, and shouted, "Yankees!"

"Don't shoot!" said Ken Dykstra. "You don't know it's Yankees!"

"I can tell it's Yankees!" Upchurch said. "We can't let 'em get any closer!"

"Wait!" said Bo Gentry. "It may be some of our men!"

"It's Yankees!" Everett Nichols shouted. And fired.

"No! Wait!" a voice cried.

Hall's nerves were strung tight. At the sound of Nichols's rifle, he squeezed the trigger and his gun belched fire.

One of the incoming riders peeled out of his saddle and hit the ground as the others pulled rein. The horses were whinnying fearfully and dancing about.

A voice from the group of riders shouted, "Cease firing! You're firing into your own men!"

Hall shouted back, "Who gave that order? Some stinkin' Yankee? Pour it into 'em, boys!"

Nerves jangled, Carney and Upchurch opened fire. One man jerked in the saddle and bent over as a bullet hit him, and another fell to the ground.

A rider came thundering at them, screaming, "I'm General A. P. Hill! Stop firing! Stop firing!"

When Hill drew up, the Fearless Four recognized him. Their blood froze in their veins as he bawled, "You fools! You've shot General Jackson!"

SIXTEEN

Captain Keith Boswell and Sergeant William Cunliffe lay on the ground—one dead and one seriously wounded. Major Sandie Pendleton's horse, fighting its bit, stepped on Cunliffe, who was unconscious, and Lieutenant Joe Morrison's horse reared in fright. Morrison struggled to contain his terrified animal as he tried to see how bad General Jackson was wounded.

Little Sorrel, alarmed by the gunshots, shouting men, and frightened horses, bolted, carrying the slumped general into the forest.

A low branch struck the general, nearly knocking him out of the saddle. But in spite of a wounded right hand, he grasped the reins and regained control, then wheeled Little Sorrel about.

As he trotted the horse toward the plank road, nearby Federals—assuming all the firing within the shadowed wilderness was aimed at them—cut loose with a fierce barrage of artillery.

Cannonballs struck trees and sod all around, and shrapnel hissed through the air.

When General Jackson had reached the road, his men were there to meet him, in spite of the bombardment. Two of them took Little Sorrell's reins, and A. P. Hill and Joe Morrison lowered Jackson from the saddle. His right hand was bleeding, and the left sleeve of his coat was soaked with blood. Bullets had hit him in the upper arm near the shoulder and in the forearm, as well as the right hand.

The Union guns suddenly went quiet as Jackson was being carried to the shelter of a huge oak tree. When they started to lay him down flat, he protested.

"No, no," he said through clenched teeth. "Let me sit up with my back to the tree."

While General Hill dispatched two men to ride to Wilderness Tavern for Dr. Hunter McGuire, Captain Jack Wilbourn of the signal corps moved in and said to Morrison, "I have some medical experience. May I look at him?"

"That all right, General?" asked Morrison.

Stonewall nodded.

Wilbourn looked around. "Could we get a lantern over here?"

As a soldier hurried away to bring the needed lantern, Hill returned and knelt beside Jackson. "We'll have Dr. McGuire here as soon as possible, General. Are you in much pain?"

Jackson grimaced and spoke with effort. "I fear my left arm is broken. There's some pain, yes. My right hand was hit too."

Hill nodded. "We'll get you fixed up as soon as possible."

Stonewall licked dry lips. "Others were hit, too, weren't they?"

"Yes, sir. Captain Boswell and Sergeant Cunliffe."

"How bad?"

"Sergeant Cunliffe is still alive. But Captain Boswell was killed instantly."

"I've got the sergeant resting comfortably, sir," said Wilbourn. "Dr. McGuire will have to treat him too."

"First," said Jackson.

"Pardon me, sir?"

"I want Dr. McGuire to take care of Sergeant Cunliffe first."

Wilbourn looked at Morrison and Hill, who both shook their heads in admiration for the general.

The sergeant arrived with the lantern, and Wilbourn cut away Jackson's left sleeve for a quick examination. To stop the flow of blood he wrapped strips of the general's sleeve around the wounds, using double cloth on the wound in the upper arm.

"So what do you think, Captain?" asked Jackson.

"Nothing life-threatening, sir," said Wilbourn. "But it doesn't look good. The bullet that hit your forearm has shattered bone, but the upper wound is worse. From what I can tell, the bullet shattered the bone just below the shoulder and all the way to the elbow joint. It severed an artery, and you've lost a lot of blood. But I think I've got it wrapped good enough to hold you till Dr. McGuire gets here."

Jackson let the news settle in his mind. "Then Dr. McGuire will have to take off the arm, won't he?"

Wilbourn wiped a hand over his face. "I really can't say, General."

Jackson closed his eyes. "How did this thing happen? It was our own men who shot us, wasn't it?"

"It was, sir," said Hill. "It's best that you don't talk now. Just sit there and rest. Dr. McGuire should be here in a few minutes."

General Hill moved about the camp, telling the men they must keep General Jackson's wounds a secret. It would only harm the morale of the Army of Northern Virginia if the troops learned that he was out of commission.

Hill then approached Captain Wilbourn and Lieutenant Ted Ransom, who were kneeling over Sergeant Cunliffe. The wind had blown the clouds away, and once again the moon was shining in its fullness. "How's he doing, Captain?" Hill asked.

Both men rose to their feet, their faces drawn.

"He just died, sir," said Wilbourn. "I thought he would make it, but he must have been bleeding internally."

Hill drew in a deep breath and let it out slowly. He looked to the spot nearby where Keith Boswell's body lay covered by a blanket. "I'll have him placed over there by Captain Boswell."

"We'll do it, sir," said Ransom.

"I have another job for you two, and I need you to move on it immediately. I need you to take the news of General Jackson's wounds to General Lee. As commander-in-chief, he must be told."

"Certainly," said Wilbourn. "We'll go right now."

"I told you earlier that we've got to keep the news from spreading…so talk with the general privately."

"Yes, sir."

"And make a wide circle so you don't get caught by the Yankees."

"We'll do that, sir," Wilbourn assured him.

"Come back as fast as you can so I'll know the message was delivered."

As Wilbourn and Ransom headed for their horses, Corporal Jim Lewis approached the sentries at the plank road.

"Hi, Jim," said Bo Gentry. "Where you been?"

"Fredericksburg. General Jackson sent me. He knew Mrs. Jackson would learn about the battle here today. I wired her to let her know he was all right."

Gentry looked away, a pained expression on his face.

"What's the matter?" Lewis asked, frowning.

The other sentries stood near, looking on.

Lewis scanned their faces. "What's happened?" he demanded, sliding from his horse's back.

"We're not at liberty to say, Jim," said Myron Flynn.

"Has something happened to the general?"

"We're not at liberty to say," said Chad Lynch. "You'd best find General Hill and ask him."

"I'll just do that!" said Lewis, leading his horse toward the camp at a fast pace.

Captain Wilbourn and Lieutenant Ransom trotted past Lewis, nodding a greeting, and soon were galloping away.

Lewis saw General Hill standing with two privates over a lifeless form on the ground. His heart lurched, and he dropped the reins and dashed toward the body. When he saw that the dead man wasn't

Stonewall Jackson, he breathed a sigh of relief, and said to Hill, "General, what happened—"

Lewis broke off as he saw the second form a few feet away, covered by a blanket. He hurried to it, pulled the blanket from the face, and recognized Captain Keith Boswell. Turning back to Hill, he said, "Where's General Jackson? What's happened here?"

Hill moved up close to Jackson's aide and said, "We've had a horrible stroke of misfortune, Jim. Some of our sentries mistook a group of our men for Yankees when they came riding in. General Jackson was leading them."

"Wh-where is he, sir? Is he…all right?"

"He's been wounded. Come. I'll take you to him."

As Hill guided Lewis toward the spot where II Corps' commander leaned against the large oak, there was a sudden boom of cannons from the Union positions, and the shrill whine of cannonballs came to their ears. Thunderous explosions followed as men began scurrying about. Shrapnel cut the air, chewed into tree bark, and rattled bushes.

"Come on!" said Hill, breaking into a run.

More cannonade followed as Hill and Lewis approached Jackson, who was surrounded by several men. Joe Morrison was kneeling beside him.

"Litter!" shouted Hill. "Somebody bring a litter! We must take General Jackson deeper into the woods!"

Lewis elbowed his way through the press and knelt on Jackson's other side. Morrison smiled at him and said to the general, whose eyes were closed, "Jim Lewis is back, General."

Jackson opened dull eyes and tried to focus on Lewis.

"How bad is it, sir?" Jim asked.

"I'm glad you're back safe," said the general, gritting his teeth in pain. "You got the wire off to Mary Anna?"

"Yes, sir."

"Good. She won't have to know about this till Dr. McGuire gets me all patched up."

Running his eyes over Jackson, Jim said, "Your right hand and left arm. Is that it, sir?"

"Please step aside, Corporal!" came Hill's voice above the sound of more exploding cannonballs.

Lewis looked up to see a man carrying a stretcher and three other men with him.

"Hurry!" said Hill to the stretcher bearers. "We've got to move the general!"

Jackson winced as the four men picked him up and placed him on the stretcher. He tried to find Jim Lewis, but his eyes were glazed over. He was going into shock.

The forest rocked from multiple explosions, and suddenly a cannonball hit close by, sending hissing shrapnel through the air. One of the bearers was hit in the side and collapsed, dropping his corner and Jackson with it. Stonewall landed hard on his wounded arm and groaned.

Lewis and Morrison were beside him instantly. "Let's get him on the litter again," said Lewis. "I'll carry this corner."

Just as they were ready to keep moving, Brigadier General William Pender, of A. P. Hill's division, rushed up to Hill. "General! We're getting heavy bombardment in several places! The Yankees are giving it to us! I need permission to pull back!"

Even in Stonewall Jackson's state of shock, he heard Pender's words and roused himself. "You must hold your ground, General Pender!" he said hoarsely. "Do not fall back! You must hold your ground!"

General Hill set level eyes on Pender. "You have your orders, General."

"Yes, sir," said Pender, then wheeled about and was gone.

Federal cannonballs continued to strike in the wilderness as Hill led the stretcher bearers through a swampy area to a spot that had dry ground amid dense trees. The Union shells had not come that far into the forest.

As they gently put Jackson down, a voice from behind called,

"General Hill. Dr. McGuire is here, sir. He has an ambulance, and Chaplain Lacy is with him."

Union artillery pounded the area as Hunter McGuire and Tucker Lacy rushed in. However, Confederate artillery was now answering, and the bombardment in the wilderness was easing up.

The chaplain went to Jackson's side while McGuire opened his medical bag.

Jackson met Lacy's gaze and moved dry lips to say, "Little setback, Preacher."

Lacy smiled. "For a tough guy like you, I'm sure that's all it is. You'll be up calling the shots in no time."

A soldier set a lantern next to the stretcher, and McGuire moved up beside the general and knelt down.

"Hello, Doc," Jackson said weakly.

"Hello, yourself, my friend. Looks like we've got some work to do on you."

"Maybe a little."

The sounds of artillery battle were gradually lessening.

Hunter reached for the lantern and placed it to get a better look at the wounds, then removed the makeshift bandages. After a quick examination he took a bandage roll out of his black bag and began rewrapping the wounds. His voice was heavy as he said, "Tom—ah…General, I may have to amputate the arm."

Jackson nodded.

"We brought an ambulance. We'll take you to Wilderness Tavern and I'll do whatever is necessary to make you better."

The artillery battle soon ended as the ambulance bearing General Jackson, Dr. McGuire, and Chaplain Lacy left the wilderness and headed across open land for Wilderness Tavern.

Major Rance Dayton was with the four heroes of Antietam as

they watched the ambulance rattle by and disappear from sight. The four men sat on the ground at the base of a tree and wept.

"Look, men," said Dayton, "nobody's going to punish you for what happened. You didn't know you were firing into our men."

"But Major," Buford Hall said in a tear-thickened voice, "we killed two good men! And…and if General Jackson dies, how are we going to live with ourselves?"

Hank Upchurch looked at the major with an expression of despair. "The South could lose the War…because we robbed them of General Jackson!"

"How are we gonna face anybody?" said Everett Nichols. "I mean, our fellow soldiers, and the people back home?"

Dayton prayed in his heart for wisdom. "You only did what you thought was right. After all, four Yankees came riding in here last night, and we don't know what they had in mind. You were naturally on edge."

"But two men are dead because we reacted too quickly, sir," said Carney. "And General Jackson will probably die!"

"Now, listen to me. All of you proved what you were made of when you saved my life at Antietam without batting an eye. You were willing to risk life and limb for me. Your fellow soldiers and thousands of civilians heard President Davis lift you up as ex-amples of what true Confederate soldiers ought to be. Sure, you hate what happened. But that doesn't change what you are.

"And what about the Yankee sergeant in the burning woods? It would've been easy to say, 'Let him burn; he's the enemy'…but you didn't. Hank…Chuck…you hazarded your lives to save another human being from a horrible death, even though he's your enemy. You other two would have done it too. Now, don't give up on your-selves."

The Fearless Four continued to hang their heads low. The major's words had little effect.

After a few moments, Dayton said, "Listen to me, men. From what I was told, the worst that could happen to General Jackson would be to lose his left arm. He's in no danger of dying from his wounds."

Hank sniffed and ran a sleeve over his nose and mouth, then said shakily, "But we love and admire the man so much, Major! We'd never knowingly do anything to cause him harm!"

"Everybody in our brigade knows that," said Dayton.

Footsteps sounded nearby, and the group looked up to see Brigadier General James Lane. All five jumped to their feet and saluted. Lane sent a glance to Dayton, then looked at the four distraught men.

"I couldn't help but hear what was being said as I came over here," Lane said. "I'm sorry you men will have to live with what you did for the rest of your lives, but let me remind you of something. You were told before you started firing that those riders could be some of our own men. Were you not?"

The four men stood in silence, remembering all the warnings from their comrades.

"And didn't one of the riders cry out, telling you that you were shooting at your own men?"

Silence.

"And didn't one of you—in spite of that voice—shout something about some stinking Yankee giving the order, and then say, 'Pour it into them, boys'? You men should have been more cautious, as were the other sentries—the ones who tried to get you to hold your fire till the riders could be identified."

When there was still no response, Lane snapped, "Well, shouldn't you have?"

Chuck Carney finally broke the men's silence. "Yes, General Lane. We should have. But what's done is done. We can't turn the clock back and start over. It was an honest mistake. We thought we were being invaded by enemy riders tonight, and we did what we thought was right. We were wrong, and we're very sorry. We'll be even more sorry if General Jackson dies. We've got enough on our consciences to last for a dozen lifetimes without that."

Dayton took a step closer to Lane. "Sir, we must not forget what these men did at Antietam, and even today in the forest fire. Don't they deserve some consideration here?"

Lane rubbed his jaw and peered at Dayton in the moonlight. "Even if you and I give them consideration based on past performance, Major, I'm afraid the rest of this army will not." With that, General Lane walked away.

"Men," said Dayton, "this war isn't over. You'll have another opportunity to show what you're really made of. Keep your chins up, and be yourselves."

At Wilderness Tavern, Dr. Hunter McGuire cleaned and bandaged Stonewall Jackson's two minor wounds, telling the general that his hand would heal completely in time, as would the forearm.

They were alone at the moment, and Jackson looked up at his friend and said, "But Hunter, if you have to take the arm, it won't matter about the forearm healing."

Hunter's lips pulled into a thin line and he nodded. "You're right about that."

Once more, Hunter did a close examination of the wound in the upper arm. With a shake of his head, he said, "I can't let gangrene set in and kill you, Tom. And there's no sense in my leaving your arm to hang like a dead piece of rope from your shoulder."

Jackson met his gaze without flinching. "So you're going to take it?"

Hunter sighed. "Not without conferring with the other doctors on my staff."

Moments later, Dr. McGuire stood with his three staff doctors as they examined the wound together. When they had each taken a good look, he said, "Tell me if I'm wrong, gentlemen. The humerus, in my opinion, is shattered beyond repair. Even if by a miracle we could get him past the danger of gangrene, he would have nothing here but a useless, dead limb."

All three doctors were in full agreement.

Hunter excused them and once again was alone with his best friend. "You heard them, Tom. I have no choice but to amputate. I'll have to take it off two inches below the shoulder."

Jackson pondered McGuire's words for a moment, and said quietly, "God's will be done."

Tears misted Hunter McGuire's eyes. He swallowed hard and gently cleared his throat. "I've got to get started, Tom. It will take a little preparation, then we'll get this over with."

He called Hilda from a room where she was resting, and asked her to prepare the chloroform, then probed with experienced fingers around the area where he would cut.

Wincing, the general said, "Hunter, I haven't asked who it was that shot me, and nobody's volunteered their names."

"I'd say it would be better if you never knew. Those men made a horrid mistake, yes, but it was an honest one."

"That's how I look at it," said Jackson. "I don't want to know who they are. And I don't want them punished or charged in any way."

Footsteps sounded at the door, and Hilda looked past Dr. McGuire to say, "Hello, Chaplain Lacy."

B. Tucker Lacy remained at the door, and Jackson's pain-filled eyes struggled to bring him into focus.

"Dr. McGuire," said Lacy, "the other surgeons told me you're going to take the arm."

"Yes," said Hunter, without looking up. "His life could be endangered if I don't."

"That's what they told me. How about we have a little prayer meeting before you begin the surgery?"

The doctor raised his head, set kind eyes on the preacher, and said, "Of course. Come over here and lead us."

General Jackson managed a weak smile as Lacy drew up to the operating table. "Thank you, Chaplain," he said. "My Jesus is close, and if something should happen that is beyond my doctor's control…I know He will take me to be with Him."

After Lacy led them in prayer, asking for God's hands to guide the doctor's, he left the room.

Hilda administered the chloroform, and when the man known as Stonewall was under, Dr. Hunter McGuire began cutting.

General Robert E. Lee was sleeping soundly in his tent, having taken powders to relieve the pains in his chest. At first the voice calling his name seemed part of his dream, but finally it broke through and awakened him.

Lee raised up on his cot and looked toward the flap. He saw the vague shadows of three men against the tent wall. One was standing closer than the other two. "Yes?" he called.

"General Lee, sir, it's Corporal Clifford Wyatt."

"What is it, Corporal?"

"I have two men from II Corps out here, sir. Captain Jack Wilbourn and Lieutenant Ted Ransom. They have something very important to see you about, or I wouldn't have disturbed you."

"All right," said Lee, "I'll be right there."

Lee had slept in his trousers and shirt. He quickly put on his boots, slipped into his coat, then pulled back the flap. "Thank you, Corporal Wyatt. Step in, gentlemen."

Lee turned to his portable desk where the lantern sat and struck a match. As the two officers stepped in behind him, they pulled the flap down.

When the wick was aglow with yellow flame, Lee dropped the glass chimney in place and said, "Now, gentlemen, what can I do for you?"

"We have a message from General Ambrose Hill, sir," said Wilbourn in a subdued voice. "I speak in a low tone because General Hill said you were the only man in this camp to hear the message."

"All right," said Lee. "I assume that what you're about to tell me has been sanctioned by General Jackson."

"Well, no, it hasn't, General. It's about General Jackson."

Lee frowned. "What do you mean?"

"General Jackson has been shot, sir."

Lee's eyes widened. "Is he alive?"

"Yes, sir. He has three wounds, sir. One in his right hand, and two in the left arm. General Hill had already sent for Dr. McGuire when we left."

"Thank God it's not worse. The Lord be praised that he wasn't killed."

"We both thank God that General Jackson is still alive, sir," said Ransom.

Shaking his head, the silver-haired general said, "So how did it happen? Snipers or what?"

Wilbourn and Ransom looked at each other.

"Captain Wilbourn," said Ransom, "since you outrank me, I'll let you answer his question."

Jack Wilbourn scrubbed a hand over his mouth and said, "Some of our sentries shot him, General."

"Our sentries!"

"Yes, sir."

Wilbourn then explained how it happened, and told Lee of the deaths of Captain Keith Boswell and Sergeant William Cunliffe.

Lee looked down at his hands, which he had unconsciously balled into fists. "Does General Lane know who did this?"

"Yes, sir," said Wilbourn.

The general rubbed his chest and said, "How goes the battle over on your side?"

"You no doubt would have had a report by now if General Jackson hadn't been shot, sir. Right now, all of General Hill's attention is on him."

"I understand. Tell me how it's going."

"We've about got the Yankees licked over there, sir," said Wilbourn. "It looks like we're going to win this one."

Lee rubbed his chest again. "Gentlemen, any victory is dearly bought that deprives us of the services of our beloved Stonewall Jackson…even temporarily."

"I agree, sir," said Wilbourn. "Well, sir, we must be getting back. General Hill asked us to return as soon as possible."

Lee nodded. "Of course. I…"

"Yes, sir?"

"From what you've told me, I believe those sentries made an honest mistake. I don't want them charged."

"We'll pass your words on to the generals, sir."

SEVENTEEN

J odie McGuire and Mary Anna Jackson were finishing kitchen cleanup after supper when they heard a knock at the apartment door.

"I'll get it," said Jodie. She opened the door to a uniformed man with corporal's stripes. "Yes, Corporal?"

"I have a wire for Mrs. Jackson, ma'am. It came to the camp about an hour ago. I believe it's from the general."

"Mrs. Jackson's in the kitchen. I'll get her."

"No need, ma'am," said the corporal, extending an envelope. "You can give it to her."

"Oh…all right. Thank you."

"My pleasure, ma'am."

Jodie closed the door and headed for the kitchen, calling out, "It's a message from your husband! It came to the camp about an hour ago."

Mary Anna rushed through the kitchen doorway and intercepted Jodie, plucking the envelope from her hand and tearing it open. When she had finished reading, Mary Anna said, "It's actually from Jim Lewis. Tom asked him to wire me from Fredericksburg and let me know he was alive and unscathed after the battle today near Chancellorsville."

"Praise the Lord!"

"And Jim adds that Hunter has set up a hospital in the Wilderness Tavern, close to Chancellorsville, and he's just fine."

"Praise the Lord again!" Jodie said.

"And we're giving the Yankees a good whipping, Jim says."

"Good! Maybe they'll go back to Washington and stay there."

"Wouldn't that be wonderful?"

"It sure would."

Mary Anna folded the paper and slipped it back into the envelope. "It was sweet of Tom to make sure I knew he was all right." Her features took on a pinched look. "Jodie, I don't know what I'd do if something happened to him…I just love him so much."

"I understand, honey. Even though Hunter isn't in the same kind of danger the general is, I still have thoughts about some cannonball dropping where he stands, or a bullet finding him. I'll be so glad when this horrid war is over."

"Won't it be wonderful when we can all live in peace?"

"It sure will," Jodie sighed. "It sure will."

Hunter McGuire finished surgery on Stonewall Jackson at 2:30 A.M., and he left Hilda to keep an eye on the patient while he met with Jim Lewis and Chaplain Lacy. The surgery had gone well, with little loss of blood, and he urged the two men to get some sleep. When he returned to the surgery room, Major Sandie Pendleton and Hilda were talking just outside the door.

"Dr. McGuire," said Hilda, "Major Pendleton insists on seeing General Jackson. I told him that even though the general is conscious, he's in no condition to talk."

"Doctor," said the youthful major, "the fate of the army and the Confederate cause itself depends on my being allowed to talk to General Jackson. Please."

"I'll let you come in and try, since you put it that way, Major," said McGuire, "but his mind can't be very clear yet."

"I must try, Doctor."

As the three moved up to the operating table, Pendleton's gaze fell on the bandaged stump of Jackson's left arm and he felt a wave of nausea.

Hunter bent over his patient. "General Jackson…"

Stonewall's eyelids fluttered, and he opened them, trying to focus on the face that went with the voice.

"General, it's Dr. McGuire. Can you understand what I'm saying?"

Jackson nodded.

"Who am I?"

Stonewall's eyes lost some of their glassy look, and he said thickly, "You're…my best friend. The best doctor…in the world."

Hunter smiled. "Listen, General. Major Pendleton is here. He needs to talk to you. Can you talk to him?"

Pendleton moved up beside McGuire to stand within the general's line of vision. "Hello, sir."

Jackson slowly moved his eyes to the major's face. "Sandie…glad to see you. What is it you need?"

"Sir, General Hill took over II Corps after you were shot."

"Yes. Good man."

"Yes, sir. But General Hill has been wounded. We suffered an artillery attack after they drove you away in the ambulance. General Hill was struck across the back of the legs by shrapnel. They're bringing him here right now."

Jackson licked dry lips. "I'm…sorry to hear that. Who's in charge now?"

"Jeb Stuart, sir. General Hill assigned command to him, even though he's never commanded anything larger than his cavalry unit. General Hill wanted Jubal Early to take his place, but he's off on a reconnaissance somewhere."

"I see," said the general.

Hilda stepped up on the other side of the table with a tin cup in her hand. "Here, General. Drink this water."

After Jackson had drained the cup, he put his attention back on the major.

"Sir," said Pendleton, "General Stuart asked me to come and talk to you if at all possible. He doesn't know the overall plan to finish off the Yankee stronghold. What instructions can I take back to him?"

The general's brow furrowed, and his eyes seemed to fog up. The effect of the chloroform was still on him, and he struggled with his thoughts. His lips quivered slightly as he said, "Major, I...can't tell you. Tell...tell General Stuart he must do...what he thinks best."

With that, Jackson's eyes closed, and he sank into a deep sleep.

"Major," Dr. McGuire said, "I suspect he'll be like this for several hours."

Pendleton nodded. "Well, I guess I'd better get back and tell General Stuart it's up to him to carry on."

At dawn, on Sunday morning, May 3, Major General Jubal Early showed up from his reconnaissance of the area only moments before Jeb Stuart was ready to launch his attack on the last Union stronghold. When Early learned of General Hill's wounds, and that Hill had assigned Stuart to head up II Corps, he told Stuart to proceed as commander of the corps. He would gladly follow his orders.

Stuart informed Early that he had ridden to General Lee and spent a few minutes showing him his battle plan, and Lee had approved it. Stuart had also learned only moments ago that somehow word of General Jackson's wounds had leaked out. Everyone in both corps knew their beloved Stonewall lay wounded at Wilderness Tavern. The news, however, did not affect them as A. P. Hill had thought it would. Instead of lowering their morale, it served to instill a greater determination to take the fight to the enemy and win.

The sun had not yet risen when both Lee and Stuart unleashed their fierce onslaught on Joe Hooker's army, which was sandwiched between the two Confederate corps. As the battle grew hot and heavy, Stuart displayed amazing proficiency, and the Federals were soon fighting like cornered, wounded animals.

Stonewall Jackson awoke just after 9:00 A.M. to a beautiful morning. He was clearheaded and sitting up in the bed in one of the hotel rooms where Hunter had had him carried in the middle of the night. Hunter and Chaplain Lacy stood beside the bed while Hilda fed him a light breakfast.

A heavy dew lay on the grassy fields. Just outside the general's window, multicolored fruit blossoms moved in the gentle breeze, and whippoorwills and robins sang. But in the distance was the rumble of cannons.

Jackson could barely remember Sandie Pendleton's visit. Hunter reminded him of it and filled him in on General Hill's wounds and the fact that Hill had turned II Corps over to Jeb Stuart. Hill was in a room down the hall and doing well now that he had been patched up.

Jackson swallowed the last of his breakfast, and Hilda left the room, carrying the tray.

"So all I told Sandie was to tell General Stuart to do what he thought best?" Jackson said.

"That's it."

Jackson turned his attention toward the window and the rumble of the big guns. He sighed. "Well, I hope Jeb makes the right decisions."

"We all do," said Lacy.

In spite of his discomfort, Stonewall said, "What a beautiful Sunday morning! I've always hoped that when it comes my time to leave this world, the Lord would let me go home on a Sunday."

Lacy chuckled. "Well, General, you're not going to heaven today. Is he, Doctor?"

"No, he isn't. In fact, in a few months he'll be back leading II Corps."

Stonewall set affectionate eyes on Hunter. "You think so, eh?"

"Tough as you are, my friend…yes."

"Dr. McGuire," came Hilda's voice from the doorway, "there's a courier here from General Lee. He would like to speak to you."

"All right. I'll talk to him out there." Then to Lacy he said, "Chaplain, you keep an eye on my patient. I'll be back shortly."

As Hunter moved toward the door, Jackson said, "Doctor…I'll want to know what this is about."

"Of course."

"And tell the courier to get a message to General Stuart. I don't want those sentries who mistook us for Yankees to be charged with any wrongdoing."

"I'll tell him, sir."

Chaplain Lacy sat down beside the general's bed and read to him from the Psalms. He had just closed his Bible again when Hunter returned and stood over Jackson.

"General Lee sends his regards to you, Tom—ah…sir."

Lacy smiled. "You two don't have to keep up formalities in my presence."

Hunter smiled. "Anyway, General Lee sends his regards and says he's praying you will recover quickly and be back at the head of II Corps soon. In the meantime, he and the Army of Northern Virginia are going to give the Yankees a whipping they will not soon forget."

Jackson tuned his ears to the thunderous sounds of cannonade some five miles away. "Sounds like he's busy at it right now."

"Another thing, Tom," said Hunter. "General Lee has ordered me to move you farther from the battlefield. He wants you totally out of danger from the fighting, and I am to stay with you at all times. The choice of where you go is up to you, as long as getting you there won't impede your recovery."

Jackson pondered Lee's order, then said, "Well…I have some dear Christian friends who live near Guiney's Station. Thomas and Clara Chandler. Is that far enough away?"

"I'm sure it is," said Hunter. "You think there will be any problem if we show up there and ask them to take us in?"

"None at all. They'll be happy to let me recuperate in their home. They have a large house and several spare bedrooms."

"All right, then. I'll have an ambulance ready shortly."

Jackson nodded. "Hunter, you did give my message to the courier for General Stuart?"

"Sure did."

He looked out the window again toward the sounds of battle. "Have you sent word to Mary Anna?"

"No. I figured to leave it up to you when you wanted her to know."

"Mmm-hmm. Well, since we're going to the Chandlers' house, Mary Anna and the baby can come see me. When we get to Guiney's Station, you could wire her."

Hunter nodded. "I'll do it. Now let me go order that ambulance."

"General," said Lacy, "I'd like to stay with you too. Do you suppose the Chandlers would let me do that?"

"Of course. They'll feel honored to have a preacher in their home." He let a sly grin curve his lips. "The Chandlers will welcome a Presbyterian preacher...but they'll only tolerate a Baptist doctor!"

Hunter gave the general a mock scowl and left the room.

On Tuesday morning, May 5, Presidential Secretary John Hay was at his desk when the door opened and an army courier entered.

"Good morning, Mr. Hay," said the courier. "I have a message for Mr. Lincoln from Major General Joseph Hooker."

Hay frowned. "I hope it isn't bad news."

"I'm afraid it is, Mr. Hay."

"I really hate to give the president more bad news...but I guess there's no choice."

"It wouldn't appear so, sir."

Hay waited until the young man was gone, then carried the

sealed envelope to the door and tapped on it before easing it open. Lincoln was at his desk.

"Sir," said Hay, "I have a message from General Hooker."

Lincoln nodded solemnly.

Hay waited as the president opened the envelope and read the message. His countenance sagged, then he looked up and said, "The Union Army of the Potomac has retreated from Chancellorsville. They've pulled back to Falmouth. We've been defeated by Lee and Jackson."

"I'm sorry, sir."

Lincoln scanned the page again and said in a low tone, "Hooker is trying to shift responsibility for the defeat to the corps leaders under his command. Says they didn't do their jobs."

"But you don't think it was that way?"

"Those major generals are soldiers tried and true. I could accept that maybe one or two of them might have failed…but all of them? I think Hooker's leadership may have been hindered by a whiskey bottle."

Lincoln placed the tips of his fingers to his temples. "What a tragedy! An army less than half the size of ours has whipped us at Chancellorsville. Oh, John…what will the country say?"

On Tuesday afternoon, General Robert E. Lee sat his horse before the weary Army of Northern Virginia, near the Chancellor mansion. The wounded who could not stand sat on the ground.

Lee raised a small Confederate flag over his head, waved it, and said so that all could hear, "You men are to be commended for a battle well fought! Outnumbered more than two to one, you showed Billy Yank how a real army can fight when they put their minds to it!"

There were cheers.

"I am aware," said Lee, "that we owe a great deal to our beloved General Stonewall Jackson for engineering this victory. It was his genius that bewildered General Hooker and his leaders and made this triumph possible. And I commend Generals Hill and Stuart for their vital efforts in carrying on when General Jackson was wounded."

The cheering was loud and prolonged.

When they quieted down again, Lee said, "I have word from Dr. Hunter McGuire that General Jackson's condition is good, for all he has been through. We plan to have him back within two or three months."

The cheers were louder yet, punctuated with wild Rebel yells, then the men went into a loud chant, crying, "Stonewall Jackson! Stonewall Jackson! Stonewall Jackson!"

Amidst the jubilation, General Lee dismissed the men to get some much-needed rest. In a few days, they would return to Richmond.

The Fearless Four stood huddled together, off to the side. They had already suffered caustic comments from many of their comrades and had been snubbed by most.

"I think I can survive this ordeal," said Chuck Carney, "now that I know General Jackson is recuperating."

"Yeah, me too," said Hank Upchurch. "It helps a whole lot to know he's going to be all right."

Buford Hall rubbed his chin. "I'd sure like to talk to General Jackson and tell him how sorry I am for all this. I think I'd feel better if I could just say it to him."

The others murmured agreement.

"And I wish there was some way we could tell the families of Captain Boswell and Sergeant Cunliffe how sorry we are."

Hank shook his head. "But how could we look them in the eye?"

"Wouldn't be easy," Buford said, "but it sure would relieve the pressure I feel down inside."

Hank's peripheral vision caught movement to his left. "Brace yourselves, boys," he said. "Here comes more trouble."

A group of some eight or nine soldiers were walking toward

them. Leading the bunch was a burly corporal from Chattanooga, Tennessee, named Mike Robinson.

"Well, lookee here, boys!" Robinson sneered. "We have the great heroes of Antietam before us!"

"Heroes?" said Private Gifford Henderson. "Hah! They oughtta be hung for what they did to General Jackson, Captain Boswell, and Sergeant Cunliffe!"

"Look," said Carney, "we made a mistake. We know that. But—"

"You made a mistake, all right!" came the voice of Bo Gentry as he and Chad Lynch, Ken Dykstra, and Myron Flynn drew up. "We tried to tell you not to fire till you could see who it was, but you wouldn't listen! As far as I'm concerned, you're heroes, all right...but for the wrong side! Wouldn't surprise me if Abe Lincoln pinned a medal on you boys for what you did!"

"You know ol' Abe will be happy when he learns General Jackson has lost an arm!" said Flynn. "He won't have to worry about fighting Stonewall for a long time!"

"If we end up losing the War," said Dykstra, "it'll be because you guys put our greatest military commander out of commission!"

"Maybe we oughtta just take these trigger-happy guys out in the swamp and forget to bring 'em back!" Robinson said.

"Hold it right there!" came the commanding voice of Major Rance Dayton.

Every eye was on the major as he crowded in between the Fearless Four and the others. His face was stern as he said, "Let me explain something to you. Both General Lee and General Jackson have said these men are not to be punished in any way for what happened, nor are they to be charged for any wrongdoing. They've declared it an honest mistake. This isn't the first time someone has been shot by his own men. And it won't be the last. It happens in every army in the world. These four men have suffered enough mental agony over this to do them for a lifetime. As their fellow soldiers, you should understand. And remember, we're all on the same side in this war. Our fight with the Union isn't over. So pull yourselves together."

The accusers gave the major an angry look, then turned abruptly and walked away.

"They're not through with us, Major," said Carney.

"Well, they'd better be!"

"It's in their eyes, sir," said Upchurch. "They'll be on us again."

"If they do, above all, don't fight them. It'll only make you look bad. Hold your tempers, and let me know it's happening."

"We'll try, sir," said Carney, "but a man can only take so much of that kind of stuff."

EIGHTEEN

The courier stood at the open door of the apartment, looking downcast, as Mary Anna read the message from Dr. Hunter McGuire.

"Oh, no!" she gasped, and her whole body seemed to sag.

Jodie rushed to her side with Julia in her arms. "Mary Anna, what is it?"

Mary Anna's voice quavered as she said, "The wire's from Hunter, Jodie. Tom's been shot.... He's been shot!"

Jodie tried to see what was written on the piece of paper. "But he's alive, isn't he?"

"Yes, thank God." Mary Anna held the wire so Jodie could read it. "Read the rest of it for me, will you, Jodie? I couldn't get past the part where Hunter said he had to amputate Tom's left arm...but at least Tom's on the road to recovery. Praise the Lord!"

Jodie quickly took in the message and noted that Stonewall was staying at the Thomas Chandler home near Guiney's Station, and Hunter and Chaplain Tucker Lacy were with him. "Do you know the Thomas Chandlers, where the general is staying, Mary Anna?"

"Yes. They used to live in Lexington and belonged to our church. We're very close friends. I know Tom feels comfortable there."

Jodie read the last few lines. "The general wants you and Julia to come to him. And Hunter wants me to come."

"We'll go immediately! Can you get off work, Jodie?"

"I'll have to ask, but I'm sure the hospital director will let me."

Both women had forgotten the courier's presence at the door. Now, as he shuffled his feet, Mary Anna gave him a startled look.

"Mrs. Jackson," he said, "would you like me to send a wire back to Dr. McGuire?"

"I'll have to go to the railroad station and get our tickets first," she replied. "I'm not sure which train they can put us on."

"Well, ma'am, since I'm a great admirer of General Jackson, let me go to the station and make reservations for you. I'll be back shortly. Then I'll know what to tell Dr. McGuire about your arrival when I wire him."

Mary Anna thanked him, and he hurried away.

Jodie encircled her friend's shoulders and said, "Now, don't you worry, honey. The general is a strong and healthy man. He'll pull through this and be back leading his men in no time."

Mary Anna raised her apron to teary eyes. "I know this is selfish of me, but I wish the loss of his arm would be enough to send him back to V.M.I. to teach."

"I know," Jodie said, giving her friend's shoulders a squeeze. "But the Lord has His mighty hand in all of this. He'll do what is best for the Jacksons."

On Wednesday morning, May 6, Dr. Hunter McGuire was at Stonewall Jackson's bedside. Jackson had slept little the night before. He was having difficulty breathing and felt intense pain in his left side.

McGuire did a thorough examination of Jackson's chest, abdomen, back, and rib cage. When he had finished, he said, "Tom, I can't find any sign of a broken rib…not even a bruise."

"So what do you think is causing the pain?"

"Well, it could be that you have some fluid in your left lung. I really don't want to put you through it yet, but it looks like I've got to go ahead and give you a menthol steam treatment. I'll have to sit you up, drape a towel over your head, and put a steaming pan of water below your face. It would be a lot easier at a table, but you can't get up and move around yet. I'll just have to rig it here on the bed."

"Well, if it'll help, I guess you'd better do it. The pain in my side is pretty bad."

There was a knock at the door, and Hunter quickly pulled the covers up on his friend before calling out, "Come in!"

Thomas Chandler and Tucker Lacy entered. Chandler had a piece of paper in his hand.

"How's our patient, Doctor?" asked Lacy.

"No broken ribs, I can tell you that. I think he's got some fluid in the left lung."

Chandler held up the paper and gave it a little shake. "Look here, Tom! A wire from Mary Anna!"

Jackson's dull eyes brightened, and he said, "Don't hold me in suspense, my friend!"

Chandler grinned. "She and Julia will arrive at Guiney's Station at 9:45 tomorrow morning!"

"Wonderful!" said Jackson, and then winced from the sudden pain in his side.

Chandler turned his gaze toward Hunter. "And guess what, Doc? Somebody you're married to is coming!"

A big smile lighted Hunter's face as he said, "Well, I wonder who that could be?"

Hunter reached into his medical bag and took out oil of peppermint, then excused himself and went to enlist Clara Chandler's help to keep hot, steaming water on the stove.

Soon, Hunter had Tucker Lacy running up and down the stairs, replenishing the cooled water with hot, as he gave Stonewall the menthol treatment.

***

Late in the afternoon, the general awakened to see his brother-in-law, Joe Morrison, sitting at his bedside along with the doctor and others.

"Joe!" he said. "What brings you here?"

Morrison rose from his chair and stood close to the general. "It's not what brought me here, Tom, it's who brought me here. I came to see how you're doing."

Jackson tested his lung by taking a deep breath. "Well, it still hurts a little, but it's better than before this quack gave me the menthol treatment."

Hunter grinned. "He must be feeling better, Joe. He's jabbing at me again."

"So," Morrison said, "I'm told that if I hang around till morning, I'll get to see my sister and my new little niece."

"Yes," Stonewall said, "and I can hardly wait!"

"And I guess I get to meet Mrs. Hunter McGuire, too."

Jackson smiled. "That means you'll see one of the prettiest little Southern belles you ever saw in your life!"

Joe looked at Hunter. "I'm sure she is. Opposites attract, you know."

Stonewall started to chuckle, then winced with pain. "Oh! Joe, don't crack funny stuff around me just yet. It hurts to laugh."

"So you think that was funny, do you?" said Hunter. "Maybe I'll just let you find a better-looking doctor!"

"That wouldn't be hard to do," said the general. "But I think I'll keep you just the same."

Joe's face took a more serious look as he said, "Tom, I was with General Lee just before coming over here. He gave me a message for you. He said, 'Tell him to make haste and get well, and to come back to me as soon as he can. He has lost his left arm, but I have lost my right arm!'"

The general blinked against sudden tears and was about to reply when Clara stepped into the room and announced, "Your number-one aide is here, General Jackson."

Jim Lewis moved past her and drew up beside the bed. "Hello, General."

"Hello, Jim! How did Mrs. Chandler know you were my number-one aide?"

"He told me so, General," said Clara, chuckling.

Jackson grinned. "So, Jim, what brings you here?"

"The main reason, of course, is to see how you're doing. Mrs. Chandler filled me in on that. But also, if I know Dr. McGuire like I think I do, he's been running short on sleep."

"Yes, he has," spoke up Lacy. "I've tried to get him to let me sit up with the general through the night, but he only let me do it for an hour and a half last night."

"Well, he's going to get himself a full night's sleep tonight," said Jim. "And that's that."

McGuire rubbed his tired eyes. "I won't argue as long as you'll promise to wake me if I'm needed."

Lewis shrugged and flashed his palms. "Hey, I'm no doctor. If you're needed, I'll call you."

Late that night, Jim Lewis was sleeping in an overstuffed chair beside Jackson's bed. A single lantern burned in the room.

His head came up with a jerk when he heard the old grand-father clock in the hall give off its double chime, signaling 2:00 A.M. He heard a moan and looked toward the general, who was drawing up his knees and rolling his head back and forth in his sleep.

Jim bolted out of the chair and laid a hand on Jackson's brow. It felt hot to the touch, and Jackson's face was flushed.

Suddenly the general's eyes opened and he squinted to bring Jim into focus. "Jim…?" he said weakly.

"General, you're running a fever, and you look pale too."

"Just a little nausea. It'll pass."

"I'm going to get Doc," Jim said, starting away.

"No! Let him sleep. He's a very tired man."

"I promised him I would call him if you needed him, sir. You're nauseated and you're running a fever. That's plenty of reason for me to wake him."

"No! I-I'll be fine. Let him sleep."

"But you're shaking, sir, and your teeth are chattering. You're fever is going higher."

"Just find a b-blanket and put it on me."

Jim went to the closet and pulled out a blanket. As he started to place it over Jackson, the general clutched his midsection and clenched his teeth in pain. Suddenly his hand went to his chest, and he moaned.

Jim quickly spread the blanket over his commander and said, "I'm going to get Doc, sir."

This time the general didn't argue.

Moments later, a weary Hunter McGuire was working furiously on Stonewall Jackson, trying to bring his temperature down. He and Jim Lewis took turns dipping cloths in cold water to bathe his wrist and the sides of his neck.

Tucker Lacy, who had been awakened by the sounds in McGuire's room when Lewis had come for him, also entered Jackson's room. "What's wrong, Doctor?"

Hunter answered without looking up. "His temperature went up, he's having pains in his stomach and chest, and he's nauseated." He wrung out water and placed the cold, wet cloth against Jackson's neck.

"What do you make of it, Doctor?" asked Lacy.

"He's had trouble breathing and increased pain in his rib cage on the left side. Those symptoms, combined with the fever, makes me think he's got pneumonia."

"Gentlemen," said Lacy, "I want to have prayer for him right now. You keep working, and I'll pray."

McGuire and Lewis continued their ministrations but followed every word in their hearts as Tucker Lacy prayed, asking God in the name of His Son to reach down and clear the pneumonia from Jackson's lung.

By sunrise, the general's temperature was almost down to normal, the nausea was gone, and the pain in his chest was less severe.

Clara Chandler brought in breakfast, and McGuire was pleased to see Jackson eat.

When Jackson had finished eating, Clara fed the other men in her large kitchen—pancakes, sausage, and hot oatmeal. Hunter, who was unwilling to leave the general alone, stayed by his side and ate his breakfast from a tray.

At 9:15, Thomas Chandler and Joe Morrison left the house in a carriage to pick up the ladies and baby Julia at Guiney's Station.

Thirty minutes later, Clara Chandler was at the door, welcoming Mary Anna, little Julia, and Jodie. She told them Dr. McGuire wanted to see them before they went upstairs to the general's room.

Joe Morrison, who was holding his little niece, placed her in Mary Anna's arms, and said, "I'll run up and stay with Tom while Doc and Jim Lewis come down."

Moments later, Hunter and Jodie were in each other's arms and stole a kiss even though they were in public. Hunter then turned to embrace Mary Anna and tweak Julia's fat little cheek. Jodie greeted Jim Lewis, whom she had met during the battle at Antietam.

When Mary Anna glanced upstairs, Hunter said, "He's had a cold for several days, Mary Anna. I've treated him for it, but it just hasn't gotten any better. That, along with his wounds, has brought on the pneumonia. We were able to get the fever down, and he's feeling much better now."

"But what about the pneumonia, Hunter?" she asked, fear touching her eyes. "Is it going to get worse?"

"Not if I can help it. I'm watching him closely. Now…even though you know his arm has been amputated, it's going to be a hard moment for you when you first see it. Stay as calm and act as normally as possible. Understand?"

"Yes," said Mary Anna, nodding her head.

Jodie laid a hand on her forearm, and said, "You'll do fine. Would you like for me to carry Julia, so you can go to him and have your moment together?"

"Yes, please," Mary Anna said with a flutter in her voice.

Jodie took the baby, kissed her forehead, and said, "Julia, we're going to take you upstairs to see your papa now."

When the group topped the stairs and moved to the door of the general's room, they stood back and let Mary Anna go in ahead of them.

Her brother was standing by the bed, and when she came in, he said to Jackson, "Look, Tom. Here she is."

The general's face lit up and a smile graced his lips as Mary Anna moved toward him.

Joe stepped aside as his sister wiped tears and leaned over to kiss her husband, and Stonewall wrapped his arm around her neck and held her close.

They remained that way for a long moment, then Mary Anna said, "Darling, I'm so thankful to the Lord that He spared your life." She kissed him again, then said, "Your little daughter came to see her papa."

Jackson looked past her and saw Jodie holding the baby. He smiled again. "Hello, Jodie."

"Hello, General," she said, handing the baby to her mother.

Mary Anna lowered little Julia so Stonewall could kiss her. While he spoke soft, sweet words to his daughter, tears flowed down his cheeks.

Mary Anna studied his drawn features while his attention was on Julia. Her heart ached as she noted the dark circles around his eyes, and it was all she could do to keep from weeping as she saw the bandaged stump where his left arm used to be.

After a few minutes, Mary Anna lifted Julia and stepped back from the bed, allowing Jodie to move closer.

As she bent down to kiss his cheek, the general squeezed her hand and said, "Thank you so much for keeping my family in your home."

"It's been my pleasure, General," Jodie said softly. As she stepped back, Hunter curved an arm around her waist.

Mary Anna placed a cool hand on her husband's brow and looked up at Hunter. "I think he's still got some fever."

"Yes, he does. But it was much higher last night. You've got a strong man there, Mary Anna."

Jackson began speaking tender, loving words to his wife and daughter as if they were the only ones in the room.

Jodie and Hunter and the others looked on, touched by the heartwarming scene.

That night, as Jodie was brushing her hair at the dresser in Hunter's room, she heard the door open and saw her husband come in. She continued to brush her hair as he crossed the room and moved up behind her. She met his eyes in the mirror and said, "All set for the night?"

"Mmm-hmm. Jim will take the first shift, Joe the second, and Tucker the third. I feel a little guilty, not taking a shift with Tom myself."

"Well, you shouldn't. From what Jim told me, you've been staying with him almost around the clock. You've got to get some rest, darling. Even rugged, handsome doctors need rest."

Hunter bent down and lifted her hair, kissing the back of her neck. She laid down the hairbrush and stood up, turning around to wrap her arms around his neck. She kissed him soundly and said, "I love you, Dr. McGuire."

He chuckled with pleasure, kissed her again, and said, "And I love you, Mrs. Dr. McGuire."

Jodie moved back in the circle of his arms so she could look him square in the eye, and said, "Hunter, I get the feeling that you're not telling the Jacksons how you really feel about his condition."

His face took on a bleak look. "You know me too well, don't you?"

"A wife is supposed to be able to read her husband. The Lord set it up that way."

"Oh, He did, eh?"

"Mmm-hmm. Now, tell your wife what you really think about the general."

Hunter sighed. "Well…I'm afraid Tom may not be strong enough to pull through."

"So the pneumonia is getting worse?"

"Yes. I've been thinking about the one and only thing I could do to possibly break the congestion."

"Cupping?"

"Yes."

"And you've held back because you would have to give him opiates?"

"Yes. If I'm going to make a positive move to save his life, I've got to do the cupping. But I don't like putting the drugs in his body. It could be dangerous."

"If you don't do it, what are his chances of pulling through?"

Hunter swallowed hard. "Nil. At best the opiates will make him delirious. He'll have some lucid moments, but he'll talk crazy until they wear off completely." He shook his head. "Jodie, I keep telling myself if I could have cured his cold before he was wounded, this pneumonia might not have happened. But then I've seen so many wounded soldiers die of pneumonia when they had no cold to begin with."

Jodie gripped his upper arms and gave him a gentle shake. "Darling, don't go blaming yourself for the general's condition. You've done everything a doctor could do."

Hunter bit his lower lip and nodded. "Cupping is the only chance he has, Jodie. I'll have to ask Tom and Mary Anna for permission to do it."

"Do you have everything you need with you?"

"Yes…in my medical bag."

"Then shouldn't we talk to them now, and do it right away, if they give permission?"

"It won't hurt to wait till morning. The cupping will wear Tom down. It's best for him to get his rest tonight."

"Oh…you're right. But maybe we should talk to Clara right now, so she'll be prepared with the hot water in the morning."

"Good idea."

"And we ought to go ahead and talk to Mary Anna tonight. If she agrees, then all we have to do is explain it to the general in the morning and go to work if he agrees."

Jodie, who was in her nightgown and robe, changed into a dress, and they went downstairs together to talk with the Chandlers.

Afterwards, when Hunter and Jodie were on their way to talk with Mary Anna, they heard voices in the general's room. They paused at the door and realized it was Mary Anna's voice they were hearing. Hunter knocked softly on the door, and they were met by Jim Lewis, who explained that the general wanted to see Mary Anna once more before he went to sleep.

Jodie took Hunter's hand and looked into his eyes. He answered her unspoken question with a nod and entered the room, pulling her gently in his wake.

While Jim Lewis stood by, Hunter told the Jacksons about the cupping treatment—the most drastic yet effective treatment to help alleviate the pneumonia. He explained that the general would be given a mixture of mercury, antimony, and opium. With the opiates in him, Hunter and Jodie would bathe the general's chest with hot water and use glass cups to draw blood to the affected area for the purpose of breaking up the congestion.

Hunter carefully explained the dangers involved with the opiates. But in spite of the risk, both Jacksons gave their permission.

By Saturday morning, some forty-eight hours after the cupping treatment, Stonewall Jackson appeared to be rallying.

Jodie was taking care of Julia elsewhere in the Chandler house, leaving Mary Anna free to stay with the general. She now stood beside his bed, holding his hand. He had been drifting in and out of a mental fog since the opiates had been administered on Thursday.

Often he would give some command as if he were on the battle-field, then he would mumble something she couldn't understand. At other times, he was lucid.

In one of his better moments, he looked up at her with lacklus-ter eyes and said, "Mary Anna, my condition is very serious, isn't it?"

"Yes, sweetheart, but you're doing better."

"I am?"

"Yes. Hunter seems encouraged, at least, and he's the doctor."

Stonewall closed his eyes for a long moment, then looked up at her again. "Mary Anna, if somehow I don't make it...if it's God's will to take me, I'm ready to go."

"Of course," she said. "But the Lord knows little Julia and I need you. He's going to let you get well."

Jackson's eyes suddenly widened, and he cried, "General Early! Form that line! Bring the artillery up! Don't let those Yankees get away!"

Mary Anna gripped his hand tightly and felt his body trembling. His eyes closed, and he coughed hard. She could hear the rattle in his chest, and perspiration formed on his brow.

At that moment, Dr. McGuire and Mary Anna's brother came in.

"How's he doing?" asked Hunter.

"I think the fever's coming back," she said.

Hours passed, and the general only grew weaker.

Late in the afternoon, Jackson was asleep while every occupant of the house but the Chandlers sat silently in his room. Baby Julia was asleep in her mother's arms.

Suddenly they heard footsteps, and the Chandlers entered the room.

"How's he doing?" whispered Thomas.

"No need to whisper," said Hunter. "He won't wake up until the opiates allow it. He isn't doing very well. I've done everything in my power to break the pneumonia, but at this point, it's worse."

"Tell them what we learned, dear," said Clara.

All eyes were on Thomas Chandler as he said, "We found out in town that word has spread all over the South about the general. Prayer services are being held everywhere—in cities, towns, and hamlets. The Southern people love this man."

Mary Anna managed a weak smile and murmured, "God bless them."

Suddenly the general jerked awake, opened glassy eyes, and shouted, "Press on, men! Press on! We've got Hooker on the run! Tell Major Hawks to send forward provisions for the men! They can't fight if they don't eat!"

Just as abruptly he went quiet, and the glaze left his eyes. He looked up to see Mary Anna standing over him with the baby in her arms. Julia had been startled from her sleep, but only cried for a few seconds.

"Papa," said Mary Anna, "here's your daughter. Want me to hold her so you can cuddle her close?"

Jackson smiled. "Yes. Please."

He kissed the baby's cheek and then suddenly looked toward the ceiling and cried, "Order General Hill to prepare for action! Pass the infantry to the front!"

That evening, the general was lucid once more, and he asked Mary Anna to read to him from the Psalms. Everyone in the house gathered in the room. When Mary Anna finished reading, Chaplain Lacy called for a circle around the bed, asking that all join hands. Little Julia was across the room, asleep in her crib.

Many tears were shed as Lacy prayed. When he said the "Amen," Stonewall Jackson ran his eyes around the circle and smiled at each one.

While Mary Anna held his hand, he talked of that moment in

his life when as a youth the gospel light shined into his darkness and he opened his heart to Jesus. With tears on his cheeks, he said, "Mary Anna, I wouldn't trade the life I've had with the Lord for anything this old world could offer in its place."

"None of us would, General," said Lacy, stepping closer to the bed. "Knowing Jesus in this life is only a prelude to the wonders of heaven."

As the hour grew later, the general's fever increased. Hunter and Jodie gave him a cool sponging, which seemed to help, but he slipped into deliriums again, and once more shouted commands to his men.

Mary Anna broke down and cried, and Jodie took her in her arms.

When the rays of the rising sun lighted the windows on Sunday morning, General Jackson was sitting up in the bed and sipping tea that Clara was spooning into his mouth. Mary Anna sat next to the bed, holding the baby.

Dr. Hunter McGuire had treated too many dying patients to be fooled by the temporary rally. He gave Jodie a meaningful look and then said, "Mary Anna, do you suppose you could get Uncle Joe to hold Julia so Jodie and I could talk to you in private for a few minutes?"

Moments later, the McGuires and Mary Anna stepped into Mary Anna's room, and Hunter closed the door. He asked her to be seated on the small sofa, and Jodie sat down beside her.

"Mary Anna," he said solemnly, "I can't keep up the facade any longer, and I know you don't want me to."

The gallant woman looked him square in the eye and said, "I know you've been trying to keep me cushioned from the facts, Hunter, and I love you for it. But I know Tom isn't going to make it. How long does he have?"

Hunter took a ragged breath and his lips were pale as he said,

"The end will come today. He won't live to see the sunset."

Jodie kept an arm around Mary Anna as the she broke down and sobbed. When she had regained some control, she said, "Tom must be told the end is near. He has a right to know."

Hunter nodded. "Yes, he does. Would you like me to tell him?"

"No. I must do it. But thank you for offering."

As Hunter and Jodie walked Mary Anna back toward the general's room, Hunter said, "I'll get the others out of the room so you can be alone with him."

"No need," she replied. "We're all like family. I would rather all of you were there."

When the McGuires and Mary Anna entered the room, Clara and Thomas Chandler were sitting with Lacy and Lewis while Joe Morrison was holding Julia so her papa could see her.

The tearstains were still evident on Mary Anna's face, and while the others looked on, she silently prayed for help. Suddenly she drew back her shoulders and moved up beside the bed, taking her husband's hand. "Darling," she said, "I have something very important to tell you."

He looked at her with attentive, loving eyes.

Mary Anna gently cleared her throat. "Hunter...Hunter tells me that very soon you will be in heaven."

Without hesitation, the hero of the South said, "I will miss you and the baby, but I prefer it."

The tears began to slip down Mary Anna's cheeks again, and every eye was fixed on the general's calm features.

Mary Anna smiled through her tears. "Well, before this day closes, you will be with the blessed Saviour in His glory."

The general gazed into her eyes and said, "What day is it, Mary Anna?"

"Sunday," she replied softly.

"Then it's all right," he said. "Praise the Lord."

Mary Anna motioned to Joe, who still held Julia. He placed the baby into her hands, and Mary Anna lowered Julia so her papa could see her once more.

"Little darling," he murmured. "Sweet one!" Then to Mary Anna he said, "Would you read my favorite passage? I will soon leave this groaning tabernacle, and mortality will be swallowed up of life."

Jodie quickly took the baby, and Mary Anna picked up her Bible with trembling hands.

Chaplain Lacy stood close by as Mary Anna read aloud 2 Corinthians 5:1–8. When she finished the passage, she repeated verse 4, her voice cracking slightly, and tears coursing freely down her cheeks:

> For we that are in this tabernacle do groan, being burdened: not for that we would be unclothed, but clothed upon, that mortality might be swallowed up of life.

There was a faint smile on the general's lips. His voice was weak as he turned his eyes on the others in the room and said, "God bless you, my dear ones. I love every one of you." He looked at Mary Anna last and smiled sweetly, saying, "I love you, my sweetheart."

There was a hush in the room.

Suddenly, the general's eyes widened and turned glassy. "General Stuart!" he cried hoarsely. "Bring up the cavalry! Hurry! Where's General Longstreet? He's on Marye's Heights with General Lee? Tell him to cut loose with the artillery! We must cross the river! By all means, we must cross the river!"

The man they called Stonewall looked toward the ceiling and said, "The river. Yes, the river…" And then, as if inviting those in the room along, he said, "Let us cross over the river and rest in the shade of the trees."

The great soldier's eyes closed, and his facial muscles sagged. There was a momentary rise and fall of his chest, then it fell and remained still.

Stonewall Jackson was gone.

NINETEEN

That Sunday, as night fell over Virginia, the stars twinkled in the velvety black sky.

The Army of Northern Virginia was camped on the Rappahannock River, just south of Fredericksburg, and the men sat around campfires, talking of their victory at Chancellorsville. Those who happened to be at the mansion when Fannie Pound Chancellor and her children returned told how glad she was that their home had sustained little damage.

Suddenly a rider thundered into the camp and dismounted. The men around the nearest campfire recognized Corporal Jim Lewis, Stonewall Jackson's aide. Lewis stepped toward them and said, "I need to talk to General Lee. Where's his tent?"

One of them pointed downriver about forty yards.

The Fearless Four, who sat alone by a nearby fire, watched Lewis thread his way toward Lee's tent.

"He sure seems in a hurry," said Hank Upchurch. "Just about has to be news about General Jackson. Why else would he ride from over there at this time of night?"

"Doesn't mean it's bad news," said Chuck Carney. "General Lee has probably given orders to keep him up to date on the general's condition."

Some fifteen minutes passed, and then Lee's aides were summoned to his tent. It wasn't long before they were moving about the camp, announcing that General Lee wanted to meet with all the men.

When the entire army was collected near Robert E. Lee's tent, the general moved to a spot on the riverbank where a large boulder stood, some four feet in height. Campfires cast their flickering light on the silver-haired general as he climbed atop the rock. When he tried to speak, he choked up, pausing for a few moments to compose himself.

"Men...I must be the bearer of very bad news. Our beloved General Stonewall Jackson has died. The general died of pneumonia—a direct result of his wounds. We...must go on in this war without him. Indeed, my right arm is gone."

A pall fell over the thousands of men like a cold, wet blanket.

General Lee forced his words past the lump in his throat and said, "We must be in prayer for Mary Anna Jackson and her baby." Tears began to stream down his cheeks. "A giant has fallen. We shall never forget him!" With that, the general moved off the rock and hurried to his tent.

There was a dead silence as the men began walking slowly back to their campfires.

Numb and sick at heart, Upchurch, Nichols, Carney, and Hall stood like statues, unable to believe that their hero was dead by their hands. Soldiers who passed by them stared with bitter eyes and angry faces.

Major Rance Dayton, who stood close by, saw it all, and his heart was heavy for the four young men. He started to go talk with them. But before he could, a group led by Mike Robinson walked up to them.

"Well, you did it!" Robinson said. "You killed Stonewall Jackson, the greatest soldier who ever put on a uniform! I hope you skunks are proud of yourselves!"

"Yeah," Gifford Henderson said, "when you're old and gray, I hope you still have nightmares about what you did!"

As other men joined the group, Bo Gentry said, "You trigger-happy dogs oughtta hang your heads in shame! We told you not to shoot! Well, I hope your insides rot till they eat you alive!"

"Stonewall killers!" cried someone in the bunch.

At that, Dayton stomped up to the group and pushed his way to the middle. "All right, that's enough! Now move on! These men feel bad enough without you taunting them!"

When the soldiers had gone, Dayton said, "I'm sorry for this, boys. Don't let them get to you."

"How do we do that, Major?" asked Buford. "We're only made of mortal flesh."

Chuck Carney's voice had a brittle edge to it as he said, "They keep it up, somebody's gonna get hurt."

The firelight revealed four bitter faces. Where once Rance Dayton had seen only hurt, he now detected anger and hatred. "Boys, listen to me," he said. "If you get physical, somebody will get hurt, and it could be you. I don't want that to happen."

"Major," Carney said, "we've taken it so far, but every man has his limit how much abuse he can take."

"Look," said Dayton, "I'm going to talk to General Lee. Something has to be done to help the men of this army see that they could have done the same thing in the same circumstances. Please...give me some time to get this situation resolved."

In its Monday, May 11, 1863, issue, the front page of the *Chicago Tribune* declared in bold print:

Under the leadership of "Fighting Joe" Hooker, the glorious Army of the Potomac is becoming more slow in its movements, more unwieldy, less confident of itself, more of a football to the enemy and less an honor to the country than any army we have yet raised.

Other Northern newspapers were saying much the same thing.

President Abraham Lincoln was signally embarrassed. The United States Congressmen could barely hold their heads up in public, and General Halleck would not even appear in public. The morale of the Union army camped at Falmouth was at an all-time low, and the people of the Northern states were losing faith in their cause.

On the other hand, though devastated at the death of their hero, the morale of the Army of Northern Virginia was at an all-time high. The return of Lieutenant General James Longstreet and his two divisions to the camp at Fredericksburg brought General Lee to the peak of strength in manpower. Lee and Longstreet—feeling deeply the loss of Jackson—began forming plans on their next move.

During this time, Major Rance Dayton went to Lee and told him what the four young men who saved his life at Antietam were facing from the soldiers because they had shot Stonewall Jackson.

Lee drew up a document exonerating the four of any misdeed. The document explained the circumstances under which the "friendly fire" took place, and Lee asked the men of the Confederate army to understand that it could have happened to any of them.

Hundreds of copies of Lee's document were printed and placed in the hands of unit leaders. The leaders were to meet with their men, read them the document, and tell them to heed it.

Major Dayton kept a sharp eye on his four friends to see how it would go after the document had been distributed. Most of the men did ease off. But Mike Robinson and his group, and the four men who had been sentries with the Fearless Four on that fateful night, kept the pressure on.

Dayton was pleased that, in spite of Robinson and his group, his friends had not retaliated.

Some ten days after the victory at Chancellorsville, Dayton was in his tent on the riverbank when he heard loud shouts and curses from upstream. The noise lasted only a few seconds, and Dayton went back to his paperwork.

Several minutes later, a young private appeared at the tent flap and said, "Major Dayton, we've got trouble out here!"

Dayton went outside to find that the Fearless Four had gotten into a fistfight with Chad Lynch, Bo Gentry, and Myron Flynn. The latter three had ended up in the river, and Bo Gentry was lying on the bank with his lungs half full of water. One of the corps doctors was trying to save his life.

Hall, Upchurch, Nichols, and Carney were standing by, and more than a hundred soldiers had gathered to see what had happened. Gentry suddenly started coughing, and the doctor announced, "He'll make it, Major, but he came plenty close to drowning."

Dayton stepped up to his friends. "What happened?" he asked.

"Same old thing, sir," replied Chuck. "They were needling us, and we just couldn't take it anymore."

"Well, you can be mighty glad Gentry didn't drown."

Hank Everett shrugged his shoulders. "If he had, it would've been his own fault." He looked past the major and said, "Uh-oh. It's General Lane."

Lane stopped where the doctor was working on Gentry and listened as Lynch and Flynn, dripping wet, told him the Fearless Four had started an argument then began throwing punches. It took them off guard, and they ended up in the river.

"They're lying through their teeth," growled Buford. "Major, we didn't start it. They did!"

"Yeah," said Everett, "we haven't retaliated before, so they figured we wouldn't this time either. Guess we showed 'em."

General Lane stomped up and said, "Major Dayton, I want you and these four men at my tent in fifteen minutes. Those other three will get dried off and be there too."

Lane gave the four an angry glance and walked away.

"Guess we're in for it now," said Chuck.

Dayton sighed. "Look, fellows, a truly big man will not let little men make him a little man like themselves. You proved at Antietam that you're big men. You mustn't let those few little men who badger you get under your skin."

"We tried that, sir," said Chuck. "We really did."

"Well, you'll have to try harder next time. I just hope General Lane isn't going to be too severe."

When the seven men were assembled before Lane in his large tent, he scolded them for fighting, saying that mature soldiers would not get into fisticuffs. He then warned of disciplinary action if any of them were ever involved in another such affair. When he dismissed them, he said, "You stay a moment, Major Dayton."

Lane waited until the seven were outside the tent, then said, "Major, you must keep a tight rein on your four friends. I mean it. If they get into another fight, I'll make them wish they'd never put on a gray uniform!"

Dayton left the tent and took the four aside. "Men," he said, "you can't ever let anybody prod you into a fight again. General Lane told me it would go very bad for you if it happens. You've got to keep a tight rein on your tempers, no matter what. You do understand what I'm saying, don't you?"

"No offense intended toward you, Major," said Chuck, "but maybe I'll come to the place where I flat just don't care what the general does."

"Chuck, please don't let that kind of attitude get a hold on you. It can only bring heartache and trouble that you don't need or want. You boys know what you mean to me. I owe you my life. I don't want you to have any more misery than you've already suffered. Just be careful."

"We appreciate your concern for us, Major. And for your sake, we'll try not to get into another fight."

Two days later, the soldiers ate their supper as usual on the riverbank, then went into Fredericksburg to walk the streets, which had become a form of entertainment since the Chancellorsville battle.

General Lee had put the drinking establishments off limits and had promised severe punishment to any man who returned to camp with liquor on his breath.

On this evening, Nichols, Upchurch, Hall, and Carney were walking the lantern-lit streets, talking of the day the War would end and they could go home to Fayetteville and put their lives back together.

Much of Fredericksburg had been destroyed by Yankee artillery back in December, and in many places reconstruction was taking place.

The four friends had reached the business district and were approaching a dark alley where new construction was being done on both sides of the street.

Abruptly, several shadowy figures emerged from the alley and blocked their path. They tensed up as they recognized Mike Robinson's bunch, along with Chad Lynch, Bo Gentry, Ken Dykstra, and Myron Flynn.

Robinson took a step ahead of the others and said, "Well, lookee who we've got here, boys! Stonewall killers!"

"Apparently General Lee's document meant nothing to you," Chuck Carney said. "We were exonerated. Or didn't you listen?"

"Maybe Lee exonerated you, but we didn't!"

"So what does that mean?" asked Upchurch, his anger mounting.

Dykstra moved up beside Robinson. "That means we're gonna punish you on our own."

Carney noticed a small pile of two-by-fours among other pieces of lumber a step or two to his right. "You'd better think twice before you try to do that," he said. "You just go on down the street and forget what you had planned."

Robinson guffawed. "I think we've got 'em scared, boys!"

Carney sprang forward, throwing his full weight into Robinson. The impact sent the big man backpedaling, and he slammed into the others, knocking most of them down.

"Over here, guys!" said Carney as he dashed to the lumber and picked up one of the two-by-fours.

While the other three men went for their own two-by-fours, Robinson charged Carney. But he was too slow. Carney swung the two-by-four, catching Robinson square in the mouth. The big man's head snapped back, and he dropped like a rock, blood pouring from his mouth.

Gifford Henderson took one look at Robinson and lunged toward Carney. But Hank Upchurch decked him with his two-by-four. The others in Robinson's group broke into a run, heading down the dark alley. Buford swore at them and threw his two-by-four as hard as he could after them.

Suddenly they heard loud voices behind them. When they turned, they saw a dozen or more soldiers, who quickly surrounded them, pointing their rifles.

The Fearless Four dropped their two-by-fours and faced the black musket bores on all sides.

Two lieutenants bent over the two men on the ground. One of them straightened up and stepped accusingly toward Carney, Hall, Nichols, and Upchurch. "You can be thankful they're still alive…though just barely."

"It was them or us," Carney said. "They laid in wait for us, here in the alley. They had plans to punish us. They said so."

"You're under arrest," said the lieutenant. "We're jailing you right here in town."

The next morning, the four heroes of Antietam were sitting glumly in their cell when they saw Deputy Sheriff Roy Bates enter the cell block with Major Rance Dayton. The four men had been placed in the same cell, which had only a pair of bunk beds. They rose to their feet at the sound of voices.

Bates gestured toward a wooden chair in a corner of the cell block and said, "You can pull that up to the bars and sit down if you want, Major."

Dayton nodded, but stepped right up to the bars. Bates returned to the office, and Dayton said, "I don't know what to say, men. I really hoped you'd be able to take the harassment without violence. Now you've really done it."

"They were going to attack us, Major," Chuck said. "It was hit first or get hit."

Dayton sighed and rubbed the back of his neck. "General Lane is going to bring assault charges against you. Several of the men in the group have already agreed to testify against you."

"Well, if they'll tell the truth," said Hank, "they'll have to say that they were lying in wait in that alley to jump us."

The major shook his head. "They're not going to admit that, I guarantee you."

"So what will an assault charge bring us?" asked Everett.

"Probably several months, maybe even years, in prison."

At the news, sick looks passed over their faces.

"Fellows," said Dayton, "I can't let you face those charges without trying to get you off."

Hank Upchurch lifted his head slightly. "What do you mean, sir?"

"Since General Lee knows the circumstances surrounding the shooting of General Jackson, Captain Boswell, and Sergeant Cunliffe, and he was partially responsible for your receiving the Presidential Commendation for your valor at Antietam, I'm going to talk to him. I'll explain to him why you went on the offensive last night. I'll see if he'll simply let you be released and allowed to leave the army. It's best that we get you away from the source of the trouble."

The four men were thanking Dayton when Sheriff George

Duncan entered the cell block. A stout man of fifty-five, with a generous paunch, Duncan said, "Major, I just found out these are the men who were honored for bravery a few months ago in Richmond by President Davis…for saving your life up at Sharpsburg."

"That's right," said Dayton.

Duncan looked at the foursome, then back at Dayton. "How could they do a thing like that, then shoot Stonewall Jackson and two other Confederate soldiers, and bludgeon two more soldiers last night?"

"It's a long story, Sheriff," said Dayton. "No time to tell it now. But they're not bad men. They got caught up in some ex-tenuating circumstances." Turning to his friends, the major said, "I'll see you tomorrow."

The next morning, Deputy Bates ushered General James Lane into the cell block, then returned to the office. The prisoners rose to their feet and approached the bars.

"I'm here in place of Major Dayton," said Lane. His countenance reflected distaste as he scanned their faces. "I have him on assignment today, and he won't be able to come. I thought it best to inform you that Major Dayton talked to General Lee. The general would not agree to release you from the army and let you go home based on past performance and present circumstances. You're going to stand trial."

With that, Lane started toward the door. He stopped after a few steps and said, "Oh. Major Dayton said to tell you he'll come and see you tomorrow."

When Lane was gone, Chuck swore and said, "I hate this stinkin' army! They're not gonna lock me up!"

"Me neither," said Hank. "We need to bust outta here."

"That's exactly what we're gonna do," said Chuck. "We'll escape when that deputy brings our supper tonight."

"So what'll we do, Chuck?" asked Everett.

"One of us will have to play sick.…"

It was after dark when General James Lane and Major Rance Dayton dismounted their horses in front of the county jail, along with the teenage boy who had ridden to fetch them.

George Duncan was waiting for them when they walked into his office. He handed the boy a Confederate dollar bill for his services and dismissed him.

"The kid said the men escaped, Sheriff," said Lane.

"That's right…and I want you to come see what they did."

Duncan took the army officers into the cell block where the body of Deputy Sheriff Roy Bates lay on the floor in a pool of blood.

Both men were stunned.

"Somehow they tricked my deputy into opening the cell door when he brought their supper," the sheriff said. "The trays are usually slid beneath the cell door. You can see the food hasn't been touched. And if you'll look closely, you'll see that they beat him to death with the butt of his revolver. One or two hard blows would certainly have knocked him out. But they must have hit him at least a dozen times. It was murder, gentlemen. Coldblooded murder. I have warrants for their arrest. When we find them, they'll hang for sure."

Rance Dayton felt sick all over, and his face was deathly white. "It's like a nightmare, Sheriff. Those four young men who so gallantly saved my life and basked in glory as heroes have become bitter, coldhearted killers. I guess you could call it a turn of glory."

Sheriff Duncan sent a wire to the sheriff of Cumberland County, North Carolina, advising him of what had happened, and to be on the lookout for the fugitives if they should return to Fayetteville. Other law agencies were alerted, with descriptions of the Fearless Four.

Duncan himself launched a manhunt, wanting desperately to catch the men who had murdered his deputy and see them hang.

Major Rance Dayton often thought of the Antietam heroes as the war continued. As far as he knew, the Fearless Four hadn't been caught. It was as if they had vanished from the earth.

Finally, the Civil War came to an end with the Union the victor on April 9, 1865.

Rance Dayton, still wanting to become a lawman in the West and to build a new life on the frontier, first made a trip to Fayetteville, North Carolina. There he met with the families of the four men who had saved his life. None of them had heard from the men since their escape from Fredericksburg in May 1863.

Dayton's purpose in returning to Fayetteville was to obtain official papers from the sheriff's department that would tell of his accomplishments as a lawman in Cumberland County. With the desired papers in hand, he took a train west.

TWENTY

In early June of 1865, a train carried Rance Dayton across Tennessee, the western tip of Kentucky, and into Illinois. He would change trains at St. Louis, Missouri, and head west to Kansas City.

As the train rolled across the flat land of Illinois, Dayton reached into his valise and took out the most recent letter he had received from Jackson County Sheriff Bart Clifford in Independence, Missouri. He smiled as he read it again, and then carefully placed it back in the valise. *Lord*, he prayed silently, *help me find the place where You want me to live, and the job You want me to have.*

When the train chugged into the depot at St. Louis, Dayton picked up his two pieces of hand luggage and stepped out of the coach. He threaded his way among the people who crowded the station platform and approached a large blackboard on the wall next to the ticket office. The chalk writing told him his train to Kansas City would be on time.

Since it was almost noon, and he had about two hours, Dayton went to the café attached to the station and ate lunch.

The train from Kansas City indeed came in on time, turned

around in the railroad yard, and hissed its way to a stop at its assigned spot in the depot.

Soon the conductor was calling for all passengers to board. Dayton climbed aboard the last car before the caboose and chose a seat about midway in the coach. He placed his luggage in the overhead rack and sat down next to the window. It looked as if the train was going to be quite full. He could see people hurrying to the other cars, and passengers entered the coach he occupied in a steady stream from both ends.

A young woman stopped at the seat directly across the aisle from Dayton, carrying her hand luggage. She sat one piece down so she could lift the other into the overhead rack.

"Excuse me, ma'am," Rance said, "would you allow me to put your luggage in the rack for you?"

The lady smiled. "Why, yes. Thank you, sir."

"You're welcome, ma'am. I'll be glad to take them down for you when we get to Kansas City."

Rance was about to ask if he could sit beside her when she looked past him and said, "Thank you, sir, but that won't be necessary. My husband's here now. Hello, darling. I was afraid you weren't going to make it."

Puffing from an apparent long run, the woman's husband put his luggage in the overhead rack and said, "Last-minute business. Got it taken care of, though."

"Darling," she said, looking at Dayton, "this nice gentleman put my luggage in the rack for me."

The man smiled at Rance and said, "Thank you for your kindness to my wife, Mr.…."

"Dayton. Rance Dayton."

"Well, thank you, Mr. Dayton. I'm Lowell Carstairs. This is Lucille."

"Glad to meet both of you," said Rance, then turned and sat down in his seat.

The coach was filling up, and now the bell on the engine began clanging—the signal that the train would soon depart.

Rance noticed a tall, square-jawed man with salt-and-pepper hair and mustache enter the front door of the coach and move down the aisle. As he came closer, the badge on his vest caught Rance's attention. The lawman stopped beside Rance and said, "The second half of this seat taken?"

"No, sir," said Rance with a smile. "Please, sit down." He read the inscription on the badge. *Deputy United States marshal.*

The deputy, whom Rance figured to be in his early fifties, placed his luggage overhead and eased onto the seat.

Outside, the conductor shouted, "All abo-o-oard!"

Rance extended his hand. "I'm Rance Dayton, sir."

The deputy gripped his hand firmly and smiled. "Deputy U.S. Marshal Dan Moore."

"Always glad to meet a lawman," said Dayton. "Before the War I was sheriff of Cumberland County, North Carolina…and had been deputy sheriff before that."

"So you're a veteran of the War. I don't have to ask which side."

"Hardly," Dayton said, chuckling.

"And something tells me you were an officer."

"Yes. Major."

"Major! And you aren't a West Pointer?"

"No."

"Well, that's great. So you fought with a North Carolina outfit, I assume."

"Yes, sir. I was commander of the Eighteenth North Carolina Regiment in Brigadier General James Lane's brigade."

The lawman frowned slightly and said, "Eighteenth North Carolina…now why does that ring a bell?"

"It probably rings a bell, Marshal, because it was some men of my regiment who mistook General Stonewall Jackson and a group of riders for Yankees, and fired at them."

Moore snapped his fingers. "Yes, that's it. So it was some of your men?"

"Yes. A real tragedy."

"Must've been hard for all of you."

"We all loved and admired General Jackson tremendously."

"Jackson sure was one of my heroes, too, I'll tell you that. So, ah…what are you doing for a living now?"

"At the moment I'm unemployed, but I'm heading west to get back into law enforcement."

"Do you have something lined up, or are you traveling west cold turkey?"

"I've been corresponding with Jackson County Sheriff Bart Clifford in Independence."

"Oh, sure! Bart Clifford. Know him well. Fine man."

"He's going to help me find a town needing a marshal, or even a deputy marshal somewhere in the West."

"Well, Bart has a lot of friends all over the West. He'll have some good contacts, that's for sure."

The train was now moving along the Mississippi River northward. Rance let his gaze settle on the wide river. "The mighty Mississippi," he said in a low voice. "Played a big part in the War."

Soon the tracks veered away from the river and turned due west, and Rance turned back to Moore. "You been a deputy U.S. marshal very long?" he asked.

"Only two months."

"Oh, really? So where did you wear a badge before then?"

"I was Douglas County sheriff in Lawrence, Kansas, up until the end of the War. Had been for ten years. And I was deputy sheriff before that."

"Lawrence…" Rance said. "Then you were there when William Quantrill and his raiders sacked and burned the city in '63."

"Yep. Those wild fools killed a hundred and fifty civilians in that raid. But in spite of the fact that Quantrill was a Confederate guerrilla, I still leaned toward the South in the War."

Dayton smiled. "Well, I'm glad you didn't let Quantrill sway your sentiments toward Dixie."

Moore laughed, then said, "You married, Dayton?"

"No, sir. I was engaged once but…it didn't work out. I'm hoping to find the right one out there where the buffalo roam. You married?"

Moore nodded. "Very happily. Nina and I have been married almost thirty years. Have a daughter and two sons…four grandchildren. A son-in-law and two daughters-in-law, of course."

Rance grinned.

"I'm glad to see you heading out West, Dayton," said Moore. "I admire you for it. The West is going to need a whole lot more like you as more people head for the frontier. It's becoming a haven for ne'er-do-wells, thieves, robbers, and troublemakers. Unfortunately, a good number of those are Civil War veterans. Just got used to violence and can't seem to live without it. So they create their own."

The two men were quiet a moment, listening to the steady clicking of the steel wheels beneath them. Then Dayton said, "Why did you decide to become a federal man? Certainly Lawrence has its share of troublemakers."

"Pressure," Moore said evenly.

"What kind of pressure?"

"The kind from Chief United States Marshal Ben Starke in Kansas City. He and I are longtime friends. Ben showed up at my office in Lawrence a week after the War was over and talked about the big influx of Civil War soldiers heading west…their lives empty and looking for excitement.

"Ben needed to beef up his staff of deputies, so being a personal friend, and knowing my arrest record, he pressured me to resign as sheriff and become one of his deputies. The reason I was in St. Louis was to take a couple of those Civil War troublemakers—Rebels, by the way—to be tried for murder in St. Louis, where they killed two men who'd beaten them in a series of poker games."

The conversation lulled for a few minutes, and Rance watched the sunlit countryside go by.

Suddenly, Moore said, "You know what, Dayton?"

"Sir?"

"If you have a better than average arrest record in Cumberland County, you ought to consider applying for a deputy U.S. marshal's position."

"Well, maybe I should. Let me get my valise out of the overhead rack, and I'll let you take a look at my record."

"I'll get it for you," said Moore, leaving the seat to stand in the aisle. "Which one is it?"

"Dark brown leather. Has my initials on it."

"Okay. Got it."

Rance took out the envelope that contained the arrest records for his years in law enforcement and handed them to Dan Moore. "Here, sir. Take a look."

Moore carefully read the records. When he looked up from the report, he glanced at Dayton and said, "Whew! My record can't come near yours! You must be plenty good at tracking down and catching fugitives."

Rance shrugged. "Maybe God gave me the nose of a bloodhound."

"I'll tell you right now, Ben Starke would jump at the chance to get a man like you. I mean it. If you decide you'd like to apply, Dayton, I'll be glad to put in a good word for you with Ben. Not that you'd need it with these credentials!"

Rance grinned and nodded slowly.

Moore slid down on the seat, tipped his hat over his face, and said, "Well, ol' Dan here is going to take a little snooze."

Rance did the same, only instead of sleeping, he began to pray silently about becoming a deputy U.S. marshal. After a while, an unmistakable peace encompassed his heart. "All right, Lord," he said in a whisper. "I'll pursue it. Thank You for Your guidance. You know I want to be in the very center of Your will."

People moved up and down the aisles, the conductor came through twice, and children played nearby, but still Dan Moore slept on.

Finally, the train slowed down for a stop at Columbia, Missouri, and the change of speed and the sound of the wheels awakened Moore. He sat up, blinking, and placed his hat on his head. "We must be coming into Columbia," he mumbled.

"That's it," Rance said. "You sleep pretty sound, don't you?"

"Been known to," Moore said, covering a yawn. "'Specially when I've been running a little short on it. And that's the way it's been the past day or two. Want to stretch your legs?"

The two men stepped off the train and walked alongside it.

"Tell you what, Deputy," said Rance, "I'm going to take you up on putting in a good word for me with Chief Starke."

A smile spread over Moore's face. "Well, great! As you know, we won't get into Kansas City until late this evening, but how about I take you and introduce you to Ben first thing in the morning?"

"I'm ready."

"What about Sheriff Clifford? When are you supposed to meet with him?"

"No set time. He knows I'm coming, but we didn't set a particular day or time. He's just expecting me to walk into his office sometime soon."

"Good. Then this won't mess up anything with him."

"Nope. If I get hired by Chief Starke, I'll simply contact Sheriff Clifford and tell him I've got a job."

Chief United States Marshal Benjamin Starke sat at his desk reading Rance Dayton's records from Cumberland County. True to his word, Dan Moore had taken Dayton to the chief's office and now waited with him as the chief considered Rance's prospects.

When he finished reading, Starke shook his head in wonder and looked over his half-moon glasses. "Mr. Dayton," he said, "this is an impressive record. I need your kind. Where have you been all my life?"

Dayton and Moore laughed.

Starke, who was a stout, bald man of sixty, shook his head again and said, "And to top it off, you made major under Robert E. Lee in a very short amount of time. If you want a job, I can place you real fast."

Dayton glanced at Moore and smiled, then said, "I'll take it, sir."

"All right. Now, we have U.S. marshal offices in several places in the West, and every one of them is shorthanded. Each office is headed up by a United States marshal and they're all accountable to this office. And this office is accountable to the U.S. marshal's headquarters in Washington D.C. We have plans for the office in Denver, Colorado, to take over the western territory now under my jurisdiction, but that's a ways off. Anyway, I can list the locations of the offices and let you pick the place you like best. Or, I can tell you where you're needed the most right now and see what you think about it."

"I'm here to serve, sir. Where do you need me the most?"

"Western Montana."

Dayton pursed his lips and cocked his head to one side. "What can you tell me about it?"

"We opened an office in Helena just about a year ago. We've had one in Billings for about five years. Gold strikes and other mining have drawn people for several years, and with population comes lawbreakers. The Billings office handles problems in eastern Montana Territory, and the Helena office handles those on the western side. Helena is situated just east of the towering and majestic Rockies."

"Towering and majestic," echoed Moore. "You really know how to do a sales job, don't you, my friend?"

"Hush up, Dan. I need this man in Helena desperately."

"Chief Starke," said Dayton, "I'll take the job. What's next?"

"You haven't asked me what the job pays."

"No lawman gets paid what he's worth, but I figure it'll be enough to keep me in food, shelter, and clothes."

Starke smiled. "It will."

"Okay. What's next?"

"You need to fill out an application, which from what I've already learned about you will only be a formality. Then you take the oath before me in the presence of two deputies. I'll commission you a deputy United States marshal, and I'll wire your new boss immediately and tell him about you. We'll have you headed west by tomorrow morning. You go by rail as far as Billings, then travel by stagecoach to Helena."

"Let's get on with it," said Rance.

Less than an hour later, all the formalities had been taken care of, and Deputy U.S. Marshal Rance Dayton received his badge and a new rifle, revolver, and gun belt. He would be provided with horse, bridle, and saddle when he arrived at his destination.

Starke sent a wire to U.S. Marshal Douglas Wright in Helena, advising him of the new man assigned to his office, along with a brief description of his qualifications.

Dan Moore looked extremely pleased with himself that he had recruited Rance Dayton for Starke. But duty called, and he excused himself, shook hands with Dayton, and left the office.

Within half an hour after the wire had been sent, Wright wired back, telling Starke to put Dayton on a train as soon as possible.

Chief Starke made reservations for Dayton with both railroad and stage lines, then wired Wright of his new man's arrival time in Helena.

When that was done, the chief sat down with Dayton at his desk, and said, "Rance, I want to explain why we need you at Helena right now. Your experience and success in tracking and capturing lawbreakers fills a real need. There's a bloody gang of outlaws terrorizing western Montana Territory. They're robbing banks, stagecoaches, stores, ranchers, and travelers. And they're heartless and ruthless. They kill anyone who dares to resist them."

"I've dealt with that kind before, sir."

Chief Starke nodded. "They also pride themselves in killing lawmen. They've been pursued by other federal men out of the Helena office. Five, in fact. And they've killed three of them. The other two saw what they were up against and resigned.

"Wright can't go after them personally and oversee the office. He has three deputies, but none of them have your experience behind a badge, or your success record. Doug Wright needs you real bad." Starke paused, then said, "Has what I've said changed your mind about going to Helena?"

Rance looked at the badge on his chest and said, "No, sir. It'll be a welcome challenge to go after that gang. Do you know who they are?"

The chief opened a desk drawer and pulled out the latest issue of *Police Gazette*, an eastern magazine about crime and punishment. Placing it on the desk in front of his new deputy, he said, "Right there on the front page. The Phantom Riders. That's them. The article tells all about what they're doing in western Montana. The article takes up three pages.

"They've also been written up in newspapers all over the West. No one knows who they are. They always wear masks when pulling their robberies and doing their killing. A few of the gang have been killed in gun battles with lawmen, but the dead ones have never been identified."

"I see," said Dayton, running his eyes over the front page. "How many men ride in the gang?"

"Anywhere from seven to ten, depending on how fast they replace a man when one of them goes down. A few times some of the gang members have been wounded when battling lawmen, but they've always escaped and taken their wounded with them."

"Sounds like they're well organized," said Dayton. "It's not going to be easy to bring them in."

"How well I know. Doug'll go over everything with you, but let me say it right here. Though you'll be tracking them alone, when you find them, you're not to try to take them by yourself. You pinpoint their hideout and go to the closest local law for help. Understand?"

"Yes, sir."

"All right," said Starke, rising to his feet. "I'll let you go to your hotel room and get some rest. I'll see you here at eight o'clock in the morning, and one of my deputies will drive you to the depot."

The day was still early, and Dayton borrowed a horse from Starke to ride to Independence. He wanted to thank Sheriff Bart Clifford in person for his willingness to help him find a lawman's job, and to let him know that he was now a deputy U.S. marshal.

The next morning, Rance left for Montana and spent the night in Cheyenne City, Wyoming, then boarded a different train for Billings and traveled all day. The following morning he boarded the Wells Fargo stage that would take him to Bozeman, where he would change stagecoaches and travel north between the Big Belt Mountains and the Rocky Mountains to Helena.

On the final leg of his journey, Rance sat in amazement as the massive Rockies came into view on his left, and the Big Belts raised their jagged peaks toward the azure sky on his right. He thrilled at the Rocky Mountain peaks that lifted their snow-capped heads, even in June, eleven and twelve thousand feet above sea level.

When the stage reached the small town of Gallatin, the passengers were allowed to get off and stretch their legs while the horses were fed and watered. Dayton decided to take a short stroll and look the town over. When he came upon a cluster of men who stood outside the town's only saloon, he heard them talking about the Phantom Riders.

One of the men noticed his badge and said, "Howdy, there, Marshal. You come in on the stage?"

"Just pausing while the horses are being serviced," said Dayton. "I'm on my way to Helena. I heard you talking about the Phantom Riders a moment ago."

"Yes, sir," spoke up a middle-aged man. "You must know about 'em."

"I do. They're part of the reason I'm going to Helena. I'm joining the U.S. marshal's office there."

"Well, good for you. I hope you put a rope around every one of their dirty necks!"

"What were you saying about them?" asked Dayton.

"Those filthy skunks robbed a bank yesterday in Missoula. Killed two bank employees who weren't even givin' 'em any trouble. Just did it outta meanness. They also wounded a bank customer. Got away before the town marshal or his deputy could appear on the scene."

As the stage bound for Helena rolled northward and the other passengers slept, Rance took his Bible out of his valise and started flipping pages. He'd read something in the Psalms recently that came back to him. He'd marked the verses and was now able to find the passage quickly. He read the two verses in Psalm 55 and let their truth grip him.

> Let death seize upon them, and let them go down quick into hell: for wickedness is in their dwellings, and among them.
> But thou, O God, shalt bring them down into the pit of destruction: bloody and deceitful men shall not live out half their days....

The new deputy United States marshal rested the Bible in his lap and stared out the window at the majestic Rockies. "Lord," he said in a whisper, "help me to bring these bloody and deceitful men to justice."

TWENTY-ONE

ance Dayton's stagecoach rolled into Helena at sundown. As the stage squealed to a halt in a cloud of dust, he noticed a small group of men standing in front of the Wells Fargo office. Then he noticed the coffin at their feet.

He stepped out of the coach, helped two ladies to alight, then reached inside for his hand luggage. As he turned around, he found himself facing a lanky man with a droopy silver mustache. The man glanced at Rance's badge and said, "Deputy Rance Dayton, I presume?"

"Yes, sir. Marshal Wright?"

"That's me," said Wright, shaking Rance's hand. "I'll have to ask you to excuse me for a moment. I've got to get a coffin loaded on the stage."

Dayton watched as the U.S. Marshal, the stage agent, and the driver and shotgunner hoisted the heavy oblong box onto the rack atop the coach.

A fresh six-up team of horses was brought from the rear of the stage station while the present team was unhitched. Marshal Wright talked to the driver for a few minutes, then came back to his new deputy and said, "Sorry about that, Dayton, but I had to make sure the driver and shotgunner understood about the coffin."

"No problem, sir."

"Let's go to the office and do what paperwork has to be done. Then we'll get you settled into a hotel room. By then, it'll be time for supper."

"Whatever you say, sir."

After filling out the necessary paperwork to establish Deputy U.S. Marshal Rance Dayton as officially working out of the Helena office, Wright said, "Now, let me tell you about the body in the coffin. That was one of my deputies—Alan Thaxter. He was from Texas, so I'm sending the body home to his family for burial."

Rance nodded. "That seems only right, sir."

"Alan was killed by the Phantom Riders…yesterday."

The marshal shook his head regretfully. "Hindsight always makes a man wise. And I sure wish I hadn't let him go after that gang alone. He really wasn't experienced enough. But when they murdered two bank employees over in Missoula a few days ago, Alan insisted I let him track them down."

"I heard about the Missoula robbery," said Rance. "They wounded a bank customer, too, if I heard right."

"You heard right. So anyway, I gave Alan permission to trail those dirty rats, with the stipulation that he not try to take them on by himself if he caught up to them. He was to get help from the closest sheriff or town marshal."

Rance nodded. "Chief Starke laid down the same orders to me, sir."

"Good. Then I won't have to school you on it, will I?"

"No, sir."

"Well, anyway…Alan caught up with them in the woods outside a town called Duncan, at the south tip of the Flathead Indian Reservation. That's about forty miles north of Missoula."

"Marshal, if he was alone, how do you know what happened?"

"Because of an eyewitness—fella named John Hammett. As instructed, my deputy went to Bob Dardin, marshal at Duncan, and asked for help to capture the gang. Dardin and his only deputy—Hammett—went with him. The three were sneaking up on the camp when they spooked a big bull moose and he charged through the campsite. The gang opened fire, my deputy and Marshal Dardin were killed, and Hammett was wounded. He lived only because the gang took off in a hurry. They probably thought there was more help on the way."

"Do you have any idea which way they're headed now?" asked Dayton.

"No, but their trail won't be hard to find. They leave dead bodies wherever they go."

"Do you want me to head out in the morning, sir?"

"Yes. We'll give you a stalwart horse and turn you loose. And Dayton...please...don't try to capture them alone. Make sure you have help."

"I will, sir."

The next morning, Rance placed his personal items in the saddle-bags, strapped on a bedroll, and rode north toward Duncan to pick up the trail of the Phantom Riders. After several miles of riding, he knew he had a strong horse in the bay gelding with the white face and stockings.

The next day, he found that the gang had swung west and begun robbing banks in towns along the east side of the Bitterroot Mountains. Marshal Wright was correct. The Phantom Riders robbed six banks in four days, and left dead people in every town.

On his fifth day out, he came close to the gang at a town called Stevensville, where they had killed a bank customer and the local marshal. Rance trailed the gang to some nearby woods and even found blood on some bushes, which corroborated an eyewitness account that the marshal had shot one of the robbers before he was killed.

The trail turned east from Stevensville, and Dayton trotted his horse toward the town of Washington Gulch. He noted a large herd of buffalo in a valley off to his right and suddenly remembered part of his conversation with Dan Moore on the train to Kansas. He'd told Moore that he was going to find the right girl out where the buffalo roam.

Well, there's the buffalo, he thought. *But where's the girl?*

Dayton bottomed out in a low spot on the road and urged the horse for more speed as they started up the hill. Suddenly he heard a series of gunshots ahead. He pushed the gelding even harder, and when he topped the hill, he saw a stagecoach stopped on the road. A man lay on the ground, and passengers were climbing out. In the distance, he saw the gang riding hard toward some dense woods.

Rance skidded to a halt and slid from the saddle near two men and a woman who were bent over the body.

"Folks," Rance said, "I'm Deputy U.S. Marshal Rance Dayton out of the Helena office. Those men were masked, weren't they?"

"Yes, they were," said one of the men. "It was the Phantom Riders, Deputy."

"They robbed us then shot the driver and the shotgunner!" said the woman. "The driver just died."

Dayton raised his eyes toward the spot where he had last seen the gang. "Look, folks, I've got to go after them. Can one of you men drive the stage into Washington Gulch?"

"We'll take care of it, Deputy," said the man who had spoken before. "Go get 'em!"

Dayton vaulted into the saddle and put the bay to a gallop. Within a few minutes, he caught sight of the galloping gang as he topped a rise. They were in a low spot at the moment, but racing toward the top of a hill.

When Dayton saw the riders again, he was much closer to them, and gaining. They couldn't be more than two miles ahead of him.

Rance wasn't sure what he would do when he closed the gap even more, but somehow he had to keep the gang in sight until they made camp that night. Then he could go for help. Moments later, he was coming up on Washington Gulch when he caught sight of the gang again. They skirted the town and Dayton did the same.

A half-hour passed, and when Dayton crested a hill and saw the gang still riding hard, he was now less than a mile behind them.

When the gang vanished once again, Rance noticed a white ranch house with white outbuildings and a red barn off to his right. The buildings sat in a wide open area dotted with trees.

So far Rance's mount showed no signs of tiring, and he pressed the horse, staying at a gallop. When they came charging over the rise and suddenly encountered an injured buffalo in the middle of the road, there was no chance to change course. The gelding's legs slammed into the buffalo, and Dayton somersaulted out of the saddle. He hit the ground hard and his head struck a large rock beside the road.

Rance Dayton awakened to a world of Montana sunshine…and his head ached something fierce.

He squinted at the bright sunlight coming through a window adorned with lace curtains. He was lying in a bed with pillows propped under his head. He closed his eyes momentarily to ease the intensity of the brilliant light, then opened them again.

Slowly he looked at different objects in the room, and then his eyes lighted on a young woman sitting in a chair beside his bed. The sun's rays coming through the window made a halo of her golden hair. She was reading a Bible and hadn't yet noticed he had regained consciousness.

Rance studied her for a moment and decided he had never seen such a beautiful woman in all his life.

Rance tried to put it all together. *How did I get here? Why does my head hurt so much? Where—?*

Suddenly it all came back. The galloping horse. The buffalo in the road. Sailing through the air. Rolling on the ground. The rock. The shower of stars. The black whirlpool. And then, sunlight coming through the window with lace curtains.

Rance's mouth was dry, and his neck felt stiff. He moved his head, and pain lanced through it, making him moan.

The girl looked up from the Bible, her eyes widening, and said, "Oh! Hello, Deputy Dayton!" Then she turned toward the open door and called, "Daddy! Mother! He's awake!"

She laid her Bible on a table and got up to stand beside the bed as the sound of footsteps came from the hall.

Rance blinked as he looked at the girl, then let his gaze swing to the door as a couple in their mid-forties hurried into the room.

"Has he said anything, Marcy?" asked the older woman.

"No, Mother."

"Deputy Dayton," said the man, "can you hear me?"

Rance ran a dry tongue over equally dry lips. "Yes, sir."

"Here, Deputy," said Marcy, turning to the nightstand. "Let me pour you a glass of water."

"My name is Mitchell Moran," the man said. "This is my wife, Elizabeth, and our daughter, Marcy."

"I...I'm glad to meet you, sir," said Rance, the slight exertion of speaking sending a lance of pain through his head. It was then that he became aware of the bandage and raised a hand to touch it with his fingertips.

"We fixed you up as best we could," said Elizabeth. "Our son, Hal, is on his way into Deer Lodge City to bring the doctor. Unless Dr. Hanson is out of town or in the midst of surgery, they should be back in a little while."

Marcy leaned toward Rance with the glass of water. "Here, Deputy...this will help take away that dryness."

Dayton took the water in small sips. When he had drained the glass, he managed a smile and said, "Thank you, ma'am."

"My pleasure," she said.

"We were coming home from Deer Lodge City," said Mitchell, "and were about to turn off the road toward home when Marcy happened to notice a big ol' cow buffalo lying in the road toward

Washington Gulch. Just as she called our attention to the cow, we spotted you lying beside the road."

Rance nodded gingerly. "My horse was at a full gallop when we topped the hill. He saw the cow, but it was too late to dodge it. Did you see my horse anywhere?"

"Nope. Just you and the cow. Horse must've run off."

"Mmm...with my saddlebags. My personal things, and my Bible."

Marcy gave her parents a quick glance, then looked away.

"Well, at least my horse must not have a broken leg," said Rance. "I'm glad for that, even if I never see him again. Say! How do you know who I am?"

"We knew by your badge that you're a deputy U.S. marshal," said Mitchell. "We pulled your wallet out of your pocket and found papers identifying you as Major Rance Dayton, II Corps, Confederate Army of Northern Virginia. So we knew your name, and a little about your past."

"My up-to-date identification was in my saddlebags. I'm working out of the U.S. marshal's office in Helena. Just started a few days ago."

"What part of the South are you from, Deputy?" Marcy asked.

"North Carolina. Fayetteville. I was sheriff of Cumberland County before the War."

"I see," she said. "So you put on a badge soon after the War ended?"

"Yes, ma'am. I decided to come west and be a lawman out here."

"Were you chasing an outlaw when you took your spill?" asked Mitchell.

"A bunch of outlaws, sir," said Rance. "Have you heard of the Phantom Riders?"

"Bunch of coldhearted killers! You were chasing them?"

"Yes, sir. My assignment is to trail them till they light somewhere, get help from the local law, and bring them in to hang."

"Well, more power to you, Deputy. We'll have to get you well real soon so you can get back after them."

"Yes, sir. Looks like I'll have to find me another horse though."

"We'll help you do that."

Rance's gaze strayed to Marcy's face. She seemed to be watching him carefully as she spoke. "You...ah mentioned you carried a Bible in your saddlebags, Deputy. Do you read the Bible a lot?"

"Every day," he said. "I noticed you were reading one when I came to."

"Oh, yes. God's given me a real hunger for His Word." She paused expectantly, and Rance smiled at her.

"That's why I read it too," he said. "I've only been saved a couple of years, but walking with Jesus these two years has been wonderful."

"Then you must've gotten saved while you were in the army," said Elizabeth.

"That's right. You all have heard of Stonewall Jackson...I served under him. He was the commander of II Corps. I was saved because of his testimony. General Jackson gave me the gospel many times and pressed home my need to be saved."

"Well, I'll be switched!" said Mitchell. "I'd heard Jackson was a Christian."

"And a very dedicated one, sir," said Dayton. "He won many of his men to Christ. And what a man of prayer! Often we would hear him praying in his tent late at night...especially when we were going into a battle the next day. He loved his men and prayed earnestly for us."

"Well! What a joy to know that our houseguest is a Christian!" said Elizabeth.

"Tell me," said Mitchell, "is there a Mrs. Dayton somewhere?"

Rance's gaze went to Marcy and she looked down.

"No, sir," he said quietly. "I've not found the right young lady yet. I figure that since I'm now one of God's children, He'll bring her into my life when the time is right."

"That's the way to look at it," said Mitchell, slipping an arm around Elizabeth's waist. "I waited till the Lord sent the most wonderful little gal in all the world into my life, then grabbed her quick!"

Elizabeth's cheeks turned pink. "Oh, Mitch...you say the sweet-est things!"

"And I mean every word of it," he said, giving her an extra squeeze.

They heard the sound of pounding hooves outside, along with the rattle of a buggy, and Marcy hurried to the window. "It's Hal and Dr. Hanson," she said.

Elizabeth hurried down the hall and led the newcomers back to Rance's room. She took hold of her seventeen-year-old son's hand and led him toward the bed, saying, "Deputy Rance Dayton, this is our son, Hal. He helped us load you into the wagon when we found you."

Rance extended his right hand, and Hal gripped it firmly.

"Glad to meet you, Hal," said Rance.

"My pleasure, sir," said the handsome youth who looked a lot like his father.

"And this is Dr. Rex Hanson, Deputy," said Elizabeth.

Dayton shook hands with the doctor, then Hanson went to work. He listened to Dayton's heart with his stethoscope, checked his ears, tested his hearing, examined his eyes, then removed the bandage from his head. Gently he pressed the tips of his fingers to Rance's skull, feeling every square inch.

"Are you having dizzy spells or nausea, Mr. Dayton?" asked the doctor.

"No, sir. Just a powerful throbbing headache."

"Mmm-hmm. I can believe that. You took quite a crack on the head. The rock must've been smooth where you hit it, because the split in the skin is minor and has already stopped bleeding. But you've got something of a knot where it's split on the left side. It'll go down in a day or two."

"Do you think there's a fracture, Doctor?" asked Marcy.

"I'm sure there isn't, Marcy."

"Praise the Lord," she said, smiling.

"I'll leave some powders for you to take, along with directions for dosage, Mr. Dayton," said Hanson. "They should relieve that headache. You do have a mild concussion, so if any kind of complication arises, please send for me."

"Should we have another bandage on his head, Doctor?" asked Elizabeth.

"I don't think it's necessary. You might clean the wound with alcohol a couple of times a day for the next three or four days. But it's already stopped bleeding, so there's no need to bandage it again."

"How soon can I ride, Doctor?" asked Dayton.

"You in a hurry?"

"Well, yes, sir. I was chasing the Phantom Riders when my horse took the tumble and threw me onto that rock."

Hanson's eyes widened. "The Phantom Riders?"

"Yes, sir. My boss at the Helena office has me on their trail. I've got to resume the pursuit as soon as possible."

The doctor scratched his head. "Well, son, with some rest that concussion will clear up in three or four days. But I'd recommend you not ride again for a week."

"But the longer I wait, the more people those murderers will kill."

"I understand, son, but if you try to resume normal activity too soon, it could be dangerous for you. If you collapse, those beasts will keep on killing even longer."

Rance closed his eyes and nodded. "All right. I'll wait a week."

By suppertime, Rance felt like getting up and walking to the table.

Hal seemed avidly interested in the Civil War, and Rance told the family some of his war experiences as they all ate. After supper, Mitch Moran read the Bible and they had a time of prayer. Rance felt right at home.

While Elizabeth and Marcy washed dishes and cleaned up the kitchen, Mitch, Hal, and Rance walked out onto the wide front porch of the ranch house and sat down on wicker chairs. There was a full moon, and the aroma of honeysuckle was in the air, along with the sound of crickets.

The men talked about the Phantom Riders for a while. The conversation had begun to wind down when the women joined them. Soon the beauty of the star-lit heavens captured their attention and they admired God's handiwork.

After a while, Elizabeth said, "Well, Papa, I think it's time we retire for the night."

Mitch agreed, and as they rose to enter the house, Hal said, "Guess I'd better turn in too."

Marcy looked at Rance. "How about you, Deputy?"

Rance drew in the sweet scent of honeysuckle and said, "I think I'll stay up for just a little while and enjoy this night air. My headache is gone, and I want to enjoy the fact that it's not hurting for a change."

"Is it all right if I sit here with you?" she asked.

"Why, of course. I'd enjoy your company."

Marcy turned to her parents and said, "I'll stay here with Mr. Dayton till he's ready to turn in. See you in the morning." She left her chair and moved to the one next to Rance.

The Morans and Hal bid them good night and entered the house.

The moon was now sending its silver light onto the porch, and the breeze toying with Marcy's long tresses made the moonlight seem to dance in her hair. The sight did strange things to Rance Dayton's heart.

"Marcy…" he said.

"Yes, Deputy?"

"Is there a young man in your life? You know, someone special?"

"Not really. There are a couple of nice young men at church that I've dated once in a while…but no one special. What about you? Has…has there ever been someone you were in love with?"

"Well, I was engaged once," said Rance. "But she decided she didn't want to marry a man who wore a badge, so she gave me back the engagement ring and married a doctor."

"Oh, I'm so sorry."

"No need to be," Rance said. "The Lord knew I was going to become a Christian, and He already had a plan for my life. Alicia wasn't in the plan. It kind of hurts when I think of being spurned like that, but it's hurting less all the time."

"I'm glad for that, Deputy."

"Marcy?"

"Hmm?"

"You can call me Rance."

"Oh. All right…Rance."

Dayton took a deep breath of the night air. "It sure is a beautiful night."

Marcy settled back in her chair and gazed up at the twinkling stars. They sat comfortably silent for a while, listening to the cricket concert.

"I sure appreciate your taking such good care of me, Marcy," Rance said after a time.

"We were glad to do it."

"Well, I appreciate what Hal and your parents did, too, but I was referring to you. I mean, it was really something to come out of my unconscious state and see such a…to see you sitting beside the bed. A fella couldn't ask for a prettier lady to take care of him."

Marcy's face tinted. "Well, thank you, Dep—Rance. You're very kind."

"I try to be, but when I said that, it wasn't kindness; it was simply telling the truth. You're a very attractive young lady."

"Well, Rance, I really should turn in. And so should you. I'm sure a good night's rest will help that concussion go away."

"You're right," he said, rising. He looked down into her soft blue eyes and added, "It may sound strange, but I'm glad my horse took that spill. Otherwise I never would've met you. And your family, of course."

Marcy walked Rance to his room, told him good night, and moved on down the hall toward her own room. As she was turning the knob, the door across the hall came open, and Hal whispered, "Hey, Marcy! Did he kiss you good night?"

Marcy glanced quickly toward Rance's door. "Of course not! Hal Moran, why do you ask such a question?"

He grinned slyly. "'Cause I saw the way he looked at you all evening. He really likes you, sis. I thought maybe he—"

"Go to bed!" she snapped. She opened her door and slipped inside, closing it quietly but firmly.

On the fourth day that Deputy U.S. Marshal Rance Dayton had been with the Moran family, Mitch and Hal pulled into the yard after a trip to town and saw Rance at the corral gate, repairing a broken hinge. Hal jumped down out of the wagon before it had come to a complete stop.

"Hey, you're supposed to be resting, Rance!" said Mitch. "What're you doing?"

Rance grinned. "Just thought I should make myself useful around here. I heard Elizabeth mention to you last night that the top hinge on this gate was broken. You said you'd get to it as soon as you could. Well, since the ladies are over visiting your neighbors, I took a look in your toolshed and found a new hinge the same size. 'Bout got it done."

"I'm much obliged, but you didn't need to do that."

"Glad to. I'm feeling much better, and since you're stuck with me three more days, I might as well earn my keep."

Mitch climbed down from the wagon much slower than his son and walked toward the back of the wagon. "We're going to miss you, my friend," he said.

"Well, thank you," said Rance over his shoulder, tightening the last heavy wood screw.

"In fact, just so you won't forget us, Hal and I picked up some gifts for you in town."

Rance turned around to see Mitch holding a beautiful new saddle, and Hal was holding a bridle and a new pair of saddlebags. "Aw, now, you didn't need to go and do a thing like that, Mitch. I—" Rance's gaze riveted on the saddlebags…the initials emblazoned on the sides were R. D. "Well, look at that, will you!"

Rance marveled at the beauty and quality of the saddle and other leather goods, and humbly thanked Mitch.

Just then the women came wheeling into the yard in the family carriage and pulled up to where the men were standing.

"Oh, so you gave them to him early!" said Elizabeth. "You weren't going to give him those until you—"

"Elizabeth! Don't say any more!"

Marcy laughed. "Daddy, you might as well go ahead and do the whole thing."

Rance's brow furrowed. "What whole thing?"

Mitch's features flushed. "Well, you know…day before yesterday you were talking about buying one of my saddle horses."

"Yes."

"And you really like the big gray gelding, don't you?"

"Yes, I do."

"Well, we had a secret family meeting last night after you went to bed, and we decided that since you're such a nice fella, and a lawman and all, we're giving the gray to you. I'd already been to the saddlery in town and bought the saddle, bridle, and saddlebags, and ordered the initials put on. We were going to give you everything at one time, but I just sorta had to go ahead and give you the gear." The older man looked down, a bit embarrassed, then said, "Anyway…the horse and this stuff is our way of saying we appreciate you, Rance."

Rance Dayton shook his head in disbelief. Finally he said, "What does a fella do with people like you?"

Mitch grinned. "Just come back and see us after you get that bunch of killers hanged!"

Rance grinned, then looked at Marcy. "You can count on it!"

∗ ∗ ∗

The next day was Sunday. Rance thoroughly enjoyed the church services in Deer Lodge City. On Monday and Tuesday he helped Mitch repair the barn roof.

On Tuesday evening after supper, Rance and Marcy took a moonlight walk in the fields. As they strolled slowly in the lush grass, Marcy said, "It's going to be hard to watch you ride away tomorrow."

"Well, I tell you, little lady, it's going to be even harder for me to ride away."

"Rance, I'm praying that the Lord will let you catch that gang soon. Not just because I want them stopped, which of course I do, but…well, because you promised to come back and see us when they were caught."

"There's nothing I want more than to come back and see you," he said softly.

The next morning, as Rance was about to leave, Hal went to the corral, saddled and bridled the gray for him, and left the horse near the corral gate. With his saddlebags draped over his shoulder, Dayton told the family good-bye at the back porch, assuring them he would come visit after the gang was brought to justice. He shook hands with Mitch and Hal, and Elizabeth embraced him affectionately.

Suddenly, all eyes were on Marcy.

"I'll walk you out to your horse, Rance," she said.

When they were halfway between the house and the barn, she stopped and brought her hand from behind her back. "I have something I want to give to you," she said.

Rance looked down and saw a brand-new Bible in her hand. "On Monday, Mother and I visited the neighbors, but we also took a little run into town. I bought you this so you'd have a Bible."

Marcy extended it to him, and Rance took it and captured her hand for a moment. "This means more to me than I could ever tell you, Marcy," he said. "I treasure the Word of God because it's His gift to us, but I will treasure this Bible for an additional reason…because it came from you."

Tears misted Marcy's eyes. "Look inside," she said.

Rance opened to the first page, which was blank except for handwriting that read:

To Rance—

I am so thankful to the Lord for bringing you into my life. Please think of me whenever you read this Bible.

Love,
Marcy

Rance Dayton thought his heart would burst when he read the last two words. He wanted to kiss her good-bye but refrained. Instead, he held the Bible over his heart, and said, "I will think of you every time I read God's Word. And I'll think of you lots of other times too. In fact, probably a thousand times a day."

Marcy raised up on tiptoe and planted a sweet, warm kiss on his cheek.

Rance placed fingertips to his cheek and said, "Marcy, if I'm not careful, I'm going to fall in love with you."

She looked up at him earnestly and said, "Be careful in your pursuit of the killers, Rance, but in your feelings toward me…don't be careful."

"I won't," he said with feeling.

With tears streaming down her cheeks, Marcy Moran watched the man she loved ride away. She didn't move from the spot until he vanished from sight.

TWENTY-TWO

Mitch Moran had provided Rance Dayton a map of Montana Territory. After studying the map Rance rode west, on a hunch, for the town of Phillipsburg.

When he got there he learned that the gang had indeed been at Phillipsburg before him and robbed the town's only bank, leaving a bank employee dead and a customer wounded. Eyewitnesses said they had ridden east out of town.

Rance soon found himself climbing through the Rockies and came upon a small unnamed settlement. The gang had ridden through there two days earlier to water their horses. After following what appeared to be the trail of several horses moving together, he finally came upon a spot where several riders had camped.

He pressed on through the next day and rode down out of the Rockies on the eastern slope. He found another campsite, and by the looks of it, they had been there only a day or so ahead of him. Dayton decided by the distance between camps that the gang was moving slowly. Maybe taking it easy for a while and laying low.

The next morning, Rance stopped in a town called Bedford, but found no one who had seen the gang. He decided to follow the road toward Jefferson City. The road threaded through dense forest, and as he rounded a bend, he came upon a stagecoach.

One middle-aged woman was trying to help another climb up into the box, but her long dress was making it difficult to climb. They paused at the sound of horse's hooves, and peered over their shoulders nervously.

The one on the ground said, "Oh, Myrtle! It's a lawman! See his badge?"

"What happened, ladies?" asked Dayton, as he dismounted.

"A gang of masked men stopped the stage. They killed the driver and shotgunner, wounded our husbands, then robbed us. We have the bodies inside the coach with our husbands. We were going to drive the stage into Jefferson City and find a doctor."

"I'll drive it in," said Dayton. "How long since this happened?"

"About twenty minutes ago."

Rance nodded. "Let me take a look at your husbands."

Both the men had taken bullets in the shoulder, but they were conscious. Rance removed the dead bodies from inside the coach and hoisted them on top. He helped the women inside with their husbands and tied his horse behind, then headed for Jefferson City.

After delivering the wounded men and their wives to the town doctor, Dayton drove the stage to the local marshal's office. The marshal was just coming out the door as Rance set the brake.

"Marshal Naylor?" Rance said, climbing down from the box.

"Yes, sir," said the lawman, who was in his late thirties.

"I'm Deputy U.S. Marshal Rance Dayton, out of the Helena office on assignment to track down the Phantom Riders. They stopped this stage about four miles north of here, killed the driver and shotgunner, and wounded two male passengers. I left them off at the doctor's office up the street, along with their wives, who were unharmed. Will you see that the stage gets to the proper people? I've got to stay after the gang."

"I'll do that, Deputy," said Naylor. "And even more. I'll round up a posse, and we'll go with you."

"I appreciate the offer, Marshal, but Chief Wright only wants one man tracking them because one man is harder to spot on their trail. My job is to locate them when they camp, then obtain help from the nearest local law."

Naylor nodded. "I understand."

"You might see to the people at the doctor's office too," Rance said.

"Will do."

With that, Dayton went to the back of the coach and untied his horse's reins, then swung into the saddle and galloped south out of town.

Marcy Moran sat alone on the front porch of her parents' ranch house near Deer Lodge City, gazing at the rolling hills where she had watched Rance Dayton ride away.

"Lord," she said, "keep Your hand on him. Bring him back to me. Please help him to bring those killers in soon. I want him to know how very much I love him. I must find a way to tell him." She prayed for several minutes, then sat quietly looking across the fields.

"What are you doing, honey?" came her father's voice.

Marcy looked up to see both parents looking down at her.

"I think she's looking for someone to come riding over those hills, Papa," said Elizabeth.

Mitchell grinned and rubbed his chin. "Now, I wonder who that might be, Mother?"

"I don't know his name," she said with a chuckle, "but his initials are Rance Dayton."

Marcy playfully swatted her mother's hand as Elizabeth sat down beside her.

"Well, I'm right now, am I not?"

It was Marcy's turn to chuckle. "Are mothers ever wrong?"

Mitch sat down on Marcy's other side and turned the chair to face her. "You really fell in love with that rugged young fella, didn't you?" he said.

"Yes, I did, Daddy. I just know he's the one the Lord has chosen for me."

"But how does Rance feel about you, Marcy?"

"He as much as said he's in love with me, just before he rode away."

"What'd he say?"

"Mitch, that's private," said Elizabeth. "Don't ask her to tell you."

"I don't mind, Mother. You both saw me kiss him on the cheek."

The parents nodded.

"Well, when I did that, he said 'Marcy, if I'm not careful, I'm going to fall in love with you.'"

"And what did you say?" asked Elizabeth.

"I told him not to be careful in his feelings toward me. And he said, 'I won't.'"

"Sounds like the real thing to me," Mitch said. "You know Mother and I like Rance. We were talking before going to sleep last night, and we both agreed that if what we thought we saw was the real thing, we'd sure welcome it. He's a fine, dedicated Christian young man."

Marcy smiled. "That's the only kind the Lord would send to me, Daddy…and it's the only kind I want."

No one spoke for a few moments, then Elizabeth said, "Honey, do you think you could stand being the wife of a lawman? It's a dangerous profession, and as a deputy U.S. marshal, he'll travel a lot."

Marcy nodded. "With the Lord in our marriage, and the love I feel for Rance, and the love I know he feels for me…I know I could stand it. I'm not saying it would be easy, but the Lord is able to give strength and grace, even to the wife of a lawman."

"Can't argue with that," Mitch said.

Rance Dayton walked into the town marshal's office in Centreville, Montana. When Marshal Ryan Thomas saw the badge on Dayton's chest he rose from his chair, saying, "Welcome to Centreville, Deputy."

Dayton introduced himself, and they shook hands.

"What can I do for you, Deputy Dayton?"

"I was talking to some men on the street out there, and they told me the Phantom Riders were here yesterday."

"Yep."

"I'm on assignment by U.S. Marshal Douglas Wright in Helena to track them down."

"Big job," said Thomas.

"Yes, sir. The men out there said someone had seen the gang members putting their masks on in the alley behind the bank, and he alerted you."

"Sure did."

"What happened then?"

"I recruited some help and gave them a gunfight. We killed two and wounded another in the thigh, but he was able to ride away. One of them was wounded in the shoulder, and the gang rode off and left him."

Rance looked surprised. "It's rare for them to leave one of their wounded behind."

"They couldn't help it," said Thomas. "We were sending so much hot lead after them, they had no choice but to take off. It was late in the day, almost dark, so I didn't form a posse."

"Well, Marshal Thomas, how about letting me talk to your prisoner."

"Be glad to, but I'll tell you right now, he won't give you any information. I tried to get it out of him. Reminded him that his pals ran off and left him to face the law and hang. But it didn't help."

"Well, I have to try. What's his name?"

"He won't tell me. Carries no identification. I understand that none of them do. The dead ones didn't either."

Dayton sighed. "Okay. Well, point me in the right direction."

Twenty minutes later, Rance left the cell block and entered the marshal's office. "You were right, Marshal. I told him the decent thing to do was to give me all the information he could so the killing spree could be stopped. You know…die with his conscience cleared. He just cussed me good and told me to get out."

"'Honor among thieves,' somebody once said," Thomas replied.

The next day, Rance Dayton was riding hard again. Marshal Thomas had told him there were ten outlaws in the gang before the shooting. They were now down to seven, and one of them was wounded.

He headed south toward Toston, which the map showed to be about a mile east of the Boulder River. As he rode, Rance prayed that the Lord would let him catch the killers soon so he could return to Marcy and ask her to marry him.

At sunset, he was about to make camp when he saw a riderless horse standing in the woods off to the side of the road. There was blood on the saddle. When he drew up, he saw a dead man lying in the bush with a bullet in his thigh.

Rance knelt beside the man and felt the flesh of his face. He was still warm. The gang couldn't be far ahead. Now they were down to six. *Odds are getting even better,* he thought.

Dayton studied the map in the fading light. He could see a pattern to the locations the gang had targeted. They would probably rob the bank in Toston next. And unless they took a day off, they would hit the bank tomorrow.

Rance thought about where he would camp if he were them and decided it would be on the east bank of the Boulder River.

Twilight fell as he headed southeast toward the river. He guided the horse across the river at a point where there was a sharp bend, hoping that if the gang was looking that way, they wouldn't see him. Cautiously, he followed the east bank, walking the gray slowly.

Clouds were gathering as the moon began to rise. Dayton slipped from the saddle and led the gray through the woods along the edge of the river. After about an hour, he caught sight of a wink-ing campfire through the trees.

He tied his horse in thick brush about a hundred yards from the camp. With the breeze rustling the tree branches and the rush of the river, a hundred yards was far enough away if the gray whinnied.

He kept to what shadows the cloud-covered moon allowed and crept up close to the camp. There were six men sitting around the fire, laughing and making jokes. The orange flames allowed Rance to see the horses they had staked out nearby among plenty of grass.

It got quiet for a moment, then one of them brought up the loss of four good men that day. "Shouldn't we go back and break Larry out of jail?" he said.

"Be too risky," said another man. "They just might be waitin' for us to do that."

Rance knew he needed to ride hard for Toston and get what help the local law could give him, but it was night, and the moon was covered. To ride hard now would be dangerous. And it would take quite a while to get to Toston, even at a full gallop. If his horse should fall…

He moved in closer, being careful not to step on a twig. He was almost close enough to make out the features of the three men who faced in his direction. The flickering fire cast dancing shadows on their faces. One of them stood up with a water pan in his hand and said, "Be back in a few minutes, guys."

Rance followed the shadowed figure and watched him kneel be-side the stream and dip the pan into the water. The rippling of the river covered Rance's footsteps as he slipped up behind the outlaw and cracked the man on the head with the barrel of his revolver. The man dropped flat on the riverbank, and the pan he had been holding filled with water and sank to the bottom. Rance slipped the outlaw's gun from its holster and threw it in the river.

He then dragged the man into the cover of brush and trees. There, working by feel more than sight, he braced the man in a sit-ting position against a slender birch and tore up his shirt to make a rope. He used the man's belt to bind his wrists behind the tree, then tied his ankles with the rope and used part of the shirt as a gag.

As Rance moved stealthily back through the trees and brush toward the fire, he saw the shadowed form of another outlaw coming his way. Rance drew up behind a pine tree and waited till the outlaw stepped past him, then slammed his gun barrel down on the man's head. He dragged him to a different spot from the other outlaw and bound him to a tree and gagged him in the same manner. Then he took the man's gun and threw it in the river.

The other four were still seated around the fire, eating their supper.

No better time than now, Rance decided. He quietly drew his revolver, cocked it, and dashed in from the surrounding darkness, commanding sharply, "All right, drop those plates and throw your hands in the air!"

Startled, the outlaws jerked their heads up and saw the gun in Dayton's hand and the firelight reflecting from his badge.

"I'm Deputy U.S. Marshal Rance Dayton, and you men are under arrest for murder and robbery! On your feet! I want those guns removed very carefully from their holsters and dropped to the ground."

All four rose slowly to their feet.

Three of the four rose a little bit slower than their fourth comrade, shocked looks capturing their faces. But no one was more shocked than Rance Dayton when he recognized Hank Upchurch, Buford Hall, and Chuck Carney.

Buford released a crooked smile and said, "Well, boys, it's our old pal, Major Dayton! You remember us, Major. We're the guys who saved your life at Antietam."

When no one moved to drop their guns, the fourth man said, "Hey, what's goin' on here? You guys saved this federal man's life in the War?"

Rance Dayton stood there, stunned. He could hardly believe he was looking into the faces of three of the Fearless Four.

"We sure did, Slim," said Carney. "He owes us. It'll be all right now. Everett'll be back any minute. He'll be glad to see the major."

"You are gonna let us go, aren't you, Major?" said Buford. "Like Chuck said, you'd be dead if it wasn't for us."

Everything these men had meant to Rance came rushing back, and he felt torn by the remembrance of their days of glory. For a few moments he let himself weigh the consequences of letting them go. If he took them in, they would be hanged. How could he end the lives of the men who were willing to risk death to save his life? Rance's heart pounded in his chest.

"Major," said Buford, "we can put our hands down now, can't we?"

Rance seemed paralyzed as the cascading thoughts of the War and his friendship with these men filled his mind. His words to them around the campfire after the Battle of Fredericksburg came back with chilling clarity: *I want to thank you guys one more time from the bottom of my heart for laying your lives on the line to save mine. You'll always be very special men in my memories, and in my life. If there is ever anything I can do for any one of you…consider it done.*

"Well, what about it, Major?" pressed Carney. "My arms are getting tired held up like this."

Rance Dayton felt a queasiness in his stomach, but his features took on firm resolve as he said, "It's not Major, Chuck. It's Deputy U.S. Marshal. I'm taking you in."

TWENTY-THREE

Marcy Moran gazed at the distant hills as she stood with her mother on the front porch.

"It'll be two weeks tomorrow since he left, Mother," she said. "I'm afraid something's happened to him."

Elizabeth put an arm around her daughter. "Now, honey, you must trust the Lord in this. He is able to take care of Rance and bring him back to you."

A tear ran down Marcy's cheek and she quickly wiped it away. "I know, Mother. It's just that…well, sometimes my faith grows a little weak."

"Marcy dear, every Christian has those times. When they come, you just hold on to what you know. Right now you can hold on to the fact that God brought that young man into your life for a purpose. Let God work out the details in His own time."

Marcy nodded and gave her mother a smile.

U.S. Marshal Douglas Wright and his deputy, Rance Dayton, turned from the gallows in Helena as the crowd began to disperse. Wright followed Dayton to the gray gelding and said, "If you do get married while you're there in Deer Lodge, wire me and let me know. After what you did for the people of this territory, you deserve a couple of weeks off."

Rance swung into the saddle. "I'll let you know, sir. If it works out as I believe it will, Marcy and I will be needing a house in Helena."

"Well, there're a few for sale here in town. I'm sure you'll find something suitable."

"Okay. I'll see you soon."

Rance wheeled the gray toward the west, trotted a ways, then drew rein. A lump welled in his throat as he looked back at the gallows and beheld the six lifeless bodies swaying slightly in the morning breeze. He focused on Carney, Hall, Nichols, and Upchurch and bit down hard on his lower lip to keep his emotions in check. But he couldn't blink back the tears that filled his eyes and spilled down his cheeks.

If only things had turned out differently, he thought. If only Stonewall Jackson had not come riding into the Confederate camp in the wilderness on that fateful night. If only the Fearless Four had listened when the other sentries told them not to shoot…

He looked at his former comrades for a long moment, then put the gray to a gallop, heading for the towering Rockies. On the other side of those mountains was the young woman the Lord had chosen for him.

Rance was facing the setting sun as the ranch house came into view. Eager to hold Marcy in his arms, he put the gray to a full gallop.

As he drew near, he thrilled to see her rise from a chair and wave to him. He gave a whoop of excitement and yanked off his hat, waving it in response.

When he drew up and pulled rein, he saw the tears glistening on her cheeks as the glow of the sunset danced in her golden hair.

He slid from the saddle, and Marcy hurried off the porch to meet him, calling his name, her arms open wide.

EPILOGUE

Historians have called the Battle of Chancellorsville "Robert E. Lee's masterpiece, and an almost perfect example of the military arts."

Facing an army of 140,000 with barely 65,000 men of his own, Lee outmaneuvered, out-thought, and out-fought the Union Army of the Potomac. Lee, of course, gave the glory to Stonewall Jackson, whose military genius had been employed to defeat the enemy.

Losses for Major General Joseph Hooker's army were: 1,606 killed, 9,762 wounded, 5,919 captured or missing. Total: 17,287.

Losses for General Robert E. Lee's army were, 1,581 killed, 8,700 wounded, 1,708 captured or missing. Total: 11,989.

When the news of Lieutenant General Thomas J. Jackson's death was released on May 10, 1863, Jackson's one-time aide, young Major Henry Kyd Douglas wrote in his diary: "A great sob swept over the Army of Northern Virginia. It was the heartbreak of the Southern Confederacy."

On Monday, May 11—the day after Jackson's death—General Robert E. Lee issued General Orders Number 61:

With deep grief, the Commanding General announces the death of Lieutenant General Thomas J. Jackson, who expired on May 10, at 3:15 P.M. The daring, skill, and energy of this great and good soldier, by decree of an all-wise Providence, are not lost to us. But while we mourn his death, we feel that his spirit still lives, and will inspire the whole army with his indomitable courage and unshaken confidence in God as our hope and strength.

Let his name be a watchword to his corps, who have followed him to victory on so many fields. Let his officers and soldiers emulate his invincible determination to do everything in the defense of our beloved country.

One historian wrote: "Stonewall Jackson's true value came to light when he began working closely with Robert E. Lee. The calm, resolute, sensitive, and scholarly Lee and the fiery but calculating Jackson formed an almost perfect military team. Jackson's masterpiece came at Chancellorsville where, defying every tenet of military science and history, he led an outnumbered army to victory in a flank march that ranks with Frederick the Great's maneuver at Leuthen as one of the greatest actions in martial records."

Stonewall Jackson's aides dressed his body in a dark civilian suit, then a military overcoat. For a shroud, Jefferson Davis provided the first example of the newly approved Confederate national flag, white with the familiar red-white-and-blue battle-flag design in the upper corner.

The morning after Jackson died, the body was taken to the parlor of the Chandler house. As the Chandlers stood looking down at the coffin, Jim Lewis came in and handed Mrs. Chandler a lock of Jackson's hair that he had cut before the lid was closed.

The coffin was taken to Richmond by train, accompanied by the widow and baby Julia, along with the McGuires, Chaplain Tucker

Lacy, Jim Lewis, and Mary Anna's brother, Joe Morrison.

The great general's body lay in state at the Confederate capitol. All the city's businesses were closed, and crowds of tearful mourners—most of whom had never laid eyes on Jackson before—came to pass by the coffin and pay tribute to their national hero.

The body was then removed to Lexington where the funeral was held on Friday, May 15, 1863, at the Presbyterian church where Jackson had faithfully served as a deacon. All Lexington and those in the surrounding countryside followed the coffin to the cemetery, and there the general was laid to rest.

At 1:00 P.M. on June 27, President Abraham Lincoln relieved Major General Joseph Hooker as commander of the Union Army of the Potomac and replaced him with Major General George G. Meade.

The Civil War would go on.

The Battle Begins…

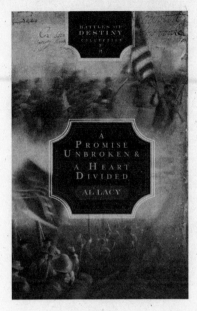

ISBN: 1-59052-945-6

Volume 1

A Promise Unbroken (Battle of Rich Mountain)
As the first winds of Civil War sweep across the Virginia countryside, the
wealthy Ruffin family is torn by forces that threaten their way of life and,
ultimately, their promises to one another. Mandrake and Orchid, slaves on
the Ruffin plantation, must also fight for the desire of their hearts.
Heartache and victory. Jealousy and racial hatred. From a prosperous
Virginia plantation to a grim jail cell outside of Lynchburg, follow the
dramatic story of love indestructible.

A Heart Divided (Battle of Mobile Bay)
Wounded early in the Civil War, Captain Ryan McGraw is nursed back to
health by army nurse Dixie Quade. In her tender care, love's seed is sown.
But with the sudden appearance of Victoria, the wife who once abandoned
Ryan, and the five-year-old son he never knew he had, come threats
endangering the lives of everyone involved. Between the deadly forces of
war and two loves, McGraw is caught with *a heart divided*.

The Battle Continues...

ISBN: 1-59052-946-4

Volume 2

Beloved Enemy (Battle of First Bull Run)
Faithful to her family and the land of her birth, young Jenny Jordan covers
for her father's Confederate spy missions. But as she grows closer to Union
solider Buck Brownell, she's torn between devotion to the South and her
feelings for the man she is forbidden to love.

Overwhelmed by pressure to assist the South, Jenny carries critical
information over enemy lines and is caught in Buck Brownell's territory.
Will he follow orders to execute the beautiful spy... or find a way to save his
beloved enemy?

Shadowed Memories (Battle of Shiloh)
Critically wounded on the field of battle, one man struggles to regain his
strength and the memories that have slipped away from him. Although he
cannot reclaim his ties to the past, he's soon caught up in the present and
the depth of his love for Hannah Rose.

Haunted by amnesia, the handsome officer realizes he may already be
married. And so, risking all that he knows and loves, he turns away to
confront his shadowed memories, including those of "Julie"—the
mysterious woman he thinks he left behind.

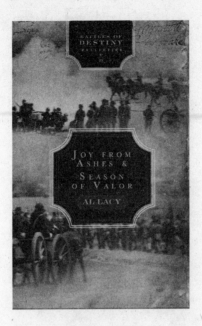

ISBN: 1-59052-947-2

Volume 3

Joy From Ashes (Battle of Fredericksburg)
While fighting to defend his home and family against Union attack, Major
Layne Dalton learns that enemy soldiers have brutalized his wife. Tragically,
the actions of three cruel-hearted Heglund brothers have caused not only
the suffering of his bride, but also the death of Layne and Melody's unborn
son. Thirsting for vengeance, the young major vows to bring judgment
upon those responsible, yet surprising circumstances make Dalton—
presumed dead by his wife and fellow soldiers—a prisoner of the very men
he swore he would destroy.

Season of Valor (Battle of Gettysburg)
As teenagers, Shane Donovan and Ashley Kilrain promise to love each other
forever. But when Ashley's parents decide to return to Ireland and take their
daughter with them, the sweethearts sadly bid each other farewell and accept
their fate.

  After several years, both have found other loves and married. So when
Ashley returns to Maine and the friendship between the two is rekindled,
Shane and Ashley find that a new kind of love is needed to overcome the
sprouting seeds of tragedy in their freshly intertwined lives.

Travel along the Trail of Tears
A Place to Call Home series

By Al & JoAnna Lacy

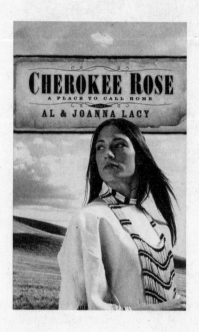

Cherokee Rose—BOOK ONE

ISBN: 1-59052-562-0

It's late summer 1838. President Martin Van Buren issues an order that the fifteen thousand Cherokee Indians living in the Smoky Mountains of North Carolina are to be evicted from their homeland. Forced to migrate to Indian Territory, the Cherokees begin their tragic, one-thousand-mile journey westward. Most of the seven thousand soldiers escorting them along the way are brutally cruel. But Cherokee Rose, an eighteen-year-old Indian girl, finds one soldier, Lieutenant Britt Claiborne, willing to stand up for them. Both Christians, Cherokee Rose discovers that Britt is also a quarter Cherokee himself. It's upon the Trail of Tears that they fall in love, dreaming of one day marrying and finding a place to call home together.

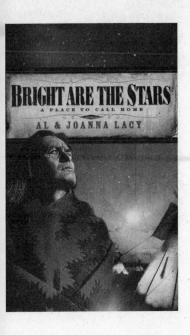

Bright Are the Stars—BOOK TWO
ISBN: 1-59052-563-9
1839. The North Carolina Cherokees are settling into their new home in Indian Territory and Britt Claiborne and Cherokee Rose are settling into married life. Britt, a quarter Cherokee Indian, is released from the United States army and joins the Cherokee Police Force where his position takes him into fearsome and heart-gripping dangers. They raise two children with much love and delight. They also lean on God through the trials of their day—including the death of the popular Cherokee Chief Sequoyah, who had translated the Bible into their language. Follow the historical events that punctuate their lives until 1889, when President Harrison announces that whites are free to enter Indian Territory, now known by the Indians as home.

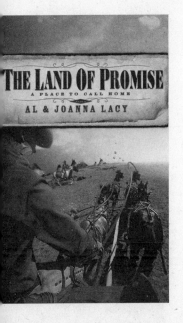

Land of Promise—BOOK THREE
ISBN: 1-59052-564-7
1889. Cherokee Rose and police chief Britt Claiborne are forced onto reservations along with their descendants and the five "civilized" tribes in the Oklahoma District. The U.S. government has told them that because of its rich, productive soil and sufficient water supply, the Oklahoma District is now white man's land of promise. With indescribable sadness and anger, the Indians look on as thousands of prospective settlers and their families enter the district and claim 160-acre sections of land in the Oklahoma land rush. This third book in the A Place to Call Home series masterfully includes the compelling stories of three white prospective-settler families introduced in Bright Are the Stars: Craig and Gloria Parker; widow Martha Ackerman with her parents and three children; and Lee and Kathy Belden with their two sons.